THE EMPEROR, THE SON and THE THIEF

ROBERT REID

THE EMPEROR
SON
the
AND the
THIEF

BOOK 1
THE EMPEROR

To my family and the many friends who keep encouraging me to continue with this new career - thank you.

ACKNOWLEDGEMENTS

Firstly, thank you to all those of you who have read "White Light Red Fire" and given me such positive feedback on the story. It is this as much as anything that has encouraged me to continue writing the story of Andore and the red fire.

So many people have reviewed 'The Emperor' at different stages in its development and given me lots of fantastic input and encouragement. It is impossible to name you all, but you know who you are, and thank you. Your suggestions have greatly improved the narrative.

Many thanks to my daughter Charis for carrying out a thorough final check of the manuscript together with giving me lots of constructive ideas for improving the story.

Grateful thanks to the editorial team who have

done a great job correcting the many mistakes in the first draft manuscripts.

To the design team, thanks for your creativity in the cover layout and detail in the map.

Finally and most importantly, thanks to my wife Phyllis for her forever love and for putting up with a missing husband hiding in his grubby office tapping away at the computer keyboard. Loved you yesterday, love you still, always have and always will.

RFR
September 2020

ABOUT THE AUTHOR

Robert (Bob) Reid grew up in Scotland's beautiful border country. Hawick was home until it was time to go to university in Edinburgh. A degree and a PhD in Chemistry followed. It was in Edinburgh that Bob met and married Phyllis. Work opportunities took them south, and their son Simon was born in Cheshire and their daughter Charis some years later in Swindon. Highworth, near Swindon, became home in 1982. It still is home and has become a special place to Bob and Phyllis.

Bob's career of forty years was initially in technical management, then general management and business consulting. Work generally took priority over creativity. Semi-retirement in early 2018 created the time, family and friends the encouragement, for Bob to develop his writing. His first novel, White Light Red Fire, was published in April 2019 and is a historical fantasy loosely based on the Scottish wars of independence of the early 14th Century. The Emperor is the first story in a trilogy. The second book, The Son, is a work in progress.

THE EMPEROR

The Emperor is set in the same lands as *White Light Red Fire* but 200 years later, in the early 1500s. The story is based in the southern lands of Kermin and Amina. An Emperor comes to power in Kermin and seeks domination of all the lands south of the island of Andore. An illegitimate son learns of his birthright and seeks revenge on his father. The son learns of the red fire that had been wielded by an alchemist in the 1300s. So begins the son's journey, which will continue in book 2, The Son. As the Emperor goes to war, sword, pike and bow are still the weapons of the day but the battleground is changing. It is the beginning of the age of gunpowder.

AMAZON REVIEWS IN PRAISE OF *WHITE LIGHT RED FIRE*

Heartfelt and inspired storytelling

If you're looking for another world to occupy the gap left by the Seven Kingdoms of Game of Thrones I can't recommend a better place to visit than the island of Andore. *White Light Red Fire* is a heady, consuming and inspiring blend of history, fantasy and folklore and is homage to the dedication and inspired storytelling of Robert Reid. Pick up a copy and prepare to commence battle.

A terrific read

This is one of the most engaging novels that I have read in a very long time. The author has created a world that draws you in from the very early stages and keeps you hooked, and caring about the outcome, until the thrilling climax. The battle scenes are realistic, very well constructed, and don't fall into the same trap as many with a magical twist that use the magic as a short cut. The multitude of characters and dominions, each with their own ambitions, lends the book an often-overlooked degree of plausibility, and is helpfully supported by maps and a character summary. You are left with a great feeling of a journey travelled, as well as an eagerness to delve further. I was given this book as a gift, but will certainly buy the sequel.

What a debut

Absolutely loved this debut novel from Robert Reid, well rounded characters and scene setting.

Was happy to be taken on the journey along with the characters, I for one will be pre ordering the next instalment.

Sit back with a glass of wine and indulge yourself. Cheers Robert, hopefully it won't be too long before I'm reading The Emperor.

Cracking good yarn with a satisfying ending

I read this book over a period of two weeks as a treat - it really was! Well-paced, not overly complicated and characters you can believe in. For fantasy and battle scene lovers like me, you will enjoy being transported to a place where people have extreme survival fears, an advanced technological age has been and gone and there are hints of the influence of a higher being. There's a touch of romance that does not distract from the whole, but links to the human experience of the characters. The story is begging for a sequel, which I will snap up as soon as it's published. I suggest you read this book and watch out for the next!

A wonderful story

Robert Reid, in my opinion, is an excellent author with a vivid imagination. His well-constructed story has so many facets in that his tale includes conflict, justice, drama, fairness and love with a mystical element thrown in. There are just enough characters to make life in this imaginary land interesting but not too many to cause confusion. The maps are also helpful, ensuring the reader does not "lose the plot" along the way and adds to a really good read. I look forward to Robert's next book with anticipation.

Captivating read

A captivating read of a fantasy story about a small nation's battle to defend itself against an oppressive enemy. It is very well written - I was hooked in the first chapter and kept engaged for the rest of the book.

Excellent to have the detailed maps and full list of characters which proved to be very helpful. If you are a fan of The Game of Thrones you'll like this book.

Robert Reid's first book and I'll certainly be looking out for the next one.

PROLOGUE

Like all Bala weddings, this was to be a simple ceremony. Alastair Munro was to conduct the proceedings and the couple's rings would be swapped from the right to the left hand.

Elbeth and Angus embraced, stepped back and each took the other's hand. The rings on the third fingers of their right hands shone with white intensity, dimmed and then reappeared on their left hands. Between their right hands a silver quaich appeared with the Cameron motto shining brightly: *Aonaibh Ri Chéile*, 'let us unite'. And united they were.

But then, as the couple lifted the ancient wedding cup to their lips, Munro once again heard his old mentor's voice from beyond the grave, and this time it carried a warning. "To your right Alastair, evil stalks the shadows!"

Alastair spun to his right to see an old beggar pointing his raised staff at the wedding party. Oien!

It could be none other. As a flash of red fire left the staff, Alastair **pushed his** hands forward, palms outward, and then drew them apart. A white wall appeared in front of him, consuming the red flame.

Oien raised his hand and another red bolt shot out, again quenched by the white light. Alastair advanced on the old alchemist and Oien hurled more and more deadly bolts of red fire. As Alastair closed on him, Oien knew that his power was as nothing to this white force. He started to beg for mercy, but Ala Moire's voice echoed in Alastair's head: "It is too late; take him in your embrace. Forgiveness, if it is to be granted, is for a greater power."

Alastair Munro took the alchemist in his arms and felt all the anger and the lust for power which had corrupted the old man's soul. He placed his arms around the other man's shoulders, clasped his hands and stepped back. The white wall now completely enclosed Oien, and as it brightened in intensity it hid him from view. Flashes of red seemed to bounce around inside the wall and then began to fade away. The wall became a shimmering wave, like a mirage in the desert. Gradually that too vanished, and all that remained where Oien had been was a piece of dull red rock.

From "White Light Red Fire"

CONTENTS

200 Years Earlier
Map of Andore

Chapter 1	Raimund	1
Chapter 2	The Rise of the Emperor	17
Chapter 3	The Painter	38
Chapter 4	Den of Thieves	51
Chapter 5	Boretar	63
Chapter 6	Aldene	87
Chapter 7	Alberon	114
Chapter 8	Aldene – A Return Journey	134
Chapter 9	Clouds of War	166
Chapter 10	The Kermin Alol	179
Chapter 11	Fatal Mistakes	198
Chapter 12	Blockade	219
Chapter 13	Winter 1507	234
Chapter 14	1508 - A New Year	252
Chapter 15	A Winter Journey	280
Chapter 16	A Change of Tactics	295
Chapter 17	All Paths Lead to Tamin	309
Chapter 18	A Time for Treaties	330
Chapter 19	Two Sons – Two Stories	364
Chapter 20	Valdin	384
Chapter 21	Lex Talionis	397
	List of Characters	422
	Geography of the Lands	425

TWO HUNDRED YEARS EARLIER

On the island of Andore, the late 13th Century of the Third Age was a time of brutal conflict. Powerful warlords fought for supremacy, kings raised armies to defend their lands and the people lived in fear. By 1298 King Dewar the Second of Ackar and Lett had quashed all resistance, and every Kingdom on Andore swore fealty to the Ackar King.

The rich country of Amina lay across the Middle Sea, south of Andore. In 1299, King Dewar led a great army over the sea intent on conquering Amina and thereby extending his dominions and further increasing his power and wealth. The two armies met on the Vale of Tember, close to the Amina capital of Tamin. The battle raged for two months and ended in stalemate. The Dewar and his army were forced to return to Andore, but the King promised he would return and conquer.

In 1300 an old alchemist called Oien arrived at the mighty stronghold of Boretar, capital of Ackar and the seat of power of the Dewar Kings. In the Second Age the alchemist had learnt how to harness the power of a rare mineral. The red stone was called othium, and in that earlier time it had been used to fuel the industrialisation of the world. The Second Age had been brought to a sudden end when meteorite storms rained down on the planet and drove man back to his earliest beginnings in caves and remote valleys.

Now the alchemist had returned, and he offered the King an alliance. The power of othium and the red fire, together with the King's armies, would destroy all who stood against them. The Dewar would be able to fulfil his promise to conquer Amina and the alchemist would again begin his journey towards world domination. First though, he needed an army to march north, because he knew that the last unexploited seams of othium lay trapped in ancient mines in the Inger Mountains.

In the peaceful province of Banora, in the country of Bala, a farmer called Alastair Munro was unaware of his inheritance. He had been gifted the power of the white light, and he would need to learn how to harness this power to withstand the evil of the red fire.

For two years the battles raged across the lands, one side fighting for conquest, the other for freedom. Othium-powered weapons wreaked havoc on defending armies.

The red fire was hard to resist, but the white light was stronger. Gradually the tide turned and the freedom fighters regained control of their lands and their cities. The stage was set for the final battle.

The opposing forces met outside the Ackar city of Erbea in 1302 and the forces of good won the day. The alchemist escaped and was about to take his revenge at a wedding ceremony when he was bound by the white light. All that remained was his heart, or maybe his soul, encapsulated in a piece of red rock.

Dewar the Third succeeded his father and the new king promised a time of peace and prosperity. History would call him the Peacemaker.

Now, two hundred years on, a new Emperor seeks to rule the world, while an illegitimate son sets out on a path towards revenge and a thief begins to learn his trade. It is time for the alchemist to return.

The Island of Andore and the Neighbouring Countries

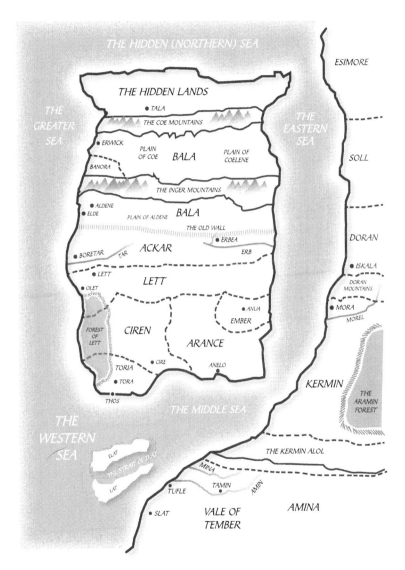

CHAPTER ONE

It was the year 1501 of the Third Age in the great city of Mora. Raimund was only six years old, and he did not understand what was happening in the next room. He could only hear his Aunt Astrid's cries of anguish, and he was scared.

Raimund had been born in Mora early in 1495, the son of a carpenter and a seamstress. The family lived in a small cottage in the Tradesmen's Quarter in the south of the city, and whilst they were not well off, nor were they poor. A skilled craftsman, Raimund's father was never short of work.

In 1501 a deadly pestilence swept through the city and mass graves were dug to the south of the city's river, the Morel. Raimund's mother was the first to have the ugly blisters burst through on her legs. At the first sign of the disease the mother knew what she had to do. Through her tears she told the boy to leave and go to his aunt's house and stay there until she came for him.

Raimund followed the small procession over the Mora Bridge and watched in confusion as the bodies of his mother and father were bundled into a huge communal grave. His aunt put her arms around him and hugged him close, sobbing silently as she saw her sister and brother-in-law deposited in the earth.

Mora was the rich capital city of the country of Kermin. Looking out from the city walls, an observer was presented with two vistas. The Kermin Plain, with its rich, fertile farmlands, lay south and east of the city. In the far distance the hills of the Kermin Alol would be just visible on a clear day. Beyond the Alol was the neighbouring kingdom of Amina and its capital city, Tamin. Looking in the opposite direction, the vista was dominated by the high Doran Mountains, which separated Kermin from its northerly neighbour, the Kingdom of Doran.

The gold mines in the Doran Mountains partly accounted for Mora's great wealth. The river Morel tumbled down from the mountains and flowed past Mora on its way to the Eastern Sea. The river was wide when it reached the city and the port at Mora bustled with activity as goods were imported from, and exported to, most of the known world.

Two retractable bridges spanned the river at the southern city gates. Initially the bridges had been designed to give Mora protection from sieges, but in the late 15th century, major conflict in the southern lands was largely a thing of the past. Now the retractable design of the bridges fulfilled another purpose; it allowed large trading vessels to pass the bridges and access the city port. The Morel continued its journey southwest to join the Eastern Sea, which separated Kermin from the countries on the large island of Andore.

The one hundred thousand residents of Mora lived in distinct quarters according to their individual professions, status and wealth. Outside the city walls a row of large warehouses lined the dockside next to the port. Behind the warehouses and just inside the city walls were the slums, where a warren of narrow, foul-smelling alleyways cluttered the southern part of the city to the east of the southern gate. The Tradesman's Quarter was less crowded and lay to the west of the gate, and it was in this area that Raimund and his family had lived. The main road from the castle wound down to the southern gate through the Merchants' Quarter and the Jewellery Quarter. The Military Quarter, with its barracks, was east of the castle, with direct entrance to the castle gates. The houses of the rich nobles of the city lay just below the castle walls to the west of the main road. The castle, with its high walls and multiple gold-plated turrets, sat on a rise looking down on the rest of the city. This was the luxurious home of Alberon, self-proclaimed Emperor of the North.

Raimund held Astrid's hand as she led him back past familiar streets to her own house on the edge of the Merchants' Quarter. The house they entered did not have the grandeur of the houses higher up the hill near the castle, but to Raimund it seemed like a palace compared to the little cottage his family had occupied in the Tradesmen's Quarter.

Astrid took Raimund to the small room that would now be his bedroom and settled him in. After drying away many tears, she persuaded him to go and play with his cousins, Erika, who was nearly four, and Egil, who was a year younger than Raimund.

Some time later, Astrid called the children downstairs for something to eat. It was only when Raimund smelt the broth that he realised how hungry he was.

The meal was almost over when Arvid, Astrid's husband, entered through the front door. He was a tall, bulky man in his late twenties, and Raimund had always been scared of him. His fear grew as the big man addressed his wife.

"So we now have another mouth to feed?" he grumbled. "We should send the orphan to the workhouse. With the pestilence in the city we are stretched enough to feed ourselves, never mind adding to our burden."

Arvid might have been a big fellow and the man

of the house, but it was soon clear that he was not the boss. Astrid held her husband in a steely gaze. "He is my sister's son, your nephew. He has nowhere else to go and he is welcome in my house." The "my" was emphasised.

Arvid sat at the table. "Get me my food, woman!" was his only reply. Astrid paused. "'Please woman' might get the response you request!" she snapped.

Raimund took a breath of relief; hopefully his aunt would be his protector.

Time heals wounds, and by the age of seven Raimund had grown used to being part of his new family. He could barely recall his father's face, but Astrid looked very like her sister and the young boy still missed his mother terribly.

Raimund was small for his age, and despite his aunt's cooking he remained as thin as a rake. The only shadow in his life was his uncle. No matter how hard he tried, Raimund could do nothing to please Arvid, and his uncle seemed to take pleasure in giving him a slap whenever Astrid was not looking.

One day Raimund found a strangely-shaped piece of metal at the back door and began using it as a pretend sword, defending himself against a long stick being wielded by his cousin Egil. Over the sound of the mock battle he did not hear Arvid step out from the house and raise his fist. The blow knocked him over onto the grass, and he sat up rubbing his cheek to see Arvid standing over him with the pretend sword hovering inches from his face.

"What do you think you're doing with this, orphan?" roared Arvid. He seldom called Raimund by name. "Do you know what this is?"

Still rubbing his cheek and holding back tears, Raimund shook his head.

"This is one of the tools of my trade, a skeleton key, and it will soon be time for you to learn about it," snapped Arvid. Giving Raimund another slap, he stomped back into the house and shouted to Astrid, "The orphan is now stealing from us. He has taken my key for a toy!"

Astrid glared at her husband, who quickly retreated and gave her his usual farewell. "I'm going out to the Tavern," he grunted.

It was shortly after Raimund's eighth birthday, over the evening meal, when Arvid announced, "The orphan is now old enough to earn his keep. He is coming with me tonight."

Astrid protested, but she knew her husband was right; it was time for Raimund to make his contribution to the family that had cared for him over the past two years.

Raimund was frightened. He had no idea what work his uncle did. He seemed to laze about the house or the taverns for most of the day and usually only left for work after the evening meal. He had wondered about the incident with the key, but he had no idea what a skeleton key was, or what trade it was used in.

Mora was cloaked in the black of a moonless night as the pair moved up through the Merchants' Quarter towards the castle walls. Raimund noticed that his uncle hugged the shadows close to the houses, avoiding the few people passing on the street. They took a sharp left turn into a broad avenue, and Raimund thought they must be in the Nobles' Quarter, a place he had never visited before. The houses looking out onto the avenue were huge; clearly only the very rich could afford to live here.

Arvid stopped in front of one of the houses. No candlelight shone through the shuttered windows. Glancing quickly left and right, he prised open one of the ground floor shutters and turned to Raimund. "You go through the window and find the front door that is just there to your right," he ordered. "Get in and check the bolts for me as I have instructed you," He waved the skeleton key threateningly in front of Raimund's face. "Then you will learn what this is for."

Raimund was shaking as his uncle shoved him through the narrow gap. Inside the house it was pitch black, but fear of his uncle pushed him on. He was trembling as he reached the front door. There was no noise in the house and the boy could only hope that the residents were either asleep or away from home. The latter seemed more likely, as the bolts on the inside of the door were not closed. This was the task his uncle had set him. If the inside bolts had been fastened, Raimund would have to slide them open and then Arvid would use the skeleton key to open the main lock and enter the house. It would mean the house was occupied and the robbery more risky, but Arvid had burgled many homes whilst the residents slept soundly in the upper rooms.

With the bolts drawn, Raimund was to find his way back to the window and let his uncle know he could open the door. In his frightened state he lost his sense of direction and turned the wrong way, away from the window he had entered through. The house was a maze of rooms and he was quickly lost. It took him some time to realise his mistake and find his way back to the window where his uncle stood in the shadows. Once there, Raimund gave a low whistle, as he had been taught. Seconds later Arvid was inside, and far from praising the boy, he cuffed him over the ear.

"What took you so long?" he grumbled. "I could have been spotted out there. I need to teach you how to work much faster." He left Raimund at the door nursing the bruise on his cheek.

It was not long before Arvid returned with his bag bulging. The pair left and Arvid used his skeleton key to lock the door from the outside.

Back at the house in the Merchants' Quarter, with the

family all asleep, Arvid could not help but boast about the rewards from the night's expedition. Out from his bag came jewellery, silver cutlery and two gold candle holders.

Arvid smiled. "Well boy, you are now a thief, but you have much to learn."

So Arvid trained his apprentice, and over the next year Raimund learned many skills. He could now quickly pick locks or move undetected through a house or shop to gather loot. He could also stealthily pick a rich noble's pocket without being detected. This latter skill was the most difficult to perfect, and Raimund spent hours practising with Arvid before his uncle allowed him to try for real in the market.

The first attempt in the merchants' market was nearly a disaster. As a rich noble was talking to the stall holder, Raimund quietly approached him from behind. The noble's purse hung from the belt at his waist, and Raimund had almost released it when the stall holder shouted a warning. Raimund froze in fear and just as the purse came free the noble swung round to grab the thief.

Arvid, who was close by, reacted faster, grabbing Raimund by the collar. "Sir, I have been watching this scoundrel for some time until I could catch him red-handed. I am with the city watch and I will take this thief back to the cells and ensure he gets the appropriate punishment. There are too many rogues on our city streets, and we must keep alert to stop them."

With a smile Arvid handed the noble's purse back to him and dragged Raimund roughly down the street. Once out of sight the boy took another blow to the head and a warning. "If you are sloppy you will get caught and next time I may not be there to get you out of trouble," he snapped.

Raimund learnt quickly and felt no guilt about his activities; after all, the family had to eat. They should have benefited from the rewards of his efforts, but Arvid quickly spent all the money in the local taverns.

By 1505 the 10-year-old had grown too big to wriggle through some of the narrow openings and his uncle began to use Egil on the night raids. Instead Raimund was sent out each day into the city to pick pockets.

One cold autumn evening, Astrid, Erika and Egil were in bed suffering from a bout of autumn fever when Arvid returned from the tavern. "Well boy, it looks like you are with me tonight," he said to Raimund. "I don't know how we'll find a window to squeeze you through, but needs must. We'll be going to the Jewellery Quarter. I am reliably told that one of the shopkeepers will be at the castle discussing a commission for the Emperor, and his shop should provide rich pickings."

A raid in the Jewellery Quarter was high risk, as the city watch patrolled the streets by night. It was around nine in the evening when the pair entered the Quarter. The cloud-filled sky blocked out the moon and it was pitch black, other than a few candles burning in some of the workshops and houses.

Arvid and Raimund clung to the shadows, constantly watching for the routine tours of the city watch. The pair reached their target undetected, and as Arvid had expected the shop and house were in complete darkness.

Arvid turned the skeleton key in the lock, but the door did not open. Clearly it was bolted on the inside.

Arvid shrugged. "All right, so someone is home and my information was flawed. It's a bit more risky, but we're here now and we might as well get on with the job. We've done this before – I just need to get you through a window."

As on their first raid, Arvid found a window and prised the shutter open. Raimund just managed to squeeze through the small gap. In moments Raimund had the bolts on the door unlocked and Arvid entered the shop. Quickly and quietly the pair scooped up handfuls of gold jewellery into the bags they both carried.

As the pair turned to leave they were taken by surprise by the shop owner. He was middle-aged and did not look as though he could overpower Arvid, although the large club he wielded showed his intention.

Raimund instinctively made a run for the door, only to be floored by a blow from the club. From his dazed prone position Raimund watched in horror as his uncle thrust his knife into the shopkeeper's chest. With blood pumping from the fatal wound, the shopkeeper fell across Raimund.

It was a few moments before the boy recovered his senses to find the smell of blood filling his nostrils. The front door was open, and his uncle was gone. Pulling himself out from under the body, Raimund could hear shouts from further down the street. It had to be the city watch.

Raimund was terrified. He might be a thief, but he was not a murderer. Blindly he ran from the house, and he kept on running until the sounds behind him died away.

It was close to midnight when Raimund realised that he had run home – not to his new home but to that of his old family, the small cottage in the Tradesmen's Quarter. The house looked run down, neglected and deserted. The small vegetable patch at the rear of the cottage, so loved and cared for by his mother, had turned into weed-filled wasteland. Raimund knew that his aunt had tried to sell the cottage; he had not known that no one had bought it.

The large red crosses on the front and back doors suggested an explanation. They indicated that people had died of the pestilence in this house; in 1501 and 1502 any such house was quarantined and left unoccupied. Late in 1503 a localised outbreak of plague had struck in the Tradesmen's Quarter and a few nearby houses bore more recent red crosses. Fear of disease and superstition that the house was cursed had seemingly deterred any new occupants. The heavy locks on both front and back doors also indicated that the authorities were reluctant to allow the cursed house to be reoccupied.

Raimund was in shock and too scared to be concerned about diseases, superstitions or curses. The large lock on the back door posed little challenge to him now that he was a skilled burglar. The door creaked open on rusty hinges, and as Raimund entered he felt as if he had stepped back in time. Apart from the fact that everything was covered in a thick layer of dust, and spiders seemed to be the main occupants, the house was just as he remembered it.

Tears ran down Raimund's face as he was flooded with memories of his childhood. His father's chair stood where it always had. His mother's apron still hung on the peg in the kitchen. In his small bedroom, the bed was still made ready.

Exhausted, Raimund sank onto the bed, and although it was now far too small for his ten-year-old frame he fell into a disturbed sleep. The night was filled with terrifying images, and he was constantly startled from sleep as over and over again the jeweller's bloodied body fell over him. Even worse, in some of the nightmares it was his father or mother falling over him with blood pouring from their mouths. It was only exhaustion that kept the boy drifting back to sleep.

Finally Raimund awoke to find himself bathed in sweat and shaking from the horrors of his dreams. He lay still for a moment, confused as to where he was in this strange though familiar room. Sunlight shone through the broken window shutters and birds were calling from the rooftops.

As he sat up, reality came rushing in. His shirt was coloured reddish brown and his hands were caked in dried blood; even his hair was stuck to his head and face by a mixture of gore and sweat. As he remembered the events of the night before, he trembled, knowing his nightmares were based on reality.

He struggled to the back door and emptied the contents of his stomach into the weeds. Then he slumped wretchedly onto the back doorstep. Taking deep breaths to calm himself, he knew he had to act. If his uncle had been caught, or he and his uncle had been recognised as they ran from the jeweller's house, then this old neglected cottage would not be a safe hiding place.

Raimund kept repeating to himself, "I might have been forced to be a thief, but I am not a murderer." Slowly the trembling stopped and he was able to consider what to do. First he had to get cleaned up and wash the blood from his hair and hands. Then he needed to destroy his clothing.

Just then he realised that he was sitting against the barrel the family had used to collect rainwater. Raimund could remember his mother's excitement when his father completed the project, which saved her the long walk each day to the nearest well. Hoping that the water reserves had remained untouched, like the house, Raimund lifted the lid and dipped the ladle into the water. Then he filled a bucket from the kitchen area and used it to clean the gore from his hands and hair.

Next he needed new clothing. He discovered a pair of hose, a doublet and a jerkin that his father had worn, and on trying them on he found they fitted, albeit rather loosely. Staring now at the blood-covered shirt that lay discarded on the floor, Raimund again repeated his mantra. He needed to dispose of this evidence, but burning the garments would create smoke and give away his presence in the house. With no other obvious solution, Raimund took a dagger which he had found tucked into the chest containing his father's clothes and sliced and shredded his old clothes before tucking them deep into the bottom of his father's chest. He covered the evidence with the rest of his father's clothes and then added other random items from the bedroom.

Raimund knew that the cottage was not necessarily a safe refuge, and he also suddenly realised how hungry he was. He had not eaten since the previous evening. Thinking that dressed in his father's clothes he must look like one of the scarecrows he had seen in the fields outside the city walls, he left the cottage, carefully closing the lock on the back door. He would check back regularly to see if there had been any activity near the building. If both he and his uncle had avoided detection then the cottage might be a future refuge, particularly once winter arrived.

Pulling the hood of his father's cloak over his head, Raimund looked out from the side of the cottage. The street was empty, so he quickly set off down the road, leaving the Tradesmen's Quarter and moving up the hill towards the Merchants' Quarter. Here he would find some pockets to pick, and then he could buy some food. However he would need to keep his wits about him, as he did not want to be accosted by his uncle and dragged back to his aunt's home. The thought of sharing a house with a murderer terrified him.

CHAPTER TWO

The Rise of the Emperor

❖ ❖ ❖ ❖

The Kingdom of Doran, Kermin's northern neighbour, was a relatively poor country consisting mostly of small farmsteads. Iskala was the capital with its large fortified castle sitting on a rocky outcrop from the mountains overlooking the town. The Doran Mountains created a natural barrier between Doran and Kermin.

Doran was unlucky in its geographical position. In the 13th and early 14th century the gold in the Doran Mountains had been found mostly on the Doran side of the border, where the gold lay close to the surface, but these seams had been exhausted over a century earlier. By the 15th century the gold seams were only found in the mines on the Kermin side of the mountains. It was this gold that had made Mora such a wealthy city, and over the years the Kings of Doran had mostly resided in Mora, only visiting Iskala during the summer months when the mountain passes were free from snow.

Treaties between Doran and Kermin had been in place for hundreds of years, and as any threat to the countries was most likely to come from the south, the standing army of Doran was permanently based near Mora. The alliance between the countries was further cemented when Elrik, King of Doran, married Princess Ingrid, the daughter of King Olsen of Kermin. In 1470 the couple were blessed with a son, who was named Alberon after his great-grandfather. When King Olsen died in 1473, with Ingrid as his only heir, the three-year-old Alberon became first in line for the Kermin throne. However his coronation would have to wait until he came of age, so in the meantime his father and mother became regents for Kermin and effectively ruled both Doran and Kermin.

The boy grew up knowing only the privileges of power and wealth, and as an only child he was spoiled by his mother and father. Ingrid often wondered what sort of king her son would make when he came to the throne. Even as a young child Alberon seemed to have two sides to his nature. He could be loving and caring, yet he could also be temperamental and fractious. He would sit engrossed as his mother read him a story and then suddenly throw a wild tantrum when he was not allowed one of the sweetmeats from the table. The tantrums worried Ingrid, as they always seemed to be laced with violence.

The boy had inherited his mother's intelligence and quickly mastered reading and writing. He also seemed to have inherited his father's cunning, often finding clever ways to irritate or avoid his parents. As to the temper, that was probably inherited from his grandfather, as King Olsen was known to be quick to anger and slow to forgive.

One summer afternoon Ingrid was watching her ten-year-old son from her rooms in the castle. The boy was in the garden catching butterflies with his net. The morning lesson had been about nature and the wonders of the natural world. Alberon had been enthralled by the drawings of the different animals and insects, particularly the colourful images of the butterflies. Ingrid smiled as she watched her son examine the red admiral that he had caught in his net, but the smile turned to shock as from a distance she watched the boy pull the wings from the insect and laugh as he threw them into the air and watched them float away on the breeze. The cold cruelty of the act horrified her.

By 1486 the sixteen-year-old Prince had grown into a young man who was certain of his destiny. He was short in stature at only five feet four inches tall and with a mop of blond hair, but his ice-blue eyes hinted at his steely determination and the streak of cruelty in his nature. The servants in the castle were wary of the Prince's temper, for a spilt drop of wine on a serving tray or a stain on a piece of silver cutlery could reward the miscreant with a slap, or the order to "Lick that until it is clean and then wash it and bring it back shining." Ingrid knew the stories, but Alberon was too clever to let her catch him mistreating a servant.

On his 20th birthday, in 1490, Alberon would be formally crowned King of Kermin, and when his father Elrik died he would also inherit the Doran crown. The wealth of Mora and the gold from the Doran Mountains would give him great riches and great power. For now however he had found love, albeit a forbidden love. Ragna, a year older than the Prince, was one of Queen Ingrid's maidservants. She was beautiful, with long auburn hair which she preferred to wear braided and banded across her head. Her brown eyes sparkled with mischief, and Alberon was smitten by her.

Ragna had been brought up in Tamin, the capital of Amina, and had travelled to Mora as a fourteen-year-old with her father Arin, a well-known painter who had been commissioned to do a portrait of the Queen. Ingrid got to know the young woman during the many portrait sittings where Ragna prepared the paints for her father. With the commission completed, Ingrid asked if the young woman would like to join her household.

Her father agreed and Ragna stayed in Mora when her father travelled back to their home in Tamin.

Ragna was ambitious as well as beautiful, and she understood that although her life in court would be comfortable, she would never have much money working as a maid. Her father's earnings were only enough to keep his small family fed and housed. At seventeen the young woman had worked out how to improve her future prospects; she would seduce the Prince. She had seen the way Alberon surreptitiously watched her when she moved round the room attending to his mother. When she turned to look him in the eye, he always blushed and quickly looked away. For Ragna it became a game, tempting Alberon's gaze with her movements, then quickly turning to catch his eye and the inevitable colouring of his face.

The Prince regularly attended his mother's quarters to read to her and to learn more about the responsibilities he would need to take on when he became King. At every opportunity Ragna would "accidentally" be in the same room as the Prince or attending Ingrid when the Prince was reading to her. Alberon was entranced by the maid, by the way she moved, her smile, the way the sunlight caught her hair.

It was a glorious mid-October day in 1486 when Ingrid called Ragna and instructed her to go and tell her son that the day's lessons were cancelled because she was feeling unwell. The Prince occupied a lavish suite of rooms on the upper floors of the castle. Ragna had never before been in this wing, and took some time to get her bearings.

Eventually she found what she thought was the correct door. Her knock met with no answer, so she decided to enter anyway. She found Alberon sitting cross-legged on the bed reading. Startled by the unexpected visitor, he snapped, "What are you doing here?"

Ragna knew the Prince's reputation with the servants and hoped that she would not find herself on the wrong end of his temper. At her smile the Prince blushed, but for once he held her eyes.

"I have a message from your mother," said Ragna. "But please tell me, what are you reading?"

Alberon felt his pulse begin to race. This girl was so beautiful. "It's a book of poems written in the early fourteenth century and to my knowledge this is one of the few copies to have survived," was his reply.

"Read some to me Alberon, please." Alberon was about to remind her that she should call him 'My Lord', but he stopped himself; this was no ordinary serving maid.

Knowing that she had the young man under her spell, Ragna risked perching on the edge of the bed close to the Prince.

"Please," she begged, giving him a winning smile. Alberon could do nothing but comply with her request. He began to read.

We met in the north on a spring day
I am sure now it was our destiny
Tender moments in the Nath
With the sand at our backs
Somehow fate set our path
A love that would last
Now in our winter years
Smile Elbeth my love
Shed no tears
White gold our rings
United we were
United we will always be
My love for you
Is for all of eternity

"It's beautiful, Alberon," Ragna whispered, leaning closer to the young Prince. Considering the reputation Alberon had with the servants, poetry was the last thing she had expected. Suddenly she felt a new attraction to the young man.

Alberon felt Ragna's closeness and took in the scent of the rose perfume she wore. Unusually her auburn hair was free, cascading down her back. She leaned closer to him, and uncertainly Alberon ran his hand through her silken hair.

Their lips touched gently. The first kiss was tentative, as neither was sure how to start, but both knew where the kiss would lead.

Later, resting in the bed, Alberon turned to Ragna. "What was the message from my mother?"

"I was sent to tell you that the Queen is unwell and your reading with her today was to be cancelled," she replied.

Alberon smiled and drew her back to him. "Probably just as well. I would now be very late in attending to her."

Over the next few weeks Ragna became a regular secret visitor to the Prince's rooms. The planned seduction had taken an unexpected course, for Ragna was surprised by how much she had grown to like the young man. To her he was gentle and caring, with a sense of humour she had not expected. His temper surfaced only occasionally when a servant knocked on the door. He would stride across the room and step outside, closing the door behind him. Then Ragna would overhear the tirade delivered to the unfortunate servant, and the angry words were often concluded by the sound of a blow. Ragna would lie in the large bed feeling rather frightened, but when Alberon returned to the room his anger would always have subsided.

Ingrid also noted a change in her son; she began to catch him daydreaming when he should have been attending to his lessons. She did not detect the glances and smiles that her son shared with her maidservant.

As the first early winter snows began to fall on Mora, Queen Ingrid noticed that her maidservant had started going absent from morning duties, claiming to be sick. The Queen was suspicious. It was not unusual for a maid to fall pregnant to one of the young nobles that attended the court; such were the opportunities and temptations in Mora. By the early days of 1487, Ragna could no longer hide the swelling of her belly, so it was no surprise when she was called to attend the Queen in her private quarters. The Queen went straight to the point.

"So Ragna, I see you are with child. I need to know who the father is so that we can ensure that you, and the child, are treated properly. Clearly the father must take responsibility, as you cannot perform your duties for me whilst carrying the baby. Such are our laws."

Ragna hesitated. She had known this moment would come. "My Lady, your son Alberon is the father of our child and he has sworn to me that we will be married."

Ingrid did well to hide her shock. Her son had clearly grown up more than she had realised. The law in Kermin was designed to protect the mother and the child, and it was quite clear and explicit; the father of the child had to take responsibility, even though in many cases the result was an unhappy marriage. Ingrid knew the law well, as she had been partly responsible for it coming into force. She had seen too many young women and their illegitimate children left penniless and forced to work the streets of Mora.

The law was clear, but Ingrid knew that there were other important considerations. In a few years' time the Prince would be crowned King of Kermin, and one day he would inherit his father's crown as ruler of Doran. If Ragna's child proved to be male, the boy would have a tenuous claim as heir and successor to Alberon's titles. To complicate matters further, the Prince, as a child, and without his knowledge, had already been promised as husband to Princess Sylva, the daughter of Berka, the King of Amina. With this marriage the dynasties of the south would be secured.

Ingrid had to act quickly before Ragna could bring the law to her side. That evening Ragna was called to the Queen's rooms to sit with her and read to her. The fire in the room burnt brightly and the room was hot. After reading aloud for thirty minutes, Ragna was glad to accept the offered glass of water. She returned to the text, but soon she found she could not keep her eyes open...

Three days later, Ragna woke in a strange yet somehow familiar bed. She was back in her father's little house in Tamin. Arin was there beside her, and as she stirred from her drug-enhanced sleep he drew his daughter to him. Realising what had happened, Ragna wept, and her unborn kicked inside her, responding to the panic she felt.

Arin held his daughter close and quietly told her that she had been sent home to bear the child. The accompanying letter from the Queen was more frightening, and he would keep it to himself for another day. The small bag of gold that had travelled with the letter would help him keep the threat secret – for now.

Alberon burst into his mother's rooms. "Where is she, what have you done with Ragna and our child?" he raged.

Ingrid gave her son a demure smile. "She has been sent home to Tamin for the birth of your child. It cannot become public knowledge here in Mora."

The young Prince was furious, and stamped his right foot on the ground like a petulant child. "Mother, you know our laws, I am the child's father and I have that responsibility!" he thundered. "I have promised Ragna that we shall be married. I love her. If you have sent her to Tamin, then I will leave immediately and find her and marry her anyway."

At that moment Elrik entered the room. He had the same ice-blue eyes as his son, and his cold stare commanded immediate attention and respect.

"Calm down, Alberon!" he snapped. "Whilst we need to adhere to our laws, it is not possible for you to marry the maid. You are already promised in marriage to Princess Sylva, the daughter of Berka, the King of Amina. Perhaps we should have told you this sooner. We will ensure that Ragna and the baby are well cared for, but they must remain in Tamin. Now stop this petulance and return to your rooms. I will discuss this with you further when you are in a mood to listen."

Alberon stormed out of the room without a word, slamming the door closed behind him. A young page boy was approaching the room at that moment, and Alberon grabbed him by the throat and hit him in the face. Blood gushed from the lad's nose, and a second strike would have landed had Elrik not followed his son out of the room. Elrik grabbed the hand and twisted the Prince's arm savagely up his back.

"Get out of here!" he roared. "I will deal with your behaviour later."

Back in his own rooms, Alberon burst into tears. Why did they not understand that he loved Ragna? Eventually he calmed down a little, and took down one of his books from a shelf. Coincidentally it was the book he had been reading a few months before when Ragna had first entered his chambers, a collection of the poems by an author of the 14th century, Angus Ferguson. Alberon studied it. The book was ancient, and woven into the cover was a motif of joined hands which merged into three words: *Aonaibh Ri Chéile.* The dedication on the inside cover was simply *"To Elbeth with Love"*. Alberon, despite his learning, had no idea what the words meant, but the love poems were soothing as he thought about his exiled lover and his unborn child.

Ragna's screams turned into sobs of relief as the new-born baby started to cry. Amelia, her mother, passed the little bundle over and Ragna held her small son for the first time. When Alberon had found out that his lover was pregnant, he had asked her to call the child Audun if the babe was male. This was a name from history, that of one of Alberon's forefathers. Audun had been the first king of Doran centuries earlier.

The baby grew into a strong and healthy child. The mop of curly blond hair complemented and somehow accentuated the boy's most distinctive feature, his ice-blue eyes. The small family were well provided for thanks to Queen Ingrid's gift of gold. In the spring of 1488, when Audun was nine months old, Ragna went to find her father in his studio. Arin had become very fond of his grandson, although he was increasingly concerned about his daughter's insistence that she should return to Mora and present her son to the boy's father. The time had come to show Ragna the letter and put an end to his daughter's impossible dreams for the child.

Ragna spoke before her father could stop her. "Father, it is spring and the roads north are clear. Audun is now old enough for us to travel back to Mora and introduce the Prince to his son."

Arin said nothing; he simply passed his daughter the letter. Ragna held her breath as she recognised the crest and seal of the royal house of Kermin. The wording was short and to the point.

At our command the maid Ragna and her child are permanently banished from the Kingdoms of Kermin and Doran. Whilst our law is clear that a child born out of wedlock is the responsibility of the father, our law is also clear that if the mother used sorcery to bewitch the father, then both mother and child will be sentenced to death. We have proof that the maid Ragna used potions and spells to bewitch our son. Prince Alberon has provided the evidence to support this claim. Whilst the death sentence was in our power to command, the Prince has pleaded for mercy. Reluctantly we have heard the Prince's plea and decided to be lenient. However, if the maid Ragna or her child are apprehended anywhere within our territories the maid will be condemned as a witch and her child a sorcerer. The penalty for witchcraft is death.

King Elrik and Queen Ingrid, Regents of Kermin

Ragna screamed. "It's lies, all of it!" she raged. "Alberon loves me and he would never have allowed me to be harmed."

Frightened by his mother's scream, Audun began to cry. Ragna started to tear up the letter, but her father quickly moved across the studio and put his arms around his daughter and her child. "Don't destroy it.

It was not the Queen's intent, but the letter is proof of Audun's birthright. It could play a part in the boy's future that the Queen has not anticipated."

Recognising her father's wisdom, Ragna folded the letter and passed it back to Arin. One day she would explain to her child who he was and what his inheritance should be.

Time eases loss, and separation is forgotten. It was a glorious day in Mora in the summer of 1490, and Alberon's twentieth birthday had passed a month earlier. Mora was decked out in splendour for his coronation. Flags flew from the city walls and the castle shone in the sunshine as the gold plate on the upper turrets reflected the summer sun. The lords and ladies of Kermin had gathered in the great hall in the castle, and the room reflected the wealth of the land. Multicoloured tapestries hung from the walls of the hall, and silver goblets filled with expensive wine greeted the guests.

Elrik and Ingrid stood beside the throne, one to each side. It was time for the regents to pass on the responsibility of kingship to the young man. Dressed in the finest clothes, Alberon proudly walked up the central aisle of the hall and knelt before his mother and father. Unusually, it was the mother who stepped forward to place the crown of Kermin on her son's head. It was her line that was now once again continuing the dynasty of the Kermin Kings.

The assembled guests cheered as the new King turned to sit on his throne. Having taken his oath to protect the lands of Kermin, one by one the lords came forward to swear their oaths of loyalty. This was a moment Alberon had dreamed of, and he gave no thought to his lost and banished lover, although he did at times wonder about the child. Did he have a bastard son or a daughter? But it really did not matter any more. It was simply the mistake of a lovestruck youth.

By the time three more years had passed, Alberon had grown into his role and its responsibilities. He had been well taught by his mother and father and had become a skilled administrator and a clever and cunning politician. It was also noted by some that the young king had inherited his grandfather's temper.

It was another glorious midsummer day, and another city was decked out in celebration. Tamin, the capital of Amina, was waiting for the arrival of the King of Kermin. As per the treaties Alberon was here to marry Sylva, the sixteen-year-old daughter of the King of Amina. Alberon had never seen the Princess, although portraits showed her as a flowering beauty with long fair hair and intelligent green eyes. Reality, as is often the case, painted a different picture. The Princess was still very young, very thin, and at five foot eight too tall for the King's liking. The portrait did however do justice to the Princess' fair hair and lovely eyes. Still, duty had to be done, and so the two were married. Alberon comforted himself with the thought that there were many slave girls in Mora who were more curvaceous and better suited to his taste.

The couple walked together from the wedding ceremony at Tamin's great church up the hill to the banquet laid out in the castle's great hall. Alberon did not notice the woman with the six-year-old boy at her side. Ragna had aged in the intervening years. The chemicals she had to mix for her father's paintings had coloured her skin, and the Queen's gold had been spent long ago. The family were poor and Ragna had to take other menial jobs to provide food for her son.

Audun was excited at the spectacle and was jumping up and down cheering with the rest of the crowd. He did not understand why his mother's grip on his hand tightened so much as she glared across the crowd at her one-time lover.

"Ouch Mother, that hurts!" he complained. "Why aren't you cheering?"

"Audun, that man is evil," she murmured in his ear. "When you are older I will explain and maybe you can right the wrong he has done to you." Audun looked at her in puzzlement.

Ragna stayed at home during the week of celebration that followed the marriage of Alberon to Sylva. She had no wish to see her former lover and his new bride. Audun did not understand why his mother would not go out and join the festivities with the rest of the family. Arin tried to persuade his daughter to let the boy join him and his wife at a street party going on just down the path from the house, but Ragna refused. She saw nothing to celebrate in this marriage.

One early evening, Alberon and Sylva were waiting for the servants to bring the evening meal. After two years of marriage the pair had become used to each other and comfortable in one another's company. Sylva had become an attractive, handsome woman. She was however almost a head taller than her husband and Alberon sometimes felt slightly inferior when he had to look up to her. Nonetheless he found her a good companion. She had a fine sense of humour, a sharp intellect and was, to his surprise, a very willing partner in the bedchamber.

Sylva in turn had grown to like her husband more than she had expected. Her first impressions on their wedding day of a spoilt, haughty young man had been proven wrong. Alberon was usually kind and considerate towards her, and he had revealed to her a surprisingly sensitive side through his love of poetry, something no one else was aware of. His dalliances with other women were one of her few causes for irritation, along with her husband's short temper, though it was seldom directed at her. Alberon, for his part, had come to respect his wife's intelligence and insight into matters politic, and she had become his closest confidante.

As the food was served, Sylva asked, "Alberon, what's this event we have to attend tomorrow?"

Her husband looked up from his plate. "Father is going to be showing off his latest present from Ackar's ironworks, his new cannon. I'm not sure why he is so fascinated by weapons when our lands have mostly been at peace for decades."

Sylva looked across the table. "Who can tell what will happen in the future? Elrik might be wise to stay up to date with the new inventions, as might you."

The spring sun shone from a clear blue sky as the procession headed across the main bridge over the river Morel. The pavilion had been set up on the Kermin Plain so that the lords and ladies could enjoy watching Elrik demonstrate his new toy. Alberon and Sylva sat together, front and centre of the pavilion. Flocks of rooks flew in clusters overhead, aerial spectators inquisitive about the activity on the ground and wondering if food would be involved.

Whilst there had been little conflict across Doran, Kermin and Amina for decades, King Elrik had a fascination for the new weapons that had first been demonstrated on the Island of Andore a few years earlier. In the early spring of 1495, a gift had arrived from the King of Ackar. It was a culverin, a form of cannon, the latest development from the ironworks in Ackar.

The beast had a twelve-foot barrel and was mounted on a large carriage. The fifteen-pound iron balls that were fired from it could travel five hundred yards when the barrel was level and two thousand yards when it was elevated.

There was a hush in the crowd as the King ignited the first charge. Then the crowd gasped as the machine roared and the iron projectile shot out across the plain. The rooks were less impressed and scattered south towards the Kermin Alol.

Elrik wanted to impress the onlookers further, so he ordered the gunners to ratchet the barrel up by ten degrees. The gun was fired again, but this time the explosion was much more devastating. Something had gone wrong with the priming of the barrel; the projectile had jammed and the explosion blew the barrel apart. The King, standing at the firehole, was struck by flying fragments of iron and killed instantly.

Queen Ingrid was devastated by the loss of her husband, but Alberon seemed largely unaffected. He told Sylva that evening, "I am sad for my mother, but the King and I were never very close."

Mora was ordered to spend a month in mourning. There was to be no laughter and no music, and all the population had to wear black on some part of their clothing.

By July 1495 it was time to move on. The old king was

still remembered, but it was time for the new one. Alberon was crowned in the castle in Iskala, the capital of Doran, and so became King of Doran and Kermin.

Alberon was not one to miss the opportunities power and wealth could buy. To the north of Doran was the Kingdom of Soll, and beyond that lay Esimore, with its tundra and reindeer herds. Esimore was of no value to the new king, but Soll, whilst also of little value, could have political possibilities. If the King of Soll would swear fealty to Alberon, his rule would extend from the far north to the Amina border at the Kermin Alol.

Under threat of an invasion from Doran, Aster, the King of Soll, agreed to swear fealty to Alberon. A large payment of gold from the Doran Mountains helped persuade Aster that his decision was right for his country.

In the spring of 1496, a second coronation was held in Mora. The new crown, in gold with precious stones embedded in the metal, shone in the sunlight beaming through the stained glass windows. So it was that Alberon claimed his new title: Emperor of the North, overlord of the new 'Empire' of Kermin, Doran and Soll. Beside him Sylva was crowned Empress.

CHAPTER THREE

The Painter

❖ ❖ ❖ ❖

As the Emperor of the North's power grew, so did his family. Sylva knew she had to establish her position as Empress, and it would be vital to her success to give Alberon his heirs. Her sons, when she bore them, would be heirs to the Northern Empire and potentially first in line to the throne of Amina, which her brother Bertalan had held since the death of their father Berka in early 1497. After five years of marriage, Bertalan and his wife Aisha were still childless.

Sylva worried about her own inability to carry to full term. She had had devastating miscarriages in 1495 and 1496, but at least she knew she could conceive. She had her own ambitions, whilst Alberon was all too aware of the dynastic possibilities in Amina, the only southern land not ruled from Mora, and the opportunities that might unfold to extend his empire, which was not as grand as the rhetoric described.

In reality Kermin was the Empire's power house, with its rich farmlands on the Kermin Plain, the busy port at Mora and the gold in the Doran Mountains. By contrast Doran and Soll were poor, and isolated as they were behind the mountains, they had little in the way of trade routes. Both countries were convenient for Alberon as they legitimised his claim to rule over an empire, but in reality the only other powerful nation in the south was Amina. Amina was rich due to the mineral wealth that was held in the southern Kermin Alol, the vast wheat fields and vineyards of the Vale of Tember and the large port of Tufle with its extensive shipyards. For every merchant vessel that sailed up the Morel to dock at Mora, four would have crossed the Middle Sea to trade at Tufle. Alberon coveted Amina's wealth and was convinced that it was the key to the next phase in the expansion of his empire. He had considered an invasion of Amina, but he was not sure what the military balance of power was, so he had decided that politics and playing a waiting game were a better strategy for now.

The birth in 1498 of the first prince, who was named Aaron, was a cause of much celebration in Mora. Elrik, his brother, was born two years later in 1500 and named after his grandfather. The two boys were heirs to the

Empire and, if Bertalan remained without a son, to the crown of Amina.

Sylva kept her own counsel, but Alberon now knew that his ambitions for the expansion of the empire could be achieved in the future. Bertalan was now the only obstacle to that ambition.

Shortly after the birth of her second son, Sylva was in the family rooms in Mora Castle looking for a book to read while the two boys were sleeping. The room reflected the riches of the Emperor's family, with tapestries picked out in gold thread adorning two of the walls. The wood burning in the large fireplace gave the room pleasant warmth, and the sunlight sparkled in rainbow colours as it shone through the great stained-glass windows.

Leading off from the main living room was the large annexe; this was the Emperor's library. Many of the books crammed onto its shelves were poetry compilations. Alberon had kept his love of poetry from his early years and indeed had published some of his own verse, under a pseudonym. It intrigued Sylva that her temperamental husband could demonstrate his softer nature in words but seldom in actions.

Sylva picked out several volumes and glanced at them, then returned them to their places on the shelf. The flowery verse did not fit her mood, which was sombre following a rare argument that morning with her husband. It had been a trivial incident over a request to visit her brother in Tamin; Alberon had refused, saying the boys were too young to make that sort of journey. When Sylva persisted, Alberon lost his temper. It was not something that happened often, but when it did it frightened Sylva.

At the end of one of the bookshelves she picked up a very old book. It was truly ancient, and woven into the cover was a motif of joined hands which merged into three words: *Aonaibh Ri Chéile.* The dedication on the inside cover was simply *"To Elbeth with Love."* The author was someone called Angus Ferguson and as Sylva read the love poems she felt a slight pang of regret, wishing that she could enjoy such a deep love with a lifelong partner.

Sylva leant back and closed her eyes to reflect on the challenges of her own marriage, and the book slipped from her lap to the ground. She left it there for a few moments, then stooped to pick it up. As she lifted the book, a folded piece of paper drifted out from the back cover and settled softly on the floor.

Sylva very carefully picked up and unfolded the paper, thinking she was handling something that could be hundreds of years old, but the unfolded sheet revealed a letter that was much more recent in origin. It was dated November 1486 and addressed to "My beloved Ragna." The writer wrote of the torment he felt at his loved one's banishment and the concern he had for their unborn baby. It continued to say that one day when he was old enough he would travel to Tamin and be reunited with his family. The letter was signed by none other than Alberon. Sylva guessed that it referred to one of her husband's flings as a youth; presumably the torment of separation had quickly passed and the letter had never been sent. A lover from fourteen years ago and a youth's heartbroken writing did not trouble her; after all, in the intervening years many other women had shared the Emperor's bed and for all she knew he might have fathered other children. However, if the child referred to in this letter had been born male, and still lived, he could be a possible threat to her own sons' right to their father's throne. Sylva knew she had to act.

It was a while later when Alberon entered the room, and he immediately noted the steely glare in his wife's eyes. Sylva may not have been completely to Alberon's tastes physically, but she was a king's daughter and Alberon appreciated her wise council and skill in court politics.

Sylva stood up. "I suppose you were never going to mention this?" she said, thrusting the letter forward. Alberon scanned the page and laughed. "I had forgotten all about this letter, it was long ago and I never sent it."

"I suppose you thought you would explain yourself when a bastard usurper arrived with an army at Mora's city gates," replied Sylva.

Alberon smiled. "It is very unlikely, my dear. My mother told me that Ragna and the child were banished to Tamin under threat of death if they returned to Kermin. The girl was proven to have used witchcraft to beguile me, which in turn negated our laws and removed me from having any responsibility for the maid or the child. She was the daughter of a poor painter living in the artist quarter in Tamin. She and the child may be dead by now, but even if the child lives the idea that he, or she, could arrive at the head of an army is preposterous."

Sylva was unmoved. "I want the threat of this child permanently removed, and I will ensure my brother carries out my instructions. I need details of the family, their names and where they live in Tamin."

Alberon sighed. "I think you are overreacting my dear, but if you wish, I will ask my mother for the details as she was the one who authorised the banishment."

Ragna's father Arin was returning home to the Painters' Quarter from a portrait sitting at one of the nobles' grand houses near Tamin Castle. As he turned the corner into Rose Street, he was shocked to see four of the King's Guard at his front door talking threateningly to his wife. Amelia was shaking her head and pointing up the hill towards the castle.

Arin ducked back out of sight. He could think of no reason for the King's Guard to be at his front door. His grandson, Audun, sometimes got into trouble as most of the young lads in the quarter did. The local constable dealt with these issues, usually with a good scolding or a clip around the ear. Was it possible that the youth had got into more serious trouble? Arin didn't think so. The Painters' Quarter was a tightly-knit community and everyone knew everyone else's business. Someone would have told him if some of the boys had done something to attract the attention of the Guard. Nonetheless Amelia had pointed up the hill towards the centre of the Quarter. Arin knew that his daughter and grandson planned to go there at some point in the day to purchase the new paint supplies he needed for his current assignment.

A sudden terrible thought struck him, and his heart missed a beat. He turned and ran through the back streets and alleyways. At the centre of the Painters' Quarter a large square was bustling with people buying goods from the market. The two large fountains glistened in the afternoon sunlight. Around the edge of the square the hostelries were busy, as most of the workers had finished their tasks for the day.

Breathless after his run, Arin cursed the crowds; his daughter and grandson could be anywhere. Then he remembered why they were coming to the centre, and the two artists' shops they would be going to where they could buy his supplies.

Finally he spotted the pair sitting at the edge of one

of the fountains, splashing each other playfully. Racing over, Arin grabbed Ragna by the hand and without explanation pulled the pair into the crowds that were milling around the market stalls.

Ragna pulled her hand away. "Father, what on earth is wrong?"

In answer Arin pointed over to the shops that Ragna and Audun had only recently left. The Guard had arrived and were obviously searching for someone. "I have no time to explain, but one or both of you are in danger. Leave here now as quietly and inconspicuously as you can. Don't go home. Go to your uncle's house on Mill Street near the south gate. I'll join you there shortly and explain, if I can."

As Ragna and Audun hurried from the square into the back streets, Arin saw the guardsmen leaving the second shop. They paused and conferred, then split up into pairs, clearly planning to continue their search.

As casually as possible, Arin wandered over to the artists' shops and innocently asked if his daughter and grandson had been to collect his supplies. In both places the answer was the same – the King's Guard had just been in looking for the boy with a warrant for his arrest. Arin felt his heart race as the terrible thought returned.

When he was not engaged on a commission, Arin worked in a small studio that he shared with three fellow artists. Here he created his own paintings, which he would occasionally manage to sell in the market. The studio was in Black Swan Alley, a short distance away from his house in Rose Street and closer to his brother's home in Mill Street.

Returning home, Arin again looked round the corner up Rose Street and saw one of the King's Guards standing at the front door of his house. Turning, he slipped unnoticed through the back streets and into his studio. It was in its usual mess, as Arin and his colleagues had had little time to tidy up. Half-finished canvases lay against the walls and the wooden floor was an art work in itself, splattered with drops of paint.

In Arin's corner of the studio was a locked wooden box where he kept some private papers and some of the money he earned from the sale of his paintings. Stuffing the bag of coins into his pocket, Arin searched for the other item he needed. Near the bottom of the box he found it, a letter stamped with the crest and seal of the royal house of Kermin. Locking the box again, he hurried down the hill to Mill Street.

Arin's sister-in-law Hilda opened the door. Raynal, Arin's brother, was still out at work in the grain stores. In a concerned voice Hilda immediately asked, "Arin, what is happening? Ragna and Audun got here an hour ago in some sort of panic."

Arin shook his head, and for some reason lowered his voice. "I'm not sure Hilda, but something is wrong and I need to speak with Ragna alone," he replied.

Hilda led Arin into the small living area and asked Audun to help her in the kitchen. Arin shouted after her, "Can you possibly make a small pack of food ready for a journey?" Hilda looked puzzled, but agreed, instructing Audun to help her.

Ragna spoke first. "Father what is it? Why did you point out the King's Guards, what were they looking for in the shops?"

Arin held up his hand. "My love I don't really know, but I fear I may be able to guess. The Guards had an arrest warrant for Audun, and unless you know of something he has done, I can think of only one thing he could be considered guilty of."

Ragna shook her head. "You know he gets into trouble sometimes with some of the other boys, but nothing serious. He is a good son, and grandson, as well you know."

Arin sighed. "Then I can only think of one possible explanation. You know that the Empress in Mora has recently given birth to a second son? I can only surmise that somehow she has found out about Audun's existence and instructed her brother, Bertalan, to seize him. If the King's men take him, I doubt we will ever see him again."

Ragna shook with a mixture of fear and fury. "So what must we do? How can we protect him?"

Arin took his daughter in his arms. "Ragna my love, you and Audun must leave Tamin at once, this evening, you are not safe here. Here is some money, take it. Go to Tufle and cross the Middle Sea to Anelo. From there, go to the city of Boretar in Ackar. You should be far enough away there to be safe, and I'm sure you can find work in the city."

Tears ran down Ragna's face. "We can't leave you and mother here and travel far to the north," she said in a trembling voice.

Arin paused and passed his daughter the letter. "You remember this? Audun has royal blood in his veins and maybe one day he can return to Mora and claim his birthright. You must go, and go now, before the south gate closes for curfew. I can't come with you as we may be recognised if we're together. I'll ask Hilda to walk with you to the gate."

Arin hugged his daughter and grandson one last time. Finally he shook the hand of a very bewildered Audun. "Have a safe journey," was all Arin could manage to say.

Early evening was a busy time at the city gates as the farmers and peasants who had come to the city markets headed out on their way home. Hilda walked to the gates with the pair and then passed them the bag of provisions that would at least keep them fed for the first stage of their journey. The guards on the city gate seemed more attentive than usual, but it was an impossible task to check every person leaving the city. Ragna and Audun passed undetected across the bridge over the river Amin, while Arin headed back to the small house in Rose Street.

On entering his front door, Arin realised that he had unexpected company. Bartos, the King's cousin and commander of the Guard, sat comfortably in the little sitting room. Amelia stood next to the small fireplace; she was shaking.

Bartos stood up. "Welcome home, Arin. Please tell me where I can find your daughter and her son. I presume that you have been with them, as you are so late returning from your work in my friend's house near the castle."

Arin shook his head. "I've been drinking with some friends in the square just up the hill. I have not seen my daughter or grandson since I left here this morning."

Bartos gave a cruel smile. "I need to find your grandson, and I think you know where he is. I would prefer that you told me now rather than have me force you to talk in the castle dungeon."

Arin shook his head. "I don't know."

Amelia watched in horror as her husband was taken away by the guards. She had no idea what her grandson had done; she had never seen the letter now safely tucked in Ragna's pocket.

Arin never returned home, and his commission for Bartos' friend was never finished, Bartos never learnt where the grandson had gone, and Bertalan had to inform his sister in Mora that he could not find the family she was searching for.

In the small tavern in Tufle, Audun asked his question again. "Please tell me mother, why did we have to leave Tamin? Where are we going? I want to go back home."

Ragna was tired from the journey, concerned about how little money she had and fed up with her son's constant questions. "Audun, I have told you that we needed to leave for your safety. You are not yet old enough for me to explain, but one day soon I will. Now it is time to sleep, because tomorrow we need to find someone to take us across the Middle Sea to Anelo. Hopefully once we are out of Amina we will be safe."

CHAPTER FOUR

The Den of Thieves

❖ ❖ ❖ ❖

Weeks passed, and the months turned into a year. Raimund, now eleven years old, had grown, and his father's loose-fitting clothes looked less baggy than they had a year earlier. He had become used to life on the streets, and practice had made him a skilled pickpocket.

At the cottage he had found a small casket that held the few pieces of jewellery that his mother had owned. Emptied of its contents, the casket was used to hold the ill-gotten gains of Raimund's thieving, and he kept it hidden in a hole at the back of the old vegetable plot, covered over with weeds.

Raimund occasionally used the cottage for shelter, especially in the depths of winter. The curse on the cottage and the red crosses seemed to deter any new occupants, but he remained concerned that his presence might be noticed by neighbours, or indeed his aunt and uncle. Aware of the risks, he only entered the cottage at night and left before dawn, always undetected and always closing the locks behind him. The spiders were left to rule the roost, as Raimund avoided any attempt to make the house appear lived in.

After the first few weeks of sleeping wherever he could find shelter, Raimund found himself gravitating each night to the docks and the slums. He had become immune to the smells and the detritus, and in the rats' nest of alleys it was easy to find a doorway or empty hovel to shelter in. Where a lock could be picked, the warehouses could offer superior accommodation. If he selected the location carefully, the warehouse could supply woollen bales for a warm night's sleep, meat and vegetables for a midnight supper and even wine to cheer up a cold winter evening.

All the skills learnt from his uncle played a part in allowing Raimund to live a relatively comfortable life on the streets. There were dangers too, of course. The slums and the port were populated by ruffians, and more than once Raimund was glad of his height and his father's dagger, which was always tucked in the belt at his waist. Whilst the dagger had been used as a threat, it had never drawn blood. He was a thief, but he was not a murderer.

Frequently Raimund could be found nonchalantly walking through the markets in the Merchants' Quarter or the Jewellery Quarter. In both markets careless shoppers would find themselves separated from their purses. He was very careful however, and only took one or two money pouches on each visit. Tall now for his age, he could not sneak through the crowds as he had as a small boy. With height came visibility in the crowds, so caution was always required.

A night-time raid on a tailor's shop in the Merchant's Quarter had increased Raimund's choice of wardrobe, which was stored in the old cottage, and he frequently changed his clothing so as not to be recognised as a regular in the markets. Being apprehended by the city watch was always a risk, but Raimund was in fact more concerned that he would be spotted by his aunt or uncle. Since the botched raid on the jeweller's shop he had not gone close to his more recent home. The memory of the bloodied body falling on him returned now only occasionally in nightmares, but Raimund had no desire, or need, to return to his aunt's home.

One morning Raimund lay lounging on some bales of cloth by the docks. He liked to watch the hustle and bustle here, but it was not an area where he worked. Whilst some of the sailors and the merchants in the crowds might have purses filled with coins, if you were caught in this area the retribution was likely to be fast and vicious. By the nature of their trade sailors were tough men, and any miscreant caught on the docks would likely suffer instant direct punishment. The sailors would not call on the city watch to intervene when they could deal with the thief themselves.

Raimund recalled an incident a year earlier when he had first considered working the docks. He saw a sailor whose purse was hanging carelessly from his belt, and this was Raimund's target. But just as he was about to move in, a shout of "Thief!" rang out from only yards away. Raimund froze in fear and then slipped back into the crowd, as it became clear that he had not been identified.

As the crowd parted, a shocking scene unfolded in front of him. The thief was being attacked by three sailors and was already lying prone on the ground with a bloody nose and mouth. They continued with their beating until finally one of the sailors dragged the man to the edge of the dock and gave him a final kick. The thief's inert body plunged into the waters below. The sailor grinned and shouted over to his shipmates, "A good wash should clean the bugger up."

That was when Raimund learned why bodies were sometimes found floating in the dockside waters.

The girl caught Raimund's eye because she seemed to be walking randomly through the crowds, sometimes with the flow of people and other times against it. At a distance she looked to be about his age. She was modestly dressed and clearly in that halfway stage between childhood and womanhood. Her long brown hair was pulled up into a tight-fitting cap, a coif. She might have been a maid to one of the noble ladies inspecting the merchandise on the harbour, or the daughter of one of the fishwives who were sorting the catch on the dock, close to where the fishing vessels were moored. However, the path she wove through the crowds suggested she was not in search of a destination or employed by any of the noble ladies.

Intrigued, Raimund roused himself from his perch and followed the girl at a discreet distance. He instantly recognised the manoeuvres; the accidental bump into the sailor, the smile and the apology. The girl was a thief, yet if she had stripped the sailor of his purse, no knife had glinted in the summer sunlight.

Memory of the beaten body being kicked off the dockside suddenly came into Raimund's head. Did the girl know how dangerous this place was if you were caught? Did she work the docks regularly? Would the sailors beat a young girl to death?

As the girl moved through the crowds towards the city's southern gate, Raimund spotted the man who he thought would be her next target. An old sailor appeared to be sleeping in the summer sun, and a canvas bag holding his possessions, and probably his money, lay carelessly at his side. The girl stopped to sit, resting against the city walls a short distance from the sailor.

Skilled in the art himself, Raimund recognised this was far riskier than picking a pocket in the crowd. He watched the girl surveying the passers-by as she waited for the moment when she could dash over and grab the bag without drawing attention to herself. Raimund leant against the city wall on the opposite side of the sleeping sailor.

A shout from the other side of the dock startled him. Two dockhands had started an argument, drawing the crowd's attention. The noise made the sailor stir from his slumber.

The girl clearly saw she needed to act quickly if she was to get her loot. She was remarkably fast, but not fast enough, because just as she grabbed the sailor's bag he in turn caught hold of her leg.

Raimund quickly moved across, and at the sight of his dagger the sailor started shouting for help. Raimund grabbed the girl's arm. "Leave the bag, we need to get out of here fast," he hissed.

The sailor's shouts were drawing the crowd's attention away from the dockyard argument, and some of those nearby realised that they were witnessing an armed robbery. Raimund's concern for the girl had now put him at mortal risk. Taking Raimund's hand, the girl dropped the bag and the pair dashed for the southern gate, chased by some of the crowd. Closely pursued, they ran into the nearest alleyway. Raimund knew these slum streets well, but the girl clearly knew them better. Dodging left and then right from alley to alley, the girl stopped at the door of a dilapidated house. Still holding Raimund's hand, she pushed the unlocked door open and quickly closed it again. Taking a moment to catch their breath, the two walked to the back door of the derelict house. This led into another alleyway, and as the pair entered the rubbish-filled street the noise behind them faded in the distance.

Confident that they had evaded their pursuers, the girl seemed to suddenly realise she was still holding the hand of a strange boy. Roughly she pulled it free, startling Raimund.

"I had no need of your help on the dock," she said angrily. "I could have got away from that old man and had his bag if you hadn't stepped in."

Raimund was at a loss. He knew that the girl would have been caught if he had not acted. With no experience of how the female mind worked, he could only splutter. "I'm sorry, my name is Raimund."

To his surprise, the girl smiled at him. "It's fine, maybe you helped a little bit. My name is Aleana. Come with me. I know someone you should meet."

Raimund was even more surprised when Aleana took his hand again as they walked down the alleyway. He began to recognise the area they were heading for. The old city walls separated the slums from the docks.

On the dockside stood rows of modern warehouses where goods were stored before their onward journeys to the markets in Mora or from the city out to the wider world. Inside the walls and closer to the slums were the older warehouses. The days when the city wall was needed for protection were long gone and many of the warehouses inside the wall were old and dilapidated. Multiple archways linked the old part to the new.

Aleana turned to her left following the old road inside the walls. Raimund felt a strange pleasure in holding the girl's hand and it occurred to him that he had spent almost a year in his own company. He hadn't really thought about it before, but now he realised he was lonely. Maybe Aleana would become his partner in crime; maybe even his friend.

As the pair entered the road that led along past the old warehouses, Aleana stopped and spoke quietly and honestly. "Look, I'm sorry for being angry with you back there. If you hadn't stepped in I would probably be in the hands of the city watch by now, or worse. I seldom work the dockside and I presume you know the dangers. Thank you." She gave his hand a light squeeze.

Raimund could feel the colour rising in his face as he responded with a question. "How did you take the first sailor's purse from him without using a knife?"

Aleana laughed and held out the thumb on her right hand. "With this." Raimund took her hand. Aleana's right thumbnail was slightly longer than normal, and more surprisingly, the end of the nail was honed to a razor-sharp edge. "This is as sharp as a knife and far less conspicuous," she said, still smiling. "Come on we don't have far to go."

As the pair moved towards the eastern city wall the warehouses became smaller, and most were now clearly unused and falling into disrepair. This was the oldest part of the city and had been the original port, but as Mora had grown in size and wealth, the area had become neglected. A century earlier and a mile downstream, around the southern city gate, the Morel had been widened. This enabled larger vessels to dock closer to the growing city. Few vessels now bothered to travel further upstream to the old port.

Aleana stopped in front of one of the old warehouses. This building appeared to be in an even worse condition than most of its neighbours. The front façade was badly cracked and the timber struts seemed to be barely holding the front wall together. Many of the roof tiles were missing and a garden of weeds sprouted there in the sunshine.

Aleana knocked on the door twice, followed by three additional short knocks. The man who opened the door was slightly shorter than Raimund, with long grey hair and a matching beard. He looked to be in his early fifties and despite the grey; he appeared to be wiry and fit. What took Raimund by surprise was the man's clothing. He was richly dressed, and Raimund thought he would not have looked out of place in the Emperor's palace.

The man smiled. "Hello Aleana, how was business today? And who is your friend?"

Aleana passed over the purse she had stolen at the dock and stood back. "Raimund, this is Rafe. Rafe, this is Raimund." She went on to explain what had happened at the dockside.

Rafe held out his hand. "Thank you Raimund, Aleana is very precious to me. She should know better than to work the docks, it's far too dangerous. Please come in and join us for supper."

Rafe opened the inner door, and Raimund gasped. The outside of the building was clearly a disguise, because the inside was warm and well appointed. The ceiling was covered in thatch and the inner walls were whole and solid. The floor was covered with what appeared to be expensive rugs, and stairs led to an upper floor which Raimund assumed housed the sleeping areas. The smell of stew made Raimund's mouth water, and it was clear that the aroma was emanating from the far end of the large room, where a small group of young people were gathered round a cooking stove. Raimund had heard of these stoves, but never seen one. Only the very rich could afford such things.

Rafe waved his hand, like a king displaying the riches of his great hall to a visitor. He smiled. "Welcome to the Den of Thieves, Raimund."

Over a generous stew supper Rafe introduced the members of "the team" as he referred to them. There were six others as well as Aleana, and they were all around the same age as Raimund. Rafe explained that the team worked the streets and markets, usually in pairs, and as well as picking pockets they also occasionally raided the warehouses along the docks where the pickings were better. Raimund now understood how the rich fabrics covering the walls and floors had been acquired.

After the meal, Rafe took Raimund aside to a quiet corner of the room and enquired, "So Raimund, tell me your story."

Raimund explained that his parents had died and related how he had been taken in by his aunt and uncle. Out of loyalty to his aunt, he did not disclose the family's name or location. He did tell Rafe that his uncle had taught him how to pick pockets and locks. He could not possibly disclose the murder, so he told Rafe he had left his uncle because of the beatings he had received. He made no mention of the deserted cottage, either; he would keep his bolt-hole secret for now.

Rafe smiled. "Thank you again for rescuing Aleana today. She was the first to come to me after her parents died in the same epidemic that took your family. She was orphaned with no home to go to and I found her wandering alone on the streets. That's why she is precious, as she is like a daughter to me. However she is also strong willed. I have forbidden her to work the docks due to the risk, but she insists she is smart enough and won't get caught. Maybe this will be a lesson for her.

"Now Raimund, one of the boys left the team a few weeks ago. He wanted to see the world and signed up on one of the ships leaving for Anelo across the Eastern Sea on Andore. So we're a hand short. Would you like to join the team?"

In his short time with Aleana, and in the house, Raimund had become acutely conscious of how lonely his past year had been. "Yes I would like that," was the reply, "although ever since leaving my uncle I have worked on my own."

Rafe smiled again. "I think Aleana can teach you how to work in a team and maybe you can teach her to be less reckless."

So it was that Raimund found a new home in the Den of Thieves, and he and Aleana became partners and best friends.

CHAPTER FIVE

❖ ❖ ❖ ❖

Ragna quietly opened the door and entered the room. She had left Audun asleep in the tavern that morning, and now when she returned her son barely recognised her. Her hair was cropped short and tucked under a man's cap, and she was dressed in loose-fitting male clothing.

Rubbing the sleep from his eyes, Audun took a moment to frame his question. "Mother, what are you doing dressed as a man?"

"Sailors can be very superstitious about having a woman on board their vessel, and we don't have enough money to pay for the transit across the Middle Sea," she explained. "From now on until we reach Anelo you must call me Ragnar and we'll tell everyone you're my nephew. We're travelling to Boretar in Ackar to take you back home to your father, my brother. You've been staying with me in Tamin to learn the trade of an artist's assistant. That last bit of the story explains the colour of my skin."

Audun shook his head, but he knew he had to agree to play the part. "I think it might be easier for me to simply call you Uncle as I'm less likely to make a mistake," he said. His mother agreed.

Tufle was Amina's main port, and the dock area was always crowded. Larger vessels that had crossed the Middle Sea from the island of Andore had their cargo unloaded onto smaller boats that transported the goods up the river Amin to the capital, Tamin. A wide range of goods travelled upstream. Spirits from Toria, wool and iron products from Ackar and hides from Bala were just some of the imports. Other boats made the opposite journey carrying Amina's produce of wheat, copper products, linen and wine to the port to be exported.

Ragna and Audun approached the dock cautiously. Tufle was not far from Tamin, and it was quite possible that the search for the pair would have moved to the port. Ragna could see no sign of a military presence, but she knew she had to quickly find a passage across the Middle Sea. If her father was correct then the Empress in Mora would insist on her brother searching every corner of his land for Alberon's illegitimate son.

Ragna and Audun mixed with the crowds on the busy harbour area. Ragna was looking for a particular type of vessel. She instinctively felt that it would be hard to keep her disguise on a big ship with a large crew. Equally she needed a vessel that was large enough to make the crossing of the Middle Sea.

The pair walked past the fishing fleet where the fishermen's wives were busy sorting the morning's catch and mending nets. Seagulls stood nearby and flew overhead, hoping to steal a snack. It was the first time that Audun had been at the port and he was almost as excited as the birds.

"Come and look mother, the fish are all flapping about and some of them are huge!" he shouted excitedly. Ragna had no time for looking at fish; the fishing boats would work at sea, but it was unlikely that any would cross it.

The main harbour was full of carracks unloading their cargo. These large ships, with their distinctive three or four masts and prominent aftcastles, were the workhorses of the seas, able to voyage even through winter storms.

Tucked in between these ships and dwarfed by them was a smaller vessel, a caravel. Ragna could make out its name on the bow; the *Swan*. Caravels were the little brothers of the carracks, lighter and more manoeuvrable, with two or three masts and lateen sails. They carried smaller loads than the carracks, but their speed gave them some advantages across the trade routes.

Ragna recognised the cargo being unloaded from the *Swan* as wine from Toria. Bales of linen stood nearby ready to load for the return journey. A thickset man with a weather-beaten face and a shock of black hair stood on the dockside overseeing the process of unloading and loading. He was presumably the master of the ship.

Ragna approached the man. "Excuse me sir..."

She got no further. "What do you want?" snapped the man. "Can't you see I'm busy here? I need to get this lot loaded and be sailing again on the midday tide."

Ragna tried to keep her voice pitched low. "My nephew and I are looking to work our passage over to Anelo on Andore."

The master paused. "Can you prepare food?" It seemed an odd question. Ragna responded hopefully, "Yes sir, I have helped in kitchens in the great houses in Tamin."

The master looked Ragna up and down. "And what can the boy do?"

"He is still young, but he's strong and can help your crew," she replied.

The master scrutinised Audun. "Well he certainly isn't getting free passage, so he'd better be a hard worker. You're in luck with your timing though, if not your destination. Our kitchen hand took sick on the journey over here and died before we reached the port. He now has a new job feeding the fish. However, we're not bound for Anelo. We're returning to Thos on the Torian coast to sell this cargo of linen, and then we reload again with wine and sail on to Boretar, in Ackar."

Ragna smiled. This was better luck for her than the master realised, and she responded quickly. "If you're agreeable, can we work our passage all the way to Boretar? I'm travelling with my nephew to take him back to his father, my brother, in Boretar. He's been in Tamin with my father to learn the trade of an artist's apprentice. I expected to be able to take passage to Anelo and then travel overland to Boretar, but if you can take us all the way that will save us time and sore feet."

Ragna hoped her story was not giving away too much of the truth. With luck the *Swan* would sail before any inquisitors arrived from Tamin.

"Well, it looks like you're in luck today," replied the master. "One of my crew is at the back of the ship loading the provisions for the journey over the Middle Sea. You'd best go and join him so that you can sort out your kitchen. The boy can stay here and help load these bales. By the way, my name is Ramon and on the *Swan* you always do what I tell you to do."

Ragna nodded in confirmation. "Thank you Captain Ramon. My name is Ragnar and my nephew's name is Audun."

The *Swan* may have seemed misnamed when moored at the dockside, but once at sea the name was less incongruous. As soon as the lateen sails on the main and front masts caught the wind, the caravel raced out into the Middle Sea. This was clearly a journey that Ramon had often made, and it seemed that the *Swan* may have made the journey many times before Ramon became her master.

Ragna was still sorting out her kitchen when the master approached her from behind. As the boat surged through the gentle waves she was having problems stacking the kitchen, and the rolling of the boat was unsettling her stomach. She had watched Ramon working with his crew and her son, and whilst he clearly expected his men to work, he did not seem cruel in his dealings with them.

The Master coughed, startling Ragna. "It looks like you don't have your sea legs yet, mistress." Ragna held her breath. "Unlike my men, I don't have any problem with having a woman aboard my ship, particularly one who can cook, but it is best that it is kept a secret between you and me. However I cannot promise to control the reaction of the crew if they find out. Your voice and your small hands are a bit of a giveaway, so you need to be very careful when close to any crew member."

Ragna smiled in relief. She was tempted to give Ramon a kiss on the cheek, but instantly realised the danger of that. She replied quietly, "Thank you, Captain."

With favourable winds and a calm sea, the crossing to the port of Thos was thankfully quick. Ragna ate little on the journey, but she did provide good fare for the crew. Audun, by contrast, suffered no sickness on the sea journey and seemed to settle well into the crew's company.

As the *Swan* approached the dockside in Thos, Audun saw a young boy playing with his ball close to the edge of the dock. The ball caught on a stone and bounced perilously near to the edge, and as the boy went to grab it he lost his footing and slipped into the water. Audun shouted, "He's fallen in, look, the young boy, there!"

Vasilli, the first mate, was first to react, and leapt from the deck getting to the child just in time to pull the boy's head back above the water. Ramon grabbed the tiller from the helmsman and held the *Swan* just clear of the dockside, giving his first mate space between the hull of the ship and the dock. Audun ran along the side of the caravel, grabbed the nearest rope and threw it over the side. Vasilli swam to the lifeline, still holding the boy's head clear of the water. Audun held the rope tight, but the tide was too strong and Vasilli and the boy were drifting further from the dock. Just in time other crew members joined the rescue, and the first mate and the boy were hauled onto the deck of the *Swan*, very wet but unharmed.

A dripping Vasilli grasped Audun in a wet hug. "Well done lad, that was a bit too close for comfort. If you hadn't reacted as quickly, this little one would have been lost." He wrapped the terrified youngster in a blanket.

Ramon came forward and patted Audun on the back. "Well done sailor, your uncle should be proud of you." Audun was slightly embarrassed by this praise, but he was delighted that the Master had called him a sailor.

Ragna worried that as the crew celebrated Audun's quick action he might give them away, but when they finally moored at the dockside her identity seemed to have remained secure.

On the dockside a grateful mother held her son close and thanked the crew for rescuing him.

As the *Swan* was unloading, Ramon came down to the galley. Ragna was surprised when Ramon passed her a small bag of coins. "You and your son, as I presume he is, have done well on the crossing," he said. "Audun's prompt action saved that boy's life, and he deserves a reward. Most of the crew will stay here in the port over the next few days and I would prefer you both to be a bit further away. Take this money and spend the next few days in Tora." The Torian capital of Tora was only a dozen miles from Thos. "We'll sail for Boretar in four days' time, so if you want to join us again be back here by mid-morning on the last day of the month."

Ragna thanked Ramon, and she and Audun spent a quiet three days in a small tavern in the Torian capital. Ragna was unsure about a return to Thos, concerned that her disguise might be discovered, but Audun was adamant. "I want to go back and see my friends on the *Swan*," he said and added, "Anyway, if I understand this island properly it will save us a long journey overland."

Ragna knew that her son was correct, and hoped that as they had avoided detection on the crossing of the Middle Sea, they would be able to maintain the deception on the journey to Boretar.

On their return, the *Swan*'s crew greeted Audun with slaps on the back and handshakes. The man the crew knew as Ragnar had always seemed reserved and had not joined the crew for meals or games. However the crew recognised that he had provided good food on the journey from Tufle, and if the cook wanted to keep to himself that was his business, although they did enjoy teasing the nephew about his rather strange uncle with his small hands and light voice.

Once again it was an easy journey. Light winds filled the sails and the waves of the Greater Sea gently rolled on the southerly breeze. For Audun it was an adventure. He was full of questions: what were those fish that seemed to fly on wings, and what were the strange beasts that were jumping and playing at the prow of the boat? The crew were amused, and teased the boy, calling him Master Questions. At night Audun loved to spend time with the helmsman, for whom he had more questions: "How do you know where to steer when there is no moon and what happens if the sky's dark with clouds?" The helmsman was happy to teach the youth how to navigate by the stars, pointing out the Plough and the North Star. When Audun was not working on the deck the helmsman also taught Audun how to use the compass.

A few days after leaving Thos, the *Swan* turned into the estuary of the river Tar. Boretar, the capital of Ackar, lay a half day further upstream. Despite the calm seas, Ragna had not fared well on the journey. She would be glad to be on solid land again.

As the crew started to unload their cargo on to the dock at Boretar, Ramon came up to Ragna. To the amazement of the crew, he took the cook's hand and gently kissed it. "Travel safely Ragna," he said, for now he knew her name. Shaking Audun's hand, he smiled. "Look after your mother." Audun did not know what to say. He had to ignore the shouted insinuations of his crew mates.

Boretar, the capital city of the lands of Ackar and Lett, was as large as Tamin and larger than Mora. Here the King's castle seemed to rise from below the ground. It was not built on a hill, but instead multiple layers of walls rose in splendour, and at the summit four great towers reached up into the sky. Ragna wondered if the King in his castle could commune directly with God from those high towers. The river Tar wound around the city in a wide sweep and Boretar's riches were inexorably linked to its port. The farmlands of Ackar and Lett were rich, and a constant stream of vessels carried goods into and out of the city.

Unlike Mora and Tamin, Boretar did not have defined quarters. Other than the area near the docks, which was like any other city's dockland, Boretar's streets were wide and explicitly boasted of the riches of the population. Ragna was concerned that in this rich city she and Audun would be out of place and thought that maybe her father had sent her to the wrong destination.

Pausing at the corner of a wide boulevard, Ragna wondered how she could find work in such a rich community. She had hoped to find an artists' quarter where she could blend in with the local population, but the dockside area now seemed a more likely place as she could find work in a tavern, and Audun could work as a dockhand. However with sailors from all lands coming and going from the port, the risk of their identity being discovered would be much greater there.

As Ragna hesitated, unsure what to do or where to go, a touch on her shoulder startled her. Spinning round, she let out a sigh of relief as she found the *Swan*'s master standing behind her.

Ramon smiled. "Well mistress, I am guessing that you have no brother here in Boretar. I assume you were leaving Tamin in a hurry for some other reason."

Ragna had no time to concoct a new fiction, so she had to rely on the truth, or at least something close to it.

Ramon had been kind to them on the journey from Tufle and had kept her true identity a secret. She hoped that she could trust him with more dangerous information.

Ragna hesitated for a moment. "Master Ramon, you are correct. The boy's father is a brute of a man and I became tired of the threats and beatings, but when I threatened to leave him and return to my parents' home he flew into a wild rage. He claimed that Audun was not his son and that he was now old enough to fetch a good price at the slave market in Tamin. I was petrified for myself and for my son. My husband threw us into a room and locked the door. We heard him storm out of the house, probably to drink himself stupid as he did most nights. I knew we had to escape and that my parents' house would be no safe refuge, as my parents are both elderly. Fortunately Audun is strong for his age, as you know from his work on your ship, and he was able to break the door open, so that very night we fled together to Tufle. The next day we joined your ship, and you know the rest of the story. Now I need to find somewhere to stay and work to earn a living." The tears welling in Ragna's eyes were real and added credibility to her story.

Ramon nodded kindly. "I may have a solution to both your problems. My trade has been very profitable this past year and I have recently purchased a new house just further down this street. Obviously I am mostly on board the *Swan*, so I need a housekeeper to look after the house whilst I am away and a cook to provide for me when I am at home. I think you could do both jobs well. Audun can join the crew on The *Swan*."

It was Ragna's turn to smile. "Thank you Master Ramon, I will do my best. However I don't think it would be safe for Audun to join your crew, as he may be recognised by his father in Tufle. Would it be too much to ask you to see if you can get him a job at the docks here in Boretar?"

Audun interrupted. "I want to join my friends on the *Swan*." He knew his mother's story was not quite true, but he also knew it had elements of the truth in it and many things were still being kept hidden from him.

Ragna's reply was equally blunt. "And then on to Tamin's slave market, I presume?"

Ramon settled the argument. "I can get Audun work with my colleagues at the docks and he will be trained by my brother to become dockmaster for the *Swan*'s mooring berth at the port. That should suffice."

The *Swan*'s captain was as good as his word, and Ragna and Audun soon settled into the rooms on the upper floor of the house on Cross Street. As he had said, Ramon was often away from home travelling the sea routes around the island of Andore and across the Middle Sea to Tufle and at times to Mora. When he was home Ramon was good company, with his stories and news from the different countries. Ragna and Audun were permitted to use any of the rooms in the house apart from Ramon's study and another private room just off the study. Ramon provided well for his housekeeper and her son and in time he almost treated them like the family he had never had.

By 1502, when Audun was fifteen, he had grown into a strong young man, tall and muscular with his fair hair pulled back in a pony tail. His most distinctive feature was his ice-blue eyes. The work at the dock was hard but paid well, and as he was now dockmaster for the *Swan's* mooring berth, Ramon added to his funds. Ramon would moor the *Swan* a short distance from Boretar's main port and one of the crew would come to instruct Audun to clear the ship's designated berth of any vessel currently occupying the mooring. Whilst the captain of the resident ship would resent the instruction to move his vessel, there was little room for argument as Ramon paid the port for his own berth. The captain knew that any refusal to move would only result in a significant fine from the port authority, and as that authority was Ramon's brother, the fine could be significant.

Audun was responsible for ensuring the *Swan's* berth was clear within thirty minutes of being informed of the ship's arrival downriver. This arrangement partly explained Ramon's success, as the *Swan* could unload, re-supply and reload faster than any competitors. Any merchant wanting fast transport for their goods would commission the *Swan* for the task.

It was an early spring evening and Audun had left the dock with the *Swan* ready to sail early the next morning. Ramon had explained that he would remain on the ship that night ready to sail with the dawn. Audun was therefore surprised when Ramon entered the living area of the house, and he rose quickly. "I thought you were sailing at first light, Ramon?"

The master shook his head. "We have a problem with the *Swan*'s rudder, so we can't sail again until midday tomorrow. I thought I would enjoy Ragna's cooking and your company for the evening before leaving tomorrow."

Ramon was surprised and annoyed to see Audun sitting reading a book. "Have you been in my study? You know that is forbidden!"

Audun was perplexed. "I know your rules and I would never break them," he replied. "I bought this book in the market this evening on my way back here from the dock." Audun saw the questioning look on the other man's face and continued, "And yes I can read, my mother and grandfather taught me." Audun held up the book so that Ramon could see the title, *A History of Sea Travel.* He continued, "I needed to read so that I could help my grandfather with his work."

Audun hesitated, as he knew he was giving away too much information about his past, but Ramon did not ask any more questions. Ramon smiled. "I wish I had known that you could read earlier as it would have made your job at the port easier. Also I could have helped you keep some of your savings. That book is not from my library, but if you're interested in history, come with me."

Ramon strode across to his study and unlocked the door. Beckoning Audun inside, he turned to the side room and showed him the library. The room was bigger than Audun had expected, and the shelves were filled with books.

Ramon walked to the centre of the room and waved his hand towards the shelves. "I collect old books. If I'd known you could read I wouldn't have prevented you coming in here. Many of these books are very old and I wanted to ensure they were kept safe. Now I know, please feel free to explore the library." He handed Audun a key to the study. "Only for you though, I'm not sure your mother would necessarily approve of your access to the history of these lands. You might want to start with this one." He handed Audun a very old book entitled *The History of Dewar the Third, The Peacemaker*.

After that, whenever he had time free from work at the dock or doing chores for his mother, Audun could be found glued to the pages of the book. He was fascinated to learn about the events that had taken place two hundred years earlier in lands he knew well. Due to the age of the volume the reading was slow, as each page needed very careful turning. Audun did all his reading in the library, to ensure no accident could happen to any of the precious books.

After a couple of weeks he had finished the story of *The Peacemaker* and went straight back to the beginning again. It was the early part of the story that most intrigued him. The young Dewar the Third, whose name was Garan, had lost his mother when he was eleven and Audun somehow felt empathy with the long-dead king, reflecting on his own life without a father. The first two chapters in the book told the story of Garan's father, Dewar the Second, and his wars of conquest. The power wielded by an old alchemist through red fire intrigued Audun. He had never before heard of this dull red rock called othium that was apparently found in the Inger Mountains of Bala. He knew that Bala lay to the north of Ackar, as Ramon sometimes sailed there to trade in the country's capital, Aldene.

The third chapter described the fierce battles around Erbea, where Dewar the Second had perished. It was the fourth chapter that Audun found most fascinating, and he read it many times over. He read how the nineteen-year-old Garan had suddenly found himself inheriting the throne, although he was a timid young man not ready for kingship – until he was somehow blessed by a man dressed in light blue, shimmering with a white light which carried a strange power. The story described how in that moment the boy had become a man and the prince had become a king. Audun had read stories of fictional heroes and villains before, but he had never thought that these magical powers could exist in the real world, his world.

The rest of the book told of the sixty years of peace and prosperity on the island of Andore that had followed, and indeed of the growth in prosperity of the land Audun considered home, Amina.

Audun found himself searching for any book in Ramon's library that could provide deeper knowledge of the history of the early fourteenth century. He wanted to know how magic, which he had thought was found only in the imagination of authors of fictional tales, had actually existed in his own world only two centuries earlier. A book called *The History of the Kermin Alol, 1270 to 1303,* gave much more detail of the battles fought near his home city of Tamin. The terrifying power of othium's red fire, wielded by the old alchemist, Oien, was described in detail in the chapters recounting the wars of 1301. *A History of the Coelete Nation* told the history of a people who had remained hidden in the far north of Bala for centuries. This volume also touched on the wars of independence that the people of Bala had fought in the early fourteenth century.

Audun wanted to learn more, but he seemed to have exhausted the library's supply of relevant material. It was chance, or perhaps fate, that drew his attention to a small table tucked into a corner alcove in the library. Two thin volumes rested on the table. The first book was ancient, and woven into the cover was a motif of joined hands which merged into three words: *Aonaibh Ri Chéile.* The dedication on the inside cover was simply "*To Elbeth with Love.*" The book contained a series of love poems, and he discarded it for the moment.

The second book seemed even older, and its pages were thin and fragile. However a strange white light seemed to radiate from them. The book's title was *The Evils of the Second Age*, and the author had a strange name, Ala Moire. Audun read this book first, taking great care with each page. From its pages he learned of the 'Council of Five' and the age of othium, when the red stone had powered conquest and aggression, followed by industrialisation and the expansion of power beyond the planet. The author wrote of the enslavement of the people of the world as they were conscripted to work in the othium mines and industrial factories. The closing lines of the book were short: "Then God intervened and the meteorite rains fell across all the lands."

These stories of the second age were beyond belief to Audun, and he had to conclude that they were myths rather than facts, although it was true that the current year, 1502, was formally described as TA 1502 – the Third Age. Maybe the descriptions of the Second Age were somehow factual.

A few days later Audun was in the library, somewhat bored with the love poems that had been written by an author called Angus Ferguson, when a call from Ragna stirred him from his reading. "Audun, I need your help in the kitchen. Master Ramon has been in the city today negotiating his next cargo and he is bringing some of the merchants here for dinner. I have too much to do and I need your assistance."

Audun obeyed his mother's call, but he forgot to leave the book of poems behind. Ragna saw it in his hand and instantly recognised the cover. With a gasp, she raised a hand to her mouth and then collapsed in a faint.

Audun dashed to his mother's side in panic and laying the book of poems on the floor he tried to revive her. As he helped her to sit up, Ragna saw the book's cover and shuddered violently. The first thing that caught her eye was the three words *Aonaibh Ri Chéile*. The words burned her soul like a brand.

Quietly she said to Audun, "Please take that thing back to where you got it. I can't bear the sight of it." Audun did not understand, but did as requested.

For the next few days Audun hardly saw his mother, as she stayed mostly in her bed. Ramon had left with the *Swan*'s hold filled with goods bound for Mora and would be away for several weeks. Audun worked his days in the docks, but he was increasingly concerned about the melancholy that seemed to have seized his mother.

A week after Ragna's fainting episode, Audun, on his return from the docks, went to see how she was feeling and asked her if he could get her anything. Ragna smiled weakly. "I need nothing other than to talk with you. Bring me the book of poems. It is time you knew more of your history."

Audun was reluctant, although he did not understand why; the book of poetry seemed to be the cause of his mother's retreat from life. But Ragna insisted, and when he returned with the book she asked him to turn to the second to last page. Audun did so, and was astounded as his mother recited the words from memory:

We met in the north on a spring day
I am sure now it was our destiny
Tender moments in the Nath
With the sand at our backs
Somehow fate set our path
A love that would last
Now in our winter years
Smile Elbeth my love
Shed no tears
White gold our rings
United we were
United we will always be
My love for you
Is for all of eternity

Audun was staggered, because he knew the book was very old and rare. He spluttered, "How can you know this rhyme, mother? It was written centuries ago."

Ragna smiled. "Your father read it to me not such a long time ago. You also need to see this." She handed Audun a letter, which he read over several times.

At our command the maid Ragna and her child are permanently banished from the Kingdoms of Kermin and Doran. Whilst our law is clear that a child born out of wedlock is the responsibility of the father, our law is also clear that if the mother used sorcery to bewitch the father then both mother and child will be sentenced to death. We have proof that the maid Ragna used potions and spells to bewitch our son. Prince Alberon has provided the evidence to support this claim. Whilst the death sentence was in our power to command, the Prince has pleaded for mercy. Reluctantly we have heard the Prince's plea and decided to be lenient. However if the maid Ragna or her child are apprehended anywhere within our territories the maid will be condemned as a witch and her child a sorcerer. The penalty for witchcraft is death.

The letter was signed *"Elrik and Ingrid, Regents of Kermin."*

Audun said nothing for a long time, until Ragna broke the silence. "Audun, there is something I must now explain to you. You are the illegitimate son of Alberon, who now calls himself Emperor of the North. His duty under the laws of Kermin was to marry me, and you would have been heir to the throne. The accusations in the letter you now hold are lies. You remember the Tamin celebrations for the wedding of the Emperor, and how I would not let you join in? Now you know why. Whilst Queen Ingrid did not intend it, this letter confirms your birthright. Keep it safe and one day I hope you will return to Mora and claim your rightful inheritance. Meantime this is our secret and you cannot tell anyone. The Empress knows of your existence, and that is the reason why we had to flee from Tamin."

Audun was speechless. So royal blood flowed in his veins? His thoughts returned to the reluctant Dewar the Third. Maybe one day, Audun thought, I will return.

The winter of 1502-1503 was one of the coldest in living memory. Ragna seemed to be dragged deeper and deeper into her melancholy and depression as snow filled Boretar's streets. The *Swan* lay in its moorings through the January and February of the New Year. The port at Boretar was locked in by ice and no vessels could leave the river Tar to reach the expanse of the Greater Sea. Ramon did all he could to help Ragna, whom he had come to love like a sister. It was to no avail; the doctors that Ramon paid for could find no cure. Perhaps her years exposed to the toxins of the Painters' chemicals had corroded her lungs. Whatever the reason, in the early March of 1503, Ragna finally succumbed.

Audun knew it was nothing to do with chemicals, but he had to keep his secret. His mother's malaise had started when she had seen Angus Ferguson's book of poetry, and he felt certain that she had died of a broken heart.

With his mother's death, Audun's determination became firmer and stronger. He silently vowed that one day he would go to Mora and avenge her death.

CHAPTER SIX

Aldene

❖ ❖ ❖ ❖

Audun felt the loss of his mother deeply, for she had been the one constant in his life. Over and over again he read the letter and the second to last page of the book of poems, and a cold desire for revenge formed deep in his soul.

Ramon liked the young man and tried to fill the gap in his life, increasingly treating him like the son he had never had. Audun continued to work at the docks through 1503, but every time he returned to the empty house on Cross Street his loneliness grew. Ramon recognised this, and despite Ragna's past concerns he felt he had to act.

As the spring of 1504 released the seaways from the winter storms, Ramon sat with Audun in the library in Cross Street. "Audun, I have a large contract to transport wool from Boretar and ship it to Thos," he said. "At Thos we pick up a cargo of wines and spirits to carry to Tufle. From Tufle we will take a mixed cargo to Elde, which is the nearest port to Aldene, the capital of Bala, and then we will return to Boretar with produce from Bala. Despite your mother's concerns about your presence in Tufle, I think it would be good for you to join the crew for the journey. We will be away from Boretar for at least a couple of months and I think you need time away from your memories here."

Audun was quick to agree, for Aldene and Bala might hold some answers to the questions that puzzled him from his readings. Why had Dewar the Third's first proclamation of his reign been to ban the strange substance called othium? Who had Angus Ferguson been, and who had the poems been written for? What did 'Aonaibh Ri Chéile' mean, and why was it on the cover of the old volume of poetry? On top of this, a return to Tufle might mean Audun could make a visit to Tamin and see if his grandparents were still alive and well.

The *Swan* left its moorings in Boretar in mid-April 1504. It was an uneventful journey to Thos and a learning experience for Audun, as Ramon had decided that now that he was seventeen years old he should learn skills beyond those of a simple deckhand. Audun was inquisitive and a fast learner. He had read books on the skills required of a helmsman and how to navigate by sun, stars and compass.

All was fine until the *Swan* came to dock at Thos. Audun did not order the sails to be lowered in time, and the ship met the dock and the rear of a large carrack at the same time with an audible crunch. On inspection it turned out that Audun had been fortunate because the retreating tide had slowed the caravel and reduced the effect of the impact. However Ramon and the captain of the carrack were quick to point out that books do not sail ships. It was a lesson Audun would remember.

The Torian port was a painful stopping point for Audun, as it brought back memories of the time he and Ragna had spent in Tora on their flight from Tamin. However he enjoyed being back in the company of the crew, despite their jibes at his prowess as a helmsman, and his feeling of loss diminished until the *Swan* docked at Tufle. Other memories rushed back as he remembered the rapid flight from Tamin and his mother's desperate search for passage across the Middle Sea.

Ramon told the crew that they could have a few days' shore leave in Tufle before the long sea journey to Elde and Aldene. Audun found the captain in the hold of the *Swan*, counting the final consignment of wine being unloaded onto the dock.

"Ramon, with your permission, I would like to travel to Tamin and see if my grandparents are safe," he said.

Ramon studied the young man. "I don't think your mother would have approved of that. She considered Tufle too much of a risk, never mind Tamin."

Audun smiled confidently. "Ramon, I am four years older and grown. Even my beard is getting thick. I don't think I'll be recognised in Tamin."

Ramon considered the young man for a moment. "Fine, you go and see if your family are safe, but be back here in two days' time. We sail in four days. You'll be needed to load the cargo and I don't want to have to waste time having to come and search for you in Tamin."

Ramon gave Audun a brief hug. "Finish your tasks here and you can go to the capital tomorrow. Take care and keep safe."

Audun left early the next morning, and saved his shoe leather by obtaining a lift with one of the boats transporting goods from Tufle to the capital. Crossing the Amin Bridge and entering through Tamin's southern gate brought back more painful memories of the hasty departure four years earlier. He remembered the fear on his grandfather's face as he and his mother were urgently pulled away from the square in the Painters' Quarter. His grandfather's last words, "Have a safe journey," seemed to hang in the air, and he could recall the tears running down his mother's face as she held him by the hand while they joined the crowds moving through this very gate. Other happier memories also flooded in: helping Arin in his studio mixing the paints, playing with friends in the alleys of the Painters' Quarter, and always in his mind his mother, helping in the house, chasing him to bed at night, just always being there, and now she was gone.

Audun quickly found the little house in Rose Street and spoke to a young woman sitting at the cottage door playing with her baby son, but the woman knew nothing of a painter who had once lived in the house.

Audun was increasingly concerned. He now of course knew that the flight from Tamin was linked to the letter from the court in Mora and his father.

He turned down Rose Street, and a few minutes later reached the studio in Black Swan Alley. The man who answered the door was colourful, or at least his apron was – it was a masterpiece composed of random splashes of paint. But he had never heard of a painter called Arin. He explained to Audun that he had rented the studio six months earlier from the owner, Bartos, Captain of the King's Guard. It had taken some time to clear the debris left by the previous occupants, as torn-up parchments and half-finished parts of paintings had been left strewn across the floor.

The painter shook his head. "I'm sorry, I have no idea who worked in the studio back then, but I do wish they had tidied up before leaving."

There was only one other place in Tamin where Audun thought he might get some answers. He made his way to Mill Street.

His great aunt Hilda was bent over working in the small vegetable plot at the rear of the house. She looked frailer than he remembered and he hesitated before approaching her. He feared for what had happened to his grandparents, and if his great aunt knew the reasons for the flight from Tamin, it might not be safe to approach her.

Hilda solved the problem. "Young man, what are you doing loitering about at my front door? There is nothing of value here for you to steal." Audun was relieved that even his great aunt did not recognise him. He replied, "I was looking for an artist called Arin who used to live in Rose Street. I believe you are related and may know of his whereabouts."

Hilda suddenly recognised who her visitor was and held her hand to her mouth. "Audun?"

"Yes, it's me," Audun replied, trying to swallow back the lump in his throat. Hilda quickly took his arm and hurried him into the house, then slumped into a chair. "Audun, what are you doing here, and where is Ragna? I don't know why you're here, but it is not safe for you to be in Tamin even now you are grown to manhood."

Audun held his questions and told Hilda about the travels to Boretar, although he limited the details. He decided that it would be better for Hilda to know only the outline of the story.

Tears welled in Hilda's eyes as Audun told her that her niece had died in Boretar. Wiping a tear away, she said, "I am so sorry Audun, I knew Ragna from birth and she was special to Raynal and me. Hilda explained that shortly after Ragna and Audun had left Tamin, Arin was arrested. She had no idea why and could only tell Audun that his grandfather was never seen again. Amelia, your grandmother, tried to find out where your grandfather was and what he had done wrong. She never found out. No one seemed to know, or those that did know were not prepared to tell her. Your grandmother's health deteriorated quickly, and I'm afraid she died, almost two years ago now. I have no idea why you and Ragna had to flee the city, or what Arin could possibly have done to be arrested by the King's Guard. I'm sorry to have to give you all this bad news Audun, but whatever Arin did it was serious enough for him to hurry you and Ragna from Tamin. I don't think it's safe for you here. You must go now, before someone recognises you."

Hilda hugged Audun for a long moment before he kissed his great aunt on the forehead and left the house and the city. He was certain he knew why his grandfather had been arrested, and now he had lost all his family. His vow became more focused and he whispered to himself, "One day I will come for you Alberon, and I will avenge my loved ones, my family."

It was a long sea voyage from Tufle to Elde, the main port of Bala. For the first leg of the journey the *Swan* travelled back across the Middle Sea, bouncing over the white-capped waves that were whipped up by a brisk westerly wind. With practical lessons learnt, Audun carefully guided the caravel into the port and docked again at Thos to top up on supplies. The *Swan* had not been fully loaded in Tufle, so Ramon decided to purchase some wine and spirits hoping he could sell these in Elde for a good profit.

Audun declined Ramon's offer to join him on a visit to Tora to discuss terms with the wine merchants. This journey had already brought too many sad memories.

Leaving Thos, the *Swan* progressed up the coast of Ciren and Lett, passing the river Tar that led to the home port of Boretar in Ackar and continuing further north to reach Elde. The long voyage was balm for Audun, as he was now given the role of second helmsman. Unhappy memories faded as he focused on the lessons that books could never teach: how to trim the sails in response to a sudden change in the wind direction, how to compensate for strong tides and how to minimise the roll of the boat by altering course to meet the waves. By the time the ship was approaching the port of Elde, Audun had become confident and accomplished in his handling of the tiller. Ramon was proud of how quickly his stepson, as he now considered Audun, had mastered his role as helmsman.

Elde, like Thos, had been built in the mid-14th century as trade flourished across the nations of Andore during the reign of the Ackar king known as the Peacemaker. Before the port had been built, all goods from Bala had to be transported by road to the markets in Erbea or in Boretar. As trade and prosperity grew the Elders in Bala commissioned the port and a broad road connected Elde to the capital, Aldene.

Audun was excited to arrive at Elde and was anxious to visit Aldene. He felt certain that he could find some answers to the many questions posed by his readings in the library at Cross Street. He was therefore delighted when Ramon announced that the *Swan* would remain moored at Elde for ten days whilst he negotiated the sale of the goods he had purchased in Thos. The crew were told that they could have shore leave in Elde or Aldene for the next week.

Early the next morning Ramon invited Audun to join him on the journey to Aldene. Bala's capital lay a dozen miles from Elde, and with merchants' wagons frequently travelling the main road to the town it was easy to beg a lift and avoid the long walk.

Audun's first glimpse of Aldene was of the old castle with its tall keep perched on the rocky crag to the west of the town. The main road ran towards the castle before turning and approaching Aldene from the south. As the merchant's wagon drew nearer to the capital it was clear to Audun that Aldene had two distinct districts. The tall town walls hid the Old Town from view, except for the castle. Clustered around the main road to the west and south was a new town that spoke of the prosperity that had developed with the opening of the port at Elde. The new town was a mixture of small cottages clustering around side streets, whilst the main road was bordered by warehouses and larger, more extensive dwellings. Ramon explained that most of Aldene's merchants lived in the new town, whilst the cottages housed many of Aldene's tradesmen and the families of farmhands who worked the fields on the plain. However their destination was the Old Town.

The pair crossed the bridge that spanned the deep ditch in front of the Old Town walls and entered by the southern gate. The tall town walls encircled Aldene, meeting in the west at the castle. Audun realised that the Old Town had been a place of refuge and defence in years gone by, and in his mind's eye he imagined great armies arrayed outside the town and laying siege to the fortress.

As they passed through the old gateway, the grey stone houses and the cobbled streets wound up towards the castle on its rocky crag. The Old Town felt less prosperous than the new town that the pair had just passed through, but the surroundings gave a sense of solidity and timeliness as though it had been like this for centuries. This was indeed the case, as Aldene's Old

Town had not developed like the cities of Mora, Tamin and Boretar, which had all been modernised over the past seventy-five years. The great southern cities all had river access to the sea, and this had driven their development. Aldene's new town had developed once the port at Elde opened leaving the Old Town much as it had always been.

Ramon and Audun walked along the main cobbled street that wound up towards the castle. Shortly before the castle, Ramon stopped at a large house with a plaque on the wall. Audun read the words, intrigued. "In memory of Gordon Graham, murdered in front of this house in 1300: Erected by order of James Cameron, 5th September 1302."

Audun was lost in thought. What had happened here over 200 years ago? Who was Gordon Graham? Had this man died in the wars of the early 14th century that Audun had read about in the histories in the Cross Street library?

His thoughts were interrupted by a cough from Ramon. Audun had been so absorbed in his ponderings that he hadn't notice the door of the house opening. Ramon spoke first.

"Audun, let me introduce you to Master Gordon Graham, who is a friend of mine and a customer. Master Graham has kindly agreed that we can lodge with him over the next few days. Gordon, this is Audun, who is ..." he paused. "Well, I suppose Audun is my stepson."

Graham offered his hand. "Welcome to Aldene Audun, I hope you enjoy your visit to our proud old town." Audun shook the offered hand and took in the appearance of his host. Graham was tall and well dressed with neatly-cut ginger hair, and Audun thought he was in his mid-forties, of a similar age to Ramon.

Without thinking, Audun blurted out, "Is the plaque on the wall for you?"

Graham could not hold back a laugh. Realising the stupidity of the question, Audun continued, "Well as you are here and not dead, and you would have to be over two hundred years old, I guess that was a very silly question."

Graham smiled again. "There's a story to be told, but not now. Ramon and I have business to discuss, so why not take the day and explore Aldene? I'll tell you about the plaque over dinner later."

Audun shook the merchant's hand again. "Thank you. I will go and explore, but I'll be back here late afternoon. I am really looking forward to hearing your story."

The old town of Aldene was much smaller than the other cities that Audun knew. Tamin and Boretar were on a grander scale and Audun had never visited the great southern city of Mora. The compactness of the town meant that exploring on foot was easy. Audun loved the old cobbled streets and the narrow alleyways that opened up to the rear of the houses where small vegetable patches were often being cultivated. In other areas the alleyways led to small squares where people sat chatting outside the taverns. Often the squares' edges were populated with shops where butchers, bakers and grocers presented their wares to the passers-by.

After stopping to buy a small loaf, Audun sat in the warm summer sun and drank in the atmosphere. Compared to the hustle and bustle of the busy southern cities, Aldene's Old Town felt quiet and secure, as though the town itself knew its place and was comfortable with it. He wondered about the plaque on the wall, and the brief references to Aldene in the books that he had read back in Cross Street, and he suspected that Aldene had not always been quite so quiet and peaceful.

Having sat for a while lost in thought, Audun turned back south away from the castle. At the southern gate he had noticed steps leading up to the old town wall. Despite their age and the fact that the Island of Andore had known little conflict in living memory, Aldene's old walls remained well maintained and strong.

From the southern wall Audun looked out over the sprawling buildings of the new town and on over to the Plain of Aldene, which stretched far into the distance. Moving east then north along the wall, Audun drew closer to the castle. The view to the north was spectacular in the summer sun. In the distance the mountain range seemed to almost reach to the sky. The mountains stretched east to west as far as the eye could see and the highest peaks still held patches of snow on their summits. Audun did not know the name of the mountain range, but from his reading of *A History of the Coelete Nation* he did know that the home lands of the Coelete lay somewhere much further to the north.

On reaching the point where the town wall joined the castle walls, Audun found a narrow stairway that led down to the esplanade and the front gate of the castle. Before taking the steps down, he noticed for the first time the flag flying proudly from the top of the castle keep, a diagonal blue cross with red edging on a white background.

When he followed the stairway down to the castle gate, he was halted by two guards. Both were armed and wore livery that matched the colours of the proud flag flying from the castle keep. The surcoats of white with their red-edged blue cross seemed to Audun to be something born out of times long past. The stern looks on the guards' faces confirmed that entry to the castle was not permitted.

Audun found a shaded spot under a tree on the edge of the esplanade and sat there quietly, taking in the surroundings and wondering what histories these walls and streets could tell.

Suddenly his thoughts were interrupted by a voice. "May I join you in the shade, young man? It's a bit warm in the sun for me these days." The speaker was old and frail, and before Audun could reply the other man sat down and offered his hand.

"My name is David Burnett, and I saw that you hoped to enter the castle. I am afraid it is forbidden, although my residence is within the castle walls. I assume that you have recently arrived here in Aldene? You were deep in thought as I came across to the shade and I wondered what it was that you were contemplating."

Audun shook the offered hand. "How do you do. My name is Audun, and yes I docked at Elde this morning on a merchant ship from Boretar. I was wondering what tales these walls could tell if they had the power of speech."

The old man smiled. "If they could talk, these walls would tell you of battles lost and won, of fear and terror, of red fire and white light, of peace and prosperity. Aldene has a history going back centuries."

Burnett paused for a second to clear his throat before continuing. "Did you take a walk around the town walls? The views are spectacular at this time of year, out over the southern plain and then on northwards to the spectacle of the Inger Mountains."

Audun was unsure where to start, so he leapt straight in. "I have read a little of the histories of the past, but little is told of Aldene. Whose flag flies at the castle top? Who are the guards, and why are they dressed in coats that seem to come from a long time in the past? Who was Gordon Graham?"

Burnett held up a wizened hand. "You go too fast, young man, with too many questions. I am out of breath just listening to you. Please, one at a time. Firstly, the flag. That is the flag of Clan Cameron and indicates that the current chief, James Ferguson, is in residence. Secondly the guard are dressed in the livery of the Red Cameron, a band of warriors that fought in the wars of independence over two centuries ago. Today, after almost two centuries of peace, the robes are largely ceremonial. However the Red Cameron does still train in case of war."

Audun held his next question and instead asked, "How is it that you have accommodation in the castle?"

Again the old man smiled. "My ancestors were captains in the Red Cameron and long ago, as a gift, one of them was granted land within the castle walls in perpetuity."

Audun could not hold back the next question. "Who was Gordon Graham? And why does he have a memorial plaque on the house down the road?"

Burnett shrugged. "Aldene has many stories to tell, but I have been out in the sun rather too long and I need to go back to my rooms and rest. You can find me here most days – I like to try to keep these old legs moving by a daily walk round the castle walls. Next time I'll be happy to tell you what I know. Until another day then, go and enjoy Aldene." With that the old man rose and walked slowly past the guards and into the castle precinct.

Somewhat later than intended, Audun returned to the house on the corner of Castle Street and Castle Walk. Gordon Graham opened the door. "Welcome back, Audun. You must have been engrossed in your exploration, as we expected you to return somewhat earlier. Never mind, you are still in plenty of time to freshen up and join us for dinner."

Audun apologised, and when he returned to the dining room an hour later his host was already seated, along with Ramon. Audun was introduced to Jane Graham, Gordon's wife. During the meal most of the talk revolved around Ramon's news from the southern countries. As a successful merchant Gordon was keen to keep up to date with news of trade across Andore and the lands further south across the Middle Sea. Jane Graham said little, but the questions she asked indicated that she was closely involved with her husband's business.

As the meal drew to an end, Ramon turned to Audun. "So how was your exploring this afternoon?"

Audun described his wanderings around the old town and his meeting with David Burnett. Gordon Graham smiled. "So you met old Burnett, did you? He can tell you far more about Aldene and Bala's history than I can. Like my ancestor, his forefathers were prominent in Bala's wars of independence in the early 14th century.

Burnett is a historian and reputedly he holds one of the largest collections of books from that period."

Ramon nodded and added, "I have met the old man a few times and in the past I've purchased books from him. Indeed some of the histories you read back in Boretar were purchased from him."

"Would I be allowed to visit his library and read any of his books?" Audun asked eagerly.

Graham shrugged. "I don't know. It's not easy to get permission to enter the castle."

"So what do you know, Master Graham, and who was your ancient namesake?"

"Audun, I am a merchant and really only interested in today and the business of the future," replied Graham. "What I know about the plaque on the wall is from the stories my father told me and what I have learned from David Burnett's explanations of the history of this house. The house has been owned by my family for hundreds of years. In the latter part of the 13th century my ancestor, also named Gordon, was resident here. That Gordon Graham was a warrior, not a merchant, and he was present in many of the battles that were fought across Andore in those days. Probably more importantly, he was mentor of one James Cameron, heir to the chief of Clan Cameron at that time, or to name him properly, Elder of Clan Cameron. James Cameron was one of the prominent knights of the late 13th and early 14th century.

"In 1300 a large army from Ackar and Lett, led by King Dewar the Second, invaded Bala looking to obtain some sort of mineral that was found in the Inger Mountains. That's the name of the mountains you will have seen to the north. I believe that in that time most of the population of Bala were evacuated to lands beyond the Inger. My ancestor was too old for the travel and stayed in Aldene. For some reason I don't know, that Gordon Graham was executed by the invaders outside the door of this house. It was shortly after the recapture of Aldene that his protégé, James Cameron, had that plaque nailed to the wall in his mentor's memory. Beyond that I haven't explored, although I'm sure Master Burnett can supply you with more of the history if you are really interested."

The next morning Audun returned to the castle forecourt, hoping that the old man was a regular visitor. An hour or two passed and Audun was considering giving up when a hand touched his shoulder.

"Are you planning to spend all your shore leave dozing under this tree?"

David Burnett had seemingly appeared from nowhere. Despite resting in the shade Audun knew he hadn't missed the old man coming through the main castle gate.

"How did you come upon me without me seeing you?" asked Audun.

The old man smiled. "When you know the history of this place there are many secret ways in and out of the castle. I saw you from my rooms in the keep and decided to surprise you. I assume you want to continue your questions of yesterday? But first tell me more about yourself."

Audun kept largely to the story his mother had used when they arrived in Boretar. The old man appeared to be dozing as Audun finished it, so he hesitated before continuing.

"As you know I am staying with my ship's captain in the house of Master Graham," he went on. "Over dinner Master Graham told me you are the most knowledgeable historian in Bala and you have a library with many books from the early 14th century. Would it be possible to visit your library and read some of the histories?"

Burnett stirred and opened one eye. "It's difficult to obtain permission to enter the castle, but why would you want to know about 14th century history?"

"My stepfather, Ramon, is captain of the *Swan* and his library has some books that I think he obtained from you."

Burnett nodded. "Yes I know Ramon, he's a good man and I know he likes to read about the olden days."

"Well, I have read several of his books, The History of the Kermin Alol, 1270 to 1303, A History of the Coelete Nation, The Evils of the Second Age, The History of

Dewar the Third, the Peacemaker, and an old book of poetry written by someone called Angus Ferguson. The stories intrigue me, but they don't answer my questions. Why was Bala invaded? Who was Angus Ferguson, and who were the poems written for? What was othium, the mineral that the invaders sought to harvest in Bala?"

Burnett laughed out loud; he was warming to the young man's enthusiasm. "Well my young friend, you certainly are full of questions. You have clearly already read enough for your interest to be genuine. Let me think. Meet me here tomorrow at nine o' clock and we'll see what is possible."

It was another clear blue-sky morning, and Audun this time was pacing round the castle esplanade. He had arrived early, but as the sun continued its rise in the sky there was no sign of David Burnett. Deciding he would wait only a few more minutes, Audun sat down again in the shade of the tree. Once again the hand on the shoulder surprised him, and once again he wondered how the old man managed to do it.

Burnett sat beside Audun and shaded his eyes from the rising sun. "It's going to be very hot today. I'm glad you could come to meet me."

Audun felt a touch of irritation. "I nearly left. You are much later than the time you suggested and I thought you might not come."

Burnett's voice became quiet and more serious. "It's fine to have enthusiasm for history young man, but the study requires patience. I know you are enthusiastic, but I wondered if you were patient. You passed my test, although by the sound of it only just. Come, I will take you to my library."

Audun fully expected the old man to lead him to some secret passage that led into the castle. Instead Master Burnett strode towards the main gate, where he spoke to the Red Cameron guards. "I have an approved visitor who I am taking to my rooms."

The two guards raised their long spears and saluted and Audun was inside the castle. From the castle gate, Burnett led the way across to the entrance to the tall keep, where again the two Red Cameron guards saluted.

Burnett's rooms were on the second floor. The old man clearly had some status in the hierarchy of Bala, as the rooms were well appointed, with warm carpets on the floors and tapestries hanging on the walls. Burnett led Audun through the main living room to a large side room with windows looking out over the old town to the south and the distant Inger Mountains to the north.

This was the library, and it was piled high with books. Stacks of them covered the floor and all the shelves. A small desk and chair sat beside a wall close to a window, the only indicators that the room had any human visitors.

Burnett waved his hand round the room as though conducting an orchestra. "So where would you like to start, young Audun?"

Audun had no idea and picked up the closest book. The title was *The best Torian wines of the late 15th Century.* Audun was not interested in the content of the book, but he was intrigued by its appearance. It was new, and the type was of a sort he had never seen before. There were several copies lying on the table. Audun knew books were very expensive and only owned by the wealthy. In addition he was one of the few people he knew who could read and write. All the books Audun had read had been copied by hand from originals or crudely printed with ink and wooden blocks. This was different; it had clear print and could be read easily.

Burnett anticipated Audun's question. "This book and several others here were created in Boretar by a new machine. It's called a printing press, and it can produce books much faster and with better quality than has ever been possible before. I purchased a similar machine a few months ago and it is just beginning to produce books. I hope to be able to print books about the history of Bala to educate the people about the challenges faced in the past by their forefathers. For now though, I don't think you are interested in reading about Torian wine. The stories you want to read are on this shelf over here. These are all histories of Bala, Aldene and the wider lands of Andore and beyond. I am going to rest in the other room. Please feel free to use the desk and chair and read all you want to."

For the rest of that day, and for two more, Audun ensconced himself in Burnett's library. There were far too many volumes for him to read them all, so he decided to scan through as many different books as possible. Several volumes had been written by a certain James Cameron who Audun assumed, correctly, was the same Cameron chief who had placed the plaque outside the wall of the house he was a guest in. The Cameron volumes included, *A Short History of the Battles of the Red Cameron, A History of Aldene and Bala, A Clan-Based Democracy* and an autobiography.

Having been authorised as David Burnett's visitor, Audun was allowed entry to the castle and the rooms in the keep. It was on the fourth day, shortly after he had started reading *The Dewar Kings – Their History*, that Burnett entered the library. Audun looked up as Burnett spoke.

"Audun, I would like you to come with me. I have something to show you, and a gift to give you. I hear from Ramon that you will be leaving tomorrow morning."

Burnett led Audun down from the second floor into the lower floors of the castle. Audun suspected that the room they entered had once been part of the castle dungeons. A large machine was clattering away in the centre of the room, with two men tending the contraption as though it was their baby.

Burnett nodded towards the machine. "Well what do you think Audun? Here is the printing press."

Audun was not sure what to say, and in the noise of the room he wasn't sure he would be heard anyway. Burnett smiled and shouted, "What, no questions? How very unusual. Come; let's go back to the quiet of my rooms where I have your present."

As the pair left the printing room they passed a small passageway on their left that appeared to lead to steps that looked as though they led even deeper under the castle keep. Audun felt a strange sense of being drawn towards the passageway. As he turned towards the steps, he was conscious of a sudden flash of red light from somewhere below, but it was quenched so quickly that he wondered if he had imagined it. It was as if a tinder box had been struck once.

A draft of warmth blew past and he sensed the whisper that echoed in the air – *"I am here, Audun…"*

Audun froze, trying to understand what he had just experienced, but the spell was broken by Burnett. "Come Audun, there is nothing down there in the castle depths other than the deep dungeons and ancient torture chambers." Audun followed as Burnett led the way back to his rooms.

Instead of going through to the library, Burnett sat on the couch in the large main room. He indicated to Audun to take the seat next to him and passed him a neatly wrapped package. Audun took the gift, not entirely sure what to do.

"Well go on, open it," Burnett urged him.

As Audun carefully unwrapped the package it quickly became clear that it was a book. It was also a new book, printed recently on a press, presumably the one they had just visited.

"As you're leaving tomorrow I thought you might appreciate this gift." Burnett smiled. "It will give you some of the answers to your many questions."

The book was printed on fine paper, the black ink startlingly clear against the white background. The cover was bound in thick printed cloth coloured red and white. The cover bore the book's title and author: *White Light Red Fire, A small nation's fight for freedom*, by Angus Ferguson.

Audun held the book reverently, not quite knowing what to say. Burnett helped him out. "You hold in your hand a copy of one of the rarest books in my collection. It tells of Bala's wars of independence between 1300 and 1304. It is written by Angus Ferguson, and much of it tells of his story and adventures. To my knowledge I have the only original copy, and somehow it seemed appropriate to make this book the first to come off the printing press. You hold it now, the first printed copy. I hope you enjoy it."

Audun remained speechless, apart from a whispered "Thank you."

"You do of course know the author's name as you have read his book of poems," Burnett continued. "This book will tell you who Angus Ferguson was and who the poems were written for. Now wrap the book back in the packaging again. It is waterproof and it'll protect the book on your journey back to Boretar. I think your captain will expect you back at Castle Street ready to return to Elde, so you'll need to save your reading for a later date." Burnett stood up and offered his hand. "With that I think it is time to say farewell my young friend; until next time perhaps."

Audun took the offered hand and paused. "David, you have been so kind to me and this gift will always be treasured. I have one last request. Could you show me some of the secret ways in and out of the castle?"

As he spoke the words, the image of the spark of red light appearing from the depths of the castle sprang to his mind again, together with the whispered words, "*I am here, Audun.*" He knew that one day he would have to return to Aldene and learn the secret of what lay in the deep dungeon below the castle.

CHAPTER SEVEN

In the late summer of 1506 a bright sun was glistening off the waters of the river Morel as Mora prepared for celebrations. The Emperor had declared that the city should have a week's holiday with festivities to celebrate his decade as Emperor of the North. The ships in the city harbour flew a multitude of flags, mostly those used at sea for signalling other vessels. The town was decked out in flowers and more flags.

Alberon had purchased vast quantities of food, wine and ale to ensure that the citizens of Mora recognised his generosity. Whilst many of the populace were happy to celebrate, some of the rich merchants were more cynical, grumbling that the Emperor's generosity was funded by the ever-increasing taxes he was imposing.

High on the castle's golden turrets, four flags flew lazily in the light summer breeze. On the central turret was the flag of Kermin. The white background with four golden stars had been the emblem of the Kingdom for centuries. To the left of the Kermin flag flew the banner of Doran, and this time the white background played host to a portrayal of a town perched on a rocky outcrop, a representation of Doran's capital, Iskala. To the right flew the red, white and blue striped flag of Amina, the emblem of Bertalan, Sylva's brother, and king of Amina.

Whilst the celebrations may have been to mark a decade of Alberon's rule, this was also a time for politics. Flying centrally and high above the others was a much larger flag. Alberon had commissioned this specially for the celebrations. On the light blue background stood a bright yellow sun, held in the hands of a tall man. Alberon was making a clear statement. He was Emperor of all things, even the sun.

Inside the Emperor's extensive living quarters, a debate was going on. Sylva was leading the discussion. "Alberon, my brother will arrive tomorrow along with Aisha. They must know that they are invited here for more than celebratory indulgence, which they could have at home in Tamin." Alberon nodded. "I have already informed Bertalan that this state visit is to celebrate my anniversary and also to review and renew the treaties that are held between Kermin and Amina."

Sylva paused for a moment, uncertain whether to give voice to her thoughts. Confident in the knowledge that her husband did at least respect her opinions on political matters, she decided to continue. "Alberon, any renewal of the treaties must include a written confirmation that our sons are the rightful heirs to the throne of Amina if my brother should die without a direct heir."

Alberon smiled. "Of course my dear, that is exactly what I plan to demand, and slightly more." Sylva looked her husband directly in the eye. It was a look that Alberon recognised, and it slightly unnerved him, as he felt his wife was looking right through him.

"My dear, you think you are clever and cunning, but sometimes you are too clever for your own good," she said. "Tell me, what does 'slightly more' mean?"

Alberon tried to return his wife's gaze, but failed. "Sylva, I want you to sit at the negotiating table. You know I appreciate your advice and wisdom, but there are some things it is better that you don't know until the negotiations are complete. After all, it is your brother we are dealing with."

Sylva did not drop her gaze. "Very well Alberon, but be careful you don't trip up on your own clever schemes."

The next morning dawned bright and clear as the royal

party from Amina approached the bridges over the Morel. Bertalan and his entourage had spent the previous night camped only a few miles from Mora on the Kermin Plain. It had been agreed between the Emperor and the King that the arrival of the Amina royalty should be the opening day of the holiday celebrations.

As the royal party approached Mora, Bertalan noted the flags flying high on the castle towers. He leant over to his wife and in a low voice said, "I think our brother-in-law, the Emperor, as he calls himself, is getting a bit too pleased with his power and his titles. I presume the light blue flag contains a message for us. He thinks he rules over all, even the heavens, and he certainly overestimates how tall he is! Well, if that is the position he wants to take in our discussions over the treaties, he will find Amina less of a willing ally."

Aisha smiled. "From the gossip I hear, your sister has a strong influence on her husband when it comes to politics. I can't imagine Sylva will want any animosity between Kermin and Amina."

Bertalan shrugged. "Maybe it is all just for show then, but I doubt it. These lands have been at peace for centuries and I hope that will continue, but if Alberon thinks his gold can purchase Amina as it did Soll, then he will be very disappointed."

The crowds lined the roads leading to the bridges and thronged the main street that wound up from the southern city gate to the castle. The royal procession was impressive. Bertalan and his queen were at the front on splendid white horses. They were followed by many of the lords and ladies of Amina, all richly dressed. The crowds cheered as the royal party progressed up towards the castle, although probably more in celebration of the holiday week than for the royal company itself.

As Bertalan and Aisha passed the Merchants' Quarter, a smaller party rode out through the castle gate. It was led by Alberon riding a huge black stallion, whilst Sylva rode a smaller piebald mare.

Bertalan again turned to his wife. "Even his horse has to be larger than any other. It may not be as big as his head seems to be getting."

Aisha grimaced. "Don't overreact, Bertalan."

As the two parties met, Sylva leaned over to embrace her brother. Alberon did the same with Aisha, albeit from a greater height. Alberon extended his hand to his brother-in-law and Bertalan's face flushed as he realised he was having to look up to meet Alberon's smile. Alberon shouted out over the din of the crowd "We welcome our friends from Amina. Let the celebrations begin."

Covers were pulled back from the large stages that had been set up at the sides of the road and at road junctions. All sorts of meats were placed on the newly lit fires and fountains flowed with wine and beer. As the crowds cheered the royal parties rode back through the castle gate.

It had only been a few months since Aleana had introduced Raimund to Rafe and the eleven-year-old had become a member of the 'team' at the Den of Thieves. For Raimund it was the happiest he could ever remember being. He was part of a family: Rafe treated him like a son and Aleana was like a sister, and better still, she had also become his very best friend. Maybe it was because they had both lost their parents when they were very young, maybe because they made a good team or maybe just because they made each other laugh, but whatever the reason, the pair were inseparable.

Raimund was tall and slightly gangly, and Aleana loved to tease him that soon they would have to heighten the entrance to the Den or he wouldn't get in through the front door. Raimund would retort, "At least I won't be up to my waist in the puddles when it rains, shorty." Aleana would laugh and give Raimund a pretend slap and say, "Go pick on someone your own size, tall person."

The pair roamed the streets or sat hand in hand watching the carracks moor at the docks, trying to guess which foreign lands the ships had come from and wondering if the two of them would ever journey far from Mora. It was there that they made their pact, and it was Aleana who raised the subject.

"Raimund, we must promise each other that if one of us leaves Mora it must be both. We must leave together." She was not sure what had made her ask for this promise, but she was growing more aware of her femininity. She loved Raimund as a brother, but something told her that her feelings for him were more than those of a sibling.

Raimund smiled and squeezed her hand. "Of course Aleana, I am after all your brother."

As the pair shared their dreams and hopes, they were unaware that their profession was about to become much more dangerous. A month earlier, under pressure from Holger, the Captain of Mora's City Guard, Alberon had instructed his chancellor, Aracir, to release funds for the recruitment of more guards. Holger had been increasingly petitioned by Mora's wealthy merchants, and the complaints were often the same: "My purse was stolen in the market place today." Less common, but becoming increasingly regular, were complaints of burglary at a warehouse or a merchant's house. Holger regularly complained to Alberon that he did not have enough resources to stem the growing tide of crime in the city. Alberon was reluctant to release funds from the city's coffers, but he had to relent when Holger presented him with a petition signed by nearly one hundred of the city's most wealthy and influential merchants.

So began a war on crime. By the midsummer of 1506, city guardsmen seemed to be in every street and on every corner. In addition to the increased presence of the guard, Alberon issued new instructions for the punishment for theft. Males over the age of eleven who were caught in the act of stealing would have their right hands cut off. Males under the age of eleven would have a capital "T" branded on their right hand and would be sold as slaves with the profits returned to the city coffers. Females of any age would have a capital "T" branded on their left hand and would also end up in the slave market at the city port.

Up until this time Mora's slave market had been largely an import business with unfortunates captured at sea by raiders, or torn from remote villages in other parts of the world, being bought as servants by Mora's rich merchants and nobles. Now a small export business started, as slave traders bought branded goods for export. The traders knew that the price they would get in Tamin or Anelo for a thief would be low, so they invented a solution. The unfortunate thief would face more discomfort as an additional brand was added; an inverted "T" joined the initial mark and the resultant "+" became quickly known as the brand of a Kermin slave rather than a thief.

These were dangerous times for Rafe and the members of the Den of Thieves. With the threat of increased punishment, several slightly older members of the team decided that the risks were too high and left for less dangerous occupations on board the carracks sailing from the port, or as dockhand runners taking messages from newly-arrived ships to the merchants in the city. To make the situation more hazardous, Holger, realising that the slums were the hiding place of rogues, increasingly sent guardsmen to raid properties there, looking for evidence of any criminal activity by the occupants. The dilapidated warehouse at the old port continued to be ignored, and no guardsman bothered to explore beyond the rotting low front door.

Whilst their refuge remained secure, Raimund and Aleana were always at risk when working the streets. They were now two of only four members remaining in Rafe's team, and Rafe had stopped all raids on property as he viewed the risks as being too great.

Raimund and Aleana had become a highly skilled partnership, and they had developed several strategies to distract a "target" whilst one or the other would remove the individual's purse. Raimund's dagger was still always at his waist, but, like Aleana, it was his razor-sharp thumbnail that now cut the purses. Rafe was insistent that they, as his "son and daughter", should only attempt to take one or at the most two purses each day, and they were to carefully assess the risks before acting, in particular looking out for any guards close by.

Three days before the holiday week began; reality delivered a sharp caution to Raimund and Aleana. A merchant was leaving the Golden Goose, an old tavern on the edge of the Merchant's Quarter, and his unsteady gait indicated that he had clearly had one or two too many jugs of ale. Raimund already had two purses tucked into the inside pocket of his jacket, and he was ready to walk on by.

Aleana grabbed his arm. "Raimund, this one is easy. He doesn't know where he's going, and look, his purse is almost falling from his belt."

"Aleana, we have two purses already and Rafe insisted we take care," replied Raimund. "The street may seem empty, but there are guards everywhere."

Aleana ignored the warning and ran across the street as though on some urgent mission. She bumped into the merchant, who stumbled. The purse was already in her hand as she apologised.

Raimund was alerted by the shout of "Stop thief." A guard had been standing nearby in a doorway and had spotted the robbery.

Aleana froze, and as the guard approached Raimund reacted. Racing across the open space, he charged, dropping his shoulder. Taking the guard by surprise, he knocked him to the ground. Grabbing Aleana by the hand, he hissed at her, "Run!"

Raimund was reminded of their escape from the old sailor on the dock a few months earlier, but this time Aleana showed no resistance and ran with him.

Unlike the previous escapade in the slums, this was an area Raimund knew well. Although there was no sound of a chase, he kept running. He turned into the doorway of an old cottage with red crosses marked on the doors, then quickly opened the locks and pulled Aleana inside.

"Aleana, that was stupid! We didn't have to take such a risk, what were you thinking of? Rafe has told us to take extra care on the streets."

Aleana didn't reply but asked her own question: "Where are we? What is this place, and how do you know how to get in?" Raimund explained that this had been his family home and it had been deserted for years. Aleana asked about the red crosses on the doors and Raimund explained. She shuddered.

"Are you sure we're safe here?" she asked.

Raimund sat in what had been his father's chair and replied, "Yes, unless you are scared of curses and ghosts."

The sunlight was filtering through the gaps in the roof, and Aleana stood in a shaft of light. The sunbeams seemed to be dancing in her hair, subtly changing her colour in multiple sparkling shades of brown. It suddenly occurred to Raimund how pretty she was.

"We'll wait here until the coast is clear and then return home to the Den," he said.

Aleana crossed the room and gave Raimund a gentle kiss on the cheek. "Thank you, brother."

For the remaining members of the Den of Thieves the holiday festivities were a welcome opportunity. It was a time of feast after the famine of the past two months.

The crowds were too large and dense for the patrolling guards to watch for attempted robberies, and the citizens were too busy partying to ensure their purses were secure. Many of Mora's drunken citizens would wake up in the morning finding that they had gained a hangover and lost their coins. A ragged tear at the base of the purse would explain the loss, and most would think that somehow in the crowds the material had been caught and ripped. Few would have blamed the tear on a sharpened thumbnail, and very few realised that they had been robbed. It was just one of those things that happened.

It was a highly profitable week for Raimund and Aleana, although they heeded Rafe's instructions now, and each target was carefully assessed before they acted. Aleana remained curious about Raimund's secret cottage, and as each shared more of their past with the other, the bonds between them grew stronger.

Whilst the festivities, the drinking and the pickpocketing continued across the city, the serious business started on the third day of the holiday. The state room in the castle was decorated with the banners of Amina, Doran and Kermin. Most notably, behind the Emperor's throne, was Alberon's own large light blue banner. The message was clear: this was the centre of power in these lands.

The two sides sat in equal numbers on opposite sides of the long table. Alberon, the self-styled Emperor of the North, sat opposite his brother-in-law, Bertalan, King of Amina. Bertalan was accompanied by Silson, Duke of Amina and Commander of Amina's armies, Bartos, Bertalan's cousin and commander of the King's guard in Tamin and Lord Ereldon, chancellor of Amina and advisor to the King. Opposite sat Lord Norward, commander of the armies of Kermin and Doran, Aracir, chancellor of Kermin and Sylva, Bertalan's sister and Alberon's wife.

Before the negotiations could begin, Bertalan had an objection. "We agreed that the negotiating team would comprise four from each side," he complained. "My wife is therefore not included, so I don't think my sister should be sitting here either."

Alberon smiled. "These lands have been at peace now for almost two hundred years and I am surprised that you needed to include two soldiers in your negotiating team. My wife is one of my wisest and most trusted advisors. She has every right to be here, and I only need Lord Norward here to represent Kermin's armed forces."

Bertalan was reminded of his wife's warning not to overreact, but he had been concerned about Alberon's ambition ever since the Kermin king had proclaimed himself Emperor of the North. And the South too, Bertalan thought to himself. As the main output from the conference was to be renewed peace treaties, Bertalan felt he needed to demonstrate Amina's military force to ensure a beneficial treaty was agreed.

All of the first day's discussions centred on trade relationships, tariffs on goods, access to ports, openness of borders and similar issues. Alberon was soon bored with these discussions, and he irritated his brother-in-law and his wife by regularly getting out of his seat and leaving the room, to return ten minutes later with a bowl of sweetmeats which he would pass round the table. Alberon wanted to move to the crux of the matter, the hereditary rights to the throne of Amina, but that negotiation was for another day.

In the trade negotiations the two chancellors were the main protagonists, although Alberon was surprised by how much insight Sylva had on matters of trade and commerce. Sylva was of course present for other matters, but her wisdom and intuition on the discussions on trade were a bonus. On the second day of the negotiations, Sylva's true role would become clearer.

Peace treaties had been in place between Kermin and Doran, and Amina, for hundreds of years. The treaties were renegotiated every five years and included restrictions on the numbers of soldiers each country had under arms and the weaponry that each could develop and deploy, together with a range of other details. Alberon knew that the King of Amina had increased the personnel in the Amina army beyond the number agreed in the previous treaty. Bertalan knew that Lord Norward had been rearming the Kermin army with modern weaponry imported from the iron foundries of Ackar. This also infringed the principles of the earlier treaties.

The negotiations on day two were largely between the commanders in chief of the armies. The Duke of Amina argued for an increase in the numbers of the armed forces in Amina based on the inferred greater threat from the Empire. Lord Norward countered with a proposal that Kermin should be allowed to buy and develop modern weaponry. Both men of course knew that in reality they were simply arguing to secure the status quo that already existed, and both countries had already broken the treaties currently in existence. For the ordinary citizens of both Kermin and Amina it would have been worrying if they had known that the treaties, when signed, would pave the way for a military expansion for both nations. Kermin could increase the size of the current forces based in Mora and the surrounding area. Kermin could also continue to purchase and develop new weapons. In return the treaty also allowed Amina to access new capability in modern weapons. Most observers would have concluded that war clouds could be looming on the horizon.

Alberon and Bertalan left the negotiations to their teams, and it was early evening when they were called back to the stateroom to approve and sign the agreements. Both appeared happy with the results and it seemed that the treaties would be signed, but then Sylva added one new term to the papers. She stood and looked across the table at her brother.

"Bertalan, there is one last item we need to agree to ensure the security of our lands," she paused for effect. "You and Aisha remain childless, which is a sorrow to me, but your succession needs to be agreed in case of any mishap or accident."

Bertalan frowned. He knew what was coming next. Sylva continued, "My sons, your nephews, are rightfully next in line for the throne of Amina. I propose that this is written into the peace treaties to further secure our countries' futures. Obviously if you and Aisha do produce a male heir, then the succession would revert to your son."

Bertalan noted the emphasis on a male successor. It was rare, but not unknown, for succession to pass to a female heir, as it had to Ingrid, Alberon's mother, although as in most cases, the Queen had acted in this instance as regent for her baby son. Bertalan also knew, although Sylva and Aisha did not, that he had fathered two bastard sons.

This was a tricky moment for the King. He knew that the nobles of Amina were very unlikely to support an illegitimate heir, and that if Aisha did not produce a son then the nobles would be most likely to recognise Aaron, Sylva's eight-year-old son, as the rightful king. Depending on the boy's age it was possible that Sylva would become regent, and by default Alberon would have power over Amina.

Bertalan frowned. "I need to think on this sister, and discuss with Aisha. You will have my response in the morning. Other than this added term, I can agree to sign the treaties in the morning."

Alberon smiled. The end of his waiting game appeared to be getting closer.

The next morning dawned cool and cloudy as rain swept in from the west on blustery showers. With the weather dampening the holiday celebrations, Raimund and Aleana stayed in the old warehouse, playing out game after game of "Game of the Goose". They pored over the board as the dice rolled, trying to be the first to get their counter to square sixty-three without landing in the hazards of the inn and the Bridge of Death. Three days of successful thievery had replenished Rafe's coffers, and the pair had no need to risk the guard or the weather.

In the castle the Amina royalty were late in arriving for the treaty signing. It had obviously been a long night for the King and his queen. Aisha in particular wore heavy, sad, tired eyes; it had been a night of tears.

As the negotiators sat at the table Alberon was tempted to question Aisha's presence, but he decided it didn't really matter. His game plan was set.

Bertalan was the first to speak. "I have reviewed the treaties and I am ready to sign them to ensure ongoing peace in our lands," he began. "The question of who ascends to the Amina throne is a concern, but it is for the future. For now I am ready to commit that my nephew Aaron, provided he is of an age, will inherit the throne. If Aaron, or his brother Elrik, is under the age of eighteen when I die then they will be declared princes in waiting and my wife, Aisha and the Duke of Amina will take regency until one of the boys comes of age. "

It was not quite what Sylva and her husband had hoped for, but Sylva thought it was enough. Bertalan looked enquiringly at the table. There were no treaties to be signed.

Alberon broke the ensuing silence. "Brother, your additional conditions are acceptable and the treaties are being redrafted to include this proposal. However I intend to insert a further clause, that from now onward, Amina will agree to submit to the law of the Emperor and the King of Amina will swear fealty to the Emperor as his overlord."

Sylva was aghast. This was not what she had planned; Alberon might just as well have torn up the treaties in front of her brother.

Bertalan looked shocked. He struck the table hard with his fist. "Amina will never be subject to a tyrant Emperor's rule!" he thundered. "We will die before allowing that to happen." He looked at his negotiating team. "I have had enough of this city and its runt of an Emperor. We leave within the hour!"

Back in the royal apartments, Sylva was livid. "What were you thinking about? You agreed that we would play the waiting game and your desire to rule Amina would have come to fruition once one of our sons inherited the throne. Aisha is as barren as a desert sand dune, and she will never produce a son. Everything was set as we had agreed, more or less, until you threw in that stupid final demand."

Alberon smiled. "Keep calm my dear. I knew the hand I was playing and I have another card that neither you nor your brother know about. When the time comes, I will play it."

Sylva retorted angrily, "So this was your "slightly more" was it? Some cunning plan that only you know about and that plan will repair the damage you have just done?"

Alberon seldom lost his temper with his wife, but now he could not maintain his self-control. "You are my wife!" he roared. "You will obey my commands and support my decisions!"

Both simultaneously rose from their seats. The tension was palpable, but Alberon was always at a disadvantage in a stand-up argument. Sylva looked down on her husband, her green eyes holding his ice-blue ones until Alberon was forced to drop his gaze.

"I am your wife, but when you make stupid decisions that could damage my sons' heritage I will have my say and you will listen!" she hissed. Without another word, Sylva left the room.

Down below, the castle forecourt was filled with bustle as the Amina royal family and their entourage prepared to leave Mora. Bertalan did not wait for farewells. With head held high, he rode out of the city.

During the remaining months of 1506, emissaries shuttled back and forth between Tamin and Mora. The pretence of seeking agreement, and peace was played by both sides. The politics were to the front, but behind the politics both sides prepared for a different solution. In the real world, the clouds of war were darkening.

CHAPTER EIGHT

Aldene - A Return Journey

❖ ❖ ❖ ❖

By 1507 trade between the countries on the island of Andore and their southern neighbours of Kermin and Amina had all but stopped as war threatened in the lands across the Middle Sea. Ancient treaties did bind the nations on Andore to support the southern lands in any conflict, but as the treaties were effectively with both Kermin and Amina, the councils across Andore declared themselves neutral in any military escalation.

With open conflict increasingly likely, the *Swan* plied its trade between Boretar and Thos in Toria and then on to Anelo in Arance. In early June 1507 the *Swan* coasted into the harbour at Boretar. The cargo of wines and spirits from Toria was destined for the merchants in Boretar, but an additional consignment purchased by Ramon was intended for his merchant friend in Aldene, Gordon Graham.

As the barrels were being unloaded a rogue cask slipped from the gangplank. Ramon, who was overseeing the unloading, was caught by surprise as the runaway barrel crashed into him. The crack was loud enough to be heard all around the port, and Ramon screamed in pain as the fibula of his right leg snapped.

That evening Ramon was resting in the large main room in the house on Cross Street when Audun returned from the port. Ramon nodded for Audun to take a seat. "Audun, to make a healthy profit on this last trip we really need to get the remaining goods to Master Graham in Aldene. You are now an experienced sailor and helmsman, and the crew respect you. I would like you to take command of the *Swan* and make the journey to Elde. Indeed I have been thinking for a few months that it may be time for me to relax a bit more. Depending on how this journey turns out, I may hand over captaincy of the *Swan* to you for a time. Certainly this sea leg will not be functional for a month or two." He pointed to the splints on the broken leg.

Audun was surprised. Over time his position as Ramon's "stepson" had added to his authority on board, but he was still one of the younger members of the crew.

"I will do my best, Captain" was his short reply.

Ramon patted Audun's shoulder. "I know you will.

Vasilli will be on hand to give you advice. Indeed he was the one who suggested that you take over command until I am fit again. Take care of the *Swan* and pass my best wishes to Master Graham, with my apologies for not being able to come in person. The prices for the barrels have already been set, so you have no need to discuss these with Gordon. Payment should be in gold coins. We have no cargo for the return journey to Boretar, so I will let you decide if any goods could be purchased in Aldene for the return journey. It has been a hard couple of months for the crew, so I suggest you give them a few days' shore leave at Elde whilst you seek a possible cargo for the return journey."

"Yes, Captain," replied Audun. He was keeping his excitement well hidden. He had been desperate for an opportunity to return to Aldene. He could still recall the strange sense of being drawn to the deeper dungeon below the city castle, the brief flash of red light and the words ringing in his head: "I am here, Audun…" More significantly he had now read and reread Angus Ferguson's book *White Light Red Fire*. It was a paragraph towards the end of the book that kept coming to Audun's mind.

Munro took the alchemist in his arms and felt the anger and the lust for power which had corrupted the old man's soul. He placed his palms together around the other's neck and stepped back. The white wall now completely enclosed Oien, and as it brightened in intensity it hid him from view. Flashes of red seemed to bounce around inside the wall and then began to fade away. The wall became a shimmering wave, like a mirage in the desert. Gradually that too vanished, and all that remained where Oien had been was a large piece of dull red rock.

Audun wondered what had happened to the piece of rock, as the final pages of *White Light Red Fire* gave no indication or explanation. For some reason he felt compelled to find the answers, and it seemed they lay somewhere below the castle keep in Aldene.

The early summer trip north on the Greater Sea was uneventful. The dolphins seemed to enjoy racing the caravel, and they provided the entertainment on the journey. The *Swan* docked at Elde on a warm afternoon in mid-June and Audun sent a runner to Aldene to inform Master Graham of the *Swan*'s arrival. The casks of wine were this time carefully unloaded from the ship and placed in the wagon Audun had hired to transport him and the goods to Aldene.

The first stop was at the warehouse in the New Town, where Gordon Graham was waiting. Graham smiled. "Welcome back to Aldene, Audun. Let's get the casks stored, and then I hope you'll join Jane and me over dinner. From Ramon's letter I believe you will be staying in Aldene for a few days to do some more business here. We would be privileged to have you stay with us in Castle Street until your business is complete."

Audun shook the proffered hand. "It would be my pleasure Gordon, thank you."

Graham replied, "Ramon's payment is in my office, so let's go back there and we can complete business for the day and settle down to a pleasant evening."

The Old Town of Aldene was bustling with activity as Gordon Graham and Audun entered through the southern gate. Bunting flags were being draped high over the town's narrow streets, flowers adorned most house fronts and larger flags fluttered in the light breeze as they hung from upper floor windows. Many of the flags flew the diagonal blue cross with red edging on a white background which Audun knew was the motif of Clan Cameron. Other flags bore a perpendicular red cross on a yellow background. When Audun asked what they were, Graham explained that the yellow flag had in the distant past been the emblem of the Coelete, the people who lived in the far north of Bala, beyond the Coe Mountains. In the mid fourteenth century the Coelete emblem had been adopted as the national emblem of Bala. Audun had arrived in Aldene at festival time when all of Bala celebrated victory in the wars of independence of the early fourteenth century.

As the pair reached the Graham's house Audun again noted the plaque on the wall: "In memory of Gordon Graham, murdered in front of this house in

1300: Erected by order of James Cameron, 5th September 1302." Having read Angus Ferguson's book many times, Audun now knew the roles both these men had played in Bala's history.

Over dinner the conversation was expansive. Gordon Graham and his wife wanted to learn anything Audun knew about the troubles brewing in Amina and Kermin. Graham's business activities reached as far as the southern lands, and he was concerned to hear that trade routes to the south were being closed down. In return Audun wanted to know what traders might be coming to Aldene in the coming week. Graham informed Audun that it was usual at festival time for hunters from Banora to come to Aldene for the festivities. Usually they brought deer pelts to trade in the markets in Aldene. The deer had been killed and the pelts prepared in the county of Banora, which lay to the northwest of the Inger Mountains.

"How is Master Burnett?" asked Audun. "I hoped I might visit him again whilst I am here."

It was Jane who replied. "I am afraid David passed away earlier this year."

Audun was genuinely saddened to learn the news. "I am sorry to hear that. Master Burnett was very kind to me on my last visit and the gift of his book was very generous."

Jane Graham smiled. "Master Burnett died knowing his legacy would live on. Over the past three years, as his printed books have become available and affordable, more of the people of Aldene and Bala have learnt to read. In David's memory, during the festival, James Ferguson will open a new library in a building close to the castle. It will be called the People's Library, and as far as we know it will be the first anywhere in the world where the ordinary citizen can take a book out on loan. David's printing press and the printers have also moved into the building and three copies of every book they print will be donated to the Library. David Burnett's legacy will live long into the future to the benefit of the people of Bala and Aldene. A plaque will be erected above the front door of the Library in David's memory." Audun smiled. He knew his old friend would rest in peace knowing his work had been completed successfully.

The subject moved on to Burnett's printed version of *White Light Red Fire*, which had become very popular in Bala. It turned out that the Grahams owned and had read a copy, so like Audun they knew the recorded history of Banora and the red stone othium. They debated whether the story was historical fact or historical fiction and agreed that it was most likely a mixture of both.

Audun cautiously raised the question of the piece of red rock that had seemed to mark the end of Oien and of the story. The Grahams both believed that this part of the recorded history was fiction and some sort of allegory of the real historical facts. However they added that a direct descendant of James Cameron, and indeed of Angus Ferguson, still called Aldene Castle home and was still the senior Elder of the clans of Bala. James Ferguson, they suggested, might know more about the facts, but it was unlikely that Audun would be able to meet him.

The three also discussed Alastair Munro, the wielder of the white light. Was this also fiction? It seemed almost certain that such a person had existed, but the concept of an alchemist harnessing red fire and a simple farmer being blessed with a white power surely had to be fiction, created to make the factual history more interesting.

The next morning Graham took Audun to an old warehouse on the western edge of the town just inside the old town wall. He explained that the warehouse had been in the ownership of Clan Duncan for centuries. From his reading of the histories, Audun knew that in the 1300s Duncan of Coe had been Elder of the lands of Coe, which included the county of Banora. From the maps Audun also knew that the Coe lands lay north of the Inger Mountains and that two hundred years earlier those lands had been brutally invaded by the forces of Ackar and Lett. The invaders had opened up the ancient mines in the Inger Mountains to extract othium.

Graham introduced Audun to Colin Duncan, the current Elder of Coe. The old warehouse was largely filled with bales of wool, apart from one corner that was stacked with deer pelts. The negotiation was quick and fair. Colin Duncan offered a reasonable price for all the deer pelts that were not already reserved. Audun agreed in addition to purchase several bales of wool.

Duncan asked, "When do you want these shipped on to Elde, and which vessel should they be marked for?"

"In three days' time please, to the *Swan* which is docked at the port," replied Audun. "I want to spend a bit more time in Aldene to enjoy the festival before heading back to Boretar."

Duncan took Audun's hand. "The deal is done and your payment is complete. Thank you. I hope you enjoy the festival and maybe I will see you in the castle at the celebrations tomorrow." Audun looked questioningly at Graham.

"Apologies Audun, I didn't know how long you planned to stay," his host replied. "Tomorrow is the main day of the festival. The Elders of Bala will meet in the morning to discuss clan matters and then James Ferguson opens the castle to an invited group of guests. The invitation list takes its precedence from the olden times. Colin will be there as an Elder. A selection of merchants, farmers, ordinary citizens, farm workers and even some of the poorest of the population are invited. Thirty people from each level of society are given an invitation and each person is allowed to bring one guest. Jane and I are invited for the first time, as the invitations are drawn by ballot. Jane is not fond of these large gatherings so I am sure she would not object if you attended as my guest in her place."

Audun was delighted. He had been wondering how to gain access to the castle now that David Burnett was gone. "Thank you Gordon, I would love to accompany you. It will remind me of my time in the castle keep with Master Burnett."

The castle gate was open as Audun and Gordon Graham crossed the esplanade. The Red Cameron Guard were carefully checking the invitations. Graham was quizzed about his guest, but his explanation was accepted and the pair entered the castle's inner courtyard.

Audun paused for a moment, remembering his visits of three years earlier and the time he had spent in David Burnett's library. He was now dressed in his best attire, and looking round he was surprised at the range of garments worn by the throng of milling guests. Merchants appeared to be richly attired, but many of the guests wore simple, modest tunics.

Colin Duncan approached. "Welcome friends, I am pleased to meet you again Audun. Please find a place to sit. Food and drink will be brought to you shortly. Some of the Elders are still in discussion over some minor clan disputes. As you can see from those already sitting on the benches, there is no hierarchy in the seating here. Richer and poorer sit cheek by jowl. So find a space and enjoy the afternoon."

Audun found himself perched between a large man with a weathered face, who was a farmer from the Ewart lands to the east of Aldene, and a pale skinny man who worked in the warehouses in the New Town. The latter clearly had limited access to a bath, so Audun was pleased that a cool wind was blowing from the north over the still snow-capped Inger Mountains.

The skinny man seemed to have little to say; either that or he was overawed by his well-dressed neighbour. By contrast the farmer was verbose. Audun never clearly caught the man's name and soon got tired of the tales of woe of a Bala farmer. He also found it hard to understand the man's strong accent. With a brief "Please excuse me" he left his seat, hoping the warehouseman was interested in farming.

Moving over to where Gordon Graham was sitting, he apologised for the interruption but informed the merchant that he was going to stretch his legs with a walk round the castle grounds. Graham nodded. "Go and explore for sure, but you will not be allowed to enter the upper floors of the castle or the keep."

"Of course, I understand," said Audun. The upper floors were not his destination.

He casually sauntered across to the main entrance to the keep. The ground floor was filled with people refreshing their plates or tankards. Red Cameron guards blocked the entry to the upper floors, but there was no obstacle to the stairs down.

The first level down was empty. This was where the printers had worked on Audun's last visit. Ink stains on the walls and floor were a reminder of their presence, but they now worked in the People's Library across from the castle. Audun then remembered that the red light had appeared as he and Master Burnett had returned to the stairway that led back to the ground floor, so he retraced his steps.

Just before he reached the upward flight of stairs, Audun found the narrow passageway on his left. It occurred to him that without the red spark it would have gone unnoticed on his previous visit.

The passageway was narrow and dark and Audun regretted not bringing a candle with him. Feeling his way along the passageway, he reached the staircase leading down into the depths of the castle. Taking his tinder box from his shoulder bag, he struck the flint and sparks fell on the char cloth, which in turn allowed him to ignite the sulphur-tipped wooden splint. It wasn't much light, but it was enough, and he carefully took the steps down into the darkness.

Once he was back on level ground he struck another flame from the tinder box and lit another splint. As he looked around in the dim light he realised that Master Burnett had been correct. Chains hung from the walls, and strange instruments were laid out in order on the central table. Clearly in times gone by this had been the castle's torture chamber. Audun wondered if this was where the unfortunate Conall Dalzell, Elder of Awick, had been left to rot two hundred years ago. He shivered at the thought. Did ghosts from the past haunt this damp, evil chamber?

The thought had no sooner entered Audun's head than the dim yellow flame on the splint suddenly burnt with a bright, intense red, and he heard a voice whisper "*Audun!*"

A cold sweat came over Audun and his heart started racing. Who was calling him, and where were they calling him to? Suddenly the thought struck him that the ghosts of the past were summoning him to his doom in the underworld.

The red fire on the splint grew stronger and singed his hand. With trembling legs and holding back the bile rising in his throat, Audun dropped the ember and ran as fast as he could back up the steps to the old print room. Taking deep breaths to calm himself, he looked back at the stairwell. Again the voice echoed in his head, this time louder and more insistently. "*I am here, Audun.*" Audun shivered again. Was it his doom or his destiny that lay deep below Aldene Castle?

When Audun reached the courtyard again, he almost immediately bumped into Gordon Graham. "There you are Audun. I thought you had got lost. The Lord and one of the other Elders are about to announce the opening of the People's Library and I knew you would not want to miss that."

Audun swallowed and forced a smile. "Thank you Gordon. I stopped for a while in the old print room remembering my friend Master Burnett. I was lost in thought I suppose."

The pair returned to the benches, where this time Graham had saved a space next to himself for Audun. They were just in time, because as they sat down two very different men appeared on the second-floor balcony of the castle keep. Graham informed Audun that the man on the left was James Ferguson. Audun might have guessed. Ferguson was a tall, red-haired man who carried about him an air of authority. The other man was of medium height with light brown hair and was dressed in light blue clothing that shimmered in the sunlight. Audun's attention was fixed on this second man, who seemed to emanate a strange power that carried with it a sense of peace.

Graham explained to Audun that this person was simply called the Eldest. "I have never seen him before, but I believe he normally only visits Bala and Aldene during the festival," he went on. "This is when the Elders from each Clan gather to discuss matters pertaining to Bala as a country. Minor Clan disputes are dealt with by the representative Elders on a regular basis, but during this annual meeting they will discuss and agree wider national topics like taxation. The Eldest presides over this meeting."

The ceremony was short and to the point. James Ferguson thanked everyone for attending the festivities in the castle and proclaimed the People's Library open. A few words were spoken in praise of David Burnett and his legacy. Audun knew his old friend would have been pleased.

Ferguson continued by explaining how the library would operate. He closed by thanking God for the two hundred years of peace on the Island of Andore, reminding the people that they were celebrating a freedom that many of their ancestors had died to achieve. The man known as the Eldest said nothing, but he swept his open hands apart in a blessing and a white cloud descended over the courtyard. As he brought his hands back together again the cloud dissipated and in his hand appeared a silver quaich, an ancient wedding cup. Even from a distance Audun could discern the words shining brightly: *Aonaibh Ri Chéile*, let us unite, the Cameron motto. He recognised the words and the symbolism of the wedding cup. *White Light Red Fire* described this cup, or one very similar, that had been held by Angus Ferguson and Elbeth Cameron two hundred years ago when they were united in marriage.

The Eldest raised the silver vessel to his mouth and after taking a sip passed it to James Ferguson, who followed suit. Audun later learnt that the ceremonial sipping from the quaich symbolised the ongoing union of the clans of Bala. The crowd in the courtyard had bowed their heads as the white cloud settled over them. Everyone gathered there, including Audun, felt a strange sense of peace. The terror Audun felt in the dungeon dissipated with the white cloud.

Gordon Graham, Jane Graham and Audun sat that evening discussing the day's events over a light supper. The two men had already drunk and eaten their fill at the banquet in the castle. Graham did much of the talking as his wife listened attentively.

Jane Graham appeared to be of a similar age to her husband and Audun thought that in her youth she must have been very pretty. Even now, approaching middle age, she was still attractive, with her long black hair pulled back from her face revealing her high cheekbones and the laughter lines at the edges of her intelligent brown eyes.

She wanted to hear all they could tell her about the person they called the Eldest. Graham had never seen the man before, and all he could do was to describe the events that had taken place at the castle. When for the third time Graham described the blessing and the white cloud, Jane held up her hand. She asked the question that Audun had pondered at the castle but had quickly dismissed: "Is it possible that this could be Alastair Munro who inherited the white power as described in *White Light Red Fire*?"

Gordon Graham was a practical man, a successful merchant, used to dealing in reality, not fantasy. He gave a snort of laughter and responded, "That would seem unlikely Jane. He would be over two hundred years old. I suppose he could be of the same blood line and by some form of right he holds the position of Eldest and has inherited some of his ancestor's power."

Audun added his opinion. "I had wondered the same when Gordon and I were at the castle, but like Gordon, I dismissed the possibility. However, since you have raised the same question, I am thinking again. Alastair Munro is reported in the book as being dressed in shimmering light blue clothing. He blessed the coronation of Dewar the Third with white light; the quaich that was raised at the ceremony today was identical, or very similar, to the one that was used at that wedding two hundred years ago, and of course Alastair Munro encapsulated the old alchemist and quenched the red fire with white light. That's a lot of coincidences."

Graham nodded. "It still seems impossible for the man to have lived for two hundred years. There must be a more rational explanation." Jane and Audun were less sure of what was possible and what was impossible.

Draining his glass of wine, Audun thanked his hosts and wished them goodnight. It had been a long day and he wanted to get to bed, to think and to sleep. He was pondering on the possibility of a person living for over two hundred years. Logic won the mental debate, and having decided to agree with Gordon, he drifted off to sleep.

The next thing he knew, he was suddenly awake and drenched in sweat. It took him a minute to get his bearings and remember that he was in the guest room in the Graham's house in Castle Street. He had been having a nightmare, and it was still vivid in his mind. Red fire was everywhere, consuming towns, cities and armies, and the same old man was always at the centre of the conflagrations. The man's robes were amber and appeared to shed sparks of fire. He wore a black cloak over the robes and his silver hair and beard glistened red in the reflection of the fire that erupted from either his hand or his staff. The reflection of the fire in his hair gave the impression that the old man's head was dripping with blood. As the cities burned, over and over the words that he had heard in the torture chamber echoed in Audun's mind: "*I am here, Audun.*"

Audun trembled as he thought back to his experience in the castle dungeon. Was it his time to be called to the underworld?

Fire and destruction haunted his dreams through the remainder of a restless night. It was not until the half-light between night and day, between sleeping and waking, that the fires subsided and the voice returned more insistently. "*I am here, Audun. You have read the histories. You should know who I am. You have a crown to win, revenge to extract and your destiny to fulfil. These things cannot be achieved without the red fire.*"

Audun sat up with a start to see the morning sun flooding into the room. The final ghostly words he had heard were still echoing round and round in his mind.

After such a restless night Audun had no appetite for breakfast, so he told the Grahams he needed to go straight out to check the status of his purchases at the Coe warehouse. He spent the rest of the morning wandering aimlessly around Aldene's streets, giving himself time to think. Who was speaking in his mind? What was the red fire, and how was it entwined with his future? What was the link to the histories?

He looked up to see that he had reached the corner of the old town walls where they joined the castle walls. He looked down to the castle forecourt and the shaded spot where he had first met David Burnett, and smiled as he remembered the old man appearing as if from nowhere to stand behind him. Maybe if his old friend had still been alive he could have helped clarify the nightmares, although as he pondered this he thought that Master Burnett's knowledge of the histories might well have caused him to try to persuade Audun to take another path. However Burnett had granted him his wish as the two had parted three years earlier, so Audun did know how to get inside the castle secretly. This corner would be his entry point, but not in broad daylight.

He made his way down the narrow stairway that led to the front gate of the castle and the esplanade. Nodding at the guards, he crossed over to the shade under the tree, sitting where he had on his last visit. Looking up at the castle, he saw the flag with its diagonal blue cross and red edging on a white background again flying proudly in the gentle breeze. Beside the motif of Clan Cameron now also flew the flag with the red cross on the yellow background, Bala's national flag. Audun wondered what that could mean.

Audun sat under the tree for most of the next hour trying to unscramble his thoughts and assert some sort of logic over his fears. If the voice and his nightmares were calling him to his doom in the underworld below the castle, then other words made no sense. Again he recalled the insistent message of the early morning: "*You have a crown to win, revenge to extract and your destiny to fulfil. These things cannot be achieved without the red fire.*" But neither could these things be achieved if he were lost to the world.

He knew the histories supposedly captured in *White Light Red Fire*. The red power in the story was wielded by an old alchemist whose name was Oien. Could the alchemist have lived locked up in a dungeon for two hundred years? It seemed impossible, but then if the Eldest was indeed Alastair Munro stepping out from the story two hundred years later, then maybe it was not.

It was then that Audun remembered the end of the story; the alchemist had been rendered powerless, encapsulated in the white light and turned into a dull lump of red stone. If Oien had been destroyed, who now controlled the red fire, who had struck the red spark in the passageway three years earlier, what were the messages in the dreams, and who was speaking to him?

He remembered his promise to himself and his family made not so long ago in Tamin: "One day I will come for you Alberon, and I will avenge my mother's death." He began to talk out loud as he was addressing himself. "If I am to have my revenge, how can I achieve it without the power to deliver my promise? If the red light in the dungeon is my path to the underworld I will have chosen badly, but if it is the power I need to deliver my promise I will have chosen wisely. Either way I need to return to the dungeon and embrace whatever fate awaits me there."

That evening Audun excused himself from dinner with the Grahams, professing to have an upset stomach. He told his hosts that he was going out for a breath of fresh air to try to settle his ailment.

It was a cloudless night and a crescent moon shone high over the Inger Mountains, bathing the streets of Aldene in a delicate white glow. Audun remembered the route he had been shown by David Burnett, although three years before he had travelled in the opposite direction, away from the castle. Burnett had taken Audun to a postern gate hidden on the north-western wall of the castle and apparently neglected by the Red Cameron. Burnett's instruction had been simple; from outside the postern gate follow the path that hugs the castle walls until you reach the point where they join the town walls. It would be a bit of a climb, but at his age he should have no problem reaching the top and dropping over onto the town wall next to the steps that led down to the castle esplanade. Then he would know where he was.

Three years before when Audun had followed Burnett's instructions, he had realised that the old man had shown him one way in and out of the castle but had not divulged his own secret routes; he knew Burnett could not have made the climb up onto the town walls.

With the delicate moonlight guiding his footsteps, Audun walked along the old walls. He had climbed onto them from steps further into the town, as walking past the guarded front gate of the castle seemed an unnecessary risk. Keeping to the shadows to avoid detection, he reached the point where the town wall and the castle wall merged. It was a six-foot climb and then a drop down to the path that wound to the north-west and in a short time he arrived at the postern gate.

He hesitated; maybe it would be locked at night, or even guarded. Gently he pushed on the rusted old frame, which opened with a loud creak of the hinges. Fearing someone may have heard, Audun quickly dashed inside, hoping that the black cloak he wore would camouflage him against the castle wall. There was no reaction to his entry other than a dog barking somewhere closer to the castle keep.

The postern gate led into the castle, close to a narrow path that wound west round the foot of the keep. Audun assumed that in the past any defenders would be on the castle walls and that the confined space on the ground level would enable defence of any breach at the gate. The path had a number of additional defensive obstacles to circumnavigate. At regular intervals the castle wall protruded out, narrowing the path further, so that it was barely wide enough for a child to pass. David Burnett had obviously been able to squeeze through these gaps, but they were too tight for Audun, who had to climb the wall and drop down on the far side to get past each barrier.

Eventually the path opened up close to the ground floor entry that Audun had explored the day before. This time he ignored the old print room, and with a beating heart he took the steps down to the dungeon. Prepared this time, he took one of the candles from his shoulder pack and with a flick of the tinder box he had light.

The torture chamber had not changed since the previous day. The only signs of activity in the room were his own footprints left in the dust from the day before. He waited, feeling increasingly agitated; there was no voice this time, and no red light. Maybe it had all been in his youthful imagination. Perhaps he had read

White Light Red Fire too many times.

He took a deep breath. He felt it would be good to be back under the watchful glow of the moon, so he started to head towards the stairs that led back to the light.

He had taken only one step in that direction when the candle flame turned from yellow to intense red and the voice returned to Audun's head: "*Audun, I am here, below.*"

Audun trembled; logic had conquered his fear, but now fear dismissed his logic. Then the voice in his head broke through the fear: "*Audun, this is your destiny. I am here waiting.*"

Suddenly a red glow appeared; it seemed to come from the edges of a large stone slab underneath the torture table. Still trembling Audun knelt down and pushed the slab. To his surprise the stone was easily pushed aside, opening up another ancient and worn stairway that led further into the depths. Audun's candle was burning out, but as it did so the red light replaced it, casting eerie shadows on the walls of the stairwell.

Fear and ambition battled for supremacy in Audun's mind. Fear shouted *"Run, return to the courtyard and the safety of the moonlight!",* whilst ambition replied, *"If you want revenge and your rightful throne, you must go on."* The moment of indecision passed as Audun heard a voice that this time echoed from the depths: "*I am here, Audun.*"

Cautiously Audun picked his way down the narrow, winding stairwell. As his feet touched flat ground, he looked around. It was clear that this space was not man made but a cave that had been here for millennia, since long before the castle had been built. Assorted human bones lay scattered on the floor. Swallowing back the rising bile, Audun realised that this had been the castle pit where in ancient times unfortunates were cast, never to see the light of day again.

In the centre of the cave was an ancient wooden box, and Audun could now see that the red light was seeping through cracks in the rotten woodwork. The rusted hinges easily gave way as Audun pulled at the box's lid. Inside the old box was a small casket, and burnt into each side of the casket was a painted red disc. The red light appeared to be shining out from the four discs.

Scared but determined, Audun opened the casket. The inside was lined with amber felt and in the centre rested a piece of red rock about the size of Audun's fist. To one side of the casket a piece of red linen was folded up. It was now clear that the red light emanated from the stone itself and not the painted sides of the casket.

The rock shimmered in the darkness with red and amber sparks spitting from the surface. The voice Audun heard now seemed to come directly from the shimmering stone.

"Audun, I know that you have read about me in the histories. I have been locked in this prison for two hundred

years. I cannot return to the world in my old form but I still have power. That power is yours now. One day we will return to Mora and you will have your revenge."

Audun stared at the shimmering stone for a long moment, trying to order his thoughts. This must be the piece of rock that had encapsulated the essence of the alchemist, Oien, two hundred years earlier. Was it Oien's disembodied voice that he was hearing? Audun picked the casket out from the old box and as he did so the red discs on the sides of the box grew in intensity until they glowed like embers in a red-hot fire. Audun could sense the power and the hatred emanating from the stone, and for a moment he wondered what evil he was in danger of releasing to the world. Maybe he should return the casket to the box and leave it here in the dungeon?

At this thought the red light intensified as if in anger, and Audun's own words came back to him: "If I am to have my revenge, how can I achieve it without the power to deliver my promise?" Audun reflected that he had chosen his way and if this was his destiny then so be it, for good or for bad.

As he covered the stone with the red linen, the intensity of the colour gradually diminished and the discs returned to their original shade, as though the stone had found some peace. Closing the lid, Audun stowed the casket in his shoulder bag and lit his second candle to illuminate his way back to the stairs and the climb back to the surface and the moonlight.

When Audun reached the now deserted print room he was about to retrace his footsteps on the narrow path around the keep, but the voice in his head halted him in mid stride: *That way is too open, Audun; there is another way that Master Burnett did not disclose to you. On the far wall push the large central slab, it should lead to our way out from the castle.* As instructed, Audun found the slab, and a gentle push opened up a gap between the inner wall of the print room and the outer wall of the keep. His candle illuminated the steps below; it looked like another passageway. Without further instructions, he followed the passageway until he reached another door, this one of wood. Again the door put up no resistance and Audun entered a large room whose walls were lined with shelves holding hundreds of books.

Instantly Audun knew he had arrived in the People's Library. Now he knew how David Burnett had crept up behind him as if appearing from nowhere. Memories of his old friend again made Audun wonder if he was doing the right thing. Images from his dreams of red fire consuming armies and cities flashed in front of him. The question formed, "Is my desire for revenge selfish? Is it worth the consequences?" The other voice was insistent: "You have made your choice. You cannot turn back." Releasing the bolts on the side door, Audun gave a sigh of relief as he stepped back into the moonlit street. His path was set.

The next day Audun bade his farewells, shaking Gordon Graham's hand and thanking him for his hospitality. Jane Graham received a warm hug. Audun had come to view the merchant's wife as a friend and respected the common sense and wisdom she showed in every discussion and on any topic. Audun wondered what Mistress Graham would have thought about the piece of red stone resting in the casket concealed in his shoulder bag. Instinctively he knew she would not have approved.

A few days later the *Swan* docked at Boretar after a quiet return voyage to her home port. During the journey Audun often checked the casket stored in the locker at the back of his cabin, but the discs on the sides of the box remained a dull red and Oien, if it was Oien, remained silent. Audun wondered at this, as the voice in the dungeon had seemed insistent that they should return to Mora. At the time he had thought the instruction was urgent, but now that the red stone had left its prison it seemed to have reverted to just that, a dull red stone. Audun knew that it could not all have been a dream or a hallucination, as the casket and the contents were real enough. If he was to have his revenge, how could he achieve it without the power to deliver his promise? For now, the power that appeared to be so potent in the dungeons of Aldene Castle seemed to have deserted him. Maybe the timing was not right, and if the spirit of Oien really was inside the stone, he was resting until other events created a better opportunity.

Suddenly it struck Audun that perhaps he was being tested as he had been by Master Burnett. He needed to be patient. Then he remembered the words he had heard in the dungeon: "One day we *will* return to Mora and you *will* have your revenge."

Audun had negotiated an excellent price for the wool and deer pelts he had purchased in Aldene. Ramon's leg was on the mend, although he still needed a crutch as he walked. Ramon had made an excellent profit from the sale of the wine and spirits to Gordon Graham, so he allowed Audun to retain the profits from the goods transported back from Aldene.

Ramon had more to add. "Audun, you have successfully captained the *Swan* to Elde and back again. Vasilli tells me you have the respect of the crew. I plan to take a year off to read the many books in the library that I never get to. I would like you to take over as Captain for a while."

It was the opportunity Audun had hoped for, although he had not expected it. His face lit up in a broad smile. "Thank you Ramon, I will take good care of your ship."

As the *Swan* returned to its moorings in Boretar, two men were in conversation in the Cameron rooms in Aldene. James Ferguson, chief of Clan Cameron, sat opposite the man dressed in light blue. The publication of David Burnett's books had answered an ancient question: why was a Ferguson the chief of Clan Cameron? The explanation was in the history books. When the warrior poet Angus Ferguson had married Elbeth Cameron, the dynastic line was set.

Ferguson was the first to speak. "Alastair I think the meeting of the Elders and the celebrations were a success. Thank you for travelling once more from Esimore to bless our gathering."

James Ferguson, despite his position, was always somewhat in awe of the other man, even though they had known each other for many years. James often wondered what it would be like to have lived for over two hundred years. The man opposite him had been there and played a pivotal role in the wars of independence.

Alastair Munro recognised the other man's discomfort and smiled. This was part of the reason he only travelled back to his homeland once a year. "Yes James, the day went well and I'm pleased that Bala's citizens still take the time to remember their history." Munro paused for a moment before continuing. "David Burnett's publication of the histories of the fight for independence gives me concern though, as events that should have remained secret are now widely known. I presume the prisoner is still safely locked in the old cave?"

James Ferguson nodded. "At least I presume so. To the best of my knowledge no one has visited the cave for years. After all Alastair, I now know from the stories, if they are correct, that all we have held in the cave for over two hundred years is simply a piece of red rock."

Alastair Munro shivered as he recalled the moment he had stopped the old alchemist from destroying James Ferguson's ancestor's wedding ceremony. He recalled the force of evil and hatred he had felt emanating from Oien as he clasped his arms around the other's neck and the white wall encircled and enclosed the old alchemist. He frowned. "Yes James, an old piece of rock, and now the published histories mix fact and fiction. I know for a fact that in that piece of rock are locked millennia of ambition, hatred and power. I would not want us to be responsible for letting Oien and the red fire of othium again terrorise the world."

James Ferguson nodded. "I'll get someone to check the cave again in the next few days." Unfortunately it would be almost a year later before that was done, and by then it would be too late.

For the rest of 1507 Audun captained the *Swan* back and

forth, trading between the ports on the island of Andore. The routine sailings were from Boretar to Thos and then on to Anelo with a repeat journey in the opposite direction. There were no return voyages to Elde.

As well as being an accomplished sailor and captain, Audun also proved to be a hard and wily negotiator, which enabled the *Swan*'s owner to make significant profits from the trading that year. Ramon was very generous to the young man who he now fully considered to be his stepson, and over the summer and autumn of 1507 Audun became relatively wealthy. He was also learning patience, although it was hard. He often checked the casket, still stowed in his locker, but the red stone remained stubbornly inert. Audun could only wait until the stone decided the time was right. He hoped the wait would not be too long.

CHAPTER NINE

Clouds of War

❖ ❖ ❖ ❖

Through the early months of 1507 the shipwrights
at Tufle were busy. King Bertalan was determined to
defend Amina from the avarice of his brother-in-law.
He was fairly certain that Kermin and Doran could
assemble a greater land force than that of Amina. In
addition Bertalan knew that Alberon had continued his
father's obsession with modern weaponry and could
field a significant number of culverins and bombards
that had been imported from the ironworks in Ackar.
These large cannon would give the forces of Kermin
and Doran significant advantage in a land battle.

Bertalan had also purchased a few cannon from
Ackar, but as conflict in the lands had seemed unlikely

until recently he had felt their purchase to be a waste of Amina's gold. He knew, however, that Kermin had a weakness. Mora had no shipyards, and all the merchant ships that sailed under the Kermin flag were built either in Tufle or in Anelo in Arance. Bertalan intended to wage at least a part of any upcoming war at sea.

Late in 1506, as the envoys shuttled between Tamin and Mora, a large carrack arrived at Tufle from Boretar. Silson, Duke of Amina, was at the port to meet the arrival. Six falconets were unloaded and mounted onto the waiting wagons to be transported out to the Vale of Tember, the wide plains to the south of Tamin. The falconet was a new design of cannon, lighter and more manoeuvrable than its cousins the culverins and bombards. Silson had learnt about them on a recent visit to Boretar, where he was trying to persuade the King of Ackar and Lett to ally with Amina if war broke out. Whilst failing in this part of his mission, he saw an opportunity; it might be possible to mount these lighter cannons in the bow of a ship.

Despite the winter weather, the Vale of Tember echoed to the sound of artillery as the Amina gunners learnt their trade from their Ackar counterparts. The gunners trained under the watchful eye of James Daunt, who had travelled with the falconets and had been seconded by the Ackar king to assist the Amina forces. Daunt was a master gunner and one of the most skilled men in the use of the new weapons.

By late April 1507, the shipwrights had completed their task and the six caravels had new reinforced prows. Although they were relatively small ships, the caravels were chosen for the task because they were highly manoeuvrable, their lateen sails giving the ships speed and the ability to sail to windward. Speed and manoeuvrability would be essential if they were to succeed in the mission Bertalan had planned for them.

The falconets left dry land to take up their positions, one on the prow of each vessel. Bertalan and Silson joined the crew on the *Warrior* for the first sea trial. As the lateen sails on the two masts caught the wind the *Warrior* raced out into the Middle Sea, bouncing over the white-crested waves. A mile out from the port an old merchant ship, which had been towed out earlier, floated innocently. At a distance of two hundred yards Silson ordered the helmsman to hold course and try to keep the *Warrior* stable. The falconet in the prow erupted with a flash of flame and the grapeshot peppered the old vessel. Benefiting from months of practice the gunners reloaded, and the one-pound ball hit the centre of the merchant ship. Silson and Bertalan smiled as the central mast of the old ship came crashing down onto the deck. It was like watching a tree felled in the forest, and it was proof enough. If Alberon wanted war, then Bertalan would respond on the sea as well as on the land.

While Bertalan was admiring the prowess of his new

naval weapons Alberon was getting increasingly frustrated. In the Council Room in Mora his senior advisors sat round the large table.

Lord Norward, Commander of the armies of Kermin and Doran, was a tall, proud man, self-centred and over confident. Norward was rich, owning swathes of fertile land in the west of Kermin and through his marriage to the daughter of the King of Soll he also owned land in the northern kingdom. It was partly Norward's influence that had persuaded King Aster to accept Alberon's gold and swear allegiance to the Empire.

By contrast Aracir, Chancellor of Kermin, was short and wiry with his eyeglass always close to hand. Appearances could be deceptive though and Aracir's raven-black eyes hinted at a steely character with a sharp intelligence.

Holger, Captain of the City Guard and the King's Guard, was clearly first and foremost a soldier. The Captain had come up through the ranks thanks to his toughness, loyalty and ability, but he was always somewhat uncomfortable in the company of the nobles of Kermin.

Morserat, Duke of Doran, had been called from Iskala to attend the conference. The fifty-year-old Duke, the brother-in-law of Elrik, Alberon's father, was Alberon's proxy ruler in Doran. He was nominally in command of the Doran forces in Kermin, but Morserat seldom visited Mora and had little time for his nephew. Iskala was his home, and the fact that Doran was cut off from Kermin for most of the winter pleased the Duke.

The last noble sitting at the table was Edin, Duke of Aramin. The young man was in his early twenties and a twitch and a stammer emphasised his nervous disposition. Edin was Alberon's cousin, and his title had been inherited a year earlier when Alberon's uncle had passed away. Edin's place at the council table was part of his inheritance, but Alberon largely ignored the young man and often wished that his uncle had lived to bring his military wisdom to the table. The old Duke had led several expeditions into the Aramin forest to try to subdue the wild tribes who lived there and bring the forest fully under the control of the Kermin throne. All attempts had failed, and Edin's title was now largely honorific, as he had never been to the Aramin Forest. The lands in east Kermin remained the domain of the Aramin tribes, who defended their forest territory fiercely. As this was a war council Sylva was not in attendance; after all, her brother was the enemy.

Alberon looked slowly round the table, holding each of his advisors for a moment in an ice-blue stare. "We have had six months of envoys crossing back and forth from here to Tamin," he said. "Despite offering some concessions to my brother-in-law, he still refuses to swear fealty to his Emperor. It is time that we took action and prepared a force to invade Amina."

Lord Norward, confident as ever, was first to offer a response. "We can raise an army and invade Amina, but to what gain, Alberon? Bertalan has already named your sons as his heirs in the event of him dying without progeny. A war will cost lives and money. All we need do is to wait for Bertalan to die and then your son can swear the allegiance you require."

Alberon held the Commander in Chief in a stare until Norward had to look away. "I am not here to ask for your opinions. I am here to tell you that I want an army mobilised and ready to march on Amina by early July."

Holger and Aracir both started to speak at the same time. Aracir nodded. "Please, you go first Captain."

"As Lord Norward has said, we can raise an army and we can march on Amina, but I doubt that Bertalan will be stupid enough to meet us on either the Kermin Plain or the Amina Plain," said Holger. "Certainly his commander, Silson, will not. We must assume that Bertalan has no ambition to invade Kermin and so his tactic will be defence, and that will happen in the Kermin Alol. That is a difficult place to deploy an invading army and an easy place to defend."

Alberon was now beginning to get angry, and to emphasise his point he stood up from the table. "I know the land and I also know our forces will outnumber those of Amina," he growled. "I want action and I want my orders obeyed. I don't want to hear more excuses for inaction!"

Aracir spoke with authority. "Alberon, we all understand your frustration at Bertalan's stubbornness, however both Lord Norward and Holger are correct in their advice. I have one other point to add. Mora is rich, but war is expensive, and people are already complaining about the increase in taxes that we have ordered in the past couple of years to purchase the cannons. The people at large don't know that we are building for war and they consider the purchase of war machines with their taxes to be foolish."

Aracir was Alberon's shrewdest and most trusted advisor, and usually Alberon listened to his advice. However Bertalan's behaviour was an insult to Alberon's pride, and his pride demanded action. He sat back down and responded in a slightly calmer voice. "I have listened to all your points. Now go and follow my commands, unless you all want to spend some time in the castle's dungeons. This meeting is closed. Go and raise my army."

Back in the family apartments, Sylva tried her best to calm her husband. "The councillors' advice is wise. Bertalan will not live forever and when his time comes Aaron or Elrik will inherit the throne. Your empire will stretch from Soll to Amina and you will be the most powerful man in the world."

Alberon looked intently at his wife and lowered his voice, speaking in a condescending tone. "My dear, you forget that the boys are seven and nine years old. I have considered other ways of removing your brother, but you should remember that last year's agreed treaty still remains unsigned and that a condition in the treaty puts Bertalan's witch of a wife and the Duke of Amina as regents until one of the boys reaches eighteen years of age. If Bertalan died today he would simply be replaced by the regents, and I would be forty-five or more before my empire was complete. I will not wait that long. Besides, I have another plan." Alberon nodded to the guard at the door, who turned to open it.

The man who entered the room was tall and muscular. His attire, the fair hair tied back in braids and the knee-length riding boots were all typical of the Horse Lords of Ember. Ember was an independent Dukedom to the east of the Kingdom of Arance on the island of Andore. It was a land of wide open plains and was famed for the quality of its horses. In Sylva's estimation the man was in his late twenties, but what caught her breath was the facial likeness to her brother Bertalan.

Alberon smiled. "Welcome Berin, meet your half-sister, and my wife, Sylva." As Berin bowed, Sylva had to fall back into her seat. She had had no knowledge of a half-brother, and she doubted that Bertalan did either. He was her father's illegitimate son, yet no one had known of his existence.

Alberon indicated for Berin to take a seat. "Berin, you had better enlighten your half-sister."

Berin nodded. "Of course" he said, turning to his sister. "Sylva, you may already know parts of my story. In 1479 our father, Berka, travelled to Boretar to discuss the increasing trade levies that Ackar and Lett were charging on goods from Amina. The levies were creating unrest in Amina, and Berka wanted to negotiate more favourable terms or he would likewise increase tariffs on Ackar and Lett imports to Amina. Whilst in Boretar our father fell in love with a young noblewoman from the Duchy of Ember. Her name was Alician. Berka did not travel back directly to Amina from Boretar but went with his lover to Anua, the capital of Ember, ostensibly to purchase horses. As you know the Ember blood stock are the most favoured horses in any of the lands.

"Berka spent a few months in Anua before returning home. Most of the horses that father purchased were young, and he was advised to leave them to develop on the rich Ember pastures before transporting them to Anua, and then to Anelo and onward across the Middle Sea to Tamin.

"Six months later, in early 1480, our father returned to Anua to collect the stock he had purchased. His timing was impeccable, although he wasn't to know it. According to my mother, who sadly died a few years ago, Berka arrived back in Anua only weeks after I was born."

Sylva had been right; Berin was twenty-seven-years old.

Berin continued. "Our father was thrilled, so my mother said, but he realised he needed to keep me a secret until the time was right to introduce me in Tamin. I suppose I could have been an embarrassment to both of my parents, but I was after all the son of a king. Berka arranged with the Duke of Ember that I should be brought up in the Royal Household and trained as an Ember Horseman. As you probably know, Sylva, although the nations on Andore have been at peace for two centuries, there are still occasional revolts or bands of outlaws terrorising the countryside. The Ember Horsemen are the peace keepers on Andore, and they will respond to a request from any of Andore's nations to suppress uprisings or banditry. Anyway, and you may know this too, our father made regular trips to Anua, continuing to purchase small numbers of horses. Each visit would last a few weeks and in many ways, for me, it felt like Berka and Alician were husband and wife.

"My mother and I only made one trip to Tamin and that was for your wedding to Alberon. We were part of the entourage of the Duke of Ember, so our presence was not suspicious. I was of course only thirteen at the time and father thought it still too early to introduce me to Amina's nobility. However Berka was also concerned that I might need protection in the future, and so during your wedding celebrations Berka introduced me to your husband. He asked Alberon to swear, as part of his wedding vows, that he would ensure that I remained safe in Anua.

"Berka and Alberon also signed an agreement that when I was twenty I would be given the title of Duke of Alol. As you know the Kermin Alol lies on the border of Kermin and Amina and this agreement was seen as a way to secure the border. Unfortunately before I came of age our father died and your brother Bertalan became king. Alberon advised that the time was not right to introduce me to the new king, so I remained in Anua, with Alberon now my patron. Alberon and I agree now is the time to claim my inheritance."

Sylva was lost for words. She had thought her husband was being impetuous in his demand for fealty from her brother, whilst all the time Alberon had a more devious plan in mind. Berin was his hidden card. If this was all true, despite being illegitimate, Berin would have the right to claim his dukedom and potentially claim a right as heir to the throne of Amina. Sylva had no doubt that Berin had also agreed to swear fealty to the Emperor. Alberon said nothing; he simply smiled.

Once Berin had left the room, Sylva turned angrily to her husband, her voice trembling with emotion. "Is this all true, Alberon? And if so, why have you kept this secret from me for so long? This bastard half-brother of mine might suit your devious plans, but he might also make a claim to the succession to the Amina throne which is rightfully that of our sons. It is very likely that the nobles in Amina would, on Bertalan's death, choose Berka's direct line, even if illegitimate, rather than crown the son of an aggressive neighbour. You think you are very clever and no doubt plan to make Berin's claim to the Alol the reason for an invasion of Amina, but all you have done is raise a competitor for Amina's crown."

Alberon held up a hand to silence his wife. "My dear, you are overreacting, and that is partly why I kept Berin's existence a secret from you. I anticipated your concerns and arguments." He walked over to his desk and picked up a sheaf of papers, which he passed to his wife. Sylva took time to study each page carefully. The top page was signed by her father, confirming Berin as Berka's son. The following pages were jointly signed by Alberon; these included the document from the wedding in which Alberon promised to watch over the boy in Anua, and the document that promised Berin the dukedom of the Alol when he reached his twentieth year.

It was the pages towards the end of the sheaf that most interested Sylva. These were co-signed by Berin and Alberon. In these documents Berin swore allegiance to the Emperor as his liege Lord. The other documents made other promises of loyalty and fealty, but it was the final document that Sylva took most note of. The paper anticipated Berin inheriting the Amina crown and confirmed that in that eventuality, Amina would fall under the overall rule of the Empire. The final lines in the document said that if the above circumstances came to pass then Berin would abdicate his crown in favour of one of the Kermin princes once one of the boys had reached eighteen years of age.

Sylva threw the papers on the floor in anger. "So you have already anticipated that Berin might accede to the Amina throne, and you believe that this piece of paper will protect our sons' right to that throne. Once Berin has power, why would he simply step away from it? He does not seem like that sort of man to me."

Alberon frowned. "I have his promise and I have the papers to support it, and if Berin should rise to the Amina throne we will cut out the regency written into the treaties."

Sylva sighed. "I hope you are not being too clever and devious, Alberon." She rose and left the room. She needed time to think about what had just taken place.

The next day Alberon introduced Berin to his war council. Berin told his story again and showed the council the agreement to invest him as Duke of Alol. The rest of the papers were not shared with the council. Having been subject to the Emperor's anger and threats the day before, the councillors remained silent, whatever their individual thoughts. Alberon had played his ace card. Kermin began to mobilise for war at the command of its Emperor and in support of an Ember Horse Lord. Unknown to his half-brother, the King of Amina, Berin had become a player in the game.

CHAPTER TEN

The Kermin Alol

❖ ❖ ❖ ❖

The hill country of the Kermin Alol marked the boundary between Amina and Kermin. It started forty miles north of the Amina capital, Tamin, and stretched for another fifty miles before opening out into the Kermin plains. It did not reach great heights, but the hills were steep with narrow valleys cutting between the slopes, many with small rivers flowing through them. The land was sparsely populated, with few occupants apart from the sheep and cattle that grazed on the hillsides.

Maps showed the Kermin Alol as belonging to Amina, but as there had been peace for so many years there was no defined border. The sheep farmers from the Alol traded equally with merchants from Kermin and Amina. There were three main trade routes through the hill country. To the east the road ran alongside the river Amin, and to the west it followed the river Mina. Both roads were relatively narrow and hugged the flat ground beside the fast-flowing rivers as they made their way south to the Middle Sea. These roads were primarily used by drovers herding their sheep to the markets in Amina or in Kermin. Larger goods were carried on horse-drawn wagons which used the wide road down the dry central valley. Any army wanting to invade Amina would need to control this central valley.

In mid-June 1507, a courier from Mora passed through the central valley on the way to Tamin, to deliver a letter addressed to Bertalan. Silson, the Duke of Amina, received it, and told the messenger to wait for a reply. He gave it to Bertalan, who snapped open the Emperor's seal in irritation. Like Alberon, Bertalan was becoming increasingly frustrated with this game of politics. The six caravels lay at anchor in Tufle and Bertalan had so far resisted Silson's request to release the *Warrior* and the other caravels until war was inevitable.

Bertalan was mystified by the letter from his brother-in-law. What caught his eye was a sentence which read: "Berin, the Duke of Alol, demands that the King of Amina recognise his birthright and acknowledges him as rightful heir to the throne of Amina."

Bertalan passed the letter to Silson. "What nonsense is Alberon concocting now?" he snapped. "I have never heard of a Duke of Alol, and how could such a person have some sort of right to the throne of Amina? We will just ignore this and send no reply."

Silson, however, had read the rest of the letter. "I think you need to read it all," he told the King. "We need to take action. The letter concludes, "If the King of Amina does not agree to reinstate the rights of the Duke of Alol by the end of June then the Empire will, unfortunately, consider itself at war with Amina."

Bertalan felt his ire rise at this mention of the Empire. "The Empire, the Emperor, who does he think he is?" he fumed.

Silson was calmer. "Clearly he sees Amina as part of his Empire, and whoever this Duke is, he is Alberon's ploy to legitimise an invasion. We need to mobilise the army and set the *Warrior* and her sisters free to control the sea."

Bertalan nodded. "Go see to it then."

A week later, another messenger arrived from Mora. The man had been told to avoid the main road and had followed the drovers' road that ran alongside the river Mina. A summer thunderstorm had left him wet and mud-spattered.

Bartos, the commander of the King's guard, met the messenger at Tamin's northern gate. Amina was preparing for war and entry to the city was now under strict control. Bartos offered the messenger time to freshen up before he met the King, but the man insisted that his message was urgent and he needed to return to Mora with a reply as soon as possible.

Bartos found the King walking in the castle courtyard, deep in conversation with Silson. Bertalan initially looked irritated by the interruption, but recognising his sister's handwriting, he led Silson to a nearby seat. Bartos remained standing nearby waiting for any reply.

Sylva had worried for weeks about writing this letter. She did not want to be a traitor to her husband but, despite having seen the written contracts, she was still worried that Berin might usurp her sons' rights to the Amina throne. In the end the latter concern won the day and Sylva's letter described for her brother the unexpected arrival in Mora of their hitherto unknown half-brother.

Bertalan's laugh was cold and contemptuous. "What nonsense, an Ember Horse Lord as my half-brother? Next Alberon will send a message that he has kissed a frog and it turned into my half-sister! This is obviously made up rubbish to give Alberon an excuse to challenge Amina. Are the *Warrior* and her sisters ready to sail?" Silson nodded. "Good, give them the order to block all entry or exit from the Morel and get our troops moving to the Alol as you planned." He turned back to Bartos. "Tell the messenger to return to my sister and say thank you. It would potentially put her at risk to send a written reply. Then go and ready your troops for war."

As Bertalan was reading his sister's letter in Tamin, a heated discussion was going on in the Emperor's rooms in Mora. Lord Norward was still trying to persuade Alberon that going to war was folly, particularly in support of the rather dubious claims made by Berin. Norward was highly sceptical of the Ember Horse Lord's claimed birthright, and with unwise arrogance he started to lecture his Emperor on the stupidity of going to war.

Alberon was getting increasingly irritated and frustrated by his pompous Commander in Chief's lecturing. He paced the room, trying to retain some degree of calm. He could not.

"Lord Norward, I am fed up with your procrastination and your lectures. The army should have been ready to march by now and yet still you want to debate, or should I say talk. I have had enough. You are relieved of your command. Although I am tempted to let you enjoy some time in the dungeon, I will be lenient for now and hold you under arrest in your house. You will not be allowed to leave the premises and you will have no visitors."

Norward was staggered. "Who then will lead the army?"

Alberon was ready with his reply. "Berin will take overall command and Holger will lead the foot soldiers."

"That impostor has no knowledge of the lands of the Alol!" spluttered Norward. "It will be a disaster."

Alberon gave a cold laugh. "At least I will have a

warrior in command rather than a procrastinating, arrogant coward." He turned to the guards. "Take him to his house and ensure he stays there, and no visitors."

July 1507 was a month of frantic activity as men gathered in the Vale of Tember outside Tamin and on the open ground south of the Morel, close to Mora's city walls. Both Kermin and Amina had small standing armies of professionals and the noble elite trained for tournaments, but neither side had significant forces under arms. There had been no need for large armies through the decades of peace in the south.

In both countries the nobles were instructed to return to their lands and call on the ancient feudal rights that committed their vassals to take up arms for their king. With his father under house arrest Lord Norward's twenty-one-year-old son, William Norward, was instructed to raise the vassals from his father's lands. Smiths' foundries in both countries laid aside the ploughshares and worked day and night producing swords, arrowheads and pike tips. Woodlands were torn down to provide shafts for pikes for the foot soldiers and lances for the cavalry, whilst elm and ash were harvested to make bows for the archers. As the raw recruits arrived at the mustering camps from the towns and the countryside, so the professionals on each side drilled them in the techniques of combat and the formations they would need to master before they took to the field in battle.

In mid-July a weary troop of Kermin cavalry rode into the camp on the plain outside Mora. The dozen troopers each held the reins of a riderless horse and several of the riders were clearly wounded.

At the head of the troop rode Edin, Duke of Aramin. The young man was pale, and the heavy white bandage running across his chest and over his right shoulder was reddish brown where the blood had dried. Like other nobles Edin had been sent to raise men from his territory, which bounded and included the Aramin forest.

As he dismounted, the Duke collapsed to the ground in pain and exhaustion. The second in command of the troop called on a wagon and Edin was carried into Mora. After his wound had been attended too by the physicians, Edin was visited by Alberon. The Emperor showed the young man little sympathy.

"Well cousin, I am told that none of your vassals have responded to your instructions and we have no Aramin archers in our ranks. Worse still, you seem to have managed to lose a dozen of my highly-trained light cavalry."

Biting back the pain from the arrow wound in his shoulder, Edin tried to reply, but his voice was weak and trembling "We didn't even get to the forest, Sire," he gasped. In between sobs, Edin described how his troop had held back a short distance from the forest edge and his trumpeter had sounded a signal announcing the presence of the Duke. The trumpet blast had no sooner faded away than troopers started falling from their mounts as a rain of arrows fell on them from the edge of the forest. Edin explained that they had no choice but to retreat, and the arrow that pierced his shoulder had struck him as he turned his mount around.

Alberon sighed. "I did suggest that you should ride with a larger force. Your father tried several times to tame the forest tribes, and he always returned with his tail between his legs. Once I have done with Amina I will need to punish those savages hiding in their precious forest. Maybe I will simply burn it down." Without another word, he turned and walked away.

While Alberon was getting Edin's report, Sylva was in her private rooms talking with a visitor. For weeks she had been fretting over the Berin question. The Horse Lord had settled into the Kermin court and was strutting around as though he was already a king. She was worried about the letter she had sent to her brother and felt that she was in some way betraying her husband; however, she knew she had to protect the future rights of her sons.

A few weeks earlier Sylva had found she had an unexpected ally, her mother-in-law, the dowager Queen Ingrid. The Queen, now in her early sixties, had withdrawn from the political arena a decade earlier and largely kept to herself in her rooms in the castle. Ingrid liked her daughter-in-law and admired her ability to influence the tempestuous nature of her son whilst ignoring his dalliances with other women. Nonetheless it was a surprise when she called on Sylva in late June.

She was quick to get to the point. "Sylva, I don't like the Horse Lord and he is a growing concern to me. He is a pretender to your brother's throne, even if his claims are legitimate, and he lords it over the other nobles as though he was already in power. Since Alberon has announced that he will command the army Berin has become even more overbearing. I am worried that he will look to steal my grandsons' inheritance, and I think we need to deal with him."

Sylva was stunned that her mother-in-law should share her worries and asked if the Queen had a plan. Ingrid had asked Sylva to be patient for a couple of weeks while she resurrected some old contacts. Now that time had passed, and Sylva sat opposite Ingrid, waiting for one of her household ladies to announce the arrival of the Queen's visitor. Sylva sat nervously, fidgeting on the edge of her seat as she wondered what her mother-in-law had planned.

Fifteen minutes later there was a quiet knock on the door and Ingrid's visitor entered the room. Sylva estimated that the man was in his early thirties. He was of medium height with close-cropped black hair, and whilst unremarkable in many ways, he bore himself with a certain quiet confidence. Sylva thought to herself that if the Queen had a task for this man, he certainly looked as if he was up to it.

The stranger bowed to the Queen and then to Sylva. Ingrid introduced him. "Sylva, this is Vidur and he is a huntsman. I will explain the background later, but for now I just want to be sure that Vidur understands his mission and to pay him the initial fee for his services."

The Queen turned to the huntsman. "Tomorrow you will go to the muster ground and present yourself to Morserat, the Duke of Doran. I have explained to the Duke that you were brought up in Iskala and trained with the Doran cavalry before joining my staff as my bodyguard. I have told him that with war approaching you wanted to join the cavalry, and as I seldom go out in public these days my need for your services had diminished. Morserat initially refused my request, claiming that only those who were fully trained could join the cavalry. However when a queen's request becomes a queen's command it would be a brave duke who disobeyed. You know what you need to do."

Vidur bowed. "Yes my lady." Ingrid passed the heavy purse to Vidur and turned to Sylva with a smile. "Accidents happen in battle. Now you may leave, Vidur." With another bow, the huntsman left the room.

Sylva looked quizzically at her mother-in-law. Ingrid smiled again. "My dear, it is best that you do not know the details of my arrangement with Vidur. Suffice to say that the huntsmen have carried out particularly sensitive missions for me, my father and my grandfather before him. Their existence was not known to my husband and is not known to Alberon, as I would be concerned that my son might not use their skills wisely. Aracir is the only member of the council who knows about the huntsmen, as he ensures that they are regularly paid their retainer."

Sylva was about to ask another question, but the Queen held up her hand. "No questions Sylva, the less you know the better, but I hope Vidur will solve our Berin problem." Without another word the dowager queen called her lady in waiting and left Sylva with her questions unanswered.

In the bright morning sun of an early August day the Kermin Plain echoed to the sound of marching feet, drum beats and the crunch of wagon wheels. The Kermin army was ten thousand men strong, and Berin rode at the front, followed by four hundred Doran light cavalry. Vidur rode in the cavalry ranks a few rows behind the Duke of Alol. The light cavalry were all armed with lances and swords, and their plate armour was worn over gambesons, thick padded jackets which added extra protection against enemy arrows.

On the flanks rode two hundred heavy cavalry armed with their long lances, and all were fully covered in armour. Morserat rode at the head of this force. In the dust of the horses the foot soldiers marched in ordered lines, pikemen, archers, crossbow men and a recently added cohort of arquebusiers.

The arquebus had been invented in Ackar a decade earlier. The long barrel was either held at the shoulder or supported on a tripod and could shoot a one-ounce iron or lead ball over three hundred yards, although accurate fire was limited to fifty yards. After firing, reloading the gun took around one minute. The arquebusiers and their new weapons were marching to war for the first time.

Behind the foot soldiers trundled the gun carriages with the cannons, the culverins and the bombards, together with the wagons carrying the ammunition, iron balls, grapeshot and powder. The cannons were also rolling towards their first battle.

After a day's march the army stopped for the night on the Kermin Plain. Holger briefed Berin on the lie of the land in the Alol with the hills, at least another day's march away, just visible in the distance. He advised Berin to bring the cannons and foot to the front of the next day's march. Engagement with the Amina forces was likely to be early on the morning of the third day. Holger's opinion was that Berin should lead with the foot soldiers and the cannon and leave the cavalry to finish the job. Berin, however, was a Horse Lord and he was skilled in leading the Ember Horse in skirmishes on open ground against outlaws or rebel forces. He was also sceptical as to how the new weapons would perform in battle, so whilst he listened to Holger's advice he continued to plan to attack first with the Doran light cavalry.

Silson, Duke of Amina, had led his troops into the Kermin Alol a week earlier and his forces were ready to deploy as soon as the Kermin army appeared in view on the plain. At five thousand men, the Amina army was half the size of the opposing force. However, whilst the lie of the land was foreign to Berin, it was homeland to Silson and he planned to use the land to balance his numerical disadvantage.

The Amina foot soldiers favoured the halberd over the pike. The halberd, at eight feet long, was half the length of the pike used by the Kermin army. Along with a sharp front spear point the halberd also had a hook and axe blade positioned just below the tip. Silson believed that the versatility of the halberd, with its ability to hook and slice, would allow his halberdiers to outmatch a pike army. He was also aware that the Kermin army would have a significant force of light cavalry. He expected these mobile troops to be deployed later in the battle, but as insurance every fourth halberdier carried the longer sixteen-foot pike. The foot soldiers on both sides also wore thick gambesons.

As dawn broke on the second day the Kermin army broke camp. Far to the north Holger could see storm clouds building over the Doran Mountains and again he advised caution, suggesting that the army should remain in camp until the gathering clouds passed over. Berin, however, was acutely aware of Alberon's desire for a quick victory over Amina. He also knew of Lord Norward's punishment for procrastination.

He turned to Holger. "Your concern is noted, but our Emperor wants a fast conclusion to this war, so we march on today and we will be ready to fight tomorrow morning."

As the Kermin troops pulled into their marching formations the first drops of rain fell on the Kermin Plain.

In the Alol, Silson also saw the threatening weather coming from the north. Whilst he thought it might give him a little more time to organise his defences, he had to act on one matter before the rain soaked the hillsides and valley. Under the command of the master gunner, James Daunt, the four culverins had arrived from Tamin the previous evening. As with Berin, Silson was unsure if these new weapons could be deployed effectively in battle. Unlike Berin, he was prepared to experiment and take Daunt's advice. On both sides of the valley, on the lower slopes, two platforms had been cut out of the hillside. The platforms had been reinforced with wooden beams to create stable bases for the cannons. If the heavy storm that was approaching soaked the ground, it would be impossible to get the culverins to their platforms.

The cannons were in place as the first raindrops fell in the Alol. The charges of saltpetre, charcoal and sulphur, along with the grapeshot bags, were wrapped with leather to protect them from the incoming weather and stored in tents next to the gun platforms. Daunt had convinced Silson that the elevated positions of the cannons would improve their effective range. Archers and Amina arquebusiers were instructed in the positions they would take the next day. The former were located behind the cannons and the latter on the wings and centre of the halberdiers. Bartos and the Amina light cavalry were not present, as they had different orders to follow.

The rain fell in torrents across the Kermin Plain, and as dusk approached flashes of lightning illuminated the skies and thunder deafened the ears. With the rain hammering on the command tent canvas, Berin consulted his commanders. The light horse and heavy cavalry were camped closest to the Alol. Berin knew from his scouts that the forward pike divisions, bedded down in their sodden tents nearby, were only two hours' march from the Alol. However, as the trampled ground behind them had turned into churned-up mud, the rear of the force had been left behind. The cannons and two thirds of the pike army were much further back, stuck in the mud.

Berin listened to the discussion. The leaders of the cavalry were pushing for a midday attack, to be led by the Doran light cavalry and followed by the heavy horse. The commanders concluded that the horsemen should be able to make enough of a dent in the Amina defences to allow the following foot soldiers to win through the valley. If the valley could be held for the rest of the day, then the remaining troops should be able to march further through the Alol and approach Tamin, the capital of Amina.

Holger remained silent, listening to the debate. Eventually Berin turned to him. "My guess is that you think differently," he observed.

Holger nodded. "Charging on into the valley with only a third of our troops would be madness. Indeed, it would be suicide. If, as I suspect, Silson is in command of the defenders, he will have them well positioned on ground he knows well. I stick with my initial advice that we wait until the cannons can be deployed in advance of an attack by the foot soldiers and that the cavalry are used to complete the victory and then we march on Tamin."

Berin shook his head. "Assuming the reports from the rear are correct, the bombards and culverins might take several days to reach us. All that will do is to give the Amina commander more time to position his forces. I have decided we will attack tomorrow. Since you are so reluctant, Holger, you will leave your guard and the foot soldiers under the command of their captains and you can return to the rear and oversee the progress of your precious cannons. We will deploy them first against the walls of Tamin. You are dismissed."

From the height of the Alol, Silson could only just see the sputtering of the Kermin camp fires in the distance. With low-lying cloud and sheets of rain, even the intermittent lightning bolts did not improve the visibility. He hoped that the next morning would dawn clear so that he could further finesse his defensive strategy.

His wish was granted, and on the third day the sun shone in a cloudless sky that stretched from the Alol to the distant Doran Mountains. Shading his eyes, Silson could see the enemy camps stretched out far back across the Kermin Plain. He immediately recognised that the progress of the rear units of the Kermin army had been halted by the rain and he assumed that they had become, literally, stuck in the mud. With the Kermin troops in the distance slowly breaking camp, he anticipated that any attack would likely be delayed for a day or maybe two.

Silson would have followed Holger's advice, and he had nearly ordered his soldiers to stand down when he saw that the activity in the forward ranks of the Kermin army indicated that they were preparing to march to war that very day. His estimation was that around four thousand Kermin troops were leaving their colleagues behind and marching towards the Alol. It was a significant force and was only just outnumbered by the Amina battalions lined up in the valley.

As the Kermin army formed ranks it was clear that the majority of the forward units were pikemen, supported by around four hundred light cavalry and a smaller contingent of heavy cavalry. If the Kermin army had cannons, they must have been left behind. Silson was glad that he had managed to get his culverins into position before the rain fell, although he still wondered about the cannons' efficacy in battle.

The sun was at its zenith when the Kermin forces approached the entry into the Kermin Alol. Berin and the light cavalry were in the vanguard. The land gradually sloped up from the Kermin Plain and then as the ground on either side grew steeper the plain merged with the valley which stretched into the far distance, with the hills marching south on either side. Some fifty miles to the south the high ground would again drop down and the valley would open up onto the Tamin Plain.

Silson had decided to position his first defensive lines close to the Kermin border, knowing that, if necessary, he could fall back further south and continue to resist the enemy's progress towards Tamin. In support of this strategy Bertalan himself was in command of a second smaller Amina force, positioned further south at a point where the hills cut the valley into a narrow pass that was only the width of the road which wound along the valley floor. This would be the second line of defence if Silson could not hold the enemy's advance ten miles further to the north. From his vantage point on the Alol, Silson watched the Kermin foot soldiers forming up in orderly lines that stretched back down onto the plain.

CHAPTER ELEVEN

Fatal Mistakes

❖ ❖ ❖ ❖

Berin held his light horse at the mouth of the valley and surveyed what he now knew would be the battleground. Looking along the valley, he assessed the deployment of the Amina battalions already lined up in their positions several hundred yards away. In front of him the valley was wide and ran straight as a die, although Berin could see that the hills in the far distance appeared to close in, presumably narrowing the route further to the south. The dirt road that ran along the middle of the valley floor was sixty yards wide, which gave plenty of space for the merchants' wagons that normally used the road to pass each other. The valley floor was ten times wider than the road itself.

Berin smiled to himself. This was ideal ground for a cavalry charge. Clearly the Duke of Amina was not as smart as Holger thought. Berin would have defended further back in the distant narrower cutting. Surveying the field again he estimated that the defending formations were about five hundred yards away.

Berin called forward Amleth, Holger's second in command, who now led the foot soldiers, to join the captains of the Doran light horse, and Morserat, Duke of Doran, who commanded the heavy cavalry. It was a short conference as Berin was not looking for a discussion; he was issuing his orders. The Doran light cavalry would lead the charge, followed by Morserat's heavy horse. The light cavalry would break the first defensive lines and then Morserat's knights would smash through the remaining defenders, followed by the Kermin pikemen and the other foot soldiers. The pikemen, with arquebusiers on the flanks, would sweep the remaining defenders away and the road to Tamin would be open.

Berin and his captains returned to their troops. This was the sort of battle Berin understood, and he had no doubt about the result. He had decided to divide the Doran cavalry into two units, each two hundred horsemen strong. He estimated that the opposing defensive front line comprised about four hundred foot soldiers. His tactic was for each cavalry unit to engage the wings of the enemy front line in a narrow wedge formation. Once the wings were broken the horsemen would circle round and join forces to engage the enemy centre from behind. Berin would lead the left wing of the attack whilst Orran, Morserat's brother, would lead the right wing.

Berin and Orran led their units forward at a trot. Both knew that once they had covered the first two hundred yards the cavalry could come in range of any archers in the Amina ranks. At that point, about three hundred yards from the defensive front line, the horsemen would rise to the gallop and then it would be lance and sword in an attempt to break the defensive line before sweeping round to join their comrades and attack the rear of the enemy centre. If this was successful, the heavy cavalry with their fifteen-foot lances would follow and drive a wedge through the centre of the defence. The foot soldiers would then march forward to finish the slaughter.

Vidur had positioned himself in the second rank of Berin's attacking force, and as the horses accelerated to a trot the huntsman rode directly behind the Duke of Alol. Berin was a little surprised when the first barbs flew into the trotting cavalry at over three hundred yards. He then saw that archers were positioned on the higher slopes on either side, giving them extra range. He also noticed the cannons on both hillsides.

It was too late to change the plan, so the cavalry broke into a gallop as more arrows filled the sky. As Berin urged his horse to greater speed it seemed as though angry bees were buzzing through the air. The Amina arquebusiers had fired their first volley from the sides and centre of the defensive wall of halberds, but the range for both shot and arrow was at the limit, and little damage was done. Berin knew that the firearms would take almost a minute to reload and by that time his cavalry would be on top of them.

Fifty yards from the front line of defenders, the Doran troopers lowered their lances as the charge raced towards the first impact. At this distance the Amina archers were impotent; they were as likely to hit their own men as they were to hit the charging horsemen.

As the charge picked up pace Vidur lowered his lance. His target was the back of the man riding directly in front of him. As the Queen had said, accidents happen in battle.

Berin's assessment of the speed with which the arquebuses could be reloaded was almost correct, but fatally, not quite. Silson knew that the arquebusiers on the wings of his halberd wall were a weak spot and they had been ordered to release their first volley and then pull back to allow the halberdiers to close the defensive wings. On either side of the defensive wall six arquebusiers had remained positioned between the halberdiers. They had instructions not to fire in the first volley but to wait until the horsemen were within fifty yards, when the shot would be far more penetrating.

The volley made some impact on the charge, with a few riders unhorsed. With hands shaking in the face of the charge, one arquebusier had struggled to get his weapon into position, and fired when the horsemen were within twenty yards. It was a random lucky shot. The one-ounce ball hit Berin centrally just above his eyes, between his helmet and face shield. The Duke of Alol was dead before he hit the ground.

To ensure his mission achieved its aim, Vidur pulled on the reins of his horse and the beast's front hooves broke the body of the prone Duke. Now certain that his mission was a success, the huntsman thrust his lance at the nearest defender, then dropped it. A cavalryman without a lance was of little use in this sort of attack, and Vidur wheeled his mount round and rode back towards the heavy cavalry and the foot soldiers still stationed at the mouth of the valley. The huntsman had been paid to complete a mission for the Queen, and he was not planning to die in battle in a war he cared little about.

As he rode back towards the main force, Vidur took out his knife and drew it across his upper arm. The wound could easily have been made by a halberd. With a cloth held over the cut, he rode past the heavy cavalry and waved the blood-soaked rag towards Amleth before making his way back towards the rear of the column where the hospital tents were located. He had no intention of stopping at the tents; he could easily stitch the wound himself.

Once he had reached the shelter of a small copse a short distance from the army, Vidur repaired his wound, removed the Doran military garments and dressed in his normal nondescript clothing. Under cover of darkness he would make his way back to Mora and report to the Queen, who would be pleased to hear his mission had been a success, even if he had been assisted by a one-ounce iron ball. The Queen would pay the rest of the huntsman's fee and her daughter-in-law would be relieved that one threat to her sons' inheritance had been removed.

Back at the front line, in the crash of horse and man, few of the Doran cavalry realised their leader had fallen. Few would have cared. The Ember Horse Lord had been forced on them by the Emperor. Berin was not one of their own, and besides the cavalry had other problems to deal with. The Doran troopers had practised attacking pike formations, and on seeing the defenders with their shorter halberds they had assumed that punching through the front line would be easy. The Doran lances dented the left wing of the Amina line, but the halberd proved to be a vicious weapon at close quarters. The spiked end did not reach as far as the Kermin pike did, but the hooked blade could snarl a lance and the reverse sweep of the axe head could be even more lethal to horse and man.

As Berin's now leaderless cavalry unit wheeled round, the right wing of the Amina front line had been pushed back but not broken. The halberdiers quickly reformed and awaited the next charge. On the other wing, Orran had successfully broken through the defence and his two hundred cavalrymen were circling round to engage the rear of the centre of the enemy line, as planned.

Orran quickly realised that the attack on the left wing had failed and his men were now potentially trapped. A second Amina defensive line was arrayed across the valley fifty yards behind the front line. Orran and his men were now dangerously positioned between the lines of Amina halberdiers.

On recognising his brother's predicament, Morserat ordered the heavy cavalry forward. The sound was like thunder rolling across the plain, and the fully armoured knights on their destriers crashed into the centre of the Amina front line, an irresistible wave of hoof and steel. Whilst the halberd was effective against light cavalry, it was about as much good against a mounted knight as shaking a stick. The knights obliterated the centre of the Amina defensive line, and as Morserat met his brother on the field his temptation was to continue the attack and engage the second line of Amina defenders. Morserat knew that the halberdiers could not resist the sheer weight of an attack by the knights, but he also recognised that if he kept moving forward he would command a small force on the wrong side of the enemy lines. Despite their power and prowess an isolated knight was an easy, all be it dangerous, target.

Reluctantly the heavy cavalry and Orran's troopers fought their way back through the destroyed centre of the Amina force and returned to Amleth and the Kermin foot soldiers who were still waiting in formation at the mouth of the valley.

It was a depleted cavalry force that reined up in front of the ranks of Kermin foot soldiers. Morserat looked back at the battlefield and the carnage caused by his knights. For a moment he considered ordering the foot soldiers forward behind a second charge from the heavy horse. Maybe the day could still be won?

But when he looked at the sky in the west, he saw that the sun was beginning to sink behind the western hills. He knew he had run out of time.

Morserat began to count the cost of the encounter to the Doran cavalry. Only just over half of the four hundred had returned. These were his own countrymen, and he cursed Berin for leading them on such an impetuous, poorly thought out and pointless charge.

When it became clear that Berin was not returning from the battle, Morserat took over command. The Duke of Alol was not missed by anyone, although the demise of his protégé might be a concern to the Emperor.

As Morserat again surveyed the battlefield, he drew the same conclusion as Holger. This was a fight for cannon and pike, not for light horse, although his heavy cavalry could play their part. Only a few knights had been killed or injured in the attack.

He sent a Doran trooper back north to inform Holger of the result of the first engagement. Holger's instructions were to bring forward the cannons and the rest of the foot soldiers as soon as possible. Morserat was a cautious man and he was content to wait until the rear of the Kermin forces had reached the front. Looking back again at the devastation caused by his knights, the Duke was confident that once his full complement of foot soldiers was ready to deploy, his force would significantly outnumber the depleted defenders. Morserat ordered the forward troops back to their camps on the Kermin Plain. The battle would commence again in the morning.

As the Kermin forces pulled back, Silson was also counting the cost to his men. Of the two thousand halberdiers at the front line, around eight hundred would take no more part in the fight. Most of the dead and wounded had met their fate under the hooves of the destriers or at the end of the knights' lances. In the skies over the Alol the crows were gathering, anticipating a fine evening feast.

Silson reflected on the outcome of the first day of the battle. Maybe he should have ordered the gunners to fire the culverins at the first attack, but Daunt had advised against that. The cannons would be effective against an infantry attack, but their impact on a fast-moving cavalry unit would be minimal. Silson also recognised the destruction wrought by the heavy cavalry, and was glad that whoever had planned the Kermin strategy had not led with the armoured knights. That was a problem for the morning. For now he had a lot of work for his men to do before the sun set.

To the south, he could see the train of wagons he had ordered moving up towards his positions.

At the rear of the Kermin column, Holger was trying to get the gun carriages and supply wagons to make faster progress across the plain. It was a challenge, as the rain from the previous day had left the ground soaked and every few hundred yards the gun carriage wheels, weighed down by the loads they carried, slid deep into the mud. Holger had sent members of his guard out to nearby farms to conscript large horses, those used for the plough, to assist the draft teams of oxen, which were now exhausted from the slow travel across the plain.

As the carriage wheels once again sank into the mud and stopped, Holger spotted a small cavalry troop to his west moving rapidly north. He had not yet been informed of the outcome of the day's battle in the Alol valley and as dusk was approaching he assumed this small force was a Doran cavalry unit heading back to Mora on some mission for Berin or Morserat. With no reason for concern, he returned to the task of freeing the gun carriages from the mud. The distraction would be costly.

Bartos and one hundred of the King's Guard were not with Silson's forces defending the central valley. Bertalan had ordered them to take the drovers' road to the west of the main valley, and Bartos and his troop had followed the road as it wound along the banks of the Mina River. His instructions were to raid the supply wagons at the rear of the Kermin column. Bertalan hoped this would disrupt the enemy supply chain and possibly cause some of the attackers to be withdrawn from the front line.

Bartos' men were equipped with lance and sword, but they had two additional weapons. Amina craftsmen had successfully developed the pistol, a new form of arquebus with a shorter barrel which, although it had a shorter range, could be fired from horseback. They also carried Doran Combustibles strapped to their saddles. The combustibles had been invented several hundred years earlier to help the Doran miners expose the gold seams in the Doran Mountains. The devices had remained largely unchanged over the centuries and were used in mines and in clearing land. Each package contained a mix of sulphur, charcoal and potassium nitrate and had a short fuse sticking out from the mouth to ignite the contents. None of the troopers knew that these devices had first been used in battle in the Alol two hundred years earlier.

As the horsemen in the west wheeled round towards the centre of the supply chain, Holger suddenly realised his mistake. These were not friends; this was an attack. Being far behind the front line, most of the men nearby were wagon drivers and the gunners who manned the cannons. There were in addition a number of pikemen there, as protection against the unlikely event of a raid on the supply chain by bandits.

Holger quickly called his limited resources to form a line in front of the gun carriages. It was a motley defence with sword and pike. Holger knew it was little protection against a cavalry attack, but somehow he had to defend the precious cannons. He called men forward from the supply wagons; the supplies could be quickly replaced from Mora, but the cannons were irreplaceable.

Bartos was leading his guardsmen to the centre of the wagon train when he saw the pikemen running forward. Briefly reining in his horse, he spotted the gun carriages sunk to their axles in the mud and realised that his attack on the supply train would be wasted if he could instead destroy the cannons. Leading by example, and knowing the guard would follow, he wheeled round to attack the defensive line arrayed in front of the gun carriages. His pistol shot floored one of the defenders, but he never drew close enough to engage with their swords and pikes. Ten yards from the wagons, Bartos began to light his combustibles and toss them into the gun carriages. His troop followed suit.

Holger, standing at the front of the defensive line, felt a shattering blow to his left shoulder, but held his position. It made little difference, as two hundred combustibles then lit up the leading supply wagons and the gun carriages. Bartos did not wait to see the results of his attack, but as he reined in to let his troopers catch up he could see the first flames beginning to consume the wagons.

Although there were pools of water lying all around, Holger had no means of quenching the fires. The Doran cavalryman carrying Morserat's instructions arrived from the front in time to see the great bombards and the culverins sink further into the mud beside the charred wrecks of their wooden carriages. An ashen-faced Holger was sitting on the wet ground getting his shoulder bandaged. Fortunately the ball had passed through the flesh and not hit bone. He instructed the Doran trooper to go back to Morserat and inform him that the cannons would not play a part in tomorrow's battle.

In the Alol, Silson had plenty of water. Wagon after wagon rolled in on the road from Tamin loaded with filled barrels. Silson did not plan to use the water to put out fires; he had another use for it, in defence.

Bartos arrived back at Silson's headquarters tent just as a waxing gibbous moon rose over the Alol. It had been a long hard ride back along the western drove road, then taking a cutting through the hills south of the main force. Bartos had paused at the narrows where Bertalan held the reserves and reported to his King. From there it was a ride past the still-rolling water wagons to report to Silson.

The Duke greeted the news with a smile. "Well done Bartos, this will change the game on the morrow. Without his cannons, whoever is leading the Kermin force will need to resort to heavy cavalry, the pikemen, archers and arquebusiers. We'll be ready for them. Your guard will remain at the rear, but they may be useful if we break the advance and force the enemy to retreat. Go now and settle your men into their camp."

At the same time as Bartos was reporting to Silson, a wounded Holger was doing the same in Morserat's tent. Despite his noble birth the Duke of Doran had always paid attention to the needs of his men. "Holger, you did all you could. We should have listened to your advice a few days ago and we would not be in this situation. My instinct is to leave this useless war behind and take our forces back to Mora, but I doubt that the Emperor would approve. Go and get that wound properly seen to and report back to me at dawn tomorrow."

The next morning brought clouds chasing south from the Doran Mountains. These were not storm clouds, but they shed a constant drizzle on the already wet Alol valley floor. It was a gift Silson could not have expected. There were no records of a real battle between pike and halberd, only the instructions from the military handbooks written from observing practice engagements. The latter's shorter reach would be a disadvantage until the pikemen were at close quarters, when the halberd was expected to be the more lethal weapon.

Silson had read the books and been trained in pike warfare, and he understood that pike cohorts relied on tight ranks and a uniform attacking front. During the night the Amina soldiers had emptied the water barrels, flooding an area fifteen feet wide that stretched right across the valley about ten steps from the Amina defensive front line. Silson hoped the ground would play an additional role in the defence of his homelands.

The Duke of Doran had spent a sleepless night worrying about strategy. It was clear from the previous day's engagement that the knights of the heavy cavalry could devastate a defensive line of halberdiers, but he had only two hundred knights under his command and these were the cream of Kermin nobility. If the knights broke through the opposing line they were likely to become isolated and would make easy targets for the Amina foot soldiers. If the heavy cavalry maintained formation they would soon outrun their supporting foot soldiers. Holger had been correct from the start; the battle could only be won by man against man fighting on foot. If the foot soldiers could win some ground, then the heavy cavalry could follow.

A watery sun broke through the cloud cover as the drums began to beat in the Kermin Plain, and thirty minutes later the pike army arrived at the mouth of the valley. The Kermin pikemen would use the central dirt road to march on solid ground to just under three hundred yards from the Amina defensive positions, avoiding the wet, soggy ground on either side of the road. At this point the front rows would halt and in orderly fashion the following troops would move right and left on to the grassy sides to create a wide attacking front. Once each cohort was in place the pike army would then march forward in unison to engage the defenders. This was classic battle tactics from the military textbooks of the past. The only apparent risk to the front line was a volley of arrows from the Amina archers that Morserat knew were positioned on the higher slopes. However he also knew that at a distance of around three hundred yards the arrows would have little power and any impact would mostly be absorbed by the troopers' gambesons. Morserat had either not known about the culverins, or forgotten about them. Maybe, being sceptical about the new weapons, he had discounted them.

Five hundred yards across the valley the Amina battalions had returned to their defensive positions of the day before. Again the flanks were manned by the arquebusiers, although having learned from the attack the previous day each man also had a halberd wedged into the ground beside him. From his elevated position beside the culverins, Silson could appreciate that the approaching force now outnumbered his defenders. He wondered if the culverin could level the playing field. He would soon find out.

The Amina gunners manning the cannons had practised in the Vale of Tember. The round iron balls could travel over five hundred yards on a flat trajectory. The more lethal grapeshot, canvas bags loaded with small iron balls which scattered on impact, had a shorter range.

James Daunt, who had travelled with the cannon from Ackar, was captain of the guns and had briefed Silson on the best way to deploy the cannon. A round of tar-coated iron balls could be fired first to stop the initial progress of the enemy. The tar would ignite on firing and the projectile would turn into a fireball. If the culverin could be reloaded quickly enough, the grapeshot round would follow.

The Kermin pikemen formed up on the hard-packed road as instructed. Each row consisted of fifty men, and as the drum beats increased in intensity so the first rows started the march to battle. From his vantage point Silson was impressed by the discipline of the march as the sun glinted from helmets, armour and pike tips. As he had anticipated, the ranks began to spread out left and right at about three hundred yards from his own front line. He estimated that the Kermin front line would be almost identical to his own, with four hundred men in each row.

As the first three rows of Kermin pike formed up, Silson ordered Daunt to light up the culverins. Morserat saw the flash of fire and belch of smoke from both sides of the valley. The beating of the drums hid the noise of the explosions that accompanied the fire and smoke. Moments later the fireballs fell from the sky just in front of the first line of the Kermin troops. The tar-soaked iron balls bounced once and then tore through the stationary ranks, cutting a fiery swath through the pikemen. The aiming of the culverins was more art than science, and one of the gunners was lucky when a fireball bounced high on the hard-packed road and smashed through the troops at the rear who were still waiting to deploy across the valley. Most of the Kermin pikemen had seen cannons being fired in practice, but this was the first time they had experienced them in war.

The Kermin formations faltered, but only briefly, as the captains pushed their men forward past their dead and wounded comrades. Silson had known that the culverins would only stall the Kermin deployment, and he hoped that their next volley would be more deadly. He knew that Daunt had to let the gun barrels cool before reloading and he wondered if this could be done in time. As the smoke drifted away into the skies above the Alol, the Kermin forces continued to line up.

The Kermin foot soldiers deployed more or less as Silson had anticipated. Twelve hundred pikemen formed in three rows, leaving a twenty-yard gap to three more rows of twelve hundred behind. This formation allowed the somewhat unwieldy pike to be used in attack rather than defence. Occasionally a gap appeared in the Kermin lines when an Amina archer managed a lucky shot. Knowing that the distance was too great, Silson was careful to save arrows; only archers positioned further forward took shots.

Eventually the Kermin troops on the road moved into their positions and the attack formation was ready. The drums fell silent and trumpets signalled the order to forward march. As the front lines started to move, the drums again took up the beat.

When the disciplined front ranks of the Kermin foot soldiers had marched forward a further hundred yards, the fire and smoke again erupted from the culverins. Not large tar-coated iron balls this time but canvas bags filled with the same one-ounce balls that were fired from the arquebus. When the bags hit the ground the canvas tore open, releasing the contents with deadly effect. The grapeshot tore into the advancing troop, causing devastating damage.

With grim determination, the first and second rows of the Kermin pikemen integrated to re-establish the front line. The culverins could not be reloaded fast enough to release a second volley. Pike advances relied on flat, dry ground to maintain the integrity of the pike wall, but before the pikemen could engage the Amina halberdiers, the ground had turned into a quagmire. Silson had prepared well. The soaked earth halted the forward march, and the pike lines broke as soldiers slipped in the mud. The pike had the advantage of reach over the halberd in orderly close combat, but as the line broke on the treacherous water-soaked ground the halberdiers stepped forward. The hooks on the halberds swept aside the pikes and the axe heads followed, slicing apart anything they connected with.

As the front lines faltered, the culverins again roared from the upper slopes. The grapeshot this time tore through the fourth rank of the Kermin advance. These were still two hundred yards from engaging their opposite numbers and the bodies filling the field further hampered their progress.

Morserat could see that only further slaughter would befall his men if they continued the attack, and the trumpets sounded a different note: pull back. The Kermin heavy cavalry had not been deployed in the fighting that day at the Alol, but the culverin and arquebus had gone to war for the first time and won. Silson knew that battlefield tactics had changed forever. The power of the black powder, gunpowder, was the weapon of the future.

CHAPTER TWELVE

In Mora Castle, Alberon was pacing the council chamber like a caged lion, and he had the roar to match. Only the chancellor, Aracir, remained in the room. Sylva and the boys kept well out of the way of the ill-tempered Emperor. Even the servants tried to avoid their master.

There was no news from the Kermin Alol, but with no weapons to attend to some of the gunners had returned to Mora and been interviewed by Aracir. Alberon was furious. "Why did they allow the attack on the cannons? Do you know how much gold they cost? Now they lie rusting on the Kermin Plain!"

Aracir nodded. "Yes my Emperor, I do."

Alberon ignored the comment. "Why have I had no

reports from the front? What is that fool Berin doing? Is there any news from Morserat?"

Aracir shook his head. "Sire, we have another problem. We should have carracks from Andore in the port, trading vessels from Thos and Anelo. There are none and have been none this past week. Clearly with the declaration of war the trade with Amina has been halted. Until a short while ago I did not understand the absence of vessels from Andore. I have just had a report from the captain of a caravel that was leaving here with bales of cloth bound for Anelo. When the caravel reached the mouth of the Morel it was threatened by two Amina war boats that were patrolling the Eastern Sea. The story has spread like wildfire around the docks and none of our captains are prepared to put to sea."

Alberon held his chancellor in a cold stare. "Your role is to come to me with solutions, not present me with problems. Get to the port and instruct one of our ships to set sail for Anelo on Andore. You will accompany the vessel and report back to me with a solution to this problem. You are dismissed."

Aracir bowed and left, leaving his angry Emperor to continue with his pacing.

Aracir had never been to sea and he had no knowledge of ships. His realm was that of gold and finance, and a sea trip was not much to his liking. The *Erth* was a three-mast carrack built for transporting large volumes of goods across the Eastern and Middle Seas. Carracks were the workhorses of the seas, large vessels capable of transporting their cargo safely even in the roughest weather. The ships were generally square-rigged on the fore and main mast and lateen rigged on the mizzen mast. They had a high rounded stern with a large aftcastle and slightly smaller forecastle.

The *Erth's* captain, Rondon, was surprised to see the richly-dressed noble approach his ship. Aracir called out. "I have instructions from the Emperor. I need you to be ready to sail in the morning for Anelo."

Rondon came down the gangway. "My Lord, rumour has it that warships patrol the exit to the Morel. I will not risk my ship and my livelihood."

Aracir passed over the purse, heavy with gold. "I am sure this can persuade you that the risk is worthwhile. Besides the *Erth* is huge, I can't see what a small war boat could do to damage such a vessel. In any case your instructions are from the Emperor, so either take the fee or I will simply call the guard and conscript the vessel."

Rondon knew he had no choice. "Yes sir, we will be ready to sail on the morning tide. I presume you are joining us on this journey?"

Aracir nodded. He had picked the three-mast carrack for the expedition for its sheer size, thinking that the bulk of the vessel would give it protection. He did not appreciate that war at sea was more about speed and mobility than it was about sheer size.

The next morning, with only the front mast rigged with its square sail, the *Erth* headed down the Morel towards the Eastern Sea. If the journey was uninterrupted, the ship would move south down the Kermin coast and then cross the Middle Sea to the Andore coast south of Arance before turning west to the port of Anelo. As the ship reached the mouth of the Morel, Rondon ordered the sails to be raised on the main mast and the mizzen mast. Instinctively he knew he needed to gain as much speed as he could.

Having no sea legs, Aracir had quickly decided that the best place to spend this journey was in the bed in the Captain's cabin. As a result the Chancellor did not witness what unfolded next.

From high on the *Erth's* aftcastle, Rondon spotted two caravels. One of them had left anchor to the north of the Morel whilst the other raced in from the south. With their lighter weight and lateen sails Rondon knew that it would be a challenge for the carrack to outrun the hunters. The *Erth* was now in full sail and with a favourable wind and the long waves with their white crests buffeting the ship's side, Rondon thought that any boarding party would be hard pressed to gain a footing on his vessel. It was the tactic that the pirates who still roamed the Greater Sea used. They would make a fast approach to the target vessel and throw grappling hooks over the gap, and then an armed boarding party would complete the job. Aracir had ordered a small contingent of Kermin infantry to join the ship, and these now manned the lower middle deck, ready to repulse any attempt to board.

The captains of the *Warrior* and her sister ship *Destroyer* had no intention of attempting to board the *Erth*; they were going to use the cannons. It required a great deal of skill from both the gunners and the helmsman to achieve accurate shots from the falconets, mounted as they were on the prows of the rolling caravels. However these men were now practised in the art. Rondon was startled to see flames shoot from the bows of the attackers at around 400 yards distance. Both shots fell short, but Rondon was now rightly very worried.

Aracir heard the explosions from his bunk. Despite his nausea, he climbed from his bed to the aftcastle to witness the first hits. The one-pound balls landed mid-deck, and under the impact the *Erth* shuddered to its keel. To the sound of straining wood, the main mast tilted and with the wind filling the sails the tall mast crashed to the deck like a felled tree. The two caravels raced past the bow of the *Erth* and after sweeping around several hundred yards away, returned to the attack. This time grapeshot peppered the decks, wounding several sailors and infantrymen.

On the *Warrior*, the captain, John Sexton, raised the flag signal to tell his opposite number on *Destroyer* to hold position. The caravels had been instructed to block the exit from the Morel, and Sexton had no wish to send fellow sailors to a watery grave. Rondon recognised the move and realised he would be allowed to return the *Erth* to Mora, but to head out to sea would likely bring destruction to his ship. Besides, the damage done meant that she would be unlikely even to limp as far as the Andore coast.

Rondon turned the carrack round and headed back to the Morel. Aracir grabbed the captain by the neck. "You have been paid by the Emperor to take us over the sea to Anelo. We still have two masts and sails. We can still make the journey."

The Chancellor felt the prick of a dagger in his back. Coolly Rondon replied, "My Lord, I care little for our Emperor, but I care a great deal about my ship. We are returning to Mora."

With nausea returning and somewhat in fear, Aracir returned to the safety of the cabin. With the blockade maintained, the caravels returned to their moorings north and south of the Morel. They had succeeded in halting the attempted break-out from Mora.

On the northern side of the Middle Sea, the other four caravels patrolled the coast of Andore, but they had not seen any action. Bertalan had informed his fellow kings in the Kingdoms on the island of Andore that whilst a state of war existed with Kermin he would stop any trade with Mora, by force if necessary. None had been needed so far.

In Mora, Alberon was prowling the castle walls. His anger had been replaced by frustration; he had had no reports back from the Kermin Alol and could only hope his forces had won. His attention was drawn to the vessel making slow progress upriver on the Morel. Even at a distance Alberon recognised that something was amiss; the carrack only had a sail on the foremast, and the main mast seemed to be missing.

He called one of the guards. "If that is the ship chancellor Aracir sailed on, I want him brought to the council chamber as soon as his feet hit the ground."

As the damaged ship moored and Aracir climbed down the gangplank, he saw the guardsmen waiting and knew he was not going to enjoy his meeting with the Emperor.

Raimund and Aleana were walking along the dockside as the *Erth* moved into view. Rumours had spread throughout the city that due to the war, no shipping was moving out of Mora and no vessels were allowed to enter the river Morel. Rafe had asked Raimund and Aleana to go down to the docks to learn more about this unusual situation, as it could have a big impact on their business.

Raimund was the first to notice that the *Erth* was damaged, and at the same time Aleana spotted the rich noble on the ship's afterdeck. Neither knew who the man was, but he might provide a better target than the light purse of a sailor. Aleana threw an arm round Raimund's neck and whispered to him. Raimund was concerned about her suggestion but only had time to say "Watch out for the guardsmen," before she moved away.

Aracir was deep in thought as he stepped from the gangplank, worried about the harsh reception he was likely to face in the castle. He had only gone ten yards when the girl ran in front. The first of the guardsmen offered her a short cuff from the butt of his spear to move her from the Chancellor's path. It was meant to be, and was, a light warning to move out of the way. Aleana, however, made the most of it and appeared to trip, feigning a heavy fall to the ground. She lay prone, groaning as though the impact had caused her serious pain.

The guardsmen were already marching on when Aracir shouted "Halt!" He could not leave the girl lying there unattended. She looked to be about the same age as his own daughter. As he bent over the girl, she seemed to groggily return to consciousness. From behind him came another shout: "My sister, what have you done to her?"

Raimund was quickly by Aleana's side and Aracir moved back to let the boy in. "I think she will be fine.

It was just a small bang on the head. Can you look after her?"

Raimund smiled at the Chancellor. "Yes sir, I think I can get her home and our mother will be able to care for her if needed."

Aracir patted the boy on the shoulder. "Well then, you best take her home." Then he moved off to join the impatiently waiting guardsmen.

Raimund carefully got Aleana to sit up and the pair watched the guardsmen move through the southern gate. Once the troop was out of sight, she stood up and, continuing the act, leant on Raimund as they headed back towards the city gate. Once they were a safe distance from the *Erth* they looked back to see the wounded ship set sail and move south down the river. Raimund gave a quiet chuckle and passed Aleana the purse, heavy with coins.

It would not be until much later, when he was back in his own house after his interrogation by the Emperor, that Aracir would realise that his purse had gone. It had been a long day, and he would have completely forgotten about the incident at the dockside.

In the council chamber Aracir sat nervously on the edge of his seat as Alberon paced the room. In a deferential voice, with hands clenched, Aracir recounted the engagement with the Kermin warships. To his surprise, Alberon stopped pacing, and slumped into one of the large chairs. "A cannon on board a caravel? Bertalan is cleverer than I would have given him credit for. Nonetheless you should have carried on and made for Anelo to prove we would not be bullied and held locked in."

Aracir lowered his head. "I tried, my Lord, but the captain would not risk his ship."

Alberon sighed. "Who was in charge? I sent you on a task and we paid the captain good gold for his voyage and you return saying the captain decided?"

Aracir paled. "When I tried to instruct the captain I was threatened with his dagger."

Alberon's voice took on an angry edge. "I consider this treason against the Empire!" he boomed. He called the guardsman from outside the room. "Take some men and go to the dock and arrest the crew of the *Erth*. They will be punished as traitors. Chancellor, you are dismissed. I need to think." After Aracir had left the chamber Alberon closed his eyes for a moment. "Very clever," he murmured, "A cannon on board a caravel."

Rondon had seen the Chancellor escorted away by the guardsmen and guessed that he and his men would be next. He immediately ordered the crew to make ready for sea again. Despite their fear and some protests, they obeyed their captain. When the guards reached the dock, the *Erth* was already sailing south on the Morel towards the Eastern Sea. Rondon knew what to expect this time, and as the *Erth* left the mouth of the Morel he flew white flags from the fore and aft mast tops. John Sexton on the *Warrior* recognised the ship at once and knew it held no threat. Pulling his ship alongside the *Erth*, he boarded the damaged vessel and shook hands with Rondon.

"I'm sorry we had to damage your ship, captain, but we're under orders from our king to stop any vessel leaving Mora," he said. "You know of course we could have sunk her, but that is not in our orders."

Rondon nodded. "Having failed to break out, I believe my crew and I are at mortal risk in Mora. I would like you to allow the *Erth* free passage to Tufle, where we can repair the vessel and be available to carry trade for your king. I have no love for the Emperor in Mora."

Sexton paused. This was not part of his orders, but he could see no harm in allowing the *Erth* to limp south to Tufle. "I agree," he said. "Johann, my second in command, will travel with you and on arrival at Tufle you will go immediately to Tamin and report to Lord Ereldon, who is King Bertalan's chief advisor."

Rondon let out a sigh of relief. With the Emperor's gold in his cabin, he could afford to have the ship repaired. He and his crew had left family in Mora, but hopefully the Emperor would not find the families guilty for their men's actions.

The guardsman had just returned from the docks to

report that the *Erth* had escaped when he was followed into the council chamber by a dishevelled Captain of the King's Guard. Holger had travelled directly from the front following the failure of the Kermin advance. The bandage on his upper arm would explain why he had not been in the front line with the troops.

Alberon summarily dismissed the news from the port. Executing the crew of the *Erth* as traitors might have sent a signal to others who refused his orders, but it was not important. He needed to know what had happened in the Alol.

Holger was not the bringer of good news. Alberon paced the room and his temper rose as Holger recounted the details of the battle. Alberon's face flushed with anger and his fists clenched and unclenched as he tried to hold back a tirade.

Holger became increasingly agitated, and his story faltered. He was the messenger, not the guilty party, and he tried to plead his case by pointing out again that his advice had been consistently ignored by Berin. Alberon forced himself to calm down and let the red mist clear. He suddenly sat down, and if his fury had been frightening, the ice-cold stare was worse.

"So the Duke of Alol will get his wish and remain forever in the Alol," he said. "Well, the arrogant Horse Lord is no great loss, and pawns are expendable. His claims on the Alol and the Amina throne were convenient, an excuse to march on Amina. Where are Morserat and the rest of the army now?"

Holger drew a deep breath and replied, "The army has withdrawn to the Kermin Plain and dug into defensive positions there. However the Amina forces seem to be content defending the higher ground and only sporadic attacks from the Amina cavalry harass the wings of our defences. The Amina cavalry are armed with some new form of arquebus, so they do not engage directly but ride in close and loose a volley of shots into our troops. These engagements cause some panic but few casualties. If Bertalan wants to invade Kermin, he shows no sign so far. Indeed our scouts' reports tell of more cannon being brought to the front at the Alol, so we assume they will hold there. I presume the Duke of Doran remains in command on the plain."

Alberon was only just holding back another tirade. "Go and get the Duke and bring him back to report to me," he snapped. "Now go, before I decide to punish you for your incompetence!"

Holger was not to know that Morserat and a troop of loyal Doran cavalry were already crossing the Morel at the ford to the north where the great river was shallower. The Duke did not expect forgiveness from the Emperor, and had decided that retreat to Iskala and his home city was the best tactic. In a month's time the snow would block the passes through the Doran Mountains. Maybe the Emperor would have calmed down by the spring. Maybe things would change for the better.

Pleased with their unexpected bounty, Raimund and Aleana started back towards the old warehouse. With the increased presence of guards on the streets, the severe punishment now administered if a thief was caught and now the war and blockade, the past few months had offered little reward for the efforts of the Den of Thieves.

Despite the poor pickings, Rafe was a cautious man and Raimund and Aleana both knew of the two boxes stored at the back of the warehouse filled with coins and rich jewels. The three were now the only members of the Den of Thieves.

As Raimund and Aleana passed the road from the southern bridge to the south gate, the first of the wagons arrived. The pair knew about the war with Amina, but apart from limiting their pickpocketing opportunities, it had not had any impact on them.

As the wagons rolled past, reality struck the onlookers. Each wagon carried its cargo of dead and wounded men, and with bright red stains spattered across their sides the wagons seemed to be dripping with blood. The sickly-sweet smell of death emanated from some of the wagons, and swarms of flies gathered around both the dead and the wounded.

Raimund and Aleana were close enough to see the pain etched in the face of a young soldier who appeared to have lost an arm. The bandage tied above where the soldier's elbow would have been was deep crimson. Other soldiers were also wrapped in bandages and whilst the sight was terrifying, the moaning, groaning and crying of the injured men was worse. It was more than Aleana could bear, and with her hands over her ears she started to run back to the security of the Den of Thieves.

Raimund was slightly less squeamish; after all he had seen blood and death before, although the memory made him shiver. Maybe Rafe's reserves in the warehouse would be called on as autumn turned to winter.

CHAPTER THIRTEEN

Winter 1507

❖ ❖ ❖ ❖

At the front lines on the Kermin Alol, there was only sporadic action with minor sorties from both sides. Bertalan had given clear instructions that he had no intention of invading Kermin, but Silson knew he needed to strengthen the defences at the Alol and give his army space to respond to any sudden counter-attack from the Kermin forces.

Now convinced of the potential of the culverins, Silson had ordered more cannons and more ammunition to be brought to the Alol from Tamin. The Kermin defensive lines had pulled back a short distance and were camped two miles from the lower slopes of the Alol. This was still too close for Silson's liking and he planned to push them further back towards Mora. Under cover of darkness four culverins had been moved down from the Alol and onto the flat ground of the Kermin plain.

In the absence of the Duke of Doran, the Kermin army was now under the command of Holger, and being much more conservative than his predecessors, he was not planning any renewed attack on the Alol, as he knew that his job now was to resist any Amina attempt to attack Mora or to put the city under siege. The Kermin forces were subject to lightning raids by the Amina cavalry, which caused minor injuries, but Kermin arquebusiers and archers generally held the pistoleers at bay. Holger had ordered the Kermin infantrymen to further reinforce their defensive positions, but he had not anticipated a redeployment of the culverins.

As a first autumn storm blew in from the north, the front lines of the Kermin forces were caught by surprise by the explosions echoing from the south and the tarred iron balls which tore into their midst. Holger knew he could not hold his positions with his forces unable to respond to the cannonades, and in an orderly manner the Kermin forces pulled further back across the plain towards Mora. The late September storms would soon turn into October rain followed by November snow, and soon any movement across the plain would become impossible. Holger also knew that his defensive positions needed to be close enough to Mora to ensure that his supply lines were secure. He set the defensive positions twenty miles south of the Morel and the city.

Silson also understood the land and the weather and was happy that the distance to the Alol was now such that any Kermin advance would be detected long before the lower slopes were approached. The Amina army pulled back to the Alol, leaving only cavalrymen patrolling the plain. By November even these men would return to the camps in the Alol, as the winter snow would hold both armies locked in their camps until spring.

It was the first week of October and the second of the two wagons was leaving the steep path that wound down from the Doran Mountains to join the main road to Mora. The wagons were carrying gold from the Doran mines to the city before the snow closed the roads. The payment was the tithe demanded by Alberon to leave the miners in peace and not conscript their mines and dwellings. A small troop of the King's guard rode with the wagons, but they were only there to dissuade bandits from any attempt to raid the convoy.

As the wagons rolled out onto the plain and joined the road to Mora, the leading guard spotted a large group of horsemen approaching from the south. Initially the captain of the escort thought the troops were reinforcements from Mora to ensure safe delivery of the gold. Too late he realised that the approaching horsemen were well-armed light cavalry dressed in the livery of Amina.

As the attacking horsemen closed in, the red, white and blue Amina flag was raised by the leading trooper and at thirty yards the first volley from the pistols despatched a number of the escort. Bartos, who was leading the raid, did not wait to engage the escort fully; instead his troopers jumped onto the gold wagons and turned them south. War was expensive, and Bertalan had decided that his brother-in-law could pay for some of Amina's costs. The helpless escort attended their wounded and could only watch as the wagons made their way across the plain towards the Kermin Alol and Amina.

October rain was falling from a dark grey cloud-laden sky. In the private rooms in Mora Castle, Alberon's mood matched the autumn weather; he was becoming increasingly agitated and his temper steadily more frayed. The temperature in the room was increasing far beyond the heat generated from the fire burning in the large fireplace.

Alberon raged at Sylva. "Why can no one bring me good news? Holger has pulled back to a mere twenty miles from here. Morserat has slunk back to Iskala. I'll have to deal with that coward one day. Your brother has stolen my gold. My cannon lie rotting in the mud of the Kermin Plain. No goods are moving in or out of the port, and any day now we will be locked in by the snow."

Sylva tried to act as peacekeeper. "Alberon, this war was a mistake. Berin was a mistake, and maybe even an impostor. All we had to do was to wait and once my brother died Amina would be ours."

"You easily forget about your brother's plan for a regency to take control," snapped Alberon. "By the time the boys are old enough to inherit the Amina throne I will be too old to enjoy the victory."

Sylva tried again. "Why don't you send a message to Bertalan and make terms for peace? Ask him to agree to the conditions set in the treaties of last year and let us end this madness."

Alberon's patience was beyond its limits. Stepping across the room, he did something he had never done before. His open palm struck his wife's face. Sylva lifted her hand to her cheek and looked aghast at her husband.

"Even you dare to defy me!" he roared. "I am the Emperor and all the lands are mine by right. Your brother is guilty of treason and once my armies conquer Amina, he will pay with his life."

Sylva spoke very quietly, her green eyes hard as emeralds. "You will never strike me again. If you do, it will be your last act." A stiletto slipped from Sylva's sleeve and the long slender blade with its needle-like point glittered in the firelight. "In case you think my threat is empty, consider the steel."

Alberon had no idea that his wife carried a weapon, but he knew her well enough to know that her threat was real. Sylva turned and walked out of the room back to her chambers.

The autumn rains fell across the Kermin plain as nature followed its seasonal course. By now the high Doran Mountains were half clad in snow and all the passes through the mountains were blocked. Holger looked up at the white peaks from the Kermin lines and spotted a pair of golden eagles soaring on the thermals. The golden eagle was Kermin's royal emblem, used primarily on the Emperor's royal seal. He wondered if the royal birds were a good omen, and Kermin's armies would fare better in the spring. As he considered the possibilities for a spring renewal of hostilities, he remembered that Morserat had returned to his capital, Iskala, taking a large portion of the Doran cavalry with him. Without the Doran forces Holger doubted that the Kermin army could mount a successful attack in the Alol in the spring.

While the October rain soaked the Kermin plain, the same weather fronts brought storms to the Eastern and Middle Seas. It was a time of year when most seagoing vessels retreated to their harbours for the winter. John Sexton on the *Warrior* had other orders. He was to ensure the blockade remained in place through the winter, although he did not expect any winter action. The caravels could easily ride out the winter storms in the shelter of the coves which they now viewed as their temporary ports. Their sister ships patrolling the Arance coast had been ordered to winter at Anelo and commence patrols again in the early spring. Sexton's concern was not the weather, but supplies. Without regular replenishment of food and water, the crews of the *Warrior* and the *Destroyer* could not remain on post over the winter.

As the last week of October was marked up in the *Warrior's* chart room, Sexton was ready to give the order to cut all rations to half portions. That morning the easterly wind was biting cold, but at least it had driven away the rain clouds. Then a call came from one of the *Warrior's* lookouts: "Sail ahoy!"

Sexton squinted through the sunlight as he called his crew to make ready to sail. Moments later he stood the crew down. He had recognised the approaching vessel as the *Erth*. The carrack dropped anchor a short distance from the caravel and lowered a rowing boat. Sexton welcomed his opposite number on board.

"Greetings Captain Rondon, your ship looks as good as new. Come to my cabin. I presume you have a story to tell and messages for me from Tamin."

Sitting comfortably in the *Warrior's* cabin, Rondon updated his colleague on his news. "After you released us to travel south we safely made the dock at Tufle. Johann arranged for us to dock close to the shipyards. Your second in command is currently on the *Erth* arranging the transport of provisions for you. From

Tufle, Johann escorted me to Tamin. I was requested to attend Lord Ereldon, who wanted to know the details of the current situation in Mora. At the end of the audience the Chancellor asked if I would put the *Erth* into the service of Amina. It was a difficult choice with both my own and my crew's families in Mora. We agreed that I would consult with my crew and return with an answer. The men understood that a return to Mora in the current circumstances was unlikely to be a safe choice. On returning to present Lord Ereldon with our answer, the Chancellor shook my hand and asked if I was a good sailor. I told him I was one of the best. He studied me for a minute as though assessing my answer. His next question was – "Can the *Erth* travel in winter?" I replied that whilst the winter seas were hazardous, the *Erth* was built to travel in most weather conditions. As you know captain, she is one of the largest vessels currently working the Middle and Eastern Seas.

"So we made a deal. Ereldon agreed that Amina would pay for the repairs to the *Erth*, I would take a commission with the Amina navy and we would run supplies to you through the winter. So here I am. With your permission, captain, we will start moving the supplies to the *Warrior* and then move north to provision the *Destroyer*."

Sexton smiled. "Well Rondon, it seems it is my good fortune that I didn't sink the *Erth* those few months ago. Please start the transport of the provisions."

A few boat trips later, the transport was complete. Standing again on the deck of the caravel, Sexton took the other man's hand. "Thank you Rondon. Please now go north to relieve my brothers on the *Destroyer*. Safe travels."

Rondon nodded. "Yes captain, and sea conditions permitting, we will return again in late November."

In Mora, Aracir was also beginning to worry about provisions. Kermin was a rich land and Mora had always been well provisioned for winter, but he was concerned that this winter things were going to change. The blockade at the mouth of the Morel meant that none of the normal autumn grain imports from Andore had reached Mora. In addition, all the normal trade from Amina that travelled through the Alol had been shut down for several months. Kermin's own fields had been left poorly tended as men had been drafted into the army. These same men, now dug in twenty miles from Mora, also needed to be fed.

After a tour of the warehouses at the port, the Chancellor requested a meeting with the Emperor. Alberon was having supper when Aracir was ushered into the royal apartments. The table was laden with various meats, fish and vegetables, and bread and cakes lay on silver platters. Sylva and the two boys were also at the table.

Alberon indicated an empty chair. "Please join us in our simple supper, Aracir. Business will wait until we have enjoyed the food and the wine." Aracir had work to do and there was no time to stop for a meal, but one did not argue with the Emperor, so he took his place.

Once the meal was over, the table cleared and the boys sent to their own rooms, Alberon turned to Aracir. "Well my Lord Chancellor, what is so important that it has to interrupt my supper?"

Aracir went straight to the point. "My Lord, I am concerned that the warehouses at the port contain less than half the level of supplies that they should have at this time of year. I fear the blockade has had more impact than we had really anticipated. We have worried about a lack of trade and our merchants have been getting increasingly agitated, but in fact our food supplies are being seriously affected. Without some form of rationing both in the city and for the army, we will not be able to feed ourselves through the coming winter."

Alberon's brow knitted into a frown. "How can we control rations to one hundred thousand souls in the city?"

Aracir was ready with his response. "We need to bring Holger and the King's Guard back from the front to reinforce the city guard. All the warehouses need to be protected twenty-four hours a day. That way we can control the distribution of food into the city. There will be no war to fight on the plain during the winter, so the troops will not be missed at the front line."

Alberon nodded. "See to it then Aracir, and one more thing; make sure the private stores in my warehouse are fully stocked before the lockdown."

Sylva gasped. "Alberon, we cannot hoard our own supplies whilst the people of the city suffer."

Alberon looked at his wife with surprise. "I am the Emperor. My people would expect me to ensure that I remain fit and happy at a time of war and shortage."

Sylva looked at her husband in disbelief, shook her head, and left the table.

November brought its usual chill, and the rooftops of the houses in Mora were dressed in their white winter covering. On the streets the snow alternated between slush during the day and hard-packed ice at night. A bitter wind blew in from the north, chilled by its passage over the Doran Mountains. Where possible, the population stayed indoors. In a normal winter the residents would have stored up for the winter to minimise the number of trips that had to be made to buy supplies from the shops, but not in the winter of 1507.

The daily routine became monotonous. Each morning a number of wagons trundled into the city from the port, each watched over by armed guards. A measured quantity of meat was delivered to each butcher's shop and similarly limited quantities of flour and other ingredients were dropped at the bakeries. All the shops were kept under guard until midday, when they opened for custom. Long queues formed from early in the morning as residents, heavily wrapped up against the bitter cold, waited to purchase their daily rations. Fortunately the regular snowfalls meant that there was no shortage of water.

Bizarrely, the only shops that were full of goods were those of the wine merchants. The last few ships to enter Mora's port before the blockade had come from Toria filled with the wines and spirits that formed the main export of that country. With little other solace, the residents of Mora drowned their misery and in each inn silent toasts were raised to the hoped-for demise of the Emperor and an end to his pointless war. An alcohol-fuelled rebellion was fermenting.

The Kermin plain wore its white blanket comfortably. The only blemishes were where the wagons trundled back and forth from Mora to the front taking the limited rations to the army. Holger had returned to oversee the rationing in Mora, and Edin, Duke of Aramin, had been given command of the army. Fortunately for the young Duke there was not much activity to supervise, as the snowfields stretched from the Doran Mountains to the southern slopes of the Kermin Alol. Indeed most of the Kermin forces had been disbanded at Edin's command. He knew from his scouts' reports that Silson had left only a small contingent defending the Alol. The scouts had counted several hundred infantrymen, together with the gunners and their cannons, in the winter camps in the Alol. They also reported that the Amina front line was still well provisioned, judging by the wagons struggling through the snow from Tamin.

Edin had pondered a raid into the Alol to try to destroy the cannon. It might have been an opportunity for him to redeem himself in the eyes of the Emperor after his failure at the Aramin forest, but having ridden out to survey the land for himself it was clear that any attempt would be spotted long before the Alol could be reached, and the range of the cannons would probably obliterate any small attacking force. Winter, it seemed, had won this phase of the war, and renewed hostilities would need to wait until the spring.

Each year the same pattern was repeated. As November turned to December, the temperatures fell even lower. The snowstorms briefly abated and a watery sun shone from clear blue skies and glistened on the snow-covered plain. By the first week in December the Morel had frozen over. Whilst their parents queued for rations, the children played games on the frozen river.

Fortunately for the population, fuel was not in short supply. Coal from the Doran Mountains was stored in some of the larger warehouses and wood from the edges of the Aramin forest was gathered each summer to add to the coal reserves. Whilst the populace were surviving on reduced rations, at least they were not freezing in their homes.

In the Den of Thieves, Rafe, Aleana and Raimund were living quite comfortably. There was plenty of fuel for the cooking stove and fires burned in the two grates on either side of the main room. Unlike the rest of Mora's residents, food was not in short supply. The old warehouse, guarded by its shabby façade held other secrets. When the old port had been the hub of activity in Mora, ingenious entrepreneurs had devised ways to avoid the port's customs officers. In those days a warren of passageways had been created below the warehouses. The practice in the past had been for the customs officials to collect tax based on the goods stored in each warehouse. As the customs men called to assess the tax due from any merchant, some of the goods mysteriously moved to another warehouse and then back again when customs officers had left. When the new port was developed and the old port fell into disuse, most of the passageways were either forgotten or had caved in.

Rafe had discovered the trap door at the back of the Den of Thieves many years ago. He had cleared the passageway and found he was in luck. One passage exited below a warehouse that sat inside the city walls and between the new and old ports. This large building had always been the store rooms for the Kings of

Kermin, and stored here were the expensive gifts that had been brought by foreign emissaries as presents for the Kings. Rafe had occasionally taken small pieces of jewellery from the stores to boost his funds if street pickings were poor; never much, and never anything that could be noticed as missing.

In the winter of 1507, the store rooms held a more valuable commodity. It was here that the Steward of the Table kept many of the provisions that would in time end up on the Emperor's dinner table. Whilst the King's Guard patrolled the street outside the Emperor's warehouse day and night, no one noticed the small quantities of food that vanished every few days. The thieves lived like kings, dining each night on the Emperor's provisions and drinking his wine.

A heavy overnight storm had filled Mora's streets with a foot of snow. The group trudged through the crisp white carpet, making their way from the Merchants' Quarter to the castle gate. The guard sheltering in the gatehouse stepped out and demanded to know their business. The leader of the group, Cristian Carter, was tall, handsome and richly dressed. He was Master of the Merchant Guild and he spoke for the group. "We are here to demand an audience with the Emperor," he announced.

The Guard smiled. "I don't think anyone presents demands to the Emperor," he stated. Carter began to argue with the guard, but by chance, at that moment Aracir arrived at the gate. The Chancellor shook the master's hand. "Master Carter, what can I do for you and your colleagues?"

Carter drew himself erect to emphasise his authority. "Lord Chancellor, we must speak with the Emperor and persuade him to seek a peace treaty with Amina. Our warehouses lie empty and with the blockade at the mouth of the Morel we have not been able to trade for months. In most years the traffic on the Morel has kept the route to the sea open, and on the rare occasions when the river has frozen over we have still managed to trade with Amina and access the sea port at Tufle. We are all living on minimal rations, and it is worse still for the poor. This madness of war must be brought to an end to allow Kermin and Mora to get back to business."

Aracir frowned. "I doubt you will get a sympathetic hearing from the Emperor, but I'll see if he will grant you an audience. However he will not entertain an audience with all of you. Master Carter, you will come with me and your colleagues can wait in the guest hall."

Aracir was at the castle to report to Alberon on the current situation with the food supplies and rationing. The Emperor was having lunch in his private rooms when Aracir knocked on the door.

"Enter, Aracir," said the Emperor. "I'm glad you are here on time despite the depth of the snow."

Aracir entered, followed by the Master of the Guild.

Alberon frowned. "You should have informed me we had a visitor, Aracir. I would have laid an extra place for lunch. What can we do for you, Master Carter of the Merchant Guild?"

It was instantly clear to Cristian Carter that the Emperor was not subject to the rationing his people were suffering. He explained that he was here representing the Guild with a request that the Emperor consider a treaty with Amina to allow the trade routes to be opened up again.

Alberon's face coloured as he tried to hold back his anger. He failed. The chair clattered on the stone floor as Alberon rounded on the tall merchant. Looking up into the now pale face of the Master of the Guild, Alberon spat out his words in fury and frustration. "I am Emperor by right of Soll, Doran, Kermin and Amina and the usurper in Tamin will fall when my armies march through the Alol in the spring. I will not have some upstart merchant advise me on my policies. Guards, escort Master Carter to the comfort of the dungeon."

The Master's face turned white with fear and as he started to fashion a response, Alberon turned again. His pointing finger stopped an inch from the Master's nose, and the ice-cold stare turned the Master's insides to water. Alberon's voice took on a soft tone, making the words more terrifying.

"Carter, your words are those of a traitor and I have identified other traitors. You will enjoy my hospitality for a few weeks. Come the New Year celebrations I will decide how to deal with your treachery. Guards, take him away. And Lord Chancellor, the next time you bring an unannounced visitor I suggest you check with me first. You are also dismissed and we will discuss the other business issues once I have finished my lunch."

Aracir left as ordered and stood in the passage for several minutes trying to control his own trembling. He had witnessed the Emperor's temper many times, but he had never seen the man so coldly frightening. His anxiety increased as he thought about some of the favours he had recently asked of the Master of the Guild.

Gradually pulling himself together, Aracir returned to the guest hall and sent the other members of the guild home with the warning that their petition had not been received positively by the Emperor and the Master of the Guild would be spending a few weeks as a guest of the Emperor. Understanding the message, the merchants hurried back through the snow to their homes.

CHAPTER FOURTEEN

1508 – A New Year

In Mora, the last few days of December 1507 were bright, cold and clear. The snow from the heavy fall the week before was gradually being pushed aside, leaving pathways along the main streets. Small crowds started to gather in some of the city squares, where they had seen notices pinned to the walls. Those that could read were pushed to the front and then allowed back through the crowd to inform the less literate citizens. The notices carried a message from the Emperor:

> *It is to our dismay that the King of Amina continues to refuse to pay homage to his rightful overlord and his country continues to rebel against the Empire.*

Our brave soldiers would by now be resident in Tamin had it not been for treachery in our own ranks. On New Year's Day I will announce my sentences for the traitors and they will be dealt with. I am proud of the stoicism of my people in these difficult times of deprivation and I can assure you that come the spring the armies of Kermin will be victorious and Amina will take its rightful place as a member of the Empire.

The notices were simply signed 'The Emperor'. Alberon had significantly and deliberately dropped the additional 'of the North'.

Sylva was sitting in Ingrid's rooms, waiting to talk to the Dowager Queen. She instantly leapt to her feet when Ingrid entered the room. "Have you heard about the notices that have just been posted in the city?"

Ingrid shook her head. "Sylva, you know I seldom leave my rooms these days and I have little interest in what is going on outside these walls. What is so urgent?"

Sylva paused to take a breath. "Alberon has announced that Kermin's failure in the battles in the Alol was due to traitors in our midst and that he will deliver punishment to those traitors on New Year's Day. Do you suppose he has found out about Vidur or my letter to my brother?"

Ingrid sat down next to her daughter-in-law. "Calm down Sylva, I don't see how Alberon could know about any of our actions. Berin was killed by an Amina shot during the battle at the Alol and Bertalan never replied to your letter other than verbally. I know my son is getting somewhat paranoid over Amina, but I think we would already know if he considered either of us guilty of treason. He must have others in his sights. I presume he has not discussed this with you?"

Sylva shook her head and absentmindedly raised her hand to the cheek where her husband had struck her.

"Alberon barely talks to me these days and completely ignores the boys. He is permanently short-tempered and can fly into a rage at the slightest thing. He refuses to discuss the war or any possible solution to ending the hostilities. I fear that this hatred of my brother is driving him slightly mad."

It was Ingrid who this time shook her head. "I wish my son had been content with his birthright as king of Doran and Kermin. This mad, foolish notion of being an all-powerful Emperor has ended centuries of peace between Kermin and Amina and left our people cold and hungry. We will need to wait and see what transpires on New Year's Day."

Whilst the Queen and the Empress were discussing their concerns in the castle, there was similar consternation in the inns of Mora. The townsfolk knew all about the disaster that had been the August battle at the Kermin Alol. For the price of a drink, wounded soldiers were happy to tell their stories of the loss of the cannons, the reckless charge led by the so-called Duke of Alol, the destruction wrought by the Amina cannon and the inglorious retreat back to the Kermin plain. Of course each soldier told a slightly different story, each emphasising their own bravery and how they had come to be wounded at the height of the battle, but despite the variations, the facts seemed to be consistent. In every inn the question was the same: how could the disaster at the Alol have been caused by traitors, and who could they be?

The answer was always clear to the crowds after a few glasses of wine: the perilous state of the nation and the deprivations in Mora were due to the Emperor, and not to some as yet unnamed traitors. Alcohol also fuelled the obvious conclusion. It was time that the people rose up and got rid of the tyrant. But come the morning, sobriety and the cold doused the flames of rebellion; the queues again formed and each citizen collected their ever-diminishing daily rations.

The first morning of 1508 dawned under a steel-grey sky with flakes of snow drifting on the gentle, but cold, breeze. The forecourt in front of the castle's main gate was buzzing with activity as carpenters hammered and sawed. By mid-morning a high platform had been erected, with steps from just outside the castle gate leading up to the flat upper level. As news of the construction got out to the city, a small crowd braved the cold and gathered around the base of the construction. However, most citizens stayed warm indoors, knowing that later in the day they would have to suffer the cold to queue outside waiting for the shops to open.

The conversation in the crowd standing around the wooden foundations was largely about what was going to happen and what the strangely-shaped plinth that sat atop the platform was to be used for. Ingrid and Sylva looked down on the scene from the windows in Ingrid's rooms. No one in Mora had witnessed an execution, but Ingrid's father had explained the pictures in an old tapestry that had hung in her grandfather's quarters. Ingrid shuddered at the memory. As a child the tapestry had always given her frightening dreams, and she feared that her nightmares were about to come to life in front of her.

"Unless I am very much mistaken we are going to witness an execution today," she murmured.

It was late morning when trumpet blasts announced the arrival of the Emperor. Alberon appeared on the battlement above the city gate wrapped in expensive furs. As the trumpet notes faded, he started his announcement.

"Citizens of Mora, our current predicament is the result of the actions of a number of traitors, and now is the time for them to pay the penalty for treason." The crowd went silent as another trumpet blast echoed. As this also faded away Alberon continued, "Berin, the so called Duke of Alol, led our troops to disaster due to his own pride and arrogance. As he fell in battle, he has already paid the price for his treason. Morserat, Duke of Doran, ran from the battlefield when our army could still have prevailed in the Alol. He is stripped of his titles and when he is arrested and returned to Mora he will be suitably punished. Rondon and the crew of the carrack named *Erth* defied my commands to break the blockade on the Morel and then fled from justice. They are banned from returning to Mora on punishment of death."

There was a ripple of noise from the crowd and some booing, as some of the crowd knew the crew of the *Erth.* Alberon continued, "Lord Norward, commander of my armies, refused to mobilise when commanded and allowed the enemy time to build their defences in the Alol. Cristian Carter, Master of the Merchant Guild pleaded with me to seek a peace treaty with the King of Amina. We have since learnt that the Master was already trading letters with his counterpart in Tamin requesting that the merchants in Tamin petition their king to invade Kermin and rout our army. These two men have been tried and found guilty of treason. I have passed my judgement, and the sentence is death."

A hush fell over the crowd as a drum roll called the

signal. The two men were blindfolded and led up the steps to the top of the platform, where the executioner waited with a great axe. At a second drum roll it became clear what the plinth was for. The axe struck twice and two heads fell from the platform to land in the snow in front of the onlookers. As the snow turned red, some of the crowd wept, whilst others deposited their breakfasts, adding further colour to the icy slush.

Alberon continued, "This is the fate that awaits anyone who is found guilty of treason to the Empire. Finally, due to the blockade, our reserves are low and there will be no New Year's feast provided in the castle this evening."

At the edge of the crowd a young nobleman had tears streaming down his face. He had not been able to watch as the axe separated his father's head from his body. William Norward knew that his father was no traitor, but he also recognised that it was probably not safe for him to return to his father's lands as it was likely that the Emperor had already confiscated them. When his father had been arrested his mother had returned to her homelands in Soll. It would be a hard journey over the snow-covered Doran Mountains, but he had to be the one to carry the news to his mother.

As the horror of what they had witnessed began to sink in, the stunned silence in the crowd was gradually replaced by a growing babble of raised voices. A few brave souls shouted out what the rest of the crowd were thinking. "The Emperor is the traitor to the people, down with the tyrant!" Snowballs began to strike the balustrade close to where Alberon was standing, and he turned to leave.

As the shouts from the crowd grew louder a number of people moved threateningly towards the castle gate. Holger had anticipated this. Norward was not liked by the people, but the Master of the Guild was known as a generous man and had often used some of his wealth to help the poor. As the rage in the crowd gathered momentum, more started to move towards the gate. The leaders stopped short as a troop of the King's Guard filed out of the castle with swords drawn. Holger's voice rose above the din of the crowd. "Return to your homes!" he shouted. "There is no entry to the castle today other than on the end of a sword. Return to your homes!"

With further shouts of defiance, the crowd gradually dispersed. Without realising it, Alberon had added more fuel to the fire of rebellion already building in the city.

The executions brought reactions closer to home, in the castle and nearby. Sylva and Ingrid had returned to the latter's rooms, and the Queen was in floods of tears. "Sylva, I think he really is going mad! What was the point of these killings? Norward was only trying to advise Alberon, and although I did not like the man's arrogance he was a loyal servant to my husband and my son. He was rightly cautious about entering the war, and he was correct that the Kermin forces would not simply walk through the Alol and capture Tamin. As for Cristian Carter, I have known him since he was a boy and liked both him and his father. He was a generous man and I cannot imagine him plotting treason. This was all about Alberon showing off his mad power. I'm worried about the consequences."

Sylva was worried about different consequences. "Ingrid, I am still afraid that if Alberon finds out about my letter to Bertalan, or about our plot to remove Berin, then we too may be labelled as traitors."

The Queen took her daughter-in-law's hand. "Sylva, as I have already said to you, I'm sure Alberon knows nothing about these events, and if he did then we would already be following those two poor men to the block and the axe. You need to keep trying to persuade Alberon to end this war and seek peace with your brother before this all escalates even further out of control."

In his grand house close to the castle, Aracir was also in a state of shock and fear. He had known Lord Norward for many years, and whilst the man was somewhat pompous he was no fool, nor was he a traitor. However it was the accusations against Cristian Carter that had the chancellor shaking. Aracir knew that the Master in Mora communicated with his counterpart in Tamin by carrier pigeons. These avian messengers played an important part in trade negotiations between the Guilds in both cities. After the defeat in the Alol and as food supplies began to diminish, Aracir had asked Carter if his pigeons could carry some messages to Tamin for him. Aracir had become increasingly concerned about the Emperor's state of mind as Alberon was becoming more and more irrational and irascible. He was also furious that the Emperor continued to feast on the reserves from his warehouse as each day the people in the city barely received sufficient rations to live on. In Aracir's personal view, the messages he had sent to Tamin were not treasonous; they were simply a plea to ask Bertalan to try to engage with Alberon to settle some sort of peace, or a relaxation in the blockades, for the sake of the people of Mora. Aracir worried about what the Master might have divulged as he was held in the castle dungeons. Inadvertently Aracir raised his hand to his neck, hoping he would not be next for the axe.

On the fifth day of the New Year, Mora's residents woke to find the city blanketed in a deep layer of fresh snow which had fallen through the night. Troopers from the city guard had been despatched to gather together working parties to try and clear the snow so that the supply wagons could move from the warehouses into the city with the rations for the day.

The same routine had been followed each day since rationing was imposed. During the morning in each quarter, queues would form outside the shops and once the supplies arrived from the warehouses the shops would open and each citizen could purchase their provisions for the day. Following Aracir's instructions, city guards remained in each shop to ensure that the limited provisions were fairly distributed. Nonetheless over the weeks a healthy black market had developed, and wealthier citizens could still enjoy more substantial meals.

With access to the Emperor's warehouse, Rafe, Aleana and Raimund were quick to capitalise on this new business opportunity. The other poor in the slums close to the Den of Thieves were less fortunate, and hunger became a call to action. By mid-morning the snow in the main thoroughfare through the city had been cleared to the boundary between the tradesman's quarter and the merchant's quarter.

It was here that the first wagon in the convoy became stuck in a deep drift of snow. The men guarding the wagon were focused on getting the provisions on the move again, knowing that the people queuing for the shops would be getting increasingly irritated and cold.

It was only when they heard shouts from the edge of the slums that the troopers realised they had been ambushed. A small crowd erupted from the side streets shouting "Death to the Emperor!" "End the war!" "Food for our children!" The crowd were armed largely with wooden sticks and clubs, although a few brandished knives and axes. The crowd fell upon the troopers like wolves on a deer. With swords drawn, the guardsmen fell back around the wagon to defend their cargo, but the crowd were too many and the troopers were forced to retreat back towards the southern gate where their comrades were drawing up in a defensive line to shield the rest of the wagons from attack.

Within a few minutes, a ton of provisions had vanished into the slums and three guardsmen lay slumped on the ground beside the now empty wagon, wounded but better off than the four members of the mob who had been pushed onto the guards' raised swords by the press from behind. The captain of the convoy of wagons decided that discretion was the better part of valour, and the remaining wagons turned back to the southern gate and the warehouses.

Across the city anger began to rise among the queues of shivering citizens as the shops remained closed. The guardsmen positioned at the front door of each shop could give no explanation for the delay in the deliveries other than perhaps that the snow had prevented the wagons from getting through to all parts of the city. In some locations fights broke out as people argued. In the tradesmen's quarter a small group gathered and decided to march to the warehouses to demand their supplies. In other quarters, particularly the more affluent districts, the cold won the day and people trudged back home through the deep snow.

As the group of tradesmen made their way through their quarter, so their numbers increased. It was a sizeable mob by the time the main road was reached and the reason for the failure of the delivery of rations became clear. A few of the women went to tend to the injured guardsmen, whilst the leaders of the group debated what to do next. Some argued for an assault on the slums to teach the 'vermin' there a lesson, while others pointed out that none of the group were armed, other than with knives, and the slums were a dangerous place these days. The calm heads won the debate and the crowd turned south towards the southern gate and the warehouses.

As the mob passed through the gate onto the dockside, the captain of the convoy was overseeing the return of the rations to the warehouses. Having witnessed what had happened an hour earlier, he ordered his men to draw swords. Undeterred, the crowd marched forward. The captain recognised that although this was an angry mob none of the group appeared to be armed, unlike the men in the earlier attack. Ordering his men to sheath their weapons, he walked over to the leading group at the front of the crowd. He recognised some of the men and knew that they were basically good, hard-working people.

The leader of the group was a tall, well-built man who the captain knew to be a blacksmith with a forge on the edge of the tradesman's district and who at times worked at the city's barracks. The captain addressed this man directly,

"Jon, I know you and your friends are angry that the rations did not reach the shops today, but the snow delayed the wagons and you have probably seen what happened when we were attacked from the slums."

Jon held up his hand and the mob gradually fell silent. Addressing the captain directly, he raised his voice so that all could hear. "Sir, we have seen what happened on the main street and some of our women are tending to your injured men."

"Thank you," replied the captain.

"Sir, without the rations our children will go hungry today and maybe for some days to come. These people are not rich and cannot afford to buy supplies from other sources. The rations are all that we have to live on and we are here to collect what we are due. We can collect our rations with your permission sir, or we can take them by force. Obviously I know your guard are armed and we may risk lives by the latter action, but we will not let our children starve and I do wonder if your men would actually use their weapons against their unarmed fellow citizens."

The captain nodded. He knew that he could not order his men to draw blood, and equally he knew that the blacksmith's threat was real. Even unarmed, the smith would be a hard man to better in a fight. The captain walked back to the guards at the wagons to give his instructions and then returned to the front of the crowd.

The people now stood in silence, except for the sound of stamping feet as they tried to keep some warmth in their bodies. This time it was the captain's voice that stilled the noise.

"My orders are to deliver your rations to the shops in your district. With the roads blocked by the snow, I can see no reason why I should not fulfil my orders here and now. The three wagons closest to us were destined for your quarter. Please form an orderly queue and we will pass out your rations. In addition I have ordered my men to give each person here double the normal ration, but this is on your promise that you will ensure those from your quarter who are not here will get their rations from you. Do I have your promise?"

The crowd clapped in acknowledgement. The captain turned to the blacksmith.

"Jon, I want you and the men who are your most trusted friends to come last in the queue. We will ensure your shares of the rations are held back, but if there is any surplus left, you and your friends will take it and ensure it goes to those in the quarter who have not already been provided for."

The blacksmith nodded. "Thank you sir."

It was mid afternoon when Holger and Aracir were granted a meeting with the Emperor. Alberon was seated in the council room in the castle enjoying a large plate of fruit and sweetmeats, while the servant who stood to the side of the room ensured that the Emperor's wine glass remained fully topped up.

"Please sit down gentlemen, and help yourselves to some of these delicious sweetmeats," said Alberon. Holger somewhat reluctantly accepted the offer and picked up a couple of the sweets. Aracir could not bring himself to eat delicacies from the Emperor's table whilst the people in the city went hungry. However he knew there was no shortage of wine in the city, so he accepted the offered glass.

Holger opened with a report on the events that had taken place earlier in the day. Alberon rose from the table and shouted at the captain, "You are in charge of the town guard and my own king's guard and you are responsible for maintaining law and order in this city. Tomorrow you will take a troop of the guard and root out the perpetrators of this crime. It is my generosity that is keeping the people fed, so this theft of rations is a direct crime against the Empire. You will find the guilty parties and they will hang from the castle walls."

Holger hung his head, not daring to look the Emperor in the eye.

Alberon continued, "In addition you will order sufficient troops back from the Kermin Plain to ensure the city streets remain safe from this slum-dwelling scum. There will be no threat from Amina whilst the winter snows continue and the army are just out there in their tents doing nothing useful."

Aracir coughed. "My Lord, the forces on the plain are small in number as the Duke of Aramin sent all, other than the professional soldiers, back to their homes before the winter locked us in. Recent reports from Edin tell of unrest and talk of rebellion amongst even the professional soldiers still on the plain. Bringing these men back to the city may add to our problems rather than solve them."

Alberon turned his ire and his icy stare on his Chancellor. "Rebellion amongst our troops? Then the Duke should crush it and deal with the leaders. A few executions should be sufficient example to dissuade any others who might be tempted to rebel."

Aracir sighed quietly to himself; it seemed that the Emperor's solution to every problem these days was a death warrant. He continued in a deferential tone, "My Lord Emperor, we also have more serious issues in the city. Even on restricted rations our warehouses will be almost completely depleted in less than two months. Unless we can bring supplies in from Andore or negotiate relief supplies from Amina, our people will be starving before the end of winter. We may be able to contain rebellion in the army, but my spies tell me that in every inn in the city the talk is the same. We cannot so easily suppress a people's revolution."

Alberon laughed. "A people's revolution? I doubt it. They love their Emperor." He continued sarcastically, "And if they are hungry, there is plenty of snow for them to eat and wine for them to drink. Gentlemen, you are dismissed."

Closing the council room door behind him, Holger grabbed Aracir by the elbow and spoke quietly. "Has he gone completely mad? From what I hear from my men, there is no love for the Emperor in the city or at the front. He sits there gorging himself and getting fat on sweetmeats whilst his people starve. I did not dare to tell him about the actions of my captain at the docks today."

Aracir moved his arm away and replied, "Your captain did well in acting as he did. There is no doubt his actions avoided bloodshed and hopefully calmed unrest in that one quarter of the city for a short while at least. You had best go and organise at least a token raid on the slums tomorrow, or you might also be enjoying the cold in the dungeons. I have other urgent business I must attend to."

When Aracir entered his office, his visitor was already comfortably seated in the Chancellor's chair. "Welcome Vidur, I trust you are well," he said. The huntsman nodded, but made no move to give up his seat. Aracir may have been the paymaster, but he was also slightly in fear of this man. He had known Vidur and his brother Valdin for years, but he had never personally given the huntsmen any task to fulfil. Under Queen Ingrid's instructions they received a monthly retainer from the

Queen's own coffers. Aracir had never asked the Queen what orders or missions she set these men, feeling it was better that he did not know. However he did know a little about the supposed ancestry of the brothers. The two men claimed to be the only living descendants of a band of assassins who had lived in caves in the Doran Mountains and had made their living accepting contracts from the nobility and protection money from the gold miners who worked in the mountains. King Olsen's father had rooted the band out decades ago when they had been found guilty of stealing the King's gold. History told that the entire band were executed in their mountain hideaway, so no one could confirm, or otherwise, the brother's claims. Whatever the truth, Vidur and his brother were clearly hard, competent men and were fully trusted by the Queen.

Ignoring the fact that the huntsman continued to occupy his seat, Aracir perched on the edge of his desk. "Vidur, I have a mission that I need you to undertake. The Queen knows nothing about this – I will pay your fee from my own purse. I want you to deliver this letter to King Bertalan in Tamin; you have no need to know the contents. This will be a dangerous assignment, and if you are caught by any of the Emperor's spies then I need you to destroy the letter."

Vidur shrugged. "My Lord, most missions my brother and I undertake for the Queen are dangerous. That is why she pays us so well. I will leave for Tamin in a couple of days' time, as I have a task for the Queen that needs to be completed before I leave."

Aracir nodded. "That will be soon enough, but no later than that."

The huntsman rose and left the room without a word. Aracir slumped into the now vacant seat and tried to control his shaking hands; if the Emperor found out what he was up to there was no doubt that he would follow his friend Cristian Carter up the steps to the platform that still stood as a reminder in the castle forecourt.

Vidur did have a mission for the Queen, but it was not what Aracir expected. The next morning the huntsman was ushered into her private apartments.

"Please have a seat, Vidur. I have no commission for you, so why this urgent request to meet?"

Vidur took the offered seat and passed Aracir's letter to the Queen. "You may not have a mission for me, but the Chancellor does." Not wanting to risk exposure if Vidur was caught, Aracir had not used his own seal on the letter and had simply dabbed a drop of candlewax to close the scroll.

The Queen took the letter. "How interesting, Vidur. You have done well to bring this to my attention." She carefully lifted the seal and read the letter, noting that it was simply signed at the end with a capital "A". The letter detailed the current situation in Mora and expounded at length on the growing unrest of the populace and the increasingly desperate shortages of food and supplies. The Queen knew nothing of the earlier letters carried by Carter's pigeons, so she assumed that this was a first attempt by Aracir to persuade the King of Amina to offer a negotiated peace, or at least lift the blockade for a short time to allow some supplies to get through to Mora. She recognised that if the letter were to be intercepted, and the author identified, there was little doubt that her son would view the act as treason. The letter did however give Ingrid an opportunity she had been waiting for, and she moved across to her desk and added a few lines below the "A". She carefully dropped a dab of candlewax to replace the seal and handed the scroll back to Vidur.

"Take care of this Vidur. It should only be given by hand, and in person, to King Bertalan. If you are detained before you can deliver the letter to the King, you must destroy it. Now go and carry out Aracir's instructions."

As Ingrid was sending Vidur on his mission, a rather worried blacksmith was being escorted up the main road towards the barracks. Jon had been at work in his smithy when the two guardsmen entered. Very politely the senior guard informed the blacksmith that the Captain of the Guard had a task that he would be grateful if Jon could carry out for him. Looking at the two armed guardsmen, Jon knew he had little choice.

He nodded to the senior guard. "Please lead on," he said.

Holger was sitting behind his desk in the small office he occupied in the barracks. "Thank you for coming, Jon."

The blacksmith shrugged. "It seemed I had no option."

Holger nodded. "My apologies for the rather blunt approach. You are correct, I need to talk to you, but you do have the option to refuse the task I am going to ask you to do for me, without any repercussions." He explained the instructions he had been given by the Emperor the day before. "Do you know any of the ringleaders that led the mob to attack the ration convoy?" he asked.

The blacksmith paused. Was this a trap wrapped up in a question? "Obviously I know some of the people who live in the slums as a number of them are my customers," he replied.

"And do you know a few men who you would trust with your life?"

Was this another trick question? "Yes, my two sons, my brother and my nephew."

"Excellent. Then this is what I would like you to do for me."

Dusk was falling over the city as Vidur led the grey horse out into the snow that was still lying deep on the streets of the Nobles' Quarter. He was dressed in a long white sheepskin coat, and he and his horse were almost invisible against the white snow. The city gates would close in the next fifteen minutes, but there was still enough time.

Vidur was leaving the city to begin his mission for Aracir. The huntsman hoped that in the dark he could cover the ground to the Alol while avoiding the forces camped in the area. He would find a copse to shelter in during the day and continue his journey the next night.

As he turned into the main street that led down to the southern gate, he was surprised to see a larger than normal troop of the King's Guard gathering at the barracks. Pulling his woollen hood over his head, the huntsman continued down the main street and crossed the southern bridge just as the city gate closed behind him.

Holger called his men together to brief them. "I am informed that the rabble from the slums intend to make a raid on the warehouses tonight. We will be there to stop that. The guards at the main gate know we are on our way and will open the gate to allow us access to the dock area where we think the slum rats have gathered during the afternoon. My informant also tells me that several of the ships in the port are privy to the plan and are currently sheltering the raiders. If the raid is successful, then the stolen provisions will be hidden in these ships until the gate opens tomorrow and they can be sequestered back into the slums. I want this raid stopped before it begins. However I am reluctant to use lethal force against our own people, so as we march down towards the city gate you will each bang your swords against your shields so that the thieves have plenty of warning of our approach. Your two captains will take the lead." Pointing to two of the other guardsmen, Holger continued, "These two men will stay behind with me and ensure that there is no attempt to break out from the slums and attack you from the rear."

Just before the troop reached the city gate, Holger and the two troopers pulled into the nearest alleyway that marked the entry to the slums. The men with Holger were the pair that had escorted the blacksmith to the barracks earlier in the day. They were two of his most trusted men, and they had already been briefed on the plan.

Just inside the alleyway, and largely hidden in the dark, stood five men with three bundles lying in the snow beside them. Holger briefly shook the blacksmith's hand. "Have you managed to do what I requested?"

"Yes sir."

Holger turned to one of the guards. "You know what to do from here." The man nodded. "Good. Now I need to follow my troopers to the docks to ensure all is in order there." He turned back to the blacksmith. "Thanks Jon, to you and your men. Your actions have possibly saved many lives. Now please help my men to get your packages back to the barracks and then come and see me tomorrow, and I will reward your bravery."

From his rooms in the castle Alberon heard the noise as the guardsmen marched towards the slums. He smiled and murmured, "I look forward to enjoying some hangings in the morning."

Satisfied that his commands were being executed, the Emperor returned to sit in front of the fire where his supper and book of poetry lay waiting. It had long been a conundrum to Sylva that her tempestuous, temperamental and power-hungry husband still kept his youthful love of poetry. It had long been his evening routine to have supper served in the library, where he would spend an hour or more reading from the many poetry books that filled the shelves. Sylva didn't understand this softer side of her husband, but it pleased her. The anger, temper and frustration of the day seemed to disappear when he was reading and he seemed like a different man when he joined her in the bedchamber.

Holger joined his troopers on the dock and caught up with the captains. "Well, have you found the scum and arrested them?"

The two captains looked slightly confused. "Sir there is no one here other than the sailors."

Holger looked across to the docked ships, where crews had gathered on the decks to shout insults at the guardsmen. Holger needed to create a little more time for the rest of his plan to come to fruition. "Maybe my informant was mistaken," he said. "Nonetheless we will patrol here for a while longer to ensure that the warehouses remain secure."

Back in the city, seven men carried three bundles through the dark streets up towards the castle and deposited them by the execution platform, which had now been converted to a scaffold. The senior guard addressed the blacksmith. "Thank you for your help. Now you had best return quickly to your homes. And remember, you know nothing about this."

"Yes sir," replied Jon. He and his companions turned back down the street, keen to get back to the warmth of their homes.

The next morning dawned crisp and clear and the rising sun sparkled on the ice crystals in the frozen snow. Alberon looked out from his room down onto the castle forecourt and let out a curse. He saw the three men hanging from the scaffold, swinging gently in the light breeze. He roared for the nearest guard. "Get your captain and escort him to the council chamber now!"

Holger had fully expected the summons and was ready when the guardsmen arrived. "I know, I am summoned to see the Emperor, lead on."

As Holger entered the council chamber Alberon rose from his seat. "What is the meaning of this? You have spoilt my morning's enjoyment. These men have already been hanged! I was looking forward to seeing them suffer for their treachery. Explain yourself!"

Holger took a deep breath, knowing he was on dangerous ground.

"My Lord, as you know there is much unrest across the city and much of the talk in the inns and taverns is of revolt. I considered that a public hanging might potentially be the spark that would ignite the crowds into action. My men raided the slums last night and arrested the three unfortunates now dangling on the end of their ropes. We had information identifying these three as the ringleaders who led the raid on the ration wagon a few days ago. Under my questioning they admitted their guilt and I pronounced their sentence and carried it out under cover of dark." Holger knew that dead men could not speak, and those twice dead certainly could not.

At that moment a hubbub rose from below. A small crowd, most poorly dressed, were gathering on the forecourt shouting insults at the guardsmen who were holding them back. Some of the shouts could be heard in the council chamber: "Kill the Emperor!" "Free our city!" "Death to the tyrant!" "We need food!"

Alberon turned to Holger. "So a night-time hanging would not stir up the crowds? It seems you have misjudged." Just then, to Alberon's surprise, the din from below died down. Looking from the council room window, he could see that for some reason the crowd was dispersing peacefully. The poor people gathered on the forecourt were not dressed for the bitter cold, and they had gathered as rumour spread through the slums that three of their leaders had been taken in the night by the Emperor's guard and executed. It was only as the crowd drew close to the scaffold that the three men hanging there were recognised. Each had died the previous day of cold and hunger.

The crowd's anger turned to quiet laughter as word was passed around. The stupid guardsmen had hung three dead men.

Alberon turned back to Holger. "Looking at the reaction down there, you may have made a wise decision, Captain. However, I should have been told before you took action. You should have sought my permission. Don't make any more mistakes like this, or you too might find yourself dancing on the end of a rope. Now cut them down. If I can't enjoy watching them die I will certainly get no pleasure in watching them rot."

CHAPTER FIFTEEN

A Winter Journey

❖ ❖ ❖ ❖

It was mid-January before Vidur reached Tamin. The journey across the Kermin Plain and through the Alol had been slow and arduous. The huntsman had needed to avoid the Kermin troops on the plain and the small contingent of the Amina army still camped beside their cannons on the slopes of the Alol.

The snow lay thick on the ground, and deep drifts often forced Vidur to retrace his steps to find an easier passage. The central valley through the Alol would have been the easiest and quickest route to Tamin, but even travelling mostly by night in a white coat which blended into the background, Vidur would almost certainly have been spotted by Amina troops. The choice had to be one of the two drover roads, and Vidur selected the western track travelling alongside the sometimes frozen river Mina. As his tracks wound behind him, it was clear that no one else had travelled this route in the depths of this winter.

Vidur had anticipated a long journey and carried two bags of supplies behind his saddle. Few men could have completed the journey between Mora and Tamin without travelling the main roads, but Vidur had successfully completed missions for his Queen in all seasons, and he was after all a huntsman. Snowshoe hares and ptarmigans, dressed in their white winter coats, supplemented his supplies, together with trout pulled from the areas of open water on the Mina. In the copses and small woods where Vidur rested during the day the snow could be cleared to allow his horse to get to the grass below. Nonetheless it was a weary traveller who slowly walked the grey horse towards Tamin's city gate.

With any threat of invasion from Kermin impossible in the winter months, the main gate into Tamin was open during daylight. As the city was much further south than Mora the winter was less harsh, and although snow still covered the ground the roadways were mostly clear.

Vidur was expecting to be halted by the guard at the city gate, but with more snow falling, the guardsmen clearly preferred the warmth of the guardroom and the huntsman walked into Tamin unnoticed. Over the years he had visited the city many times, and he had no difficulty following the familiar streets to the small square at the edge of the merchants' quarter. The Black Bull was not a luxurious hostelry, but it was warm and comfortable and the innkeeper knew the huntsman, although not by his real name.

As Vidur tied the horse up in front of the inn, the innkeeper bustled out into the snow. "Welcome back Master Ferdinand, I'll have your normal room prepared for you immediately and I'll get your horse settled down in the stables. This is a wicked time of year to be travelling, your business in Tamin must be very urgent?"

Vidur said nothing at first, but shed his heavy woollen coat and followed the innkeeper into the tap room. As he warmed himself in front of the blazing fire, the innkeeper brought across a foaming tankard of his best ale and repeated his question. Innkeepers the world over liked to keep up with any gossip.

Vidur placed the tankard on a table. "Yes Connor, I have urgent business to attend to here in Tamin, but it is rather sensitive."

Intrigued, the innkeeper leant forward and spoke in a whisper. "You can trust me to keep a secret, Master Ferdinand, and I may be able to help."

Vidur sighed, as if reluctant to divulge his reason for visiting Tamin in midwinter, although he knew that the innkeeper could not keep a secret. "Very well, as long as you promise not to tell anyone. I have learnt that my nephew has been arrested and has been accused of stealing from the nobleman to whom he is a squire. The lad is only fourteen and I doubt the accusation has any truth to it, as I send the boy regular sums for his upkeep and I can think of no reason why he would revert to thievery. I am here to try to speak to Bartos, the Captain of the Guard, and to understand the truth of this matter before the boy is punished. I hope to be able to pay a fine to have the lad released and take him back to his parents in Slat."

As far as the innkeeper knew, his guest was a merchant from Slat, a small town that lay close to the Middle Sea some thirty miles south of Tamin. Connor clapped his hands together in delight. "I'm glad you told me of this, Master Ferdinand. Every few days the Captain stops here for a drink after his rounds, and I can introduce you. Tell me, who is the nobleman who accuses your nephew? I'll probably know him too. I serve the best ale in Tamin and many people visit the Black Bull.

Vidur shook his head. "I'm sorry, I cannot divulge the nobleman's name, but it would be helpful if you could point out the Captain for me when he next calls in."

Over the next couple of days numerous guardsmen stopped for a drink at the Black Bull, but there was no sign of the King's cousin. It was mid-afternoon on the third day when Bartos arrived with two of his senior officers. Connor could not contain his excitement at being able to help, and instead of simply pointing out the Captain, he dashed over to Bartos.

"Sir, the customer sitting over there needs to talk with you about his young nephew who has been wrongly arrested," he said. "He is a rich merchant."

Bartos looked over at the man sitting at the corner table with his tankard in front of him. The huntsman was dressed in his normal drab clothing and did not look like a rich merchant.

Bartos shrugged. "I don't deal with peasants who claim they have been wronged, tell him to go to the jail and ask after this nephew there."

The three guardsmen sat at a table at the far side of the tap room and soon forgot about the man sitting in the far corner, so they did not notice as Vidur slipped out of the room.

Connor had been helpful after all, and Vidur now knew who his target was. Donning his long white coat, the huntsman slipped out of one of the side doors of the inn and headed towards the castle. It was only a hunch, but hopefully, having finished his ale, the Captain of the Guard would be returning to the castle.

It was a good guess, and an hour later, with dusk edging towards dark, Vidur spotted the three men leaving the Black Bull and moving up towards where he was concealed in a doorway not far from the castle gate. Bartos shook his colleagues' hands as they moved off along the road that led to the barracks, then he walked on alone.

After a couple of jugs of ale the Captain was not as alert as he would normally be and was taken completely by surprise as Vidur stepped out from the doorway right in front of him. In the moment of surprise Bartos did not recognise the white-clad man as the same person who had been sitting in the corner of the tap room at the Black Bull, so instinct took charge. This had to be a paid killer, and his life was at risk. Bartos' right hand got to his sword, but the huntsman was much quicker. In a flash of white he had wrenched the Captain's arm from the sword and forced it up his back. At the same moment the dagger came to the Captain's neck.

On another day, and if the huntsman's mission had been different, Bartos' instinct would have been correct, and he would be dead. Not on this day. The huntsman spoke quietly. "Easy Captain, I am here to deliver a letter from Mora to the King. My instructions are to hand it to Bertalan personally. Now you will take me to him."

As he was slowly released, Bartos considered attacking his assailant, but the prick of the dagger in his back told him that this stranger was not to be denied. Nonetheless, bravado held sway for a moment. "You will not get past the guards at the castle gate when I shout to them," he said loudly. Vidur quietly replied,

"That is your choice sir, but you will be dead long before I am."

Bertalan was sitting at his desk in front of a pile of paperwork when Bartos knocked and entered. "Cousin, I hope this is very important," said Bertalan. "I asked not to be disturbed, you can see how many documents I have to read through and sign."

Bartos indicated Vidur beside him. "This man claims to be from Mora with a letter that he says must be delivered to you in person." Bartos feared that this stranger might be an assassin and his commission might be to kill the King.

Bartos took a step towards the King, away from the dagger at his back, but when he spun round to face Vidur, the point of the dagger was already at his throat. Bertalan, now also concerned, rose from his seat. "What is this?"

Vidur spoke; there was no need to divulge his true name. "My Lord King, my name is Ferdinand and as your cousin says, I bring a letter from Mora that I am tasked to deliver to you by hand." Vidur held out the letter.

Bertalan looked at it warily for a minute, then instructed Bartos to leave them. Bartos raised his voice in concern. "My Lord, he may be here to kill you under instruction from Alberon."

Bertalan smiled. "Well cousin, if that was his mission

then you didn't try too hard to stop him, and if this Ferdinand, or whatever his name is, had wanted it, we would both be dead by now. Leave us."

As Bartos left the room, Vidur sheathed the dagger and walked across to pass the letter to the King. Bertalan noted the crude wax seal as he opened the letter. For a moment he wondered if Bartos was correct; who would send a letter without a seal of authority? The huntsman had not moved.

"No noble seal on this, which is unusual. Who sent you?" Bertalan asked.

Vidur shook his head. "I don't know my Lord, I was paid in advance for the mission and the letter was passed to me by a servant."

Bertalan started to read and noted the "A" signature at the bottom. "Ah, so the Chancellor continues his pleading for a truce or for a lift of the blockade. I wondered why his letters had stopped coming to pester me, but then I see from this that the Master of the Guild in Mora is no longer able to send his pigeons to his colleague here in Tamin. I will not waste my time writing a reply, but I think I can trust you to pass on my message. You can tell Aracir that I plan to starve the people of Mora until they rise up and get rid of that stupid brother-in-law of mine. Only then will the blockade be lifted."

Bertalan was not going to continue reading Aracir's pleas as he had seen them a dozen times before, but then the postscript at the end of the letter caught his attention. The added lines were short and to the point. *"Come the spring we need you to march your armies on to Mora. The populace will welcome you and the city will not resist."* It was a female's handwriting, and Bertalan knew it was not his sister's script. Bertalan thought for a minute. The wording was a request couched in an order. Whoever had written the lines was used to being obeyed. Suddenly it occurred to him that the writing must be that of Queen Ingrid.

He turned back to Vidur. "You can tell your queen that I have no desire to conquer Kermin or deliver Mora from its Emperor. If the people of Mora have a will, then they can find the way, without my army's help. I will not waste the blood of my men on something I have no desire to own, unlike Alberon."

Vidur nodded. He had completed his mission, at least in one direction, but he needed safe passage for the return journey. "I will ensure your messages are delivered, my Lord, but I am not sure if your cousin will be keen to grant me safe passage out of Tamin."

Bertalan nodded. "Yes, that would be understandable, as undoubtedly you have embarrassed him."

Bertalan sent a guard to ask Bartos to return to the office. Bartos felt some relief that his concern for the safety of the king had been unnecessary. As soon as he arrived, Bertalan gave his order. "Bartos, please escort this gentleman back to his lodgings and ensure that he gets safely on his way in the morning. He is now under my command to take my responses back to Mora and he is not to be hindered on his journey."

Bartos accompanied Vidur to the castle gate, where he grabbed the huntsman by the arm. "I must obey my king, but if I had my way you would now be headed for the castle dungeon, not the Black Bull," he said. "I will look out for you, Master Ferdinand, and if you ever return to Tamin my sword will be ready to greet you."

Vidur pulled his arm away and gave a cold smile. "It is unusual for a man to seek his own death, but if that is what you request I will be happy to oblige. Until the next time then."

The huntsman turned away and walked back to the Black Bull. It would be another long journey back to Mora to report to the Chancellor and the Queen.

It was late in the month when Vidur arrived back in Mora, after another arduous winter journey. As the huntsman approached the southern bridge he noticed the fires burning a hundred yards south of the banks of the Morel. He knew that in his absence, winter had not been kind to the people of Mora. The fires were thawing the frozen ground so that the earth could be opened up to deposit the bodies that Vidur could see lying on the snow. The first deaths from famine and cold were the blockade's innocent casualties.

Vidur first made his way to Aracir's house and

passed on Bertalan's message. The Chancellor was not particularly surprised, as his previous requests had been met with a similar response.

When Vidur reported to the Queen, Ingrid was more vocal in her response. "Did you read what I added to Aracir's letter?" she asked.

"No, my Lady."

"Well I asked him to attack Mora as soon as the weather clears. Does that surprise you?" Vidur did not reply, so the Queen continued. "My son has shut himself away in his rooms and all matters of state are being ignored. The people are beginning to starve and the only way I can see out of this mess is for an Amina army to capture Mora. Bertalan could set his nephew, my grandson, on the throne and we could settle back to the peace and prosperity that the Emperor has so thoughtlessly discarded. Do you think that is treason, Vidur?"

Vidur smiled. "Almost certainly my Lady, but as of now I don't see that the Emperor has many alternatives."

In his private rooms in the castle, Alberon had retreated behind closed doors. His wife, his mother and his advisors had all been excluded. Only the servants were allowed entry to bring him his food. For over two weeks, he had fretted over his predicament. In six weeks' time the snow would begin to melt and it might be possible to engage again with his enemy. However, he recognised that this was wishful thinking. He had no cannons to deploy, the majority of the Doran light cavalry had followed their Duke back to Iskala and the Kermin forces still camped on the Kermin Plain were in little better condition than their fellow citizens in the city. They were on one-third rations and would probably hardly be able to march back to the Alol, never mind win a battle there.

Alberon swore to himself. It seemed that his brother-in-law had all the cards. He would have to come up with a different plan, but what?

February brought little relief to the citizens of Mora. Surprisingly food could still be bought, at black market prices, although no one was sure where the supplies came from. It was rumoured that some enterprising sailors had, at night, managed to avoid the blockade at the mouth of the Morel and make the treacherous journey over the Eastern Sea to Andore. They had returned, again at night, and landed their goods in sheltered bays north of the Morel where the black market traders bartered for the cargo. Some ships' masters were, according to rumour, getting very rich on the proceeds.

Meanwhile, the poor in the slums and in the tradesmen's quarter had to rely on the limited supplies delivered each day from the now close to empty warehouses, and rat stew was becoming an increasingly common dish. In addition to food shortages, Aracir was worried about the level of fuel in storage. The reserves of coal and wood in the warehouses were now seriously depleted. If he could stretch the food supplies a bit further and find other sources of fuel, he thought the people of Mora could possibly survive until the spring, but what then? The Chancellor and the Emperor were both searching for some solution to the same problem.

At the same time as Aracir was pondering, Audun was, for the third time, guiding the *Swan* into a cove north of the Morel, some miles away from the sheltered bay where *Destroyer* was moored. The lights from the shore guided the ship's passage through the night and Audun knew that his cargo of grain, salted meat and flour would earn him and his crew a significant bounty. Ramon would not have approved, and indeed the *Swan* was in breach of the treaties and the blockade agreed between Bertalan and the rulers of the kingdoms on Andore. It was however a lucrative business, and Audun had earned more in a month than Ramon would have earned in three.

Audun soothed his conscience by imagining the relief his supplies would give to the people of Mora. Of course he could not see the daily crossings from the city to the mass graves where those who had succumbed to starvation or cold were laid to rest.

In the Den of Thieves, the winter was passing reasonably

comfortably. Rafe's reserves of gold coin and jewellery could easily pay for additional supplies on the black market, and the underground passageway to the Emperor's stores provided another source of food and wine. However, whilst living in comfort, Rafe, Raimund and Aleana could not simply ignore the poverty of their neighbours. Every few nights, when there was no movement on the streets, Raimund and Aleana would sneak out from the Den with bags filled with food. In the morning some lucky slum dweller would find provisions tucked into the snow at their front door. They were selective however, and most of the recipients of their gifts were families with young children.

It was towards the end of the month that Mora's problems came closer to home. Aracir thought he had a solution to at least one of his problems. The old disused warehouses along the south-eastern edge of the city should have been demolished years before, but now they could perhaps be of some value. Aracir could create space for new warehouses when peace returned, if it ever did, and in the meantime the demolished buildings could add wood to the depleted supplies of fuel.

Aracir knew full well about the black market that helped keep the rich warm and fed, so his orders were that whatever was found during the demolitions that could be used should be distributed locally amongst the poor people in the slums.

Two days later Rafe left the Den of Thieves to investigate the noise of hammering from further down the street, closer to the new port. He talked to one of the workman, who explained his orders. Aracir's solution had potentially become Rafe's problem.

CHAPTER SIXTEEN

A Change of Tactics

❖ ❖ ❖ ❖

Early March 1508 brought some relief to the beleaguered citizens of Mora. The bitter north wind that had been blowing in over the snow-covered Doran Mountains swung to the south and west, bringing warmer weather and some rain. As the snow began to melt, and the Morel's water became ice free, everyone hoped that spring was going to come early, even though an early spring could also mean a renewal of the hostilities in the Kermin Alol. Fishermen returned to their boats on the Morel and their daily catch bolstered the meagre rations that had just about kept starvation at bay for most people. As the roads gradually cleared additional supplies of dried meat and vegetables arrived from the farms on the Kermin Plain.

Wood and coal also began to arrive in the city, and the demolition of the old warehouses stopped a few doors away from the Den of Thieves. Rafe hoped that his hideaway would be safe for a while longer, although he had no doubt that at some point the entire row of old buildings would be pulled down.

As the days warmed, and lengthened, Alberon hoped that life in Mora would return to some sort of normality. He was mistaken. The snow and winter cold had kept the people off the streets, but now protests were daily events throughout the city and the chants from crowds were all the same: "No more war!" "Down with the Emperor!" "Death to the tyrant!" Holger and his guardsmen ensured that the protests were mainly peaceful, but it was a close-run at times. News from the front was no better, as Edin reported an increasing number of troops deserting and returning to their homes. These renegades were of greater concern to Holger, for these were hard men and they were armed. In the few cases where the peaceful protests erupted into violence the disillusioned soldiers were in the vanguard. The guards made some arrests, but Holger kept the details from his Emperor, knowing that further executions were only likely to make the situation worse. Edin's reports also told of increased Amina activity in the Alol and more cannons being brought to the front. Alberon was caught in a trap of his own making; he needed a different plan, a new strategy, and a change of tactics.

A late March sun illuminated the council room in Mora Castle, sparkling off the silver goblets and plates that were laid out on the long table. The guests were already seated, but Alberon's place at the head of the table was still empty. The Emperor's seat was draped in the light blue banner with the image of the tall man holding the yellow sun which reminded everyone of the Emperor's power. It was an unusual gathering and none of the attendees knew why they had been called to the council room.

A number of the Masters of the City Guilds sat nervously on one side of the table next to some of Kermin's senior nobles. The Masters and noblemen had not forgotten the fate of Cristian Carter and Lord Norward. They had accepted their invitations reluctantly, having concluded that ignoring the Emperor's invitation could be more dangerous than attending.

Opposite these wealthy and influential men sat members of Alberon's inner council. Edin had been called back from the front; Aracir and Holger were seated next in line, with Ingrid and Sylva closest to the empty chair at the head of the table. In whispers Ingrid enquired if Sylva knew what Alberon had planned, but the Empress had no idea.

A deep silence hung over the gathering as servants brought food and wine to the table. When the meal was nearly over, Ingrid again whispered to Sylva, "Where is he? What are we doing here eating in silence?"

Sylva shrugged; she didn't know.

Almost on cue, Alberon walked into the room. Sylva gasped. Her husband liked to wear expensive, colourful clothes and here he was dressed in a dark grey tunic with a black cloak around his shoulders. He looked more like a humble tradesman going to a funeral than an Emperor. Alberon was many things, but humble he was not. He knew how to make an impression though.

Alberon smiled as he walked slowly through the silent room. He could sense the mix of emotions in his guests, some scared, some resentful and some inquisitive, and it pleased him.

Reaching the chair at the head of the table, he lifted the blue banner from the seat, folded it carefully and laid it to one side. Then he took his seat, crossed his arms and leant back, milking the moment, the silence, the trepidation and the anticipation.

After a moment Alberon leant forward, ice-blue eyes scanning each face. "Ladies and gentlemen, I hope you have enjoyed my food and my wine. Now I will explain why I have invited you here. We have experienced a difficult winter and my people have remained strong and stoic in the face of cold and hunger. Even your Emperor's table has been almost empty some days."

This barb brought a murmur from around the table. The food that had just been served was the richest many of the visitors had eaten in weeks.

Alberon paused, looking round the table again to see if anyone was brave enough to gainsay him. None were, so he continued.

"The war with Amina has gone badly for us, betrayed as we were by the traitors in our midst." Another murmur rose from the table, and this one was slightly louder. Sylva knew her husband and recognised that he was toying with his audience. Alberon was arrogant and self-centred, but he was also cunning, and this act of pomposity must be for a reason.

After another moment's silence, Alberon carried on. "As the spring thaws continue, the campaign on the Kermin Plain and the Alol could be resumed."

Edin turned the comment he was about to make into a cough. He knew how low the morale was amongst the Kermin forces, and this, combined with the lack of cannons and the absence of the Doran cavalry, would make any resumption of hostilities pure madness. Alberon glared at his cousin before he spoke again.

"I am certain that my brave soldiers would prevail in the Alol in time. However my people have suffered enough through the winter and the deprivations brought by the blockade. Amina and her King should be proud to be invited to join the Empire, but I have decided that the issue will not be resolved by stalemate and death on the Alol. I therefore plan to travel to Tamin and meet with King Bertalan."

Sylva and Ingrid both let out quiet sighs of relief. At last Alberon was seeing some sense; but he wasn't finished. "I am persuaded that my role should be to bring peace again to our lands, light instead of the darkness of the past months. I hope that my brother-in-law will see the sense in my proposals and Kermin and Amina can once again be friends. I will be issuing specific instructions to some of you over the next few days." With that the Emperor rose from his seat and left the room, taking his folded banner with him.

As various conversations broke out among those gathered in the room, the servants brought more wine to lubricate the discussions. Sharing the same thoughts, Ingrid turned to Sylva. "Humble and caring for the people, a seeker for peace and light? I know my son. He is proud, devious and cunning, and behind his pompous words lies some different plan, of that I am certain."

Sylva nodded in agreement.

It was late afternoon when Alberon agreed to see his wife and mother. He virtually never met with both women together on matters of state or politics, as he knew that the two women could combine to form an irresistible force. His mother was too wise and experienced in political games and could almost always pick flaws in any of his plans, whilst his wife, whom he had largely ignored over the past couple of months, had a cutting logic, and she had slightly frightened him when she had wielded the blade after he had struck her. Not that Alberon would admit to either weakness.

It was Ingrid who spoke first, and she went straight to the point. "What was that all about in the Council Room today? A lavish lunch served with ample wine and a pretty speech that was a sham? I know you Alberon, you can play humble and conciliatory, but you don't fool me for one second."

Before Alberon could reply, Sylva cut in. "What are you going to do, walk up to Tamin city gates and say sorry? My brother will probably throw you into a dungeon, if not execute you on the spot. Are you completely forgetting that you were the one who declared war on Amina, and Bertalan has shown restraint when his troops could have marched to our gates and held Mora under an even more destructive siege?"

Alberon held up his hands. "Ladies, please take a breath and let me respond. Your observations are all correct and I have been worrying over our situation for the past two months. We have been unfortunate in the war."

"That is something of an understatement," interjected Sylva.

Alberon was about to raise his voice, but regained control. "Please let me continue. Since we lost our cannons, Bertalan has us completely outgunned. His forces hold the high ground in the Alol and we have a depleted and half-starved army. The Doran cavalry have retreated behind the mountains to Iskala and the route to the sea from the Morel is blocked. Sylva, your brother has outmanoeuvred me, and grudgingly I admire him for that. I have considered many options and have come to the conclusion that there is only one choice, and that is to meet with King Bertalan and come to some form of agreement around the original treaties. The war was a mistake, Berin was a mistake. I don't like to admit my failure, but I should have paid heed to your advice. When Aaron becomes king of Amina, then my Empire will be complete. I will need to be patient, not one of my strengths as you both know. For now we need time to rebuild and open up trade again."

It was Ingrid who cut in this time. "And were the executions a mistake too, or just unfortunate?"

This time Alberon did raise his voice a level. "No mother, they were proven traitors, although I may reconsider my sentences on the Duke of Doran and the crew of the Erth. Now leave me, I have work to do."

Sylva and Ingrid walked back to the Queen's rooms in silence. Behind the closed doors, Ingrid spoke first. "Time to rebuild? I doubt Alberon means only trade. As for patience, Aaron is only ten years old and I cannot imagine my son waiting at least another eight years to fulfil his dream of completing his Empire."

Sylva had a different worry, although it also related to her eldest son. "What if Bertalan decides to have Alberon executed? It would leave Aaron as a young king, with all the difficulties that involves. Also, Alberon and I may not have the most loving marriage, but he is my husband and despite all his flaws I am fond of him. I fear he is putting himself in great danger."

Ingrid calmed her daughter-in-law. "If the worst should happen a young king is not an impossible situation. Remember I was regent for many years when Alberon was under age. Besides, had your brother wanted to win Kermin for himself, then he had the opportunity last autumn. If there's a danger for Alberon I think it's more likely to be here in Mora than in Tamin." Ingrid could not, of course, divulge the message from Bertalan that Vidur had given her, nor could she know how right she would be in the future.

Over the following days Alberon met with members of his council and passed out his orders. First in the council room was Edin. Alberon started with a question, not an order. "I noted your inadvertent cough the other day and I presume you do not think there is any possibility of the army being recalled and marching successfully through the Alol?"

Edin was scared of his cousin and did not want to present himself as a coward, but he knew all he could really do was present the truth. He stammered through his reply. "Sire, as you said at the meeting, our army, still camped on the plain, is now few in number. Many have deserted and the others that I sent home for the winter have not returned."

Alberon was about to take the young man to task for allowing the desertions, but held his ire. Edin continued, "Even if we had all the forces at our command, any advance towards the Alol would end in slaughter. The Amina cannons are now dug in to the north of the Alol and our foot soldiers would be annihilated long before they got close enough to engage. In addition the Amina cavalry roam the plain at will, and without the Doran light horse we would have no defence."

Alberon nodded; of course he already knew the situation. He handed Edin a small package sealed with the royal symbol of a golden eagle in flight.

"Cousin, I need you to take this and deliver it to Silson, or whoever is in command of the Amina forces on the Alol. You will need to travel under a white flag with a small contingent of Kermin cavalry. It is essential that these letters are delivered to Bertalan before the middle of the coming month, as I plan to arrive at Tufle in the last week of April. Do not fail me on this mission." With that threat in his mind, the Duke of Aramin was dismissed.

Later that afternoon a young man was ushered into the council chamber. He was tall and thin with a shock of brown hair and was clearly very nervous. Soren was Orran's son and the Duke of Doran's nephew. He had attended the meeting in the council rooms a few days earlier. As the most junior of the noblemen in the room that day, he had said very little, but Alberon had invited him for a reason. Alberon left the young man standing, rather enjoying his obvious discomfort. "So Soren, you heard my speech a couple of days ago and I need to repair some of the damage done over the winter. Clearly you did not ride with your father and uncle back to Iskala. Were you present at the battle on the Alol?"

Soren blushed. "No sire, I wanted to join my father and the Doran troops, but it was my uncle who refused me, saying he needed someone to stay here in Mora and look after our people and properties here."

Alberon nodded. "I suppose that was wise of Morserat. The battle in the Alol was no place for a boy."

Soren flinched and drew himself to his full height. "Sire, I am eighteen years old and I have almost finished my training for full acceptance into the Doran cavalry. I was perfectly capable of fighting in the Alol, but I had to follow my uncle's orders like any other soldier."

Alberon smiled, quietly impressed by the young man's bravado. "So I assume you are a competent horseman?" he asked. Soren nodded. "Good, then I have a task I need you to carry out for me. With spring coming early, some of the passes through the Doran Mountains should be opening up. I need you to take this letter to your uncle, and it's important that it gets to him by the middle of the month. I have decided to pardon the Duke for retreating from the battle at the Alol. His actions probably preserved some of our best warriors. I am requesting that he bring the Doran cavalry back to the Kermin Plain by the end of the month. It will be a hard journey to Iskala but I am confident that you can complete my task."

Soren saluted the Emperor. "Your letter will be delivered on time my Lord. I guarantee it."

Alberon smiled. "You'd best go and get ready then and leave as soon as possible."

Soren saluted a second time. "Yes sir."

The pattern was repeated the next day, when Holger was the first to be called to meet the Emperor.

"Take a seat, Captain. I have a number of tasks I need you to do for me over the next few days. Firstly though, remind me how long it will take us to sail to Tufle?"

Holger hesitated a moment. "Well, it depends on the weather. Normally a few days, but remember the Amina ships at the blockade – we will need to outrun them if we can."

Alberon had anticipated the answer, although it was some years since he had taken the sea route to Amina. Overland, on the main road through the Alol, was the normal route, but clearly it was not currently an option. "Good. Then I need you to get the *Eagle* ready to sail in ten days' time," he ordered. The *Eagle* was the Emperor's flagship, a luxuriously-furnished carrack.

"My Lord, if we ready the *Eagle* at the dock then it will be a clear signal that you plan to leave the castle," replied Holger. "As you know, the people are angry and it may not be safe for you to venture out from the protection provided here. My guardsmen can probably hold off any direct attack, but we cannot stop the insults that the rabble might decide to throw at you."

Alberon had already considered this. "I hear the insults from the castle forecourt every day and I am not afraid of words. However you are correct, we need to proceed with some caution. You will have the ship moored in the old port. The night before we depart I want you to have Amleth and a dozen of the most loyal of my guard ready to escort me safely to my warehouse on the edge of the old port. The troopers and I will spend the night in the warehouse and board the *Eagle* early the next morning. The city gates will remain closed that morning until the ship has departed. Now, I expect to be away for a couple of weeks and you will take overall charge in Mora in my absence. That assumes of course that I can secure some form of agreement with Bertalan. I have some other tasks you will complete for me before I return to Mora."

An hour later, as Holger left the council room, Aracir was standing outside the door waiting to take his place. Alberon ushered the Chancellor in to take a seat.

"Aracir, I plan to sail for Amina in ten days' time and you will be accompanying me," he told him. "I have already decided on the terms I will offer Bertalan to secure a peace treaty, but I am certain he will bargain for more. In his position of strength, I certainly would. I want you to be my chief negotiator and I will discuss the details with you on the journey."

Aracir bowed and left the room. Remembering his last sea voyage, the Chancellor was not looking forward to an even longer one.

Alberon had one last person that he needed to brief about his plans, but that would wait until it was nearly time to sail.

CHAPTER SEVENTEEN

All Paths Lead to Jamin

❖ ❖ ❖ ❖

The last week of April heralded the onrush of spring, with warmer days and gentle winds. On the Kermin Plain the snows had mostly melted and in Mora the streets were clear and the Morel was ice free. As the days lengthened, so the conditions in the city improved. Supplies from the farmlands to the south and west of the city could now be brought by road and boat, so gradually the shelves in the shops began to fill and the emergency rationing was ended. Across the city the warmer weather also heralded more protests against the Emperor. Holger was increasingly worried about Alberon's planned transfer from the castle to the warehouse at the docks.

Whilst Holger was fretting about how to safely transport his Emperor to the Eagle, Edin was pacing the floor in a guest room in Tamin Castle. The journey across the Kermin Plain had been unexpectedly easy, as the snow-covered ground was increasingly turning to green again. Riding under a white flag, the Duke first arrived at the Amina front line. It was clear that Silson and Bertalan had been busy during the winter months as a row of eight culverins were dug into positions along the front. Edin was not over-familiar with these new weapons, but even to his untrained eye it was obvious that volleys of grapeshot from this deployment would be lethal to any advancing infantry. Clearly Bertalan had used the winter to strengthen his defensive positions.

James Daunt was the most senior commander at the front and he was the first to question the Duke. The ten Kermin cavalrymen who rode with Edin were not a threat, but Daunt considered that they may have accompanied the Duke to spy on the Amina positions and report back when they returned to Mora. Daunt knew that his cannon deployment was arranged to engage with an infantry attack and the positions were weaker if a cavalry force could break through on the flanks.

Calling across a captain of the Amina cavalry, Daunt issued his instructions. "Captain, you will take twenty of your men and escort the Duke of Aramin to Tamin, where you will take him to the Commander in Chief. As for his ten colleagues here, you will take them to the camp in the Alol and find them comfortable accommodation, but I want them kept there until I understand the Duke's mission to Tamin better."

Edin began to protest. "My men were to escort me safely here and should now be free to return to Mora."

This simply confirmed Daunt's suspicions. "Your men will stay as my guests until I am given the order that it is safe to send them back to Mora," he snapped.

So, as ordered, Edin arrived in Tamin at the end of the second week of April. Having been escorted to Silson's office in Tamin Castle, he passed over the package he had been tasked with delivering. Silson noted the seal on the package, the soaring golden eagle which was the royal emblem of Kermin. Edin was left under guard in Silson's quarters whilst the Commander in Chief sought out his king.

Bertalan took the package from Silson. "I wonder what nonsense Alberon is sending us now?" he said. "Maybe he has found another impostor who claims rights to my throne. With the weather clearing he is probably looking to renew hostilities. Are our forces ready to deploy as soon as they are needed?"

Silson nodded. "Yes sire. The cannons are already on the plain and in the back-up lines in the Alol. My spies tell me that Morserat is still banished and under threat of death, so the Doran cavalry remain in hiding in Iskala. Alberon's only option would be to use his infantry, and any infantry attack on the plain would simply be wiped out. Bartos and some of our cavalry units make occasional scouting sorties out across the plain and there is no indication of any activity in the Kermin camps, indeed my informants tell me it has been a hard winter for the troops on the Kermin Plain and for the citizens in Mora. However the Duke of Aramin should be able to enlighten us as I believe he has been in charge of the Kermin army, although in truth he seems a bit young for such a role."

Bertalan started to tear open the package. "So we are prepared, excellent. Now let's see what my brother-in-law has to say to me." He took his time to read the first letter and then unfolded the rest of the package. "Well, well, Alberon plans to visit us here at the end of the month. His letter apologises for his mistake in declaring war on Amina and says he would like to negotiate a peace with us." He took a thick sheaf of papers from the pack and waved it. "And this is the treaty we agreed in 1506 with all references to the Emperor and the Empire removed, and it is signed by Alberon below his seal. What do you make of that?"

Silson considered the question for a moment before replying. "I think the Emperor has taken the only choice open to him. He will know that he cannot possibly challenge us in the field without cavalry and even more so without cannons. His people and his army have come close to starvation during the winter as the blockades have remained in place. He would have to break the sea blockade at the mouth of the Morel to rearm, and whilst our caravels patrol the seas that option is really not viable. If he is planning to come then I suggest that we receive him and see what he proposes, ensuring that the deal we might make is mostly to the benefit of Amina."

Bertalan frowned. "I am tempted to let him come and throw him into our deepest dungeon."

Silson shook his head. "I don't think that would be a good idea. Kermin is weakened and defeated, but they are still a proud nation. Throwing their king into prison whilst he is on a peace mission might renew their energy to continue the war. We would be better to prepare our demands and agree a peace. However Alberon is devious and cunning and I don't think we should fully trust him."

Bertalan recalled Ingrid's words requesting him to invade and capture Mora and saying the people of the city would support him. However Bertalan also knew his sister and suspected that Sylva might not take kindly to any harm coming to her husband.

Bertalan nodded. "All right, we are agreed. We will receive Alberon coolly on his arrival, and in the meantime please bring the Duke of Aramin to me in the morning, as I would like to learn more about the current situation in Mora."

That evening Bertalan discussed events with his wife.

Aisha was instantly suspicious about her brother-in-law's motives. "Bertalan, if the situation in Kermin is as reported by Silson we need to demonstrate to Alberon our power and strength. Whatever treaty we may finally agree has to be crafted in such a way that it both punishes and embarrasses Alberon. I will not allow you to simply countersign the treaties that we walked away from two years ago. The first demonstration of our resolve and intent can begin tomorrow when you meet the Duke of Aramin."

The next morning Silson led Edin through the corridors of Tamin Castle. Edin was surprised when Silson stopped at the entrance to the grand hall and knocked on the door. "Enter" was the command, and Edin was ushered into the hall. Bertalan, King of Amina, sat on his throne at the far end of the room, fully dressed for war. When the King stood, the plate armour rattled under his surcoat, which was embellished with the grey wolf emblem of the kings of Amina. A gauntleted hand beckoned Edin to approach the throne.

Edin was scared; this was not how he had expected to meet the King. As he reached the first of the steps leading up to the throne, a second command came from behind the steel helmet. "You will kneel before me."

Edin did as commanded and his fear grew when he heard the rasp of steel as the King drew his sword. Fearing the worst, Edin lowered his head.

Inside his helmet Bertalan smiled before speaking. "You can see that Amina is ready to go to war again, and this time I look forward to seeing Mora burn. Tomorrow we will meet again and you will tell me all that you know about the situation in Mora and the deployment of the Kermin forces on the plain."

Relief swept over Edin as he realised that he was not about to be executed. Silson helped the trembling Duke to his feet, and taking his arm he supported him as he walked hesitantly back out of the hall. As the door closed behind them Bertalan removed his helmet. "How good it is to have a clever wife!" he laughed.

The next day a still fearful Duke was again led through the castle, this time to the King's own quarters. Servants brought food and wine as Edin waited in trepidation. This time Bertalan was richly dressed, but without the armour, though he still wore the surcoat as a reminder of the previous day. As ordered, Edin told Bertalan all he knew about the situation in Mora and the demoralised state of the Kermin army. Bertalan concluded the meeting by saying, "Thank you Duke, your information has been very helpful and now you will stay as my guest here in Tamin. When your Emperor arrives in Tufle you will go to meet him. You will tell him that Bertalan is dressed ready for war and the conquest of Kermin." Ten days later Edin was pacing the floor in his room, still wondering what he would say to Alberon when he arrived in Tufle.

Two days before Alberon's departure for Tufle, a lone horseman rode through Mora's southern gate and made his way to the castle. Soren had been as good as his word; somehow he had made his way across the Doran Mountains and back in less than two weeks. Holger met the young man at the castle gate and, as he knew Soren's mission, quickly escorted him to the council room.

Alberon rose to greet the weary traveller. "Well Soren, you claimed to be an accomplished horseman, but you must have had wings to get to Iskala and back in such a short time."

Soren bowed to the Emperor. "Sire, the high mountain passes are still blocked but there is a route to Doran following a little-known path that runs close to the source of the Morel as it flows south from the mountains. It is not a route that can be travelled by a large force, but it is possible for a few horsemen to get through the mountains even in the depths of winter."

Alberon was surprised; he had always thought that Iskala was closed off behind the snow-covered mountains for most of the year. "So what was the response of your uncle to my letter and pardon?"

Morserat had commanded his nephew to repeat his reply word for word, and Soren was concerned about the Emperor's reaction. However he was a soldier and knew he had to follow his uncle's orders. Slightly hesitantly, Soren began. "The Duke of Doran thanks the Emperor for his forgiveness. The Duke's actions towards the end of the campaign last summer were necessary, as the battle in the Alol was already lost thanks to the reckless behaviour of the man the Emperor had put in command of the army. I was not prepared to put the lives of more of my cavalrymen at risk against a better-armed and better-prepared enemy. We did not retreat from the front out of fear but out of necessity. I did not think that the Emperor would understand the criticality of the situation, so I returned to Iskala with my cavalry. The wisdom of my action has been confirmed by the news I have had of the fate of my fellow councillor, Lord Norward."

Alberon was getting slightly irritated with this lengthy response. "Yes, yes, so Morserat was concerned for his own skin if he had returned to Mora, but will he lead the light cavalry back to reinforce the troops on the Kermin Plain? Did he respond to my offer that he would be granted overall command of the Kermin forces as my commander in chief?"

Soren knew he would have to depart from his script. "Yes my Lord, my uncle will lead the Doran cavalry back to the plain once the main passes are open, but that will not be possible for at least another month, depending on the weather. In the meantime my father is leading a troop of one hundred Doran light cavalry who are following my route through the narrow pass along the Morel. They should reach Mora in three or four days' time."

Alberon nodded. "That will suffice. Now I need you to ride back to join your father and tell him I need the Doran cavalry to show their presence on the plain in view of the Amina forces. However I do not want them to engage in any action; I just need them to be visible to the enemy."

Soren knew he must now try to deliver the most important part of his uncle's message. Bravely he continued, "My uncle also instructed me to tell you that his troops will have been briefed to respond to any threat on his life. He told me to tell you that if any attempt is made to apprehend him, or otherwise threaten his life, then the Doran forces have been instructed to change sides and join the Amina cavalry."

Alberon's face reddened and his voice rose. "So your uncle threatens me, does he?"

Soren raised his hand in apology. "My Lord I am only my uncle's messenger, I am not privy to his thoughts."

Alberon calmed down. "Well at least he has accepted my invitation to lead my army when the time comes. Now rest in the castle tonight and tomorrow seek out your father and pass on my instructions, messenger."

Soren nearly responded, but held back. He would report to Orran, Morserat's brother, in the morning, because he knew that his father and the Doran force were camped closer to Mora than he had divulged to the Emperor.

The day before departing for Tamin, Alberon needed to speak with someone else, and this was a conversation that he was not looking forward to. During the winter months he had mostly ignored his wife. Sylva had demanded that he join her and their two sons regularly for evening meals to at least maintain some pretence for the boys about their marriage. Alberon knew his wife disapproved of many of his actions of the winter, particularly the executions, and he considered Sylva's attitude as both a betrayal and an insult. As a result he was keeping his distance from her, knowing how quickly her words could stoke his anger. He was also aware that he could act irrationally when he lost his temper, and whenever he considered this he remembered the stiletto. He decided it was best to meet his wife on neutral ground, and had asked her to meet him in the council room.

Twenty minutes after the time he had requested, Sylva entered the room. Alberon had to control his temper; she was late and did not even have the courtesy to knock before entering.

Sylva got quickly to the point. "You have more or less ignored me for months, so why this sudden request to meet on the day before you leave for Tamin?" Alberon felt his anger flaring up again at this abruptness, but he knew this was not the time to raise his voice, so he too went straight to the point. "It is the journey to Tamin that I need to speak with you about. Aaron will be joining me on the trip. It's time he got to know his uncle and the capital in which he may one day be crowned as king."

This took Sylva by surprise, and it took her a moment to find her words.

"Alberon, he is only ten and it will be many years before he needs to go to Tamin. You have no idea how you might be received by my brother, and I will not have my son put in danger through your stupidity. He is not going."

Alberon was losing his self-control. He rose from his seat and took a step towards his wife. "I was a king at three years old, I am your husband and I am your Emperor. You will do as I command."

He stepped forward again and caught a glint of steel from Sylva's knife. "You may be all those things, but I am his mother!" she snapped. "He is not going with you, and please don't forget my promise."

Alberon took a step backwards, and taking deep breaths to calm himself, he sat back down. His one regret about the past six months was the distance he had created between himself and his wife. Over their fifteen years of marriage he had grown to respect Sylva for her intellect and wisdom, and indeed her companionship. He concluded that it was the pressures of the past months that had caused him to vent his anger in her presence, something he had never done previously, and the consequence had been the threat, backed by the stiletto.

Forcing himself to control his anger, he continued more quietly, "Sylva, I need the boy with me to ensure your brother signs the treaties. Bertalan may be reluctant to come to any agreement with me, so I will ask our son to countersign the documents as a commitment for today and for the future. He will be making the commitment as the future king of Kermin and the current heir to the throne of Amina."

Sylva paused. She was a mother, but she was also skilled in the art of politics, and in this instance she actually agreed with her husband's proposition. Nonetheless it was her maternal instinct that won through.

"I will not allow you to take him. What if my brother decides to hold Aaron as a hostage to ensure you keep to any treaty you agree? It is too great a risk both to our son and to Kermin. What if the *Eagle* were to sink in a storm? Both the Emperor and his heir would perish. What would that mean for Kermin? I can't allow it."

Alberon took a different tack. "I'm sorry for ignoring you and the boys over the past months. You know how difficult it has been for me."

Sylva was not to be so easily mollified. "Not as difficult as the months have been for our people."

Alberon stifled a sharp response and spoke again quietly. "Sylva, you want to bring an end to this situation that I have created with your brother. To achieve that end I think I need to have Aaron with me when I meet with Bertalan, if only to reinforce my change of heart."

The politician in Sylva could see the sense in what he was saying, but her reply remained sharp. "You forget how well I know you, Alberon. A change of heart? Contrition? That is very unlike you. I am sure you have another plan besides this impersonation of a peacekeeper. However, in this instance you may be correct. I will consider your command and give you my decision later this afternoon. If I do let my son go with you then you'd better make sure you bring him back safely. Remember, you have never yet seen me truly angry."

Alberon thought again of that glint of steel. "He will be safe, I promise," he said. As Sylva rose to leave she had the last words: "You should be careful about making promises you may not have the power to keep."

That night thick cloud blocked out any light from the waxing crescent moon as Amleth, Holger's second in command, led a small party through Mora's dark streets down to the Emperor's warehouse. In the centre of a dozen guardsmen Alberon and Aaron marched side by side, both dressed in guards' uniforms. Aracir was also in the centre, dressed as usual with a dark red cloak covering his shoulders. Any observer would have concluded that the guardsmen were escorting the Chancellor on some form of business and would not suspect the presence of the Emperor in the group.

They reached the old warehouse without incident other than a few insults thrown at the Chancellor from passers-by. The ground floor of the building had been prepared by the Steward to ensure that the Emperor could spend a relaxing night before crossing the dock the next morning to board the *Eagle*.

Prior to sitting down to enjoy his evening meal, Alberon had to find something he hoped had been stored in the warehouse. The first floor held most of the treasures that had been given to the Kermin royal family over the years, and Aracir held the inventory. On a corner shelf was a large gold brooch, a gift from Bertalan on Alberon's marriage to Sylva. The brooch's gold circle was bisected by two hands clasped in a greeting; above the hands was the eagle emblem of Kermin and in the lower half the gold was embossed with the grey wolf of Amina. It was symbolic of the joining of the houses of Amina and Kermin represented by Alberon and Sylva's marriage. Alberon felt that wearing the brooch when he met with Bertalan might be a reminder of the promise to unify the countries.

As Alberon picked up the brooch Aracir looked at his inventory and noted that some small pieces appeared to be missing. He would need to investigate this further once he returned from Tamin.

Neither Aracir nor Alberon knew that they were not the only ones in the warehouse that night. As the guard had entered on the ground floor the thieves had been on the floor above, deciding which few treasures they should select to add to the pieces now stored in the Den of Thieves. With their escape route through the tunnel on the lower floor no longer accessible, Raimund and Aleana had quietly and quickly moved up to the top floor, where they hoped they would remain undetected until these new visitors left.

It was a cold, uncomfortable night for the two thirteen-year-olds. The top floor of the warehouse was empty and the wooden floor made a hard bed. They did not dare to light any candles in case they give their presence away. All they could do was to huddle together in the dark for warmth.

As the first light of the new morning leaked through the eaves on the warehouse roof, Raimund was first to wake, and quietly moving to the edge of the staircase, he could hear the visitors leaving. Always inquisitive, he moved down a level and through a crack in the timbers he watched a small troop of the King's Guard cross the dock to board a carrack moored opposite in the old port. Raimund thought he recognised one of the nobles in the centre of the group, but couldn't think why. The two people walking next to this man were also richly dressed. The one in the centre seemed to be the person in charge, whilst the other was a young boy. Raimund guessed that the boy was about his own age, maybe slightly younger.

With the coast now clear, Raimund went back upstairs and woke Aleana. Rafe was mightily relieved when the pair entered the Den of Thieves. He gave each of them a hug. "Thank goodness you are both safe, you had me very worried. Do you know who was visiting the warehouse last night?"

Raimund replied, "I saw a small number of the Guard and three noblemen leave this morning. I thought I recognised one of the nobles, but I don't know why. When they arrived yesterday evening we were fortunate that they made a lot of noise and we had time to move and hide on the top floor. During the evening they all stayed mostly on the ground floor, although we did hear two voices on the floor below us. They seemed to be searching for something."

Rafe gave a sigh of relief. "You both did well, and you were lucky. I was worried when you didn't return here promptly last night. After an hour I was wondering if somehow you had been apprehended, so I crept quietly along the passageway to check on the situation. Your visitors were none other than the Emperor and his Chancellor, and my guess is that the boy was one of the young princes. I don't know why they were dining in the warehouse, very strange."

Raimund suddenly remembered. "The Chancellor? I think it was his purse we took a few months ago as he disembarked from the *Erth*. That would be why I thought I recognised him. Anyway, this morning they left and crossed the dock to board a large carrack moored at the port."

So it was that rumours started to circulate in Mora that the Emperor had fled the city.

The next day dawned bright and clear. The overnight clouds had been dispersed by the gentle breeze which filled the *Eagle*'s foresail as the carrack made its way past the two retracted bridges and travelled south and west, following the Morel as it flowed towards the Eastern Sea. Aracir recalled his previous sea journey on the *Erth*, and he was already feeling slightly queasy. By contrast Aaron was in a state of high excitement and raced back and forth, getting under the feet of the seamen who were stowing the ropes and manning the sails.

Aracir was not to know that the *Erth* had been at the mouth of the Morel only two days earlier. Rondon had been instructed by Lord Ereldon to once again take supplies to the *Warrior* and the *Destroyer*, and he had also been given a letter from the King addressed to the captain of the *Warrior*. John Sexton now knew that the Emperor's flagship was likely to arrive at the mouth of the Morel in the next few days. Sexton was instructed to escort the *Eagle* to Tufle and leave the *Destroyer* patrolling the Eastern Sea.

It was mid-afternoon when the *Eagle* left the river Morel and picked up speed as the wind strengthened. Almost immediately the captain pointed out a caravel racing north towards them. Aracir had retired to bed, so he was not on deck to point out to the captain the threat carried on the bow of the caravel.

As the *Warrior* closed in on the larger ship Alberon saw the cannon, and in a panic he ordered Aaron to leave the deck. Alberon had to once again grudgingly acknowledge that he had been outwitted by his brother-in-law. He had never dreamed of encountering a ship armed with a cannon.

As the caravel tacked and the bow pointed directly at the *Eagle*, Alberon's heart missed a beat. What if Bertalan's orders were simply to sink the *Eagle* and end the Empire problem once and for all? Bertalan was not to know that his nephew was also on board the flagship.

The *Eagle* flew the Kermin flag from the mainmast, but on the foremast and mizzenmast large white flags flew in the breeze. Bertalan had indeed considered that sending his brother-in-law to a watery grave might be a solution, but had decided that this would only fuel another ground war for which he had no desire.

The *Warrior* again tacked and Alberon let out a short sigh of relief as the cannon now pointed away from the *Eagle*. A set of flags was hoisted on the caravel and the *Eagle's* captain studied them. "We are being told to continue to Tufle and the caravel will follow us," he told Alberon.

To reinforce the instruction, Sexton manoeuvred the *Warrior* to a position fifty yards behind the *Eagle*, with the falconet now pointing directly at the stern of the larger ship.

With the early coming of spring, and the improving situation in Mora, running black market supplies across the Eastern Sea had become less profitable. By March Audun had returned the *Swan* to normal duties travelling back and forth between Anelo, Toria and Boretar with various cargoes. Ramon stayed in Boretar negotiating the contracts whilst Audun remained in command of the *Swan*.

In early April, Audun and Ramon were sitting comfortably in the house on Cross Street discussing the next voyage. The *Swan* was already loaded and ready to sail, carrying a cargo of wool and cured hides that were bound for Anelo, but Ramon was discussing a change in plan with Audun. Ramon had been told by the merchant whose wares he was shipping that market prices in Toria were better than those in Arance, so Audun's destination would now be Thos.

Audun questioned the man he now fully considered to be his stepfather. "Ramon, our contract was delivery to Anelo and the shorter journey to Thos will presumably reduce our profit."

Ramon nodded. "Yes it will, but it means we can run our own cargo of wines and spirits from Thos to Tufle. With the war in the south fewer merchant ships have been crossing to Amina and a cargo of Torian goods should make us a better profit." He passed a bag of gold coins across to Audun. "This should be enough to purchase our own cargo, and if you negotiate a decent price in Tora we should be able to double or treble our investment when you sell it on in Tamin."

Audun was not about to argue. Perhaps a return to the city of his birth would help him focus again on his destiny and reignite his vows for revenge. His thoughts returned to his last visit to Aldene and the red stone. The casket was still stowed in the locker in his cabin on the *Swan*, but he seldom looked inside it. It had been almost a year now, and the casket still contained just a dull piece of red rock.

CHAPTER EIGHTEEN

A Time for Treaties

❖ ❖ ❖ ❖

The sun was setting on the Western Sea as the *Eagle* approached the port of Tufle. Alberon hoped the timing was auspicious, as the following day would be the first of May and Tamin would be celebrating the festival of Beltane, the coming of summer.

John Sexton on the *Warrior* followed his instructions, holding the caravel at sea until the *Eagle* docked and then turning the ship back north to continue the blockade at the Morel. Alberon was happy to see the threat of the cannon move away, but it was also a reminder of his mission, to get the seas reopened for Kermin's shipping.

While the sailors prepared the ship for time in port Alberon and Aaron walked the deck, enjoying the early evening warmth. Alberon was pointing out Tufle landmarks to Aaron as they reached the prow. A large carrack moored directly in front was flying the Amina flag from the main mast, and it took Alberon some moments to realise that this was the *Erth*. Alberon had decided to pardon the crew for their treachery in defying his instructions to break through the Morel blockade, and now seemed as good a time as any to show his benevolence. Leaving Aaron watching the sailors at work, he made his way back to the aftcastle in search of Aracir.

From his cabin at the stern of the *Erth*, Rondon had watched the Emperor's flagship enter Tufle's port. He had considered preparing his ship for a quick departure, but then, assessing the situation, he had decided to stay put. After all he was flying the Amina flag and was under the protection of the Amina king, so little threat could be posed by the Emperor's arrival, assuming of course that the Emperor was on board his flagship.

That evening there was a polite knock on Rondon's cabin door. It was Aracir, following Alberon's instructions.

Rondon rose from his chair. "Welcome back on board the *Erth*, Lord Chancellor."

Aracir shuddered, remembering when this man had held a dagger to his throat. "I am instructed to request you to come over to the *Eagle* and join the Emperor for supper," he said.

Rondon smiled. "Rumour has it that my crew and I have been exiled by the Emperor on pain of death if we were to return to Mora. It would be rather foolish of me to simply walk into captivity."

Aracir held up his hand and explained that Alberon had decided to pardon all on board the *Erth*. Rondon nodded. "Please tell the Emperor that I would be delighted to serve him supper here in my cabin."

When Aracir reported back, Alberon was furious. "How dare the impudent wretch! I will reinstate my order exiling him and his crew."

Aracir was, as ever, the calmer of the two. "My Lord, you had these men condemned to death. It is understandable that their captain will not simply walk into a potential trap."

So it was that two hours later Alberon had just finished a remarkably good supper accompanied by even better wine, and Rondon had accepted the Emperor's reprieve, knowing his crew would be pleased to be able to go back home to their families in Mora. Alberon had one last request. "Now that we understand the situation captain, I would like you to lower the Amina flags on your masts and replace them with the Kermin flag."

Rondon considered for a moment. "My Lord, I cannot do that. The *Erth* is, for the present, commissioned by Lord Ereldon and I would need his permission to change the flags. In addition, if as you hope, we are instructed to sail back to Mora in the near future we will need the gunboats at the Morel to know we are friendly and not making an attempt to break the blockade."

Alberon knew that Rondon's concerns were sensible, and indeed he did not care what flag the carrack flew when at sea, but he did require a statement whilst the *Erth* lay at berth in Tufle. He rose from the table. "Thank you for an excellent supper captain. As a favour to me, please fly the Kermin flag for the next few days whilst I am here in Tamin. You can revert to the Amina emblem when you are sailing back to Mora." With that the Emperor returned to the *Eagle*.

The next morning Beltane kept her promise and the warm sun sparkled on the waters of the Middle Sea. All along the harbour the boats flew pennants in random order, not passing messages but simply welcoming the holiday. Market traders were setting up their stalls and some of the May Day dancers were practising their routines close to the warehouses.

Alberon was waiting; the night before, he had sent Amleth ahead to Tamin to inform Bertalan of his arrival at Tufle. Looking across the deck to the *Erth*, he was pleased to see the Kermin flag flying from the foremast, although he was annoyed that the Amina flag still took prominence on the main mast.

Alberon was waiting for Bertalan, or at least one of Amina's senior nobles, to come to greet him and escort him to Tamin. He was dressed as he had been a few weeks earlier in Mora's council room; not in sackcloth and ashes, but it was as close as Alberon could force himself to come. He hated the dark grey tunic and the black cloak, but he had to give the impression that he regretted his actions. The gold brooch glinting in the sunlight was the only emblem of his power and wealth. Humility and contrition, that was the message the Emperor reluctantly wanted to portray. Humiliation was not what he was prepared for.

Alberon's temper rose as he was kept waiting. Surely his brother-in-law would send him an official welcoming party?

It was mid-morning when a lone horseman rode up to the *Eagle*. It was Edin, Duke of Aramin, mounted on an old farm horse and leading an even older mount.

"Greetings my Lord, welcome to Amina," he said in a trembling voice.

Alberon stared hard at his cousin for a few moments, making the other drop his gaze. "What is this, a royal welcome? Where are my carriage and the formal entourage to meet me? Am I supposed to ride into Tamin on that old nag?"

Edin lowered his head. "Yes sire, I am afraid that on Bertalan's orders I have to escort you, and only you, to Tamin."

Alberon's first instinct was to order the *Eagle* to leave port and return to Mora. Then he remembered the caravels at the mouth of the Morel and the cannons, and knew he had run out of options.

Audun had not been in Tamin since his previous visit four years earlier. The *Swan* had docked at Tufle in the last week in April and his trade was now completed. The caravel was loaded and ready to sail for Boretar, but as the planned departure date coincided with the May Day holiday, he had decided to delay by a couple of days so that he and the crew could enjoy some holiday relaxation.

Returning to Tufle and Tamin still brought back painful memories. Audun had hoped that his great aunt and uncle would still be living in the house in Mill Street, but the current occupants only knew that they had purchased the house from an elderly couple and had no idea where his relatives may have relocated to.

The Bear Tavern stood close to Tamin's main street, and Audun was sitting alone outside the inn staring into his jug of ale, lost in thought. His hope had been that his return to Amina would renew his purpose and his desire for revenge, but this had been overtaken by his memories. The crowds in the main street started cheering as some of the Beltane celebrants paraded up the street. Audun remembered the six-year-old boy who wanted to join the wedding celebrations and was forbidden to by his mother. In that moment he could almost feel his mother's hand tightly gripping his and her words instantly came to mind: *"Audun, that man is evil and when you are older I will explain and maybe you can right the wrong he has done to you."*

Other memories came tumbling through: his grandfather and his paintings; his mother mixing her father's paint; the flight to Boretar via Tufle; the kindness of Ramon and Hilda's explanation of what had happened to his grandparents. As the memories flashed by, other images came to mind, the letter from the Kermin Regents' and the old poem, both stored in his locker alongside the casket with the red stone. Taking a long swig of ale, he let the memories drift away. All that remained was his promise to himself: *"One day I will avenge my family."*

Audun suddenly realised that the noise from the crowd had changed. The cheers had turned to jeers, and angry shouts echoed through the alleyways. Quickly he drained his tankard and headed for the disturbance. Pushing his way through to the front of the crowd, he saw two men riding towards him heading for the castle. One, in a black cloak, sat erect in the saddle glaring at the crowd as he rode past. Audun heard the insults from the crowd: "Warmaker!" "Enemy scum!" but it was the last taunt that really caught Audun's attention: "Not much of an Emperor now, are you?"

Ragna's words from the past again echoed in Audun's mind: "Audun, that man is evil and when you are older I will explain and maybe you can right the wrong he has done to you." In an instant, realisation dawned. This was his father, mounted on an old nag, but defiant despite the humiliation.

Audun felt that Alberon's glare was focused directly at him as the two mounted men rode past. He smiled back at the disdainful glare and mouthed his own response: *"One day I will come for you Alberon, and I will have my revenge."* Alberon rode past oblivious. He had long forgotten his early lover and her unborn child.

Edin was relieved when they reached the castle gate. Alberon had not spoken a word on the journey from Tufle, but Edin could feel his cousin's rage and anticipated that he would be the focus of Alberon's fury once they were alone.

Bartos was at the gate to meet them, but he offered no warm welcome. One of his lieutenants was waiting as the two men dismounted. Bertalan had clearly given his instructions, and the lieutenant saluted Edin and asked him to follow. Edin was returned to his rooms in the castle.

Alberon turned on Bartos, releasing his pent-up fury. "Take me to Bertalan NOW!"

Bartos shrugged. "Those are not my instructions, sire. Please follow me."

Alberon grabbed the Captain by the shoulder and spun him round. "TAKE ME TO YOUR KING NOW!" he roared.

Bartos pulled away. "I cannot do that sire, the King is resting and is not to be disturbed. I will take you to your rooms and the King will see you in the morning."

Alberon was apoplectic with rage, and needed to vent his anger and frustration. Ignoring the two guardsmen behind him, he drew the jewelled dagger that was sheathed at his waist. Bartos did not need the warning shout from the guard; he spun round with his own blade glinting in the afternoon sun. "That would be a very silly thing to do, my lord," he said.

Alberon did not step back. Instead he roared at the Captain, "I am your Emperor! It is treason to threaten me!"

Bartos was unrelenting but polite. "Please sheath the dagger and follow me, my Lord Emperor. I believe your empire is defeated and your people are starving."

Of course Alberon knew that Bartos was correct, and this final insult drained his fury. Maybe this visit was not such a good idea. Once more, he reminded himself that this was his only option. Sheathing the dagger, he followed Bartos into the castle.

If Alberon thought his humiliation was complete, he was mistaken. Bartos led him to an older part of the castle and opened the door to what would be his quarters for the next few nights. The room was small, dusty and smelt of damp. Clearly Bertalan was making a point; the meeting in the morning, if it happened, would not be a meeting of equals, but the victor lording it over the vanquished.

Alberon's evening meal was undoubtedly better than the fare being served on many of the tables in Mora, but it was hardly fitting for a king, never mind an Emperor. Exhausted, he retired to bed, but he got little rest, as his dreams were filled with faces yelling insults at him. Sometimes the mob seemed to be lining the streets in Mora, and then the background would change and it would be the crowd yelling at him as he entered Tamin.

In the morning he would recall one particular face, a young man with ice-blue eyes who always stood at the front of the mob. Strangely, the man's face seemed familiar, or perhaps it was the eyes, so like his own.

Across the city, in his room in the Bear Tavern, the same young man was also having a restless night. Audun's dreams were filled with fire. Cities that he didn't recognise were being consumed by the flames and the old man was always at the centre of the conflagrations as the fire erupted from either his hand or his staff. On waking, the words he had last heard in Aldene, almost a year ago, echoed in his mind. *The power is yours now Audun. We will return to Mora and you will have your revenge.* Was his time of waiting over?

The next morning, Alberon was woken early. The servant bringing his breakfast also carried a note from his brother-in-law. Ignoring the food, Alberon tore open the seal and read the note. Was this to be more humiliation?

Bertalan's words were surprisingly conciliatory: *"Brother, we need to negotiate an end to this war which has damaged both our countries. This is a task for you and me and not our advisors. We will meet later this morning and start our discussions. I apologise for the reception you received yesterday. The Beltane festival was probably not the best day to arrive, considering the crowds celebrating in the streets."* Alberon was sceptical, as the holiday was not a reason for Bertalan to make him ride into Tamin on an old nag or to provide such poor quarters for his night's rest. Nonetheless he was here now and all he could hope for was to bargain for a peace beneficial to Kermin.

At ten that morning Alberon was once again waiting when Lord Ereldon knocked and entered. "My Lord, I am to escort you to meet with my king. Please follow me." Alberon was surprised when the Amina Chancellor ignored the corridor that led to the newer, refurbished areas of the castle and instead turned left and started to climb an old spiral staircase which Alberon assumed led to one of the many high castle turrets that looked out over Tamin. The stairs were old and worn, and there were many of them.

Finally, somewhat breathless from the climb, Alberon was ushered into the turret room. Pausing at the door, he took in his surroundings. This might be the oldest part of the castle, but this circular room was expensively furnished. Tapestries were draped on one of the walls, a log fire in the opposite wall provided warmth and two chairs were set opposite each other at a single table. The windows provided views over the city and beyond, and Alberon could make out the masts of the *Eagle* and the *Erth* in distant Tufle.

Ereldon again broke the silence. "Please take a seat, my Lord. The King will be with you shortly." With that, the Chancellor left and Alberon heard the key turn in the lock. He tried to calm his thoughts. Was this some new form of trap? The turret room could only be accessed by the single staircase, and the only door to it was locked. He took one of the seats and once again waited.

Thirty minutes later, Alberon's nerves were beginning to fray, and the noise of metal grating on metal as someone climbed the staircase intensified his tension. A thought struck him with a sudden jolt – was this where his brother-in-law intended to have him murdered? Thought turned to action. The only weapon he had was the jewelled dagger at his waist, but if he was going to be attacked he would go down fighting. Rising from his seat with the dagger pointing to the door, he prepared himself to meet his death.

The door lock quietly clicked, but seconds passed and the door did not open. Was this another part of Bertalan's game?

Just as Alberon thought his imagination was playing

tricks on him, the door was thrown open and Bertalan stepped into the open space, fully dressed in chain mail under the grey wolf surcoat, the sword at his side clattering against the door. He indicated the seat at the table. "Sit brother, I am dressed ready for war if this is what you desire, but I hope you have come to talk of regret and of peace. At least you are dressed like one who is showing penitence."

Bertalan noted the gold brooch clasping Alberon's cloak, but decided not to mention the wedding gift. "Please put your dagger away Alberon, it is of no use here."

Alberon bit back his angry reply. He knew Bertalan was probably correct; the dagger would be of little use against armour, although the temptation to try was difficult to resist. After a moment's pause, he sheathed the blade and returned to his seat.

"This is my hideaway, and only Ereldon knows about it," said Bertalan. "Believe it or not, the Chancellor will bring us food and wine during the day, and we will stay here until we have agreed the treaties. You will not have access to the rest of the castle until we have settled our differences. Your rooms are down the stairs below us, so that you can be brought here as needed each day in secret. Now where will we start?"

As the two kings faced each other across the table, far below in the city Audun was wandering the streets, going over his memories and etching them more clearly in his mind. Unconsciously he followed the route he had taken that fateful day eight years earlier. Pausing outside the small house in Rose Street, he could still visualise his grandmother and grandfather sitting at the front door in the summer sun.

He walked on up through the Painters' Quarter and browsed in the artists shops he had visited with his mother. Then, sitting at the edge of the fountain in the square, he recalled how agitated his grandfather had been as he pulled Ragna and him away and into the crowds in the market place.

Walking back towards the southern gate, Audun took a detour via Black Swan Alley. It looked different from the way he remembered it, and he asked a passer-by about it; the man told him that two years earlier a fire had destroyed some of the buildings. As a result Audun couldn't identify exactly where his grandfather's studio had been, but he could still recall the smell of the paint in the room and watching his grandfather concentrating on his next masterpiece.

From the alley, Audun retraced his steps and paused again outside the small house in Mill Street. He wondered if Hilda and Raynal were still living in some other part of Tamin. He could still see the fright in Arin's face as his grandfather hugged Ragna and then turned to shake his own hand. As he walked out through the southern gate, Audun could remember it all as if it had happened yesterday; his confusion as to why he and his mother were fleeing from home, the journey to Tufle and the onward travel to his new home in Boretar. Of course, now he knew the reason, and it was time to plan his revenge.

Returning to the port, Audun passed by the large carrack flying the Kermin colours from its masts. A quick enquiry of a dockhand confirmed his suspicions; this was his father's flagship.

Audun of course had no way of knowing that two of the targets for his revenge were sitting high above him in the castle turret. Alberon was about to start the discussion, but before he could begin Bertalan held up a mailed hand. "As I have said, Amina is ready to resume hostilities, and my information tells me that Kermin is not. You started this silly adventure with your lust for power and empire. Conversely I am King of Amina and I have no desire to conquer Kermin, although I'm sure that if I issued the order my army could be at Mora's gates in a few days, together with my cannons."

Alberon was about to respond to this clear threat, but again Bertalan acted first. Taking off the mailed glove, he slammed it onto the table. "In case you are thinking I am making an idle threat, consider it a promise. With the blockade still in place, your people will continue to starve and your army have no weapons to resist if I bring my cannons forward."

Bertalan stood up with his chain mail clanking, amplifying the threat. He walked over to a nearby shelf and picked up a sheaf of papers, slowly placing these down beside the glove. "These are the treaties we didn't sign two years ago, the versions carried here by the Duke of Aramin bearing your seal and signature. I may be prepared to sign them now, but only if you accept my additional conditions."

Alberon was somewhat flustered by his brother-in-law's aggression, and his response was weaker than he would have liked. "We are not entirely helpless, Bertalan," he said. "The Doran cavalry are returning to the front from Iskala and should by now be riding on the Kermin plain. I have spoken with the master of the *Erth*, and he is willing to fly the Kermin flag again and break the blockade."

Bertalan stood and looked out over to the port. "I have spoken several times to Master Rondon and I doubt he will risk his ship again when faced with the caravels and their cannons. I also note that the Kermin flag is flying on the *Erth* subservient to the Amina flag, as is appropriate. Finally, in the unlikely situation that my land forces could be held back, I would simply instruct the *Warrior* and *Destroyer* to sail up the Morel and use their falconets against the city walls and any defenders. Brother, I control the land and I control the sea. I know you are only here because you have run out of options."

It was too much. Alberon lost control of his temper and shouted, "I am the Emperor and you will treat me as such. I demand your respect!"

Bertalan smiled. "Of course you do my Lord Emperor, and I am duly reprimanded. Now let's talk about reality shall we?" Moving back across the room, he pulled a single sheet of paper from the shelf. This he passed to his brother-in-law. "I will leave you time to consider your response. We will meet again tomorrow to agree the terms." With that, he rose and left the room.

Alberon was again caught off balance. Had he got it wrong when Bertalan had said they would stay locked in the tower until they came to mutual agreement? Clearly mutual agreement was not what the King of Amina had in mind. He was issuing his demands, his retribution.

Some time later, Ereldon arrived with food and wine. Alberon paid it the same amount of attention as he had to Bertalan's demands – none.

Meanwhile Audun was back in his cabin on the *Swan*, holding an old letter and a book of poems. Setting both in front of him on his table, he took up the goose quill and started copying the words. In truth he did not need the originals in front of him, as the words of both were etched on his soul. The old letter was faded, but it still clearly held the eagle seal of the royal family of Kermin. The book of poems had been recently printed and he had purchased it from the library in Aldene on his previous visit.

Having completed his writing, he tied up the letter, finishing it with a candlewax seal, left the *Swan* and walked along the dock to the Emperor's flagship. A richly-dressed boy of about ten years old was playing with a ball on the dock next to the *Eagle*. Audun called him over and asked, "Are you with the crew of this ship?"

The boy pulled himself proudly to his full height. "No, I am not with the crew. I am here with my father, the Emperor."

Audun suddenly felt a flood of conflicting emotions. So this was one of his stepbrothers, he guessed the elder, and if he remembered correctly the boy's name was Aaron. Should he hate this boy as he hated the father? It would only take a moment to push the lad over the edge of the dock and no one would notice. However this was his brother, and Audun knew Aaron could not be held guilty for his father's sins.

In a moment of confusion, Audun passed over the sealed roll of paper. "Please make sure to deliver this letter to our father when he returns."

The boy was polite. "Yes sir, I will take it now and place it in his cabin."

Audun returned to the *Swan* in a state of shock and confusion. He had just spoken with his stepbrother, and he shuddered for a second when he remembered what he had considered doing to the boy. Still, he knew he could not let emotion subsume his plans.

Back in his cabin, he remembered the previous night and the dreams that were filled with the red fire: *"The power is yours now. We will return to Mora and you will have your revenge."* Was his time for waiting over?

Going to his locker, Audun lifted out the casket. The dull red discs on the outside appeared to be darkly glowing, but maybe it was just a trick of the light. He opened the casket and lifted off the red linen cloth covering the stone. Then he took a step back. The dull red rock seemed to be in a state of metamorphosis. The bottom half of the stone had remained unchanged and was still a rough piece of red rock, but the upper hemisphere had become smooth and unblemished; the dome was now a deep red mirror that reflected the sunlight coming in through the cabin window.

As Audun stepped closer, he could see the flashes of amber that made the dome appear alive – alive with power. The *Swan* was due to sail for Boretar in the morning, but Audun wondered if this was a message that it was now time to go to Mora.

Eventually Alberon stirred himself and picked up the piece of paper that outlined Bertalan's demands. The Amina King did not waste paper on flowery words. The list came straight to the point.

To agree to a cessation in hostilities and the signing of the treaties drafted in 1506, Amina demands the following from Kermin:

1) *The Kermin Alol has, for centuries, been nominally Amina territory but practically the land has been shared between Amina and Kermin with no formal border. Kermin will agree to formally cede these lands to Amina and the new border between the countries will be set on the Kermin Plain five miles north of the Kermin Alol.*

2) *In compensation for the Amina lives lost in the battle in the Alol in 1507, Kermin will pay a fine of three wagon loads of gold. This is to be delivered to Tamin by the end of August 1508 and the treaties will only be formally adopted once this compensation is paid.*

3) *Kermin will agree not to rearm with cannons imported from Ackar until 1513.*

4) *Doran forces will be instructed to return to Iskala and remain in their Doran homelands until the summer of 1510.*

5) *Aaron, son of the King of Kermin and nephew of the King of Amina, is currently the proposed heir to the throne of Amina. To ensure that the future king is fully educated in the customs of his future kingdom he will remain in Tamin until he reaches*

the age of fifteen. Edin, the Duke of Aramin will also remain in Tamin to tutor and mentor the boy.

6) *In an alteration to the 1506 treaties, Prince Aaron will not inherit the throne of Amina until he reaches his twenty-first birthday. If required the Duke of Amina and Queen Aisha will hold regency until the Prince comes of age.*

7) *The self-titled Emperor of the North will agree that Amina is a separate kingdom and will never be incorporated into the so-called Empire by force.*

If the King of Kermin agrees to these demands by countersigning this document, then Amina will agree a cessation of hostilities and a withdrawal of the blockades until the end of August 1508, when the full treaties can be further modified, ratified and signed.

Alongside the grey wolf seal of Amina, the document was signed 'Bertalan, King of Amina'.

Alberon read the document again, more carefully. The demands were preposterous, and not at all in line with what he was prepared to agree with. He screwed the paper into a ball and was about to throw it into the fire when he paused and asked himself a question: what *was* he prepared to agree to?

Straightening out the sheet, he read it again, slowly considering each demand independently. Gradually it dawned on him that his brother-in-law was not as clever as it first appeared. The Kermin Alol was already under Amina control, and Bertalan's cannons were already positioned more than five miles into the Kermin Plain, so agreeing to clause one would actually result in a short withdrawal of the Amina forces. The demand for the gold was a high price, but with access to the seams of the precious metal in the Doran Mountains, it could be met.

Clause three caused Alberon to smile. In 1507, as war became increasingly inevitable, he had sent a small contingent of Kermin master craftsmen to Ackar to learn how to forge and assemble cannons. He would have no need to import them, as once the blockade was removed the smiths could return to their forges in Kermin and he would build his own cannons and so avoid the condition in this clause. Ordering the Doran forces back to Iskala would leave his ground forces depleted, but now that Alberon knew there was a pass through the mountains that would be open most of the year this clause could be ignored.

Clauses five and six were the most difficult. Sylva would be furious to learn that her ten-year-old son was to be held, effectively as a hostage, in Tamin for five years. Alberon hoped that Bertalan had no knowledge of Aaron's presence on the *Eagle*. He was less concerned about his cousin; Edin had been a disappointment and would not be missed. Indeed Alberon wondered if the Duke had committed treachery by divulging too much information to Bertalan during the past few weeks while he had been held in Tamin. It then occurred to Alberon that clause six was also weak, as it extended the time before Aaron could come to the throne of Amina but it ignored the existence of the younger son, Elrik.

As for clause seven, well that was just words; Amina would one day be part of the Empire, through force of arms or through one of his son's inheritance. Alberon read the list of demands once more. Then he screwed the paper up and threw it into the centre of the fire.

The next day followed the same routine. After being woken early, Alberon was escorted by Ereldon back up to the turret room and again left to wait. He was feeling miserable; he was fed up of wearing the clothes of a penitent, tired of being kept waiting again and pessimistic that he would be able to negotiate any better conditions with his brother-in-law.

With nothing else to do, he pulled one of the seats away from the table and sat himself at the window that looked out over Tamin. In the distance he spotted white sails filling with the wind as what looked to be a caravel headed out to sea. He wished he could be back on the

Eagle with the winds hastening him home to the comfort of his own castle in Mora.

There was no way the Emperor could know, but the captain of that caravel had spent a sleepless night considering his options. Twice during the night Audun had gone to look into the casket and found that the stone's metamorphosis appeared to have stopped or slowed. Even the amber sparks in the smooth upper hemisphere appeared to have died down. Audun considered his two options: a return to Boretar with the cargo as planned, or a detour via Mora. With the image of his father's face in his mind and the memories of the pain this man, and the Amina king, had caused his family, his emotions were driving him towards the Mora option. However, he was well aware of the blockade and the caravels that patrolled the entrance to the Morel. For now, Boretar was the sensible and safe destination, but Mora would be where he would seek his revenge.

Lost in thought, Alberon was startled when the door to the tower room was abruptly unlocked and opened. The Amina king stepped into the room, this time without the chain mail but still clad in his surcoat. For a brief moment Alberon imagined the grey wolf coming to life and attacking him.

Bertalan spoke before taking his seat at the table. "Well brother, I assume my conditions have been consumed to ash in the fire, so I have brought another copy. I had hoped that the brooch you are wearing on your chest indicated that you were prepared to rebuild our friendship and the friendship between our nations. Maybe I was wrong."

Alberon concealed a smile; maybe it had been a good idea to wear the wedding present after all.

"I came here to negotiate a peace between our lands, not to receive a list of outrageous demands," growled Alberon.

Bertalan could not resist a jibe. "You came here dressed as a penitent and a pilgrim, not as a king wanting to negotiate," he retorted. He succeeded in making Alberon lose his temper. Rising from his seat at the window, the Emperor pushed his chair over and advanced on his brother-in-law with dagger drawn, clearly bent on ending this charade here and now.

Bertalan remained sitting, unperturbed. "A dagger once again Alberon, and again, not a good idea. You need to learn to control your temper. I am unarmed and no doubt you could murder me, but what then? You would spend the rest of your life in one of Tamin's dungeons, and your son would join you. My sister would not be pleased that you had killed her brother, yet she would come to plead mercy for you. It would not be forthcoming. Aisha and Silson have their instructions.

I may be unarmed, but I am still the power here. Put that puny thing away. Pick up the chair and sit down before I change my mind and order my forces to march on Mora."

Alberon had no response other than his anger. He raised his hand high and drove the dagger point first into the table. Bertalan calmly extracted it, tossed it in the air and caught it by the tip, then passed it handle first back to Alberon.

"Sit brother, it is time to get to the details of the peace treaties and those "outrageous" demands, as you call them."

It took Alberon a moment to process Bertalan's words: "And your son will join you." Did the King somehow know that Aaron was already close by on the *Eagle*?

The two men remained closeted in the turret room for the rest of the day. Alberon pressed hard for a relaxation in Bertalan's seven conditions. He argued that the Kermin Alol was the main trade route between the countries and could not be wholly ceded to Amina. The amount of gold that Bertalan was demanding was way beyond what was held in the treasury in Mora. To try to gain some advantage, he agreed to the clauses related to the cannon and the Doran forces but issued his own demand that the Amina army had to withdraw from the Kermin Plain and the Alol.

So it went on, with Alberon trying to extract more favourable terms and Bertalan remaining unyielding.

Dusk was beginning to cast shadows in the room, and neither man had mentioned the young prince who was heir to both thrones.

Finally Alberon moved to these clauses. "It is impossible for me to agree to the clauses that involve my son, particularly the fifth. Sylva will never agree to me transporting Aaron here to be held as your prisoner for the next five years."

Bertalan smiled, and Alberon felt a shiver of unease. "It will not be necessary for you to ask my sister for her permission. I could simply send Bartos and a troop of my guard to the *Eagle* and Aaron would be settled in his rooms here by morning."

Alberon was stunned. This was not his plan, and he tried to bluff his way out of it. "That's ridiculous! Why would I drag my son all the way here for no reason?"

Bertalan smiled again. "I have trusted men who monitor all the comings and goings in Tufle. They report that a very richly-dressed boy of about ten plays every day on the deck of the *Eagle* and on the adjacent dockside. When the ship arrived in Tufle, the same boy was observed walking hand in hand with you along the deck as you pointed out some of the landmarks. I presume you did not pick up some orphan as you left Mora and give him your clothes in exchange for his?"

Alberon now deeply regretted his decision to wear the grey tunic and black cloak. Instead of showing his repentance, it had made him look like a soft-headed fool.

"This is just nonsense! My son is at home in Mora and the boy on the deck is Aracir's son."

Bertalan looked straight into Alberon's eyes. "Of course he is, but let's just assume for the sake of argument that Aaron is pretending to be Aracir's son. If that is so I think you should invite him to the signing of the treaties, assuming we can get to that point. At this moment Aaron is heir to both our thrones, and I will require him to countersign the treaties alongside both our seals. In that way we ensure that the treaties bind our nations through to the next generation."

Alberon was staggered. Had Bertalan read his mind, or had someone informed him?

Bertalan continued, "It's getting late and I'm tired of debate. Tomorrow Bartos and a troop of guardsmen will escort you back to the *Eagle.* I will then consider my conditions and your requests and decide if I am prepared to be a little bit more lenient. I'll send Ereldon to you with revised documents tomorrow afternoon and you can consider your position. On the sixth of the month, Bartos will escort Aracir here to deliver your response. The treaties will all be dated the seventh of May, the day when we will formally sign the documents, if we have reached agreement. That should give you a few days to brief Aracir's son on his role in the proceedings."

With that Bertalan departed, leaving Alberon alone with his thoughts. The Emperor sat in the gathering darkness for another hour racking his brain and searching for alternative solutions or different strategies, but none came to mind.

The next morning Alberon was escorted to a guest room in the centre of the castle. He was relieved to see that Bertalan had supplied him with fresh clothes, and although the green of the doublet and hose was not a colour he would have chosen, anything was better than the grey he had been wearing for so long. Bertalan had also left another less subtle message; the jerkin was made from grey wolfskin.

Refreshed and dressed more like a king, Alberon waited for Bartos. This time he was not kept long and the captain entered the room with a slight bow to the Emperor. "Sire, it is time we moved you back to Tufle. We will be accompanied by a contingent of troopers to ensure that there is no repeat of the scenes when you arrived here in Tamin. Half the troop will stay at the dock close to the *Eagle* to ensure there are no protests there. Unfortunately the people of Amina have no love for you, my Lord."

Alberon grunted. "Let's get on with it then, captain." He doubted if the move was for his protection; rather it was to ensure that he did not decide to pack up and sail away.

The troop reached Tufle and the *Eagle* without incident. On the short journey Alberon enjoyed the wind blowing in his hair and the smell of the salty air.

He had not realised how imprisoned he had felt during his time in Tamin Castle's turret.

Immediately upon boarding the *Eagle*, he called for Aracir to join him in his cabin to discuss Bertalan's conditions. Sitting at his desk, the first thing he noticed was a rolled-up scroll of paper with a candlewax seal.

At that moment Aracir entered the cabin. "Do you know what is in this letter, Chancellor?" Alberon asked.

"No sire, I have not been in your cabin since you left for Tamin."

Alberon shrugged. "It is probably of no importance then." He pushed the scroll to the side of the desk. "Sit Aracir, we have much to discuss and decide." He began to brief Aracir on the discussions of the previous two days. On hearing the conditions that had been demanded by the King of Amina, Aracir shook his head. "Three wagons of gold by August? That is impossible. It would empty the treasury, and although the gold in the mines in the Doran Mountains is yours by right, as a result of the blockades we have no means of paying the miners."

The gold mines had been owned by the crown for decades, but the miners were not slaves. Each miner was paid a small portion of the gold he collected and an equal weight in supplies of food, clothes and wine. Alberon waved his Chancellor's concern aside. "Aracir, you rightly worry about the finances, but I am more worried about the condition demanded regarding my son. I cannot return to Mora and leave Aaron here. As for the gold, well, the miners will have to work harder, and if necessary we will deploy troops to ensure they deliver what we need."

Aracir did of course know why Aaron had been brought on the journey. "I thought the boy was brought here to countersign the treaties?" he said. "That is surely what you wanted. And as for the gold, turning the miners into slaves could have the opposite effect and cause some sort of rebellion."

Alberon's temper flared. "My son is here for a specific reason, and it is not to be incarcerated in Tamin Castle for the next five years."

The discussion was interrupted by a knock at the cabin door and Lord Ereldon entered. "My Lords, I am here to deliver a revised version of my king's demands and a copy of the original 1506 treaties modified to incorporate these demands," he said, his tone formal as always. Without another word Ereldon turned and left.

For the next two hours Alberon and Aracir studied the papers. Bertalan had relaxed some of his demands. A reduction to two wagons of gold placated Aracir somewhat. Aaron would only be required to reside in Tamin for three years but could return to Mora for a few weeks each summer, and the Amina border would now be at the northern end of the Kermin Alol and not on the Kermin Plain. In other places the demands had been strengthened. Elrik was now included in clause six, and clause seven was more severe: Alberon would agree to relinquish the title of Emperor and return to being titled King of Doran and Kermin.

It was early evening when Alberon held up his hand. "I am tired of reading this set of impudent demands. I need to sleep on it; we will meet again in the morning to agree our response."

Alberon would get little sleep that night, but not for any reason he could have anticipated.

As he moved the treaty documents to the side of the desk he knocked over the scroll of paper he had noticed earlier in the day. He was tempted to leave it on the floor as it was getting late, but piqued by his curiosity, he picked it up and broke open the seal. The package contained three sheets of paper, and he rolled them out to read them. The first page was a poem that he had long since forgotten about:

We met in the north on a spring day
I am sure now it was our destiny
Tender moments in the Nath
With the sand at our backs
Somehow fate set our path
A love that would last
Now in our winter years
Smile, Elbeth my love
Shed no tears
White gold our rings

United we were
United we will always be
My love for you
Is for all of eternity.

The next sheet was a copy of a letter he had never seen before.

At our command the maid and her child are permanently banished from the Kingdoms of Kermin and Doran. Whilst our law is clear that a child born out of wedlock is the responsibility of the father, our law is also clear that if the mother used sorcery to bewitch the father then both mother and child will be sentenced to death. We have proof that the maid used potions and spells to bewitch our son. Prince Alberon has provided the evidence to support this claim. Whilst the death sentence was in our power to command, the Prince has pleaded for mercy. Reluctantly we have heard the Prince's plea and decided to be lenient. However if the maid or her child is apprehended anywhere within our territories the maid will be condemned as a witch and her child a sorcerer. The penalty for witchcraft is death.

King Elrik and Queen Ingrid, Regents of Kermin.

The third sheet contained only one word: "*REVENGE*".

By now Alberon was shaking. He had long ago forgotten about his young lover and her unborn child. Sylva's angry words of eight years ago suddenly came to mind: "I suppose you thought you would explain yourself when a bastard usurper arrived with an army at the castle gates." The girl's child would now be a grown man, assuming he still lived, but surely it was not possible that he could threaten to take the throne.

Alberon had a disturbed night. Sylva's words kept coming to mind, and his restless dreams were again filled with images of the fury of the crowds in both Mora and Tamin. Increasingly at the front of the mob he saw the young man with the ice-blue eyes. In waking moments he tried to recall the detail of the man's face, but he could not see beyond the eyes, so much like his own. Then, for some reason, Alberon remembered the face and the smile and the words that almost seemed to be delivered in a whisper: *"One day I will come for you Alberon, and I will have my revenge."* Was it possible?

CHAPTER NINETEEN

Two Sons, Two Stories

❖ ❖ ❖ ❖

The next morning Alberon called Aracir to his cabin. He held up the scroll, which he had now resealed. "Where did this come from? I need to know."

Aracir was at a loss. "I have no idea, sire. To my knowledge no one has left the ship or boarded it since your departure for the city. Why, is it important information?"

Clearly Alberon could not divulge the contents of the letter, but he needed to know how it had been delivered. "Someone must have had access to my cabin and someone else must have been on the dock to receive the letter," he barked.

Aracir paused for a moment to think. "The only person who has been on shore is your son. He sometimes plays there with his ball."

Alberon asked Aracir to fetch Aaron and then to leave him alone with his son. Once the cabin door was closed, Alberon turned to the boy. "Aaron, do you recognise this?"

The boy nodded. "Yes father, the captain of a ship docked nearby asked me to deliver it to you."

Alberon knew his son had done nothing wrong, but he could not help but raise his voice. "When was this delivered? What was he like? What did he say? Tell me!"

Aaron took a step back, frightened by his father's anger, but he was the son of a king and straightened himself as he replied. "He was nice, father. It was yesterday or maybe the day before. He kicked the ball with me for a minute, and then asked me if I was one of the crew. I told him I was not and that I was your son. He then asked me to take the letter and leave it for you."

Alberon tried not to show his anger and concern. "What exactly did he say, my boy?"

Aaron struggled to recall the other man's words. "Father, I can't remember exactly, he just said 'please deliver this letter to your father for me'. He paused, trying hard to recall the exact words, and then he remembered. "Yes, I remember, and I thought it slightly strange at the time. His exact words were, 'please deliver this letter to our father for me'."

It was Alberon's turn to step back. "Describe him to me, particularly his face."

Aaron suddenly realised what he had just said and asked the obvious question. "Why did the man say 'our father'? Is the man somehow my brother? He seemed nice and kind."

Alberon was flustered. He faltered over his reply. "It was probably just a mistake… or maybe you misheard. Your only brother, Elrik, is at home in Mora. Now please describe the man to me."

Aaron tried his best. He remembered particularly the blue eyes, and that was good enough. The face Aaron described was almost exactly the same as the face in Alberon's dreams. Alberon could now visualise the man mouthing the words, 'One day I will come for you Alberon and I will have my revenge'. He must indeed be his own illegitimate son. It still seemed impossible, or at least very unlikely, but no one else could know this past or have such evidence of it.

He asked Aaron to return to his games, and was left alone. He needed time to think and to try to remember.

He reopened the scroll and re-read the second page. He remembered that this was how his parents had justified the banishment of the maid, but he had no memory of potions or witchcraft. He did remember being furious with his parents. He tried to cast his mind back, and flustered as he was, memories returned in snippets. The maid had been his first lover and she was very pretty, but what was her name?

Out of respect for his mother's memory, Audun had felt compelled to omit Ragna's name when he copied this sheet from the original version. Alberon remembered being besotted by the maid. He had been in love for the first time, he remembered the poem, but her name eluded him.

Closing his eyes, Alberon tried to journey back in time. Long auburn hair and a hint of rose perfume triggered memory, but not a name. Then he remembered her promise, that if the child was a boy she would name him Audun. In memory, one name connected with another; Ragna, his mother's maid. Was this really possible, the past coming back to seek revenge?

Alberon called some of the *Eagle*'s crew to his cabin. The men were wary about an order to meet with the Emperor, but he quickly came to the point.

"Do any of you know a ship's captain called Audun? It is possible that his ship was moored here in the port until yesterday."

The men were all sailors and they knew many of their brothers who travelled back and forth across the seas. Yes, many of them knew Audun, the captain of the caravel the *Swan*, whose home port was Boretar. Some could confirm that she had left Tufle on the high tide the day before. Alberon remembered watching a caravel's sails billowing in the wind as he looked out from the turret room in Tamin. Had that been his son Audun, departing for another port? When would he set sail for Mora, and with what intent?

Again he was left alone, and ignoring the Amina treaties he pondered this new threat. Reading the Regent's letter once more, he smiled. Presumably unwittingly, his son had provided him with a solution. If Audun were to set foot in Kermin or Doran, then the letter would be the evidence. It could prove that he had been born of a witch and by definition was himself a sorcerer. The sentence would be death.

Alberon stowed the scroll in the box with his private papers and went back to the Amina treaties.

It was mid-afternoon when Aracir knocked on the cabin door. "My Lord, it is time to send our response to Bertalan," he said. "Bartos is waiting to escort me to the city."

Alberon rose from his seat and passed the treaties to Aracir. "I think this is the best we will get. Please tell my brother-in-law that I will sign the treaties as written, including his demands, but also tell him that I expect a royal reception when I arrive in Tamin tomorrow. I want no repeat of the outrage of my reception of a few days ago. And Aracir, as you leave, please ask Aaron to join me here." It was time for Alberon to tell his son about the role he would need to play the next day and the consequences. He hoped that Aaron would not ask any further questions about the letter.

As was fitting for pomp and ceremony, the seventh of May dawned bright and clear. Bertalan decided to overplay Alberon's request, and the Amina King and Queen Aisha rode into Tufle's port with a full cohort of mounted guardsmen. At the head of the troop, riders carried the striped flag of Amina alongside the four golden stars of the Kermin flag. Bertalan also decided to reverse the welcome he had received in Mora two years earlier, and whilst the two horses draped in Kermin livery were fine beasts, they were noticeably smaller than the steeds on which Bertalan and his Queen were mounted.

Alberon was again showing his mastery of subtle innuendo. He wore doublet and hose embroidered in gold thread, but over the doublet he had retained the wolfskin jerkin and over the jerkin his fur-trimmed red cloak was embroidered with a golden eagle in full flight. When Alberon mounted his horse and the sea breeze caught the cloak, it did indeed appear as if the eagle was taking wing and flying proudly over the grey wolf. Bertalan noted the imagery and frowned.

As the entourage turned to return to Tamin, Aaron was mounted next to his aunt. The boy was excited to be part of such pageantry and was talking endlessly with

Aisha. In front of these two, Bertalan and Alberon rode side by side in silence.

Aracir and Ereldon were at Tamin's city gates to greet the royal party. The two chancellors had been working on the final details of the treaties. As the royal party rode up through the city towards the castle, the crowds on the sides of the road were cheering. Alberon thought this excitement was all for their king, who they considered the victor. Irrationally, he scanned the faces in the crowd, searching for one in particular, although he knew that face would now be somewhere on the island of Andore, Thos or possibly back home in Boretar. He knew that when he returned to Mora he would need to send someone to Boretar to learn more about this Captain Audun.

Once inside the castle, the two chancellors and the kings made their way to the council chamber to prepare for the formal signing of the treaties. Aaron was taken to his quarters by his aunt. Alberon had told him that he would be staying in Tamin for a while after the *Eagle* sailed for Mora, but he did not explain how long the boy would remain with his aunt and uncle. Aaron was pleased. The rooms were spacious and certainly suitable for a prince.

As he was exploring, Edin entered the room and greeted his cousin. Aaron liked the Duke and was happy that he would stay in Tamin as his mentor. Edin was fun and not like the other stuffy old nobles in Alberon's court back in Mora.

Whilst one son was familiarising himself with his new surroundings, the other was in his cabin on the *Swan*, which was indeed now moored in the port of Thos. As the cargo was unloaded Audun left the overseeing of this to Vasilli, his first mate. Locked in his cabin, Audun lifted the casket with the red discs onto his table and was sitting as if mesmerised, staring at the contents. The red stone remained in some state of transformation, the upper half a perfect red orb and the lower half rough red stone. Clearly Oien, if indeed it was the alchemist's essence encapsulated in the stone, did not think the time was right to reignite the power and thereby help Audun fulfil his vows. However, Audun realised that his actions at Tufle, which he now thought might have been premature, must have started events moving. His father would now know of his existence and his desire for revenge. It was quite likely that the Emperor also knew his name and the identity of his ship. Audun regretted saying "our father" rather than "your father" when he had passed his letter to Aaron, but that could not be helped now.

He stared hopefully at the stone, again but it remained silent and unchanging. What was the next step of his plan? What should his next actions be? If the treaties, which were rumoured to be why his father was in Tamin, were signed, then presumably the blockade at the Morel would be lifted and he could take the *Swan* to Mora. He could easily alter the outbound cargo for the new destination. That seemed the most sensible next step towards taking him closer to the target for his revenge.

Just as Audun felt he had made his decision, the upper hemisphere of the orb glowed and disembodied words echoed in his head. *"It is too soon Audun; for now you must return to Boretar. You acted hastily and not wisely. Read the last lines of the letter."* The instruction was clear. He rummaged through his belongings to find the letter and instantly the message made sense: *"However, if the maid or her child is apprehended anywhere within our territories the maid will be condemned as a witch and her child a sorcerer. The penalty for witchcraft is death."* Audun realised that he had divulged his identity and occupation too soon. If, or more likely when, he returned to Mora, it would need to be incognito.

Aracir and Ereldon had finessed the treaties and the two kings now had to agree to the final changes. There were not many. The two wagons filled with gold were to be delivered to Tamin a month apart, the first by the end of August and the second by the end of September. Aaron would stay in Tamin for eight months each year, but he would be allowed to spend one month at home every quarter. Elrik was also to learn Amina's customs and join his brother for three months each spring. The boundary between the two countries would remain at the northern end of the Kermin Alol, but Kermin would agree that it would not engage in any military activity within ten miles of the border. Goods coming through the Alol from Kermin would be subjected to tariffs, and so it went on. Alberon was getting bored.

"Enough!" he said to Bertalan. "Let's just get on with it and sign these damn things. However, before I do, I have one last demand. If my sons are to be kept here and schooled in Amina's customs, then it is only right that they are publicly proclaimed as heirs to the Amina throne."

Bertalan nodded. "That is acceptable, and I have one last gift for you, brother. As we speak, the *Erth* is being loaded with supplies for the people of Mora, food, grain, seeds and other necessities. This was a particular request from my sister, and I am happy to oblige. Rondon will also carry a message to the *Warrior* to instruct the gunships to relax the blockade, although they will remain on patrol in case you decide to renege on any of our agreements. In addition, once the *Erth* has unloaded its cargo you will allow any members of the crew's families who wish it to join the ship and return here. For now the *Erth* will continue to fly the Amina flag."

"So be it, now let's get on with it," replied Alberon. This last 'gift' caused Alberon a moment's thought. If his wife had somehow been in contact with her brother, then what else had she divulged to him?

The grand hall in Tamin Castle was decorated for a large gathering. On one side of the hall were the multiple emblems of Amina, and on the opposite side the flag and motifs of Kermin. Rather incongruously, the only furniture in the hall was a single table with four seats on the Amina side and two on the Kermin side. A single chair was positioned at the head of the table. In the centre of the table lay the paperwork, the treaties. Bertalan, Silson and Ereldon were already seated on the Amina side of the table, while Alberon and Aracir sat opposite.

They had only been there a few minutes when Aisha led Aaron into the room. The boy was motioned to his seat, symbolically at the head of the table, whilst his aunt took the empty chair on the Amina side. Aaron felt somewhat overwhelmed, but he was a prince, his father's son, and he had to act as such.

The treaties moved back and forth across the table as Alberon, Bertalan and the chancellors signed various pages beside their individual seals. It was only the final page that Aaron had to countersign. The papers were passed to him and he paused with quill in hand. "Father, Uncle, I am not sure it is right for me to sign these agreements without having had the opportunity to read the documents," he said.

Both kings hid their smiles; Sylva had clearly trained the boy well in the art of politics. Bertalan was first to react. "Aaron, you are wise for your age, but I know your father has already explained to you what is written in the treaties. The commitments made in the documents are between Amina and Kermin in the names of your father and me. Your countersignature is simply a confirmation that you will broadly comply with the terms when you inherit either of our thrones. I will ensure that copies of all the documents are sent to your rooms so that you can review them at your leisure. Should you disagree in any way with the contents, then your father and I will consider your requested revisions." So with that, Amina and Kermin were once more at peace, at least for now.

It was a time for farewells, and Aaron was trying to be brave. He and Alberon had ridden back to the *Eagle* the evening after the treaties had been signed. Bertalan had agreed that the boy could return to the ship, but had insisted Aracir remain in Tamin until his nephew returned to the city. The *Eagle* would remain at dock in Tufle until the *Erth's* cargo was fully loaded. The date for departure was set for the tenth of May, and that day had come. Bertalan had decided to make the most of the public declaration that Aaron was to formally become heir to the Amina throne, and had declared the day a holiday.

It was a proud and richly dressed entourage that rode onto Tufle's dock that morning. Aracir rode between the Amina king and his Queen. At the dockside the Chancellor dismounted and handed the reins of his magnificent horse over to Alberon. The crowd cheered as Alberon lifted Aaron up and onto the saddle. Bertalan clasped Aaron's hand and then turned his horse round and led the party back towards the city.

It occurred to Alberon that his son was positioned as though he was truly the son of the royal family. He was slightly irritated that the crowds cheered again as the party rode past, remembering the jeering reception he had received on his journey to the city only ten days earlier. Still, he had work to do to prepare his own capital for his return. Back in his cabin he wrote a short note and after collecting the pigeon from its cage he tied the letter to the bird's foot and let it fly. The avian messenger should reach Holger a few days before the *Eagle* reached port in Mora.

The *Eagle* and the *Erth* left Tufle together, and once the ships reached the Middle Sea, the *Erth* took the lead. Rondon had orders from Bertalan for John Sexton, and he also had his own instructions to deliver. These were to ensure the *Erth* would make a safe return from Mora.

Two days later the *Warrior* appeared just north of the two ships. Sexton boarded the *Erth* and shook hands with the Captain. "Well Rondon, this is a surprise. Are you going home at last?"

Rondon explained what had happened at Tufle and passed Sexton the King's orders. Bertalan's note was short and to the point: *"The Warrior will allow passage to the Morel for both the Erth and the Eagle. Once the cargo on the Erth has been unloaded at Mora, Rondon has been instructed to bring the families of the Erth's crew on board and return with them to Tufle. The families are to be relocated in the Amina port and the Erth will continue to sail under the Amina flag. Once the Erth has returned to the mouth of the Morel, the Warrior and the Destroyer are to relax the blockade but remain on station until peace is secure. The gunboats will carry out random checks on foreign ships entering the Morel to ensure that no weapons are being imported to Kermin."*

Sexton shared these instructions with Rondon, who replied, "Lord Ereldon has given me similar instructions, but with one additional order that could not be written down. If I have not returned here by the seventeenth of May you are to take the *Warrior* up the Morel and point the cannon at the city."

Sexton looked somewhat surprised, as he could not see how a weapon mounted at the prow of the ship could threaten a city. He replied, "I hope your families are delighted to see you and your men again. I will look out for you returning south in five days' time."

As the *Warrior* pulled away, Alberon again wondered how Bertalan had thought of putting a cannon on board a ship. The *Eagle* and the *Erth* set off north, turning towards the Morel.

The carrier pigeon reached Mora Castle two days before the *Eagle* was expected. Holger released the message taped to the bird's foot: *"The treaties are signed; you know what I now need you to do"*. Holger did know and was prepared.

The next morning guardsmen went through the city pinning posters to trees and houses in the squares and main streets. Citizens gathered to read the notice from their Emperor. By using that title Alberon had already broken one of the terms of the treaties, although he had not known the clause would be incorporated in the treaties when he had left Holger his instructions.

The poster read: *"Your Emperor is returning home having negotiated favourable peace terms with the King of Amina. Hostilities between our two countries are now at an end. I have been magnanimous with my brother-in-law, forgiving him for allowing his army to invade Kermin. In return King Bertalan has agreed to lift the blockade at the mouth of the Morel and normal trade routes will be open to our merchant ships. The forces in the Kermin Alol will stand down and the overland route from Mora to Tamin will once more allow free passage for trade between our countries. I know it has been a hard twelve months for my people and I thank you for your bravery and stoicism through these difficult times. Now is the time to recover and rebuild"*.

Wisely, as it turned out, Alberon had decided to sign the poster *"Alberon, King of Kermin and Doran"*. He intended the poster to show his people that he was still fully in control of the country's destiny and, despite its humiliating defeat in the war, Kermin remained powerful. He knew that when Bertalan heard about the posters the Amina King would be angry, but Alberon thought he could easily apologise, correctly claiming the posters had been displayed before he had returned to Mora and had the chance to alter the wording. Holger could take the blame. Alberon also knew that he could not fool all of the people, but he did expect to fool some of them.

Two he could not fool were his mother and his wife, who discussed it in the Queen's rooms in the castle. Ingrid pointed out to Sylva that this was just propaganda ahead of Alberon's return. Sylva responded, "It may be propaganda, but it must also be lies. There is no reason for my brother to be generous in the negotiations and I doubt very much that he would be in any mood for accepting Alberon's forgiveness! Never mind, at least my son will be home tomorrow."

Early the next morning Sylva spotted masts in the distance, still some way southwest along the Morel. She called Holger and ordered him to gather a small troop of guardsmen. She would meet her son, and as an afterthought her husband, at the port.

Soren had also had instructions from his uncle to meet the Emperor on his arrival and a troop of Doran Cavalry were already forming a guard of honour on the dockside. Soren's father and uncle were still sceptical about the Emperor's forgiveness and remained with the majority of the cavalry on the Kermin Plain.

As the two ships came towards the dock, a large crowd had already gathered. This of course meant an opportunity for Raimund and Aleana to ply their trade. The *Eagle* docked first, to polite clapping from the crowd. The *Erth* followed with a more exuberant welcome, and Alberon wondered if it had been wise to bring both vessels to the port at the same time. It was too late now.

He stepped down the gangplank from the Eagle to find his wife waiting at the foot of the steps. Sylva looked behind her husband. "Where is my son? Where is Aaron?"

This was a reception Alberon had expected, and playing to the crowd, he took his wife in his arms, stepped back and gave a royal wave. The crowd's response was muted, so Sylva's words were clear: "Where is Aaron? Tell me now!"

Alberon spoke quietly so that Sylva could only just make out the words. "Now is not the time or the place my dear, I will explain when we are back in the castle. For now we need to appear as victorious leaders returned to our city."

Sylva was about to snap a furious reply when a loud cheer went up from the crowd. The *Erth* had now tied up behind the *Eagle*. At that moment Soren walked down between lines formed by the Doran cavalry, leading Alberon's favourite stallion and another fine horse. The second mount was of course meant for the absent Aaron.

Soren bowed. "Your escort is ready sire."

Alberon smiled. "So Soren, once more the messenger. I presume you will give me news of your father and uncle when I invite you to meet with me later in the castle."

Soren bowed once more. "Yes sire."

As though it had all been part of the plan, Alberon escorted his wife to the extra horse and helped her mount, then with a flourish he mounted the stallion. With a shouted order from Soren, the Doran cavalrymen pulled their mounts into position and with a clatter of hooves they led the party through the crowds and back to the castle. Behind them on the dock, Alberon heard the cheers grow louder. He presumed the crew of the *Erth* were being welcomed home. With a word in passing, Alberon had informed Holger of the *Erth*'s cargo, and what had been the Empresses' escort now closed in around the ship to ensure the precious cargo was correctly moved to the appropriate warehouses.

As soon as Sylva and Alberon were alone in their private quarters, Sylva spoke. Her voice was low, but there was steel in her green eyes.

"Now tell me why our son has not returned home. Why is he still in Tamin, or did you just accidentally lose him?"

Alberon responded with a different question which took Sylva by surprise. "Why did you send a message to your brother asking him to send relief supplies to Mora? Your request was granted and the supplies travelled with us on the *Erth*. What else did you tell him about my plans? He seemed to be always a step ahead of me in the negotiations."

Sylva was caught slightly off guard, but she was quick to retaliate. "I know nothing of messages to my brother, but I do know you seem to have lost our son." Her right hand fingered the left sleeve of her dress. Alberon knew what was hidden there and held up his hand.

"Enough! Now sit down and I will explain," he said. He outlined Bertalan's request without indicating that it was a condition of the peace treaties. "Sylva, this was actually a wise request. If our son is to become the Amina King, then he needs to be prepared and educated in their customs. Initially your brother wanted Aaron to stay in Amina for many years. I persuaded him to come to a more agreeable arrangement. Time in Tamin and time here, and you can visit him any time you want to. Now tell me, what about the supplies on the *Erth*?"

Sylva hesitated for a moment. This could be treacherous ground. "I acquired one of Master Carter's pigeons and released it as you started your journey to

Tamin. It was a simple request to my brother, asking him to consider our people, and if a treaty was agreed could he please send seeds so that we could ensure we have a harvest to gather in the autumn and grain to replenish our stores for this summer. Nothing more, no royal secrets were divulged, I promise."

To Sylva's relief and surprise, her husband smiled. "You did well Sylva. We need this summer to rebuild, restock and prepare for next year." He left the word "rearm" unsaid.

CHAPTER TWENTY

Valdin

The *Erth* departed Mora as scheduled on the morning
of the sixteenth of May. Most of the crew's families had
boarded the ship, as it seemed likely that Tufle would
be the Erth's home port for the foreseeable future. In
addition the promise of accommodation in Tufle, made
by the Amina King, seemed to offer a new start to
the families that had suffered the deprivations of the
recently-passed winter.

It was mid-afternoon when the ship left the mouth
of the Morel, and a short distance into the Eastern Sea
the *Warrior* pulled alongside. John Sexton was on the
foredeck and offered a formal salute followed by a wave.
On the *Erth* Rondon returned the salute and waited. He

had asked his fellow captain a favour when they had met five days earlier. Sexton was happy to oblige and guided the *Warrior* a short distance away from the larger ship. Intrigued, most of the families crowded onto the deck of the *Erth*.

A puff of smoke issued from the falconet at the prow of the *Warrior*, followed by a loud bang, and then three hundred yards in front of them there was a great splash as the cannonball hit the surface. There were gasps from the watchers on board the *Erth*. Rondon watched. If this was the future of warfare at sea, he might need to consider how best to arm his own ship for such a threat.

Alberon paid no heed to the departure of the *Erth*. Despite his generous pardon for Rondon and his crew, it was clear that from now on the carrack would be flying the Amina flag. One day he would repay that treachery, but for now he had other problems to deal with. Shortly after his return to Mora, he had met with Soren and instructed him to ride out to the Kermin Plain and request that his uncle return to Mora for further instructions.

While the *Erth* was pulling away from the dock in Mora, a large contingent of Doran cavalry clattered across the southern bridge and headed up the hill towards the castle. Morserat had been at the head of his cavalry unit, but he was now sitting in the council room opposite his Emperor.

Alberon opened the conversation. "Welcome Duke, you are travelling with a surprisingly large force considering we are now at peace with Amina. Have you left any men patrolling the Kermin Plain?"

Morserat shrugged. "As you say my Lord, if we are now at peace with Amina then there is little need for my men to be riding on the Plain. My captains have their instructions."

Alberon recognised the disguised threat but ignored it. "Morserat, I made a mistake last year as we prepared for war. I should have heeded your advice at that time, but what is done is now done. The transgressions of the past are forgiven and we must plan for the future. You are now my Commander in Chief and I need you to understand the details of our situation." He went on to brief the Duke on the details of the treaties. Morserat was pleased to hear that they required him to withdraw his forces back to Iskala. Alberon noted the Duke's faint smile, but he had other plans in mind.

"Duke, I need you to take a troop of Doran Cavalry into the Alol to confirm the withdrawal of the Amina forces back behind what is now the newly defined border. You will not engage with the enemy but simply make sure that the agreed terms are complied with."

Morserat noted the use of the word 'enemy'; peace might have been agreed, but clearly the Emperor was only planning a pause in hostilities.

Alberon continued, "Once you have confirmed that

they have withdrawn to the border, we will comply with the other part of the treaty and you will send the majority of the Doran Cavalry back to Iskala. You, however, will stay here in Mora and I want a division of your men to remain here in Kermin. You will have them incorporated into the Kermin cavalry divisions, ready on this side of the mountains for when I need to deploy them." As Morserat had concluded, the Emperor's peace would only last until he was rearmed and ready to mount another invasion of Amina.

In the last week of May the capital of Bala was preparing for the annual independence celebrations. Aldene was bustling with activity. Bunting flags were being draped high over the town's narrow streets, flowers adorned most house fronts and larger flags fluttered in the light breeze as they hung from upper floor windows. Many of the flags flew the diagonal blue cross with red edging on a white background, the motif of Clan Cameron. Other flags were the red cross on a yellow background, Bala's national flag.

Alastair Munro had made his annual trip back to Bala from Esimore and would lead the meeting of the Clan Elders the next day. For now, he was comfortably seated in the family rooms in the castle, listening to James Ferguson as the latter recounted some of the events that had occurred in Bala and the wider world during the past twelve months. Munro actually knew much of what happened across the world despite his relative isolation in Esimore, but this annual ritual helped the Cameron chief relax in the company of his two-hundred-year-old mentor.

Once Ferguson had finished telling his news, Munro echoed the question of twelve months earlier: "Is the stone still safe in the deep cave? Did you check as I requested?"

James Ferguson remembered the request, but he had forgotten to take any action. After all, this was ancient history, and the few times he had gone to the dungeon all he found was an old wooden box which did not seem like much of a threat. The Cameron chief shook his head. "Sorry Alastair, I did not remember to carry out your request, but what is it about a lump of dull red rock that worries you so much?"

Munro paused before responding. "James, from the history books you now know that two hundred years ago, if that "dull red rock" had succeeded, you would not be sitting here now. The white light encapsulated the power of the alchemist, but I doubt it was enough to destroy the evil that resided in the heart and soul of Oien. Remember that Oien had lived for millennia, far longer than I have, and he was patient. After the meteorite rains ended the second age, he waited more than a thousand years until he could corrupt a new ruler's power to manipulate another time of othium-fuelled destruction. The centuries of peace have been broken by the ambitions of the Emperor in Mora. A new peace may have been agreed in the south, but what I worry about is that which I know and fear. Whatever remains locked in that "lump of old rock" as you call it, maybe the alchemist's heart or his soul, then I worry that it also still retains his ambition, his hatred and the red power."

"I have not been gifted the wisdom to understand how Oien lived through the millennia except that it is related to the power of othium. However, my knowledge of the history of two hundred years ago informs my fears. The alchemist first of all needs military might that can be bent to his will. For two centuries none of the countries have built up such forces, and none have had an ambition for power and domination. The desires of the Emperor in Mora remind me too much of the aspirations of Dewar the Second in 1300. The Emperor's lust for power and his army might be the trigger Oien has been waiting for. We will go now and check that the lump of old rock remains at rest in the lower dungeon."

But when Munro and Ferguson inspected the ancient cave below the dungeons, all they found was an old wooden box. The casket containing the red stone had gone.

The cycle of the seasons carried on as ever, regardless of the hopes and fears of the people. As the summer of 1508 moved on to the autumn and then to winter, normality gradually returned to Kermin and Amina. The conditions set in the May treaties were largely complied with. The wagons filled with gold from the mines in the Doran Mountains trundled through the Kermin Alol in August and September, protected on both occasions by a large force of Doran cavalry. Morserat led both convoys, and when the August payment arrived and Bertalan challenged him, the Duke persuaded the King that the Doran troops were only present due to the need to have elite soldiers escort the gold, and this was not intended as a break of the conditions written in the treaties.

Sylva travelled regularly to Tamin, often with her younger son Elrik, who also began to learn about Amina's customs. In Mora, conditions improved as trade once more opened up with the wider world, although many of the population remained resentful as the Emperor increased taxes to try to recover some of the costs of the war and the retribution payment demanded by his brother-in-law. Sporadic protests still broke out in various parts of the city, but Holger had orders to quash them, with force if necessary. The Captain of the Guard was respected by the people of Mora, particularly after his careful handling of some of the flashpoint situations during the previous winter. As a result most demonstrators dispersed peacefully at Holger's request.

In the castle Alberon cared little about the ill will of his people. Holger could deal with the protests and if necessary a few executions could be ordered. To emphasise his point, Alberon had ordered that the gallows on the castle forecourt should remain in place.

As winter approached, Bertalan decided that the patrols at the mouth of the Morel could be ended. Rondon and the *Erth* returned to the trade routes across the Middle Sea as the *Warrior* and *Destroyer* returned to port in Tufle. Alberon had ordered Holger to maintain a guard watch on port and to inform him immediately if a caravel called the *Swan* arrived at Mora.

The news Holger brought was different. The captain of a Kermin vessel returning from Tufle reported that the gunboats were no longer on patrol and were now docked in their home port. It was a moment Alberon had waited for. He needed the sea route from Boretar to be free from searches so that his master craftsmen could return from Ackar with their equipment. He already had plans to build his own ironworks. The smiths would return to their new home, Sparsholt, on the Doran Plain. Once their forges were constructed, the smiths could start to rebuild his war machines. Alberon needed cannons, lots of them.

Bertalan's decision to bring the gunboats back home had not been random. He knew that to the north the first snows would be falling on the Kermin Plain and the first ice would be forming on the Morel. Any attempt by Alberon to acquire new armaments from the factories in

Ackar would have to wait until the spring. In addition it was unlikely that Alberon had the funds to pay for new weapons. The gunboats would resume their patrols as soon as the first buds of spring broke through their white winter coat.

In his private rooms in Mora Castle, Alberon was considering the same problem. Somehow he would need to transport the smiths and their materials back to Mora across winter seas and before any resumption of the stop and search patrols at the Morel estuary. In his mind it was linked with another problem: his illegitimate son, Audun, the captain of the *Swan*.

The first snow was indeed falling in Mora when Aracir was called to attend the Emperor. "Lord Chancellor, I need a man we can trust to carry out a mission for me. I cannot divulge the details of the mission except that it will require a winter journey from here to Boretar to deliver a message for me."

Aracir thought for a moment. "My Lord, I can only think that we could send one of the guardsmen or Holger himself. They have all been loyal through this past year of troubles."

Alberon shook his head. "No, it needs to be someone with no obvious connection to Mora, or to the throne, like a thief in the night. In the past I suppose I would have hired an assassin, if my great-grandfather had not wiped them all out."

Aracir suddenly realised that he did know such a man; indeed he knew two of them, the huntsmen.

Alberon interrupted. "To be clear, Aracir, this is not an assignment with my name on it. I will reveal the identity of the person commissioning the task when we meet again and you have identified a messenger. I do not want to know who you select to carry out this business"

The next morning, both Valdin and Vidur met with the Chancellor. Aracir outlined what little he knew of the Emperor's task. "I need one of you to carry a message to Boretar. At the moment that is all I know, but I am instructed to pay whatever is needed to have someone complete this mission."

Vidur shook his head. "I have completed one winter journey for you and I have no desire to spend another winter freezing on the Kermin Plain and the Alol. Besides, at this time of year the route to Boretar is probably via Tamin and I upset one or two important people there on my last visit."

Valdin was slightly younger than his brother, taller, well-built and more arrogant. "If my brother is scared of a bit of cold and a few unhappy people in Tamin, I am not." He smiled. "The price will be high, but if your sponsor can afford it, then I can deliver the message."

Later that morning Aracir reported back to Alberon that he had identified someone who would take the message to Boretar. But he was curious. "What is so important that it must be carried to Boretar in the winter?" he asked the Emperor. "Why not wait until the spring and send a messenger by sea?"

Alberon held up his hand to stop the Chancellor. "It is vital that my message reaches its destination in Boretar before the spring. The messenger must leave here under cover of darkness so that no one can connect his mission to me. It is also essential that he avoids travelling via Tamin or Tufle, in case he is intercepted. Return later this afternoon and I will have a package prepared for your messenger."

Aracir turned to leave, but Alberon spoke again. "As an aside, is your man capable of murder?"

Aracir was quite certain of the answer to this question. "Yes my Lord, he is, as were his ancestors."

Alberon spent the rest of the afternoon procrastinating. There were choices to be made, but which were the correct ones? He needed to get the craftsmen together with their equipment and tools back to Mora before the Amina gunboats started their stop and search patrols again. He correctly guessed that the Kermin gunboats would be most likely to return to the mouth of the Morel in the spring. That meant he had possibly until March to get the smiths back to Mora. Then there was the problem of the boy. Maybe Aracir's answer to his final question provided the permanent solution to that complication. Should he order the execution of his own bastard son?

When Aracir returned to the Emperor's room, a package was waiting for him. It was wrapped in leather, and oddly it carried the galloping horse seal of Berin, the long-dead Duke of Alol. He looked quizzically at Alberon.

Alberon smiled. "Yes, the seal is slightly odd, but I cannot allow the documents in this package to be traced back to me, particularly if they were to be discovered by my brother-in-law."

Aracir frowned. "But if Bertalan were to acquire this package, surely he would know it was false and that Berin perished during the battle in the Alol."

In response Alberon laughed. "He may think that, but I don't think he would know for sure."

Aracir took the package. He knew Alberon was devious and cunning, but this seemed somewhat mad.

Alberon then handed Aracir the letter that was to be carried with the parcel. This was not sealed, and Aracir read the instructions that he would shortly pass over to Valdin:

You will take this package to Boretar and only on reaching the Ackar capital will you open it for your further instructions. If at all possible you will avoid travelling via Tamin or Tufle. In the event that you are apprehended during your journey you will do everything in your power to protect the package and if necessary, you will destroy it.

The letter was signed Berin, Duke of Alol. Alberon smiled again. "You see, sometimes even the dead have their uses. Now go and get your messenger on the road. He must reach Boretar before the full snow moon in February. If he is later than that, he should destroy the package and return here to report back to you. You will add this final instruction verbally, it is not written down."

The horseman was mounted on a fine grey stallion and he crossed the Morel Bridge onto the Kermin Plain just as the sun was setting. He had many miles ahead of him. Aracir had been stunned by the size of the fee Valdin had demanded, but the Chancellor had little choice; he had his instructions from the Emperor. The stallion was part of the fee and had come from Alberon's own stables.

CHAPTER TWENTY ONE

Valdin was fortunate; the winter of 1508 was less severe than the previous one, and as he did not have to avoid the various military outposts, he made good progress. The instruction to avoid Tamin and Tufle created a small problem, as Tufle was the obvious embarkation point for travel on to the island of Andore. By the end of November he had crossed the Kermin Alol by the eastern drove road. He was south of the Aramin forest and well to the east of Tamin.

His destination was Slat, the small, sleepy town thirty miles south of Tamin. Slat had one advantage and one disadvantage as a location. For many years Valdin's brother had owned a house there. It was useful when Vidur had business in Tamin and needed to use his second identity as Ferdinand, the merchant from Slat. Slat's disadvantage was that its small port, located a few miles away at the Middle Sea, was mostly used by fishing vessels and only occasionally by larger ships. Despite the gold he carried to fund the costs of his travels, Valdin knew he might need to spend a week or two in Slat before he could buy passage to one of the ports on Andore. Still, he was ahead of his planned schedule, and a few days' rest in Slat would energise him for the rest of his journey.

He hoped to buy passage to Thos in Toria, and then it would be a hard winter's ride through Ciren and Lett before he could reach Boretar. He had made the journey in the past on a mission to the Ackar capital for Queen Ingrid, but that had been in the summer. He also knew the cross-country journey carried risks; a lone horseman on a handsome stallion would potentially be a target for bandits. Valdin was not really worried about these risks; he was well armed, and besides his sword and daggers he carried four charged pistols at his belt. These had been purchased by Vidur on his visit to Tamin the previous winter. Besides, the grey stallion could more than likely outrun any threat.

Once Valdin had settled into his brother's house in Slat, he paid a boy to keep watch at the port and alert him if any sea-going vessels docked there. Eight days passed, and he was beginning to get worried. If no seagoing vessel docked in Slat's harbour in the next couple of days, he would need to risk breaking his instructions and travel via Tufle. Of course, another option was to destroy the package and return to Mora, but half of his fee had been held back by Aracir and would only be paid on the successful completion of his mission.

Valdin was not a curious man, and it did not occur to him to open the sealed package. He did not recognise the galloping horse seal, but he did know it was not the Emperor's or that of the Dowager Queen, who normally commissioned him and his brother for sensitive tasks. It didn't matter; he was being paid handsomely and the stallion was a bonus.

Valdin was considering his options: another round of drinks at the local inn or prepare for a journey back north. The warmth of the inn seemed the most tempting, but then there came a knock at the door. He opened it to find the boy he had hired standing there panting. "Sir, a caravel has just pulled into the port, and it looks like it's got a problem with the foremast. I thought I'd best let you know at once."

Valdin tossed the boy the coins he had promised him and called on one of the servants to ready the stallion. Thirty minutes later he was riding onto the dock of the small harbour. A caravel was the best that Valdin could have hoped for, as the harbour at Slat was too shallow to allow the larger carracks to find a berth. When goods were being shipped from Slat to the carracks, the fishermen ferried the cargoes from the port to the vessels moored further out in the Middle Sea. Winter storms often made these transports impossible, but a caravel was perfect. Valdin knew this was a lucky gift, and he also knew that as long as the caravel was not too badly damaged it would hopefully be heading for one of the ports on Aldene.

Valdin hailed the men gathered round the base of the caravel's foremast. One young man left the others and walked to the side of the ship. "Yes sir, what can we do for you?" He appeared to be in his early twenties and carried himself with a certain confidence.

Valdin dismounted and asked, "Are you the captain of this ship?"

The young man nodded. "Yes sir I am."

"I am hoping to buy passage to one of the ports on the island of Andore. I have no preference for which one, but I can pay handsomely if you can transport me."

At that moment the stallion seemed to become impatient with the wait and started snorting and stamping his hooves on the ground. The captain regarded the animal for a moment before replying.

"We are planning to go to Thos in Toria, and we would have been there by now but for a problem with the foremast. It's nothing too serious, but I didn't want to risk it failing if a storm was to come down through the Middle Sea as we crossed. It simply needs some firm binding and resetting in its base. Depending on the weather, we should be ready to sail again in a couple of days. For the right price I can transport you to Thos, but I can't take the horse. We have no stalls big enough to house the beast, and besides we are pretty much fully loaded. He is a handsome animal, but he also seems to be somewhat temperamental. We would not be able to keep him calm on a sea journey."

Valdin paused. He was reluctant to leave the stallion in Slat, knowing that the journey from Thos to Boretar would be very demanding of a lesser animal. On the other hand, he had enough gold to purchase a fresh mount in Thos and the stallion could be stabled safely here at his brother's house.

After a short negotiation a price for the passage was agreed and the young man stepped from the ship to shake Valdin's hand and confirm the deal. "We will leave as soon as the mast is repaired and the weather is favourable, hopefully in the next few days, so you need to be able to get on board at short notice."

The horseman took the offered hand. "We have a deal then. If you will allow it, I have a boy who can come and stay here on the caravel, and he can come and get me as soon as you're ready to embark. Once you send him to me, I will be here with you in less than an hour. By the way, my name is Valdin."

The captain noted the strange tattoo on the other man's palm and wrist as he responded. "My name is Audun. Make sure you're ready when you receive my message, we will not wait for you."

It was then that Valdin noted the name of the caravel: the *Swan*.

For the next few days gales blew in from the north carrying sleet and snow. Valdin knew that the *Swan* would not leave harbour in such conditions even if the foremast was fully repaired. However the huntsman also knew that time was ticking by, and if he was to get from Thos to Boretar before February's full snow moon he needed to be on the journey soon. Again Valdin considered turning north to Tufle; a carrack would probably be able to ride out the winter storms, whilst a caravel was less stable on winter seas.

Slat was preparing for the celebrations of the winter solstice in four days' time when the boy again knocked on the huntsman's door. "Sir, there is supposed to be a break in the bad weather and the caravel plans to leave within the hour."

Valdin hastily packed his bag, including the leather package, and on one of his brother's horses he made haste to the port. He made it just in time, as the crew were beginning to set the sails on the *Swan*'s foremast. Rapidly dismounting, Valdin shouted out to Audun, "Wait! I am ready to join you."

Audun held the ship close to the dockside as Valdin leapt angrily on board. "I thought you were going to give me enough time to get here, captain?"

Audun shrugged and shouted back, "You have not

paid me any advance and I have a cargo that I must get to Thos. There is a short break in the weather and we must catch it. Anyway you are here, so what's the fuss?"

A few moments later the *Swan* pulled away from the port. With the wind moving from the north to the northeast, the ship's sails filled and it raced out into the Middle Sea. The route to Thos would take the caravel close to the islands of Lat and Elat. These were treacherous waters and sailors tried to keep their vessels well to the north of the islands. The tide race and the often prevalent northeasterly winds could quickly drive even a large ship perilously close to the shallow waters separating the islands. At certain times of year the sea conditions could create large whirlpools at the entry to the narrows, and these could swallow a ship whole.

Audun had read of the devastating consequences of an accident in the shallows between the islands two hundred years earlier. He also remembered that this was where Oien had first learnt how to harness the power of othium, or at least that was the myth written in the ancient books.

Although the winter storm had abated, the sea was still rough, with large white-capped waves whipped up by the wind. Valdin was a landsman, not a sailor, and he soon retired to the small cabin under the prow of the ship. Audun however was constantly on deck, ensuring the sail settings were correct and that the helmsman held the best course to minimise the impact of the waves and hold the caravel far enough to the north. With its shallow keel the ship was susceptible to waves hitting it broadside, but the helmsman had sailed these seas for many years and knew how to pick a relatively steady course.

It was early afternoon when the island of Lat was first seen in the distance on the port side. Shortly after, the sister island of Elat came into view. That was when Audun sensed that Oien was speaking to him, and the words that echoed in his head distracted him for a moment: *My home islands are near. The tsunami created near here once destroyed my plans and ambitions. It will not happen this time and one day I will return home.* As the voice faded, two thoughts struck Audun: the history books must indeed be true, and one day the alchemist would return home. Audun wondered what the latter sentence meant for his own desires and ambitions. Time would tell.

The crossing to Thos was rough but uneventful, and a day later the *Swan* docked at the Torian port. During the crossing of the Middle Sea Audun and Valdin had not spoken a word to each other; the captain had been too busy and the huntsman too seasick. All Audun knew was that his passenger had come from Mora to complete some sort of mission on Andore.

Audun was keen to know more about Kermin's capital city, his father's home. Valdin had his bag packed and was about to step ashore when Audun called over to him. "Valdin, the day is getting late and I think you will need to purchase a horse and provisions for your onward journey. You are welcome to stay here onboard for the night and set off tomorrow. I know an inn with excellent food where we could eat, and I will pay if you will allow me."

Valdin thought about this. The young man was correct; if he was to start his onward journey to Boretar he would need at least a day to prepare and indeed he might need to travel the short distance inland to Tora to find a suitable mount for the long journey north. He stepped back on board the ship and stowed his belongings back in the cabin. Walking back to the aft deck, he nodded to Audun. "Well why not? I presume you will be paying with the gold you robbed from me for such an easy passage."

Audun smiled. "Of course I will, but your passage here to Thos would have been much more expensive on foot or on horseback."

Valdin laughed, an unusual event for the normally serious huntsman. "You're right, stepping over those waves would have required longer legs than mine, or those of a horse."

The Sailor's Rest was aptly named. The tavern's location was a few streets inland from the dock area, so it was normally quieter than the establishments close to the port, which were in most cases simply drinking dens for the passing sailors. Audun was a regular, and at times he stayed in the tavern if he wanted a few days away from the *Swan*.

The proprietor greeted him warmly. "Welcome Captain, your normal table is reserved for you." Audun liked the peace in the tavern and his corner table was well away from the main bar area, so he managed to avoid sea stories when he was enjoying his meal.

Once the two men were settled at their table, Audun started the conversation. "So tell me about Mora. I have never had the chance to visit Kermin's great city."

Valdin was somewhat surprised, as most sailors had been to Mora's port. "You are captain of a cargo ship and have never carried goods to Mora?"

"My stepfather is owner and master of the *Swan* and I only took on my current responsibility when he got injured. This was at the time when the war between Kermin and Amina broke out and I had no wish to risk his ship to get through the blockade. For the past year we have been travelling between the ports in Aldene, with occasional trips across the Middle Sea to Tufle."

Audun asked again. So what's Mora like? I am hoping to travel there soon now that peace has been agreed."

Valdin was not much of a conversationalist, but he was proud of his home city and the excellent ale helped him to relax. He went on to describe Mora, the swing bridges and their history, the old port and the new one, the markets, the streets and looking down on it all the castle, with its gold-plated turrets, the palace of the Emperor.

Audun was reluctant to jump directly to his next obvious question, so he kept to safe ground. "Why would an Emperor plate the turrets of his castle in gold?"

To Valdin the answer was obvious. "Because Mora and the Emperor are rich beyond measure, due to the gold in the Doran Mountains."

Audun went on to ask questions about the gold mines, Kermin and the Kermin Alol, until he at last felt that he could ask the questions he really sought answers to.

"What is the Emperor like? Have you met him? What do the people think of him?" he asked. Then he realised that he should hold himself in check. He remembered his old friend David Burnett telling him he needed more patience and that he was inclined to ask too many questions all at once.

Valdin smiled. "One at a time Audun please, and I will try to answer, but then I have some questions for you. I have never met the Emperor, although I have carried out missions for his mother and for Aracir, the Kermin Chancellor. So I only know how the people talk of him. Alberon is arrogant and devious, so I am told, and only cares about his own power and wealth. He has little concern for the ordinary people and they have no love for him. It was different with Elrik and his queen – they were much loved by the people of Mora and Kermin."

Audun remembered the Regent's signature on the letter in his cabin. The people might love the Dowager Queen and the memories of her husband, but for Audun they had been responsible for the death of his mother. He asked another, more direct question. "Is it the Queen's business that brings you on this long winter journey?"

Valdin shook his head. "No, I am under instruction from the Chancellor." Now it was his turn for questions. "I am wondering how one so young can be captain of the *Swan*?"

Audun stuck with his mother's story, the brutal father, the rescue by his stepfather, the broken leg and his home in Boretar. It was the final part of the account that caught the huntsman's attention.

"I didn't realise the *Swan*'s home port was Boretar. Audun, you could save me a long ride if Boretar is your next port of call."

Audun smiled. "It might be, and we could take you, if you have enough gold to pay."

Valdin frowned. "Please don't play games with me captain. I need to get to Boretar before the snow moon, and if that is your destination then I can pay." Audun pulled back a little. The man in front of him was clearly not one to be toyed with; the pistols at his belt were the most obvious indicator of this. He decided to be more serious.

"We do have a cargo to load here and it's bound for Boretar, but January is not usually a time for a caravel to venture onto the Greater Sea. The crossing of the Middle Sea was rough, but the Greater Sea can be a beast in winter. If the weather clears for a time we may try to make a run for it, but if not we'll stay here in Thos until there's a clear spell. We might even have to wait here until early spring. If we had not had the problem with the mast, we'd be in Boretar by now. Of course, if that had not happened you would still be in Slat. "

For Valdin it was a difficult balancing act. He could perhaps wait a week and still complete the journey overland in time. Any longer and he would miss his deadline. "When will you know if there is an opportunity to sail for Boretar?" he asked.

Audun shrugged. "I'm sorry Valdin, I really don't know. I can't foresee the weather. It will take us a day or two to load the cargo, and after that we wait, a day, a week, a month, I don't know. However it is possible that a carrack will call here on its way to Boretar. The bigger ships have deeper keels than caravels, so they're better equipped to deal with the storms on the Greater Sea."

The *Swan* was soon loaded and ready to sail, but strong gales now coming from the west forced Audun to stay in port. Five days passed and Valdin was beginning to prepare for the land journey when a large carrack pulled into Thos. The *Amin*, one of the largest carracks working the Middle and Greater Seas, was sailing from Anelo to Boretar via Thos. Audun introduced Valdin to the *Amin's* captain and a day later he wished the huntsman a safe journey.

Valdin shook the offered hand and added, "Maybe I'll get the chance to buy you dinner in Boretar, if you can get there before I sail back to Mora."

Audun laughed. "What, and let me spend more of your gold? I know some very expensive taverns in Boretar."

Valdin smiled. "Maybe that is not such a good suggestion then!" With that he boarded the *Amin* and Audun returned to the Sailor's Rest to await more clement weather.

Valdin arrived in Boretar late in the second week in January hoping that he still had time to complete his mission before the snow moon. An added bonus from the journey was that the *Amin* was shipping some of the famed Ember stallions from Anelo to the winter market in Boretar. Being on board the ship gave Valdin the pick of the horses, and he selected a black stallion which he called Onyx, after the stone of power.

He was used to following the Queen's instructions to the letter, so he had done as ordered, and only now, on reaching Boretar, did he pull Aracir's package out from his saddlebag. The package contained a single sheet of paper, two additional sealed letters and a second smaller package. The sealed letters and the small package were numbered one to three. The first letter was addressed to Master Wayland Henry at Ackar Iron Works, while the second was addressed to the Master of the *Swan*. Valdin wondered at the strange coincidence. As far as he knew the *Swan* was still in the harbour at Thos, but the letter was addressed to its Master, and Valdin knew this was Audun's stepfather whose name, he remembered, was Ramon.

If Valdin considered the second letter a coincidence, the small package made him wonder more about chance and fate. It was addressed to Audun, the captain of the *Swan*. All the items in the package contained the same seal, a galloping horse, and the same signature, that of Berin, Duke of Alol. Valdin unfolded the single sheet of paper which he correctly assumed would contain his next instructions.

His first task was to deliver the letter to Wayland Henry. Valdin was pleased he had purchased the stallion. The Ackar ironworks were the best part of a day's ride south of Boretar, close to the Lett border. For centuries Ackar and Lett had been a single kingdom ruled from Boretar. The location of the ironworks kept the plumes of black smoke that emanated from the multitude of forges well away from the King and the rich merchants who lived in Boretar; there was however also a practicality involved in the location. The furnaces produced metal components and equipment used in agricultural machinery, armaments and in shipbuilding. Ackar and Lett's ships were all built in the large dockyards in Olet, where the port opened up directly on to the Greater Sea. With their central location the products from the ironworks could easily reach city, farmlands and dockyard.

Onyx covered the ground from Boretar quickly, seemingly enjoying the freedom of the gallop after the weeks cooped up in his pen on the *Amin*. The first phase of the journey was through Ackar's farmlands with the winter wheat lying waiting for the summer sun. The numerous watermills on the tributaries of the Tar River still turned, as grain stored in the autumn was processed for the bakers in Boretar. However, horse and rider were both coughing as they drew close to the ironworks, where dense, acrid smoke filled the air.

From a rise a short distance away, Valdin took in the view. The valley was smothered in smoke, and flames leapt to the sky as the smiths primed their furnaces. Valdin never thought about the underworld, but the smoke and flames filling the view reminded him of the popular idea of hell. He shuddered. This was a place to get quickly in and out of.

Some brief enquiries directed the huntsman to some forges close to the northern edge of the works. There he found Wayland Henry. The smith was huge, with muscles that spoke of the effort required to work his trade.

Valdin handed over the letter, which was gripped by a soot-blackened hand. Wayland passed it back to the huntsman. "You'd better read it for me. I am not good with my letters."

Valdin did as requested. He read: "You are instructed to prepare all the components and equipment you have made here and have it ready for transport to Boretar within two weeks". Valdin looked up at Wayland. "Interestingly your instructions are linked to mine," he said. "You must give me a list of all that will need to be shipped. I have to commission a caravel called the *Swan* to transport the equipment to Mora. The ship must arrive there before the end of March."

Wayland shook his head. "I am no expert on shipping, but I very much doubt that a caravel could take the load in winter seas. We'll be moving large iron tubes, heavy wooden cores, iron strapping bands and many iron balls. A caravel will not carry this weight in heavy seas, but by all means speak to the master of the ship and ask his advice."

Wayland took Valdin on a tour of the workshops and introduced him to the five other smiths who would at last be travelling back home to their families in Mora. Valdin noted all the equipment and estimated the weights. "I need to return to Boretar and talk to the owner of the *Swan* about the commission. I will return here in a week's time and you must then be ready to move to Boretar."

"Yes sir," was the smith's only reply.

Valdin turned Onyx back north, and both were happier when the air became clean again. It was now time to deliver the second letter to the master of the *Swan*.

The next afternoon Valdin was sitting opposite Ramon in the house on Cross Street. Ramon was examining the letter. "Who is this Berin, Duke of Alol?"

Valdin shrugged. "I don't know, my instructions come from Aracir, Chancellor of Kermin."

Ramon looked up. "Why this very specific request to transport these goods on the *Swan*? Winter voyages on a caravel are risky, particularly on the Greater Sea." Valdin did not mention that he already knew about the *Swan* and winter voyages. Ramon continued, "To the best of my knowledge the *Swan* is still docked in one of the southern ports, either Anelo or Thos or possibly even Tufle. My captain will not risk the ship as long as these westerly gales continue. If these goods need to be transported in the next week or two, it is highly unlikely to be on the *Swan*. Now tell me, what is this special cargo that you are prepared to pay such a high commission to transport?"

Valdin outlined the details of the equipment he had seen at the forges. Ramon shook his head. "A large weight of iron? Even if the *Swan* was in port we would not load this cargo. It would be too heavy. I presume this is mostly agricultural equipment to enable Kermin's farmers to recover following the war?"

Valdin did not really know. He had his suspicions, but he did not want to divulge them to the ship owner. "Yes sir, I think so."

"I guess then that the Chancellor wants the goods in Mora at the start of spring ready for the planting season?"

Valdin shrugged. "Sir, I am only the messenger and I am not privy to the Chancellor's, or the Duke's, plans."

Ramon had his own suspicions. "I may have an alternative solution for you, but I need to consider it and decide if the commission is worth the risk. Return here tomorrow and we can discuss the subject further."

During the summer of 1508 Ramon had gradually become bored with the books in his library. He needed a new project, and he also needed to feel the sea wind in his hair once again. He had discussed his plans with Audun. Thanks to Audun's skills in striking profitable deals, their business had thrived during Ramon's enforced retirement. As the news of the cessation of the war in the south reached Boretar, Ramon and Audun had agreed that the winter would bring new opportunities in rebuilding the trade routes between Boretar, Andore and Mora. Both also agreed that winter trade would require them to purchase a larger vessel. The carrack had spent months in the dry dock at Olet being refurbished, and Ramon was frustrated that the work had suffered delays which meant that only now, in late January, was the ship ready to put to sea. Audun and Ramon had agreed that Ramon would captain the carrack whilst Audun would continue to command the *Swan*.

For reasons Ramon did not understand, Audun had insisted that if the carrack was to be mostly transporting its cargo from Andore's ports on to Mora, then it should be named *Lex Talionis*. Ramon understood the meaning of the words – "an eye for an eye" or "the law of retaliation" – but he had no idea why Audun had been so insistent on this particular name.

From Valdin's description of the cargo in the offered contract, Ramon also knew with certainty that it would not be agricultural equipment he would be transporting for the Kermin Chancellor and the Duke. Transporting what Ramon thought the cargo really was would have much higher potential risks, but then again, if *Lex Talionis* could make the journey in a few weeks, before the winter weather broke, then the value of the contract would make the carrack's first journey spectacularly profitable. One thing Ramon had not shared with Audun was the large debt that he had incurred in paying for the carrack and the delays in the refurbishment had further driven up the costs. Whilst the offered contract carried significant risks, it would also clear the debt with gold to spare.

The next morning Valdin was again sitting opposite Ramon, who came quickly to the point. "I have considered this contract and I do have a possible solution for you. It is impossible for the *Swan* to fulfil the contract, but I have another vessel at Olet that could be ready to sail within two weeks."

Valdin shook his head. "My instructions are explicit that the goods have to be transported on the *Swan*."

Ramon laughed. "I don't think the Duke or the Chancellor have much experience of the sea. Your instructions are completely contradictory – a winter voyage with a heavy load on a caravel? Even in calm summer waters the *Swan* would be dangerously low in the water with such a load. If you insist I can try to commission another caravel, if I can find a captain stupid enough to risk the voyage. My guess is that you would not get as far south as Olet before you would have to swim."

Valdin had to decide: the cargo or the ship? It had to be the cargo that was more important. He raised a hand and responded, "Captain I think my contract is for the transport of the cargo. I don't understand the reason for the definition of the specific vessel. Do we have a deal for the carrack?"

Ramon was still unsure if this contract was worth the risk, but he decided to play the final card. "I presume you have enough gold with you to negotiate a worthwhile deal for me?"

Valdin nodded. "I hope so sir."

Ramon frowned and leant forward. "Valdin, we both know what you are instructed to ship to Mora and it is not meant for the farmers. I will be putting my new ship at great risk. I will only accept the contract if the price is right, and it will be very high."

Valdin knew that if he was to get the iron to Mora before the end of March Ramon's offer was the only one he was likely to receive. The price was agreed, the gold was transferred to safe keeping in Ramon's library and a letter of additional payment due on delivery in Mora, was signed, countersigned, and passed to the huntsman.

Ramon concluded, "Good, then I will see you in two weeks' time in Olet and you should be sailing as you are instructed just before the snow moon."

As Valdin rose to leave, he remembered the third package. Without giving away the fact that he had sailed on the vessel, he handed it to Ramon. "This, I believe, was to be passed to the captain of the *Swan* on our departure for Mora. I guess as you are now to be captaining us on the voyage, then it is meant for you." Ramon took the package and replied that he would look at the instructions before the carrack left Olet.

Once Valdin had left the room, Ramon picked up the small package. He immediately noticed that the cover was addressed very specifically to his stepson. Why would the Chancellor of Kermin, or the Duke of Alol, address a package specifically to Audun, and why the insistence that the *Swan* should carry the cargo, regardless of her suitability?

Ramon leant back in his chair and pondered. Maybe this journey was too full of unknown risks, but then the agreed payment would more than cover the debts incurred in the purchase and the refurbishment of the carrack, and of course he wanted to be at sea again.

Despite the fact that the package was specifically addressed to his stepson, Ramon decided to open it up, in case it held further instructions related to the contract he had just agreed. Inside there were no instructions, only a recently printed copy of a book that Ramon recognised. The cover title had been reworked and presented the work as *Poems from the Bard of Bala.* The cover motif was unchanged from the ancient, original version that Ramon kept in his library, a motif of joined hands which merged into the three words *Aonaibh Ri Chéile.* He vaguely remembered some connection between this book of poems and the decline and death of Ragna, Audun's mother, but he could not recall Audun ever telling him about the details. Maybe his stepson had deeper secrets from his past that Ramon had not discovered.

One thought led to another. If Valdin's contract and the papers came from the authorities in Mora, was this related to Audun's past and his insistence on the naming of the carrack? Ramon had read many of the myths of ancient history, and he knew that Audun was also well versed in old texts. Ramon knew Lex Talionis was an ancient story that had originated from the wild tribes that still inhabited the Aramin forest in the east of Kermin. The old scripts had been discovered a decade ago in an ancient burial site in the east of the Kermin Alol, just south of the forest. The hieroglyphs had been deciphered by a scholar in Amina, and Ramon had an early copy of the translation that Audun almost certainly would have read.

"Lex Talionis: A story of deceit, of fire and revenge." Ramon opened his copy of the book. Maybe he could learn something here, and some way to warn his stepson if he was in danger. The story was a long ballad about one of the ancient kings of the Aramin. Althred was the anointed king of the Aramin and was worshipped as a god. His golden palace was situated at the centre of Aram, the capital of the Kingdom. Ramon knew that some adventurers had gone to search the Aramin forest for the golden city, but few had returned alive. The Aramin forest was still a wild place inhabited by the Aramin tribesmen.

Ramon read on. Althred had a newborn son, heir to his throne and blessed by the gods. His name, and here Ramon paused, was Adun. The babe was only a year old when foreign armies invaded the lands. The ballad told that Althred's second wife, Karun, was hungry for power and jealous of the baby recently born to the regent Queen. Karun led the enemy through the forest to reach Aram and laughed as the city burned. The poem described the power of a red fire, the destruction of Aram and the death of the King. The baby was smuggled out of Aram under the cloak of a poor washer woman, and the myth held that one day the child would return and revenge his father.

The translation ended abruptly. Maybe the final part of the story had never been found, maybe never written down or maybe the poet felt this ending was all that was needed. The ballad closed with the final lines:

Lex Talionis
An eye for an eye
A tooth for a tooth
A life for a life
Not my revenge
Justice
Not for revenge
For justice

Lex Talionis
Not for what is now
But for what was done
Betrayal of love
Escape of a son
Not for revenge
For justice
For what was done.

LIST OF CHARACTERS

In alphabetic order

Aaron – first son of Alberon and Sylva

Aisha – wife of Bertalan

Alastair Munro – Known as The Eldest of Bala

Alberon – Son of Elrik and Ingrid and heir to the Kermin throne. Later to become Emperor of the North

Aleana – A member of the Den of Thieves

Alician – Berin's mother and Berka's lover

Amelia – Arin's wife and Ragna's mother

Amleth – Holger's second in command of the Guard in Mora

Angus Ferguson – 14th century warrior poet

Aracir – Chancellor of Kermin

Arin – Ragna's father

Arvid – Raimund's uncle

Aster – King of Soll

Astrid – Raimund's aunt

Audun – Ragna and Alberon's son

Bartos – Commander of the King's Guard in Tamin and cousin of Bertalan

Berka – King of Amina, father to Bertalan, Sylva and Berin

Berin – Illegitimate son of Berka and half brother to Bertalan and Sylva

Bertalan – son and heir to Berka and brother of Sylva

Colin Duncan of Coe – Elder of Coe and Banora

Connor – an innkeeper in Tamin

Cristian Carter – Master of the Merchant Guild

David Burnett – an old historian living in Aldene

Elrik – King of Doran, husband to Ingrid and Regent of Kermin, Alberon's father

Elrik – second son of Alberon and Sylva named after his grandfather

Lord Ereldon – chancellor of Amina and advisor to the King.

Erica and Egil – Raimund's cousins

Edin – Duke of Aramin and Alberon's cousin

Gordon Graham – a merchant in Aldene

Hilda – Arin's sister in law

Holger – Captain of the City Guard in Mora and Captain of the King's Guard

Ingrid – Daughter of King Olsen of Kermin and wife of Elrik

James Daunt – Captain of the Ackar and Amina gunners

James Ferguson – Chief of Clan Cameron, Senior Elder of Bala and Lord of Aldene

Jane Graham – Gordon Graham's wife

Johann – John Sexton's second in command

John Sexton – Captain of the Warrior

Jon – a blacksmith in Mora

Morserat – Duke of Doran

Lord Norward – Commander in Chief of the armies of Kermin and Doran

Oien – An alchemist from the Second Age

Olsen – King of Kermin

Orran – Morserat's brother and Soren's father – a captain of the Doran light cavalry

Rafe – Master of the Den of Thieves

Ragna – Queen Ingrid's maid and Audun's mother

Raimund – A thief

Ramon – Master of The *Swan*

Raynal – Arin's brother and Ragna's uncle

Rondon – Captain of the Erth

Silson – Duke of Amina and Commander in Chief of the Amina armies

Sylva – Daughter of Berka, King of Amina, to become wife of Alberon

Soren – Nephew of Morserat, son of Orran

Valdin – Vidur's brother and fellow huntsman

Vasilli – First mate on The *Swan*

Vidur – a huntsman (also known as Ferdinand)

Wayland Henry – A Kermin Master smith

William Norward – Lord Norward's son

GEOGRAPHY OF THE LANDS

The large island of Andore is home to several
independent countries. In the north, Bala has its border
with Ackar at the old wall. South of Ackar is Lett, whilst
further south are Toria, Ciren and Arance. Ember is an
independent Dukedom in the east of Arance. To the
northeast the island is bounded by the Eastern Sea, which
separates the island from the eastern lands of Esimore,
Soll, Doran and Kermin. To the south is the Middle Sea
across which is Andore's southern neighbour, Amina.
Lying between Middle Sea and the Western Sea are the
islands of Elat and Lat. The Greater Sea runs the length
of the island to the west. By the early 16th Century there
had been little conflict between the nations. The legacy
of the King called the Peacemaker had lasted for nearly
two hundred years.

KERMIN AND DORAN

Kermin and Doran have long lived in harmony with
ancient treaties committing each to the protection of the
other. Marriages between the two royal families further
cemented the bonds between the countries. Doran is
the most northerly of these lands and is separated from
Kermin by the Doran Mountains. Doran is a relatively
poor country with small farms scattered across the
Doran Plain. The capital, Iskala, sits on a rocky outcrop

on the northern slopes of the Doran Mountains. Winter snow blocks the high mountain passes and for four months each year Doran is cut off from its southern neighbour.

Kermin by contrast is a rich country. The Kermin Plain is home to fertile farmlands and extensive pastures. The gold in the Doran Mountains is mined on the Kermin side of the border and this provides much of the Emperor's wealth. Kermin's capital, Mora, is an impressive city sitting on the banks of the river Morel which flows southwest from the Doran Mountains into the Eastern Sea. The Morel is wide as it flows past the city and the port bustles with activity as goods are imported from, and exported to, most of the known world. To the east of Kermin is the large Aramin forest, home to the Aramin tribes. The border between Kermin and Amina is the Kermin Alol, which is rugged hill country, populated mostly by herds of sheep and cattle. The hills rise steeply from the valleys, cutting the Alol into several distinct sectors with the trade roads hugging the valley floors.

AMINA

South of the Kermin Alol is Amina with its vineyards, wheat fields and acres of flax. Tamin is the capital city, and the Amin River flows close to the city walls. Further north the river Mina flows south and west from the

Kermin Alol into the Middle Sea. Amina's port is Tufle, and further south near the coast is the small town of Slat. The port at Tufle is connected to Tamin by the river Amin and a constant stream of small boats transport goods too and from the city. Wheat, wine and linen are amongst Amina's main exports. Carracks and caravels constantly crisscross the Middle Sea making Tufle the busiest port in any of the lands and a key source of Amina's wealth. Tufle also has the largest ship building yards in the south and most of the vessels sailing the Middle Sea and the Eastern Sea were built in Tufle. The Vale of Tember stretches out to the south of Tamin and is the country's breadbasket.

ACKAR AND LETT

Ackar is the richest country on the island of Andore, with large farms and a busy river port at the capital, Boretar. The Tar River flows through Boretar's port to the Greater Sea. To the north east, closer to the border with Bala, is the second city of Erbea. The Erb flows past Erbea after it has been joined from the north by the Bari. Ackar is the most populous of the countries and is rich with the trade that flows in and out of Boretar. In the mid 13th century Ackar nobles gradually extended their power into their southern neighbour. By 1280 the countries agreed to a union and so Ackar and Lett became the most powerful country on the island.

Lett is slightly smaller than its northern neighbour and less wealthy. The capital city is named after the country, and lies inland. Olet is the country's port on the Greater Sea and the extensive shipyards at Olet build most of the vessels that ply their trade up and down that sea. The shipyards get their raw materials from the Forest of Lett, which extends down beyond the Lett border into Ciren and on south into Toria. South of Boretar and close to the border with Lett are the Ackar ironworks. The ironworks produce metal components and equipment used in agriculture, shipbuilding and armaments. These products are widely exported from the port at Olet.

BALA

Bala's border starts north of Ackar at the old wall. Bala is segmented by two great mountain ranges. North of the capital, Aldene, are the Inger Mountains and in the far north the Coe Mountains. The only route through the Inger Mountains is the Pass of Ing. Winter snow means that the pass is blocked for several months each year. To the northwest of The Inger Mountains is the province of Banora. Bala's capital is smaller than the great southern cities of Boretar, Tamin and Mora. Aldene has two distinct districts; The Old Town, with its grey stone houses, cobbled streets and the castle perched on its rocky crag, is encircled by the old town walls and has remained unchanged for centuries. Outside the town walls is the New Town with its warehouses and the homes of Bala's merchants. The New Town had been built in the late 14th century following the development of Bala's only port at Elde. A broad road connects the port to the town. Bala is a reasonably prosperous country due to its exports of woollen products and deer pelts.

TORIA, CIREN AND ARANCE

Ciren and Arance share a border with Lett, their northern neighbour. Toria borders Ciren to the west and Arance borders it to the east. Arance has rich farmlands and in the east the province of Ember, whose capital is Anua, is home to the Ember Horse Lords. Ember is renowned for its thoroughbred horse stock and Ember stallions grace the stables of the royal families in every country.

Ciren is rich in natural resources with the Forest of Lett providing the wood for the shipwrights in Olet. Ciren mines supply the iron ore for the Ackar ironworks and its quarries the stones for Boretar's buildings. Ciren's capital is the small town of Cire.

Toria is a small country perched on the southwest edge of the island of Andore. Toria is blessed with a benevolent climate and its vineyards, fields of rye and potato farms produce the raw materials for its main exports. Toria's wineries and distilleries provide the finest wines and spirits and are exported widely. Toria's busy port at Thos looks out across the Western Sea and in the distance the island of Elat can be seen on the horizon. The other great port on the southern coast of Andore is Anelo in the south of Arance. Here the Ember horses are loaded onto carracks for their journey to the horse markets in Boretar.

ELAT AND LAT

Lying between the southern shores of Toria and the northern shores of Amina are the twin islands of Elat and Lat. The islands are of little value other than as possible staging posts for crossing the Middle Sea. The water lying between the islands forms a shallow channel connecting the Middle Sea to the Western Sea, the Straits of Elat. However this water is too shallow for any large boat to navigate and holds no value. The islands do however hold a curiosity, as the water in the shallows evaporates in the summer months so the water turn purple as the salt becomes concentrated in the narrows.

ESIMORE AND SOLL

Esimore and Soll are situated in the far north and are separated from Andore by the Eastern Sea. Esimore is the most northern country and it is largely tundra, with great herds of reindeer roaming free and tended by the few nomadic herdsmen who call the land home.

The northern tundra runs across the border between Esimore and Soll and the reindeer are not constrained by any frontier. As a result Soll's main source of income comes from the reindeer hides that are exported south to Doran and Kermin. To the south Soll borders Doran and like its neighbour it is a poor land dotted with peasant's small crofts. Winters here are long and cold and most of the population are subsistence farmers. In 1496 under threat of invasion from the south and bribed by Kermin gold the King of Soll swore fealty to the Kermin King and Soll became the third member of the Empire.

Printed in Great Britain
by Amazon